IN OUR TIME

IN OUR TIME

PAUL JOSEPH LEDERER

FIVE STAR
A part of Gale, Cengage Learning

GALE
CENGAGE Learning·

Farmington Hills, Mich • San Francisco • New York • Waterville, Maine
Meriden, Conn • Mason, Ohio • Chicago

GALE
CENGAGE Learning®

LIBRARY OF CONGRESS CATALOGING-IN-PUBLICATION DATA

Names: Lederer, Paul Joseph author.
Title: In our time / Paul Joseph Lederer.
Description: Waterville, Me. : Five Star, a part of Cengage Learning, Inc. 2016.
Identifiers: LCCN 2016024341| ISBN 9781432832766 (hardcover) | ISBN 143283276X (hardcover) | ISBN 9781432832704 (ebook) | ISBN 9781432832700 (ebook) | ISBN 9781432833398 (ebook) | ISBN 1432833391 (ebook)
Subjects: LCSH: Cherokee Indians—Oklahoma—Fiction. | Families—Fiction. | GSAFD: Historical fiction | Domestic fiction | Western stories
Classification: LCC PS3559.R6 I53 2016 | DDC 813/.54—dc23
LC record available at https://lccn.loc.gov/2016024341

First Edition. First Printing: November 2016
Find us on Facebook– https://www.facebook.com/FiveStarCengage
Visit our website– http://www.gale.cengage.com/fivestar/
Contact Five Star™ Publishing at FiveStar@cengage.com

Printed in the United States of America
1 2 3 4 5 6 7 20 19 18 17 16

IN OUR TIME

PROLOGUE

Not so long ago on a cold drizzly Saturday morning with the rain streaking the windows, Tina Black came across a long-forgotten letter from her grandmother in the cool reaches of the dim attic. She was little interested initially. Tina was still young and not much interested in the fading memories of older people. Nevertheless, with little else to do on this dreary morning, she perched on the leather-bound trunk and unfolded the yellowing pages from the past.

Dear Tina,

I know you are still very young for this, but older people have this predilection for passing on ancient stories even when they have no relevance to your modern world.

Would you believe it! We felt the same way in our time. We had so many new conveniences and marvels: the telephone, the automobile, airplanes, and films. It was so exciting and daunting at once, especially to the older folks who knew what our Cherokee heritage was about; that it needed to be preserved at all costs—but time was upon us with all of its drama and sweep. And there was only time to try to keep up with change.

It was so very exciting, Dear. I was born on December 31, 1899, heralding the new century. And you will become a woman of the new century!

Only now and then, as I grew older, did I understand what people like Sky Dog (whom we always just called "The Old

7

Man") meant when he warned that we were rushing away from our heritage as we stormed brazenly into the present, the future. The Old Man had one saying I did not understand then and only now appreciate, "It is not the white man who has finally defeated us, but progress."

Oh, but did we savor progress! How exciting the first electric lights in town were.

We tried so hard to keep stride, but, really, in those times we didn't have the skills to do so.

I just wanted to write a little bit of how it was in our time and how we struggled with it. And perhaps to relive a little of how, despite the hardships, I loved that vanished time.

CHAPTER ONE

Joe Gah hnee gee suh—our home.

1916—Indian Territory (Oklahoma)

In Summer the fleeting clouds shadowed the golden land and at sunset the hills turned to deep rose and violet. The grass was long, sweet-smelling, and wildlife abounded near Otter Creek. Sometimes massive black tornado shadows rose in the southwest and swept across the land, and winter buried the countryside in deep snow.

But it was a magical and wonderful place to grow up for the Adair children.

Raccoon and deer, fox and wildcats still abounded. The islands in the stream were alive with birds. Otter Creek was rife with catfish, crappies, and bluegill. The land beyond was still empty and wild, but there was also the wonder and magic of the new century, the new world rushing toward them on the Cherokee Nation.

In Tahlequah they had electricity and telephones that let you talk across the miles.

The automobile had arrived; and one day despite the old Cherokee's grave doubts, they saw a machine carrying a man buzz and stutter low across the sky, heading toward the oil fields where the Texas men had begun drilling. In Tahlequah too, they had radios where you could hear music all the way from Oklahoma City. They even had a small building where, for the price of a nickel, you could see the new wonder—motion pictures.

That was Tahlequah, the big city where already there were five hotels, five different stores, two smiths, a tailor shop, and a sawmill.

The Adair children visited Tahlequah only seldom, but they were aware of the growth, the changes so rapidly challenging their time and their world that it was breathtakingly exciting.

They were from the tiny, scattered town of Broken Post to the southeast where things endlessly remained the same, as if not only the people but the land itself resisted change. (Even as adults they told people they were from Tahlequah rather than Broken Post, as if Tahlequah meant anything to anyone off the Nation.)

Broken Post did have its own store. It was divided into three sections. On one wing was the feed and grain store, on the other was the saddlery and the blacksmith's shop. In the center, facing the rutted dirt road with its sun-blistered false front, was the dry good store. Liquor was sold at the rear.

There were three Adair children: Shanna the oldest, then Tom, then the baby, Elizabeth, each ten months apart in age from the next. It was a small family for that time, in that place, but the Adairs had never suffered a miscarriage or lost an infant—also unique in that time and that place—so they considered themselves fortunate.

Shanna was pretty—more than pretty as she matured—and she was well aware of it from a very early age; she was constantly remarked upon by neighbors, family, and friends. Tom was quiet, distant one might say. At seventeen, he was slight for his age, but sinewy and quick. He ran like a jackrabbit and was proud of that and his hunting prowess. He was encouraged to hunt by his grandfather and Roy, his father, and had gone off by himself since he was eight or nine to bring home rabbits, quail, dove, and even deer. Elizabeth was studious and shy. She blinked often and one eye seemed to be unfocused. Obviously she needed glasses, but in that time Roy and Sarah could afford no such luxury even had there been an optometrist in the county. Besides, for children and especially girl children such an expenditure was considered an inappropriate use of the small resources of a family. She was a pleasant girl, her feelings easily hurt, easily bolstered. She was the type of girl of whom one might say, "She'll make some man a good wife some day." Patient and sincere, her thoughts went far deeper than her school-age friends could understand.

Roy and Sarah Adair did their best to raise them on a treeless plot of land near Broken Post. Their three-bedroom, randomly expanded log house was hot in the summer as the iron stove blazed cherry-red in the kitchen and the days grew stifling. In the rainy season the roof leaked abominably and Sarah Adair spent half of her time cleaning up the mud that would seep into the house. Still, their fortune was greater than that of many of their neighbors on the Nation.

Down along Otter Creek there was very little usable timber. At one time it had been pine country, but white speculators had cut most of it down. Now the only trees in quantity were in the oak grove a quarter of a mile south of the Adair farm surrounding Oak Knoll owned by the Black family. There was a lot of post oak and blackjack scattered around, and many willows and sycamores down along the creek itself—all useless for lumber— and a few small stands of pine across Otter Creek along the red bluffs, but basically the land was now barren and timberless.

The Cherokees living south of Tahlequah had sunken, almost without noticing it, into poverty. Near Tulsa the Glenn Pool oil strike had been made, making instant millionaires of a handful of fortunate Indians. One man they knew was making three thousand dollars a month just for sitting on his porch watching

the ducklike heads of the Texas oil pumps spotted across his al-
lotted lands.

Roy Adair seldom made fifty dollars a month to support his
family. But then he was a full blood and refused his government
allotment. The children were still too young to understand the
inequities; they had not yet reached the age of cynicism.

When their father and some of his cronies would sit around
the kitchen table and discuss the "Damned Dawes Commission" and the white speculators until their voices grew loud and
hoarse with anger and they began to mutter quietly in the old
tongue, the children would go or be sent outside to play. The
children knew, of course, that there were outlaws like the
Nighthawks and the Snakes, the Kee-too-wahs (the full-blood
association) out there harassing and even beating their enemies,
but none of it meant much to children of their age. They were
more interested in the arrival of the new age with all of its
technological gifts; a new time had come and they wished to be
a part of its promised glamor and not a remembrance of the
old.

Airplanes sputtered overhead; Crazy Man, the oil-rich Creek,
swept down the dusty road to Tahlequah in his Stutz motorcar;
the radio at the Roberts' house played dance music from St.
Louis, which drifted all the way to the Adair farm on clear summer evenings. They had gone to see a funny little man with a
smudge of a mustache named Chaplin wiggle and mug, and
they laughed so hard their stomachs hurt.

The old times were fading; this then was theirs.

The road to Tahlequah followed Otter Creek until it reached
the big pond on the Roberts' farm; then it was forced to swing
west and pass Old Man Hill. The children, who hitched their
rides by jumping on the tailgates of passing wagons, would sit
and laugh as they passed The Old Man.

Everyone knew The Old Man, though no one remembered

his real name. He had refused to accept any white allotments, left his small farm, and moved to the top of the low, brushy knoll where he sat alone day and night, looking out across the land. People said he ate alone, slept alone. No one had ever seen him in Broken Post.

Tom said, "Folks say he's looking for buffalo, waiting for them to come back."

Shanna looked toward the dark knoll, her legs swinging from the tailgate like elegant scissors. "There's never been any buffalo here, I bet."

"Yes there was," Elizabeth said. "There's still some away over on Blue River." The others paid no attention to the baby of the family.

The truth was that Sky Dog, which was The Old Man's given name, did watch for buffalo from the knoll. He lived simply on a diet of rabbit, quail, chia flour, nopalitos, and pinyon nuts. There was no place in his diet for white man's food; there was no place in his heart for the times that were approaching. He sat and watched the crimson and gold sundown, the truck gasping its way along the road below, then he rose and walked back to his primitive bark wigwam, lit his pipe, and watched the First Promise star gleam through the smokehole in his roof. And he waited . . .

That was the summer of the execution.

It was Joe-Boy Parker that the sheriff of the county Indian Police accused of being a Nighthawk and killing the Federal agent, the white man Jacoby. Judge Peter Braxton, late of Chicago, had listened to the conflicting, inaccurate statements of two witnesses for at least fifteen minutes and then dropped his gavel, condemning Joe-Boy to death. The people were in fear of the Four Mothers Society and the Nighthawks who had vowed to drive off all whites and breeds. Joe-Boy was to be an example.

If the trial itself was an exercise in brevity, the hanging itself was a daylong event.

Bright banners and balloons filled the air; vendors sold roast corn and barbecue.

Children laughed and wove among the crowd, playing tag. Most of the women wore their best church dresses, waiting to watch Sheriff Max Lomas hang Joe-Boy Parker by the neck until he was dead.

The Adair family was there to witness it. Roy said nothing as he stared darkly at the scaffolding and carnival crowd with his black, expressionless eyes. The children laughed and shrieked as if it were a Sennett comedy. It had no reality to them.

Elizabeth did notice that her father was not standing with his friends, Black Jack and Warren Weaver, who came over on Saturday nights to play cards or darts or sit smoking black tobacco as they spoke in low tones.

"Everyone should know where I stand," she heard her father say to her mother.

"Those who matter know," her mother answered. She gripped Roy's arm tightly, her eyes not frightened, only sorrowful. Her broad mouth was turned down at the corners.

As a girl she had played with Joe-Boy's sisters. She felt Roy's muscles tighten beneath her grip, felt him start forward toward the scaffold. "Think of the children, Roy, please!"

"They'll know soon enough. They should be taught now—especially Tom. White justice . . . !" he said in a savage undertone.

Sarah's grip tightened still more and she shushed Roy, nodding toward Elizabeth who had emerged unseen from the crowd of spectators.

"Not now, Roy, please. Stay with me. It can do no good."

Roy did not answer. He remained tense and uneasy, glaring at the gallows. Slowly, he breathed out. He drew Elizabeth to him and rested his strong, work-knotted hand on her head. She looked up at him, understanding none of it.

The shouts and loud conversation around them fell to a murmur. One unseen boy cheered. There was the tiniest smattering of applause as the jailhouse door opened on iron hinges and Joe-Boy Parker, his hands strapped behind him, was led forward to the platform, the sheriff and two deputies armed with shotguns, guarding him.

Joe-Boy wore a rolled red bandana around his head. It had slipped low so that it nearly covered his black, vengeful eyes. His red shirt was open and they could see the muscles flex across his powerful chest as he strained against his bonds. The hot wind had risen and a dust devil spun down the street, causing those in the crowd to cover their eyes.

A tumbleweed raced in its wake and bounced up onto and over the scaffold as Joe-Boy climbed the three steps to stand in the wavering shadow of the waiting noose. Reverend Thatcher was there with his Bible in his hand, but Joe-Boy snarled something inaudible and the white preacher turned away, his face scarlet.

Sheriff Lomas, in his fawn-colored Stetson and tan, piping-decorated suit, stepped behind Joe-Boy and slipped the noose over the convicted Cherokee's head. It was then that tragedy turned to travesty.

The barrel-chested sheriff stepped back to make the end of the line fast and Joe-Boy took to his heels. The Indian leaped from the platform, jerking the rope from the sheriff's hands, and darted down the street at a dead run. The deputies raised their shotguns, but there was no way to fire at Joe-Boy with the massed crowd.

Women screamed; some of the men cheered. Children began to run along after the escaping prisoner; dogs darted out from alleyways to join in the chase, snapping at men, at each other in their excitement. A startled horse, loosely hitched, reared up from the rail and bucked away, wild-eyed, down the street, towing a careening buggy behind.

"Go, Joe-Boy!" a man yelled enthusiastically.

"You can make it!"

Cursing wildly, Sheriff Lomas chased after his escaping prisoner. Running in Western boots, his speed was no match for the younger, moccasined Cherokee, but just as Joe-Boy reached the ice house, the sheriff managed to step down hard on the rope that still trailed from the escapee's neck. Joe-Boy was jerked to a strangling halt, landing on his back in the middle of the dusty street. He sat up, stunned for a moment, then tried to rise and take flight again. He got halfway up, clawing at the tightened noose around his throat, before Sheriff Lomas, sweating profusely and still cursing, reached him.

"You dumb bastard," they heard Lomas say. Then he drew his .44 revolver from its holster and shot Joe-Boy in the head. Panting, the sheriff backed away, straightening his Stetson. He ordered his deputy, "Get the damn rope and call the coroner."

Somehow it seemed much more terrible than a hanging, which was, after all, a lawful sentence. Even the most fervent reveler fell somberly silent. A lost red balloon drifted past, floating high and away. Elizabeth saw her father, his face as dark as death and as fixed as stone, staring at Sheriff Lomas's back as the big man strode away.

Roy Adair spoke not a single word on the way home to Broken Post. The three children sat in the back of the wagon, intimidated by their father's mood, afraid to speak above a whisper.

That evening Elizabeth lay prone on the bed in the room the two girls shared, her toes wriggling. Shanna sat brushing her long hair before the bevel-cut oval mirror. Her brush halted in its downward motion. Just two weeks shy of her eigtheeenth birthday, her beauty was stunning even to her younger sister.

"It was terrible," Shanna said petulantly. "Whyever did Father take us? I thought it would be fun at first."

"I don't think that's why he took us," Elizabeth said softly.

Her older sister glanced at her in the mirror and began brushing her hair vigorously again. "What do you mean, Elizabeth?"

"I don't think he wanted to take us at all . . . except to teach us something."

"What?" Shanna tossed her glossy black hair over her shoulders where it cascaded like an obsidian waterfall. "What could be learned at a spectacle like that?"

"Something we're too young to understand," Elizabeth said, rolling onto her back to look out at the night sky beyond the window.

"Then how could we learn it! Honestly, Elizabeth, you can be so silly at times," Shanna said, banging down her tortoiseshell brush in disgust. She rose and smoothed her blue cotton skirt, turning before the mirror.

"Are you going somewhere?" Elizabeth asked.

"To Tina's to listen to their crystal set. Last night they got Denver on it. Honestly, I don't know why Father doesn't buy one for us."

Elizabeth didn't answer. She had closed her eyes, but that only made matters worse.

Instead of closing out the real world, she could see more clearly the image of Joe-Boy Parker lying in the dust of the street, his mouth open in shock, the dark blood spilling from his skull drawing blue bottle flies as the people turned away or rushed toward the scene to witness a man in death.

Shanna flitted out, the screen door banging, and Elizabeth rose to go out into the twilit yard. A pale half-moon rose lazily in the east, gilding the softly flowing Otter Creek. Her stomach felt hollow and tight. In the west, a lone star shone through the orange-gold evening haze like a distant memory. She walked toward the twin oaks where Roy Adair had fashioned a bench circling the trees, and sat, staring at the tangle of their dark and evil roots.

One of the bitch Maggie's pups had followed her and sat between her ankles waiting in fuzzy anticipation for some affection. Stupid little ball of fur, head cocked, tiny pink tongue dangling. It had no name. The two bitches had so many litters no one paid any attention, except the time one of them was mounted by a coyote and Roy had put all the puppies down, saying he'd never be able to trust any of them around the chickens.

The world went slowly dark; the moon seemed cold and mocking. She dropped a hand to the pup's muzzle and it bit innocently at her fingers with needle-sharp teeth. The night was too still; from far beyond Oak Knoll to the south she could hear the Roberts's crystal radio slur and crackle, reaching for reception from the long copper wire strung across their yard. Not so distantly she heard a coyote yap, and the fuzzy pup cringed until she picked it up and cradled it in her arms. The puppy, its stubby tail wagging, furiously licked at her face, wriggling in relieved ecstasy as if only she could save it from some terrible fate and had, indeed, done so . . .

No one had saved Joe-Boy Parker.

Elizabeth rose and, still cradling the pup in her arms, started back toward the low house where cedar smoke rose white against a midnight-blue sky. She was nearly to the back door when she paused and halted. Black Jack, Warren Weaver, and another man she didn't know had arrived on horseback. Her father and mother always shooed Elizabeth away when the men were having one of their councils. Besides, Black Jack always drank too much whiskey, making Elizabeth uncomfortable.

The puppy squirmed in her arms and Elizabeth put it down

to run to its mother's nipples. She walked away from the house, toward the creek, still painfully uncertain of what the day's events had meant.

Looking back toward the house, she could see her mother's nearly fragile figure moving behind the yellow lace of the windows. There were late dove shadows across the last streak of color in the western sky and a raucous cricket chorus sounded in the grass.

Something—she knew not what—caused her to murmur a small prayer as she continued on. Christ and her small sins and the blood of Joe-Boy all seemed to merge in a confused, complicated swirl. Black Jack roared with anger behind her. Her mother shushed him; her father spoke in a low even voice. The low brassy light along the western horizon was overwhelmed by darkness and the deadening sky settled, smothering secret sins.

She leaned against the broken oak at the river's edge and listened to the night words. They had quit speaking English inside the house and now used the old tongue. Grandfather Deerfoot had tried to teach the Cherokee tongue to the children, but none of them had any real interest in learning it any more than they had an interest in hearing the tale of his mother dying on the Trail of Tears. It was all so long ago it had lost any real meaning.

Elizabeth stayed out much too late, dreaming star dreams. The men had argued and Black Jack had gotten drunk, as usual. Sometime after midnight they rode away silently; even the horses' hoofs made no sound against the loam of the riverbank trail. Shanna had walked home from Tina Roberts's house. Entering the house she found Tom asleep by the softly glowing embers in the fireplace. Still Elizabeth did not go to sleep. Restlessly she went out once more. The pup, its belly full of milk, had returned, and she scooped it up, walking through the moon shadows and the mosquitoes, the darting, feeding night birds, trying to read the mysteries of the stars. Without doing so intentionally, she passed beneath her parents' window and heard them talking quietly.

". . . Still," Sarah said in a strangely muffled voice, "keep it from the children, Roy. They are so young."

"Yes," Roy Adair answered in a voice uncharacteristically soft. It was not the authoritative voice she recognized as her father's. She knew sometimes in their room alone her parents spoke with gentle, almost secretive words, but this was not the same as those, either. "I will ride tonight, but for now . . . Time makes such insidious inroads, my love. I feel so old at times. Make me feel younger."

There was a silence then, which was no silence, and Elizabeth hurried toward her bed, the night too mysterious and deep to be investigated further.

"Hey, Tom! Oh, Tom! Where are you?"

Tom flung open the window to his bedroom and stared sleepily out at the dawn light and Billy Bird standing there grinning, a slim silhouette with a small shotgun and a huge straw hat. His black-spotted white dog, Old Warrior, sat beside Billy, laughing a dog's dangling-tongue laugh.

"What's the matter with you, Billy?" Tom hissed, hanging halfway out the screenless window.

"What's the matter with me? We were going hunting this morning, remember? You asked me."

"Okay," Tom said sleepily. A yawn stretched his mouth. "I forgot. But none of that yellin'. My dad'll tan me and you too."

"Sure, just hurry up. We're already past sunrise. Rabbits'll be taking to their holes."

The window closed and Billy tossed sticks for Old Warrior until Tom, still draped in sleep, hair mussed, .410 shotgun in his hand, stuffing shells into the pockets of his loose poplin shirt, slipped out of the back door, careful to keep the screen from banging on its spring.

" 'Bout time," Billy Bird said. A perpetually smiling boy, he had terrible buck teeth and walked with a limp caused by a clubfoot. He and Tom had been best friends forever.

"Okay, I already said I was sorry," Tom Adair replied. From the other pocket of his shirt, he pulled three milk biscuits. He gave one to Bill and they walked on, silently chewing.

"Want to try The Split?" Billy Bird asked. "Janet Lightning told me she saw three foxes up there last week."

"She's crazy," Tom commented, "but why not, sure. Good a place as any."

They walked another hundred yards before Bill said quietly, "I think she's pretty smart." Tom glanced at his friend and grinned, punching him on the shoulder.

"And beautiful?"

"Stop it, Tom," Bill said. "I don't say nothin' about Lorna Paxton, do I?"

"No, and you better not," Tom said, stiffening. "or I just might have to whip you, and that would be a shame."

"Over a girl, it would be," Billy agreed, grinning his bucktoothed grin, and the two walked on, breaking open their shotguns, loading, falling silent so as not to frighten the game away.

They passed the schoolhouse deep in the pooled shadows of the huge oaks surrounding it. On the porch stood Mrs. Hoyt, her arms crossed against the cool of morning, her frail figure pathetically at odds with the long wild land beyond. Bill nudged Tom as they passed.

"Look at that poor critter."

Tom glanced at the bespectacled white teacher in the patterned cotton dress and shrugged. "She's all ready to start pounding it into their skulls and the sun ain't barely up."

"They'll never get me in there," Bill said with some passion.

"Me, neither. I woulda gone to the tribal schools my dad told me about; but not that one."

"My daddy says they ought to have burned it down." Bill shouldered his rifle as a cottontail started from the brush, but he didn't have a clean shot and he lowered the .410, ammunition being too dear to waste on a "maybe" shot. Old Warrior took off to give chase for a short distance, but there was no chance for him to catch the swerving rabbit.

The dog returned, panting, and fell in behind Bill. Warrior was a good old dog. He had been trained a long time ago not to bark at the game, not to run in front of the shotguns' muzzles. He had had one ear nocked once by buckshot as a pup, and that was all the lesson he had needed. Tom was still looking toward the school where within the hour, Mrs. Hoyt would start clanging her brass handbell, summoning the children who never came. What had brought that sad person to the Nation?

"My sister Elizabeth goes to school every day," Tom said mockingly.

"Yeah, well, there you go. Tom! Look at the kids who go there. Jeannie Bear, sure. Little snoop. Lorna Paxton . . ."

"I told you not to say a word against her," Tom warned.

"I didn't, Tom. I'm just stating the fact. There's Dumb John Mountain Song. He could go for a hundred years and never learn his alphabet. His mother sends him to get him out of the way. And there's Allyn Jefferson—the sissy. Wears a tie to school too! I ask you what's a boy fourteen years old still doing in school?"

Tom shook his head. "It's not for me. I like this just fine. Give me a shotgun and a fish hook and I'm a happy man."

"Me too. Look, Tom." They were nearing the eastern bluffs of Otter Creek and the cabin where crazy Alfred Inkatha lived. He was there now, running around his contraption, six or seven little grandkids in his wake, all shrieking with excitement. His contraption was his concept of what an aeroplane should be like. Ten-foot wings it had, covered with feathers he stuck to the wood with mucilage he boiled down himself from dead animal's hoofs. He knew some white men had taken flight, had seen a picture of the machine and figured the white men were stupid not to know that there was a reason birds had feathers—could they fly without them? Of course not. Alfred saw the boys passing and he cupped his hands to his mouth and yelled.

"Going hunting, heh! Going to get some geese?"

"Just rabbits, Alfred Inkatha!" Tom shouted back. "No geese."

"I could use some goose feathers if you shoot some geese. Grouse is okay!" he continued to yell. "Grouse is okay if you can't find no geese, but geese is better."

"Okay, Alfred Inkatha," Tom shouted, "if we find some."

The two boys went on, laughing and screwing up their faces in imitation of Alfred Inkatha's excitable expression. Nearing The Split, a narrow brushy canyon, they divided, Tom taking the left of the canyon, Billy Bird the right. When one of them would startle a rabbit out of the brush, it would automatically run down the ravine and up the other side into the shotgun range of the other. They never failed with this maneuver, and today they had three cottontails and one brush rabbit before an hour had passed. Tom had his two hanging from his belt by leather laces poked through their Achilles tendons. They never went far into The Split, it became rapidly too steep for comfortable walking. But it was cool and wild-smelling, the scents of sage, chia, and sumac blending together in the still-shadowed ravine. They sat for a while on a flat rock, Tom plucking new grass from beside the rock, chewing on it.

"We could try for cats," Bill suggested, but Tom shook his head.

"Stop for catfish and the rabbits'll go bad, Bill."

"I suppose. It's a good day to just hang around Wigwam

Island, though."

"Maybe we could try it tomorrow. Got to get the bunnies home to Mom." There was a covey of quail in the brush not twenty feet below them. They could see them running along the ground. Toss a rock in the brush and they'd take to wing. Be surprising if you didn't take down two with one shell, but as much as Tom liked quail, he hated plucking them. He liked rabbits. Take your pocketknife and cut a circle around their ankles. Then you just peel 'em. Like taking off a sweater. When you get to the head, you cut it all off, go back and get the tail, gut 'em, and you're done. Tom could do a cottontail in less than a minute, easy. Plucking little birds, now that was a different matter.

"Want to get some snakes, Tom?" Bill asked, leaning back lazily, propping himself up on one elbow.

"Mom don't want no more skins in the house."

Bill nodded. They hadn't done it for awhile, but they knew where a big den of rattlers was. The way to get them was to tie a hunting knife to the end of a stick. You heat the blade of the knife with a match and stick it into the den. A rattler senses the heat and strikes, splitting his own skull open. Tom had a drawer full of rattles at home.

"Let's get on back, Bill," Tom said through a yawn. "I ain't had breakfast."

"All right," Bill answered, yawning in response. They walked over the divide, not liking to go back the same way they had come—you don't need to see the same things every day. Cresting out of the valley they walked through the cool shade of one of the last big pine stands in the county, the scent of the big trees rich in their nostrils. Beyond they could see Fletcher's Pond like a spattering of sky. A crow taunted them and squirrels leaped from branch to branch among the bluish tall pines.

"Tom!" Bill stopped abruptly and threw out an arm to halt

Tom's progress. Bill's voice sounded shaky. Tom looked ahead, saw nothing, but gripped the stock of his .410 more tightly.

"What is it, Bill?" he asked in a near-whisper. "Wildcat?"

"No . . . don't you see it?"

"See what?"

"Right ahead, come on."

Tom peered into the forest shadows and then he, too, saw it. But what was it? They walked slowly forward toward the dark shape hanging between the trees. Bill whispered, "I think it's a man, Tom. I think it's a dead man."

Tom Adair didn't answer. He had already come to the same conclusion. The reason it had been hard to identify for what it was initially was because the man was hanging upside down, his legs tied to two pine tree boughs, his head dangling, arms touching the pine-needle-littered earth. The boys crept nearer.

"What happened to him, Tom?"

"I don't know—shut up!"

The man's shirt had fallen open, his big white belly spilling out. His hair hung toward the ground. His eyes were open and clouded like those of the rabbits hanging from Tom's belt. There was dried blood across his neck and jaw. A wire noose had been wrapped around his neck and drawn tight. His tongue protruded from his purple lips. His face was dark with trapped blood.

"Tom." Billy Bird touched his arm. "I think it's the sheriff. I think it's Sheriff Lomas."

Tom handed his shotgun to Billy and crouched down, studying the dark bloated face. He carefully lifted the shirtfront that had folded over on itself and caught the silver gleam of a badge. He dropped the shirt again as if the fabric were hot.

Straightening, he told Billy, "You're right. It is the sheriff. What do we do now?"

"We got to tell somebody," Bill said, looking around frantically.

"Who, Bill?"

"Someone, I dunno. They got to catch whoever done this."

"Well, damn all, Bill—who do you think done it! It was Nighthawks. The sheriff killed Joe-Boy and they got him back. Was your dad home last night, Bill?"

"He was . . . well, maybe I heard him riding out late." Bill said. His mouth was dry; he was having trouble talking. He couldn't take his eyes away from the dangling dead man.

"Well, Bill, my dad rode out too. I heard him. He was gone for a good three hours." He shook his head. "We can't tell nobody, Bill. And nobody's ever going to find him way up in these hills."

"Somebody ought to . . ."

"Somebody can! But it ain't going to be us, Billy Bird. We didn't see nothin'. We got to swear to keep it a secret between us."

"I do swear to, Tom . . . now can we get out of here? I don't like the feeling in my stomach."

Tom knew what he meant. They walked on quickly, weaving through the pines as they worked their way downslope. Neither of the boys said a word until they had emerged from the pines.

"Let's not take the road, Bill," Tom said.

"No," Billy Bird agreed. He peered into the sun, orienting himself. "We go straight ahead, though, we got to go across The Old Man's knoll."

"So?"

"So, he spooks me, Tom. He just sits and stares and stares . . . they say he eats bugs," he added irrelevantly.

"He don't eat bugs, and if he did, who cares—that's the shortest way and I want to get home. You can walk within three feet of him and he don't know you're there, anyway. Whistle up Warrior and let's go."

They walked slowly up the gradual incline of Old Man Hill.

There was a game path cut by deer that made its meandering way up the knoll through live oaks and stunted cedar. The new grass was bright and the purple lupine was beginning to come out.

Warrior, too tired to rove, followed at their heels. They could see Otter Creek below, making its sinuous silver way southward, the banks clotted with sycamores, willow, and white oak trees. Lost in the haze was the mile-long Wigwam Island, and farther, the dark specks on the water which were called The Hundred Islands, though Tom and Bill had once spent a day counting them and there were thirty-eight. They crested the knoll to see a thin twisted ribbon of smoke rising from The Old Man's camp.

"Let's give it wide berth, Tom," Billy said nervously.

"If you want!" Tom snapped. The morning's experience had affected them differently. Billy wanted to complain or talk foolishly. Tom had grown short-tempered. Neither spoke of the real reason for their discomfort with the day. They could see The Old Man now, sitting in front of his crude shelter, legs crossed, hands loose, eyes watching the far reaches of the land beyond the creek where all was gold and deep red, wild oats rising up from the clay along the blue-green of the river strip.

"I'll be, he does eat bugs—and lizards!" Billy broke into a high-pitched giggle and Tom glanced at him uncertainly. He knew what was bothering Billy. He himself had been thinking, *My father might have done that, my father might have done that.* As they trudged up the hill, letting it fall into the cadence of his strides. He was suddenly afraid to close his eyes for fear of seeing the upside-down man projected in his mind.

"Maybe we ought to give him a rabbit," Tom said.

"Why? There's plenty of bugs around!"

"Shut up, Billy, will you? The joke's worn thin."

The two boys, their shotguns in the crooks of their arms, approached The Old Man's camp, the white dog lagging.

"Jesus," Billy said, "look at that shack."

The ramshackle bark hut tilted dramatically to one side. It seemed any vagrant gust of wind could level it. The Old Man's fire burned low within and the smell of roasting game birds—dove or quail—drifted to them through the still air. The Old Man's white hair, like smoke around his skull, was drawn into a single braid that ran down his back. He had a blanket over his shoulders, no shirt, a pair of black jeans, and worn moccasins. A necklace of bear claws was visible where the blanket parted to reveal his shallow chest.

"All he needs is some feathers," Billy whispered.

Tom said nothing. He had the sudden urge to talk to The Old Man. They were, after all, crossing his land. It seemed rude to speak not at all. His voice was tight as they approached the old Indian, but he said clearly, "Hello, Old Man. It is a good day."

Dark, impenetrable eyes drifted to Tom's face. The Old Man nodded. "It is a good day. Did you bury the dead man?"

"No . . ." It was so unexpected a question, he could find nothing to add. The old Cherokee nodded.

"Too bad. You should have buried him. Coyotes will eat him. No man should be devoured by wild dogs."

And then he said no more. He shifted his eyes back to the long Oklahoma distances and might as well have been on the moon, so far from the young men was he. Billy jabbed the immobilized Tom Adair roughly in the ribs, and they walked on, moving toward their homes in the valley below.

They spoke hardly at all the rest of the way.

The day and its events had traveled far beyond ordinary speech. Reaching home, Tom went into the kitchen, rapidly dressed his rabbits, placing them in the icebox in a paper bag. Then, after burying the entrails and heads, he washed his hands and slipped into his bedroom to lie, hands clasped beyond his head, dreaming thunderous daydreams.

A soft tap on his door turned his head. "Come in," he said and Roy Adair entered the room to stand in puzzlement over his son.

"Ten o'clock in the morning and you're in bed? You feel all right?"

"Feel fine, Dad," Tom said, but his eyes slid away from his father's gaze. Roy felt his son's forehead.

"Well, all right. Only two rabbits, Tom? They won't go far."

"Wasn't much luck today." Still Tom looked toward the window, looking past the heavy red curtains toward the big black oak tree where jays hopped from branch to branch and squawked at one another or at the squirrels intruding on their territory.

"Well . . ." Roy hesitated, ". . . rest up then. Maybe you'll split some kindling for your mother later."

"Yes, sir. I'll be sure to," Tom answered.

Roy backed out of the room, closing the door gently, leaving Tom in semi-darkness. Sarah was in the kitchen cutting up the rabbits when Roy found her. "What's the matter with Tom?"

"Is something the matter with him?" she asked in surprise, the knife poised.

"Something. I dunno," Roy said. He sat at the tiny kitchen table with its red-checked cloth and rubbed his head. "Just don't feel up to snuff, I guess."

"He's getting to that age, Roy," Sarah said, pulling down the flour canister. She began to make a batter for the fried rabbit. "Maybe he's young to us, but I hear he has a powerful interest in that little Lorna Paxton.

Roy laughed out loud and moved to his wife, slipping his arms around her, looking down into her eyes. There was flour on her nose and he kissed it away. "Is that it, woman? Why do females think everything must have to do with romance? And if there's not enough romance, they start inventing it for themselves and other people."

"I?" Sarah asked coyly. She tilted her head to one side.

"You what?"

"I invent romance or I don't have enough?"

"Have you enough?" Roy asked, kissing her small round ear lightly. She swayed against him and smiled dreamily.

"All any woman could need, now get out of here before romance interferes with my motherly chores!"

Roy Adair went out to stand on the small porch, the gusting breeze off of Otter Creek lifting his black hair, still untouched by silver, off his shoulders. Tom bothered him. It was nothing, he knew. A touch of flu, a lovebug bite, but as he walked toward the barn he felt uncomfortable with the day. It was guilt nagging him, Roy knew—if only Black Jack hadn't gotten so drunk and crazy; they had only intended to scare Sheriff Lomas and teach him a lesson—but Tom could not possibly know anything about last night's events—he was tormenting himself over nothing. Roy shrugged off the mood and went into the horse-scented barn to pitch the animals some fresh clover hay. He whistled as he went, his good spirits returning.

Elizabeth heard the clanging of the big brass handbell Mrs. Hoyt rang for school and she rushed on, her pigtails flying. She did not like to be late, but Shanna would not get out of her way that morning as she tried to dress hurriedly and make herself a lunch.

Elizabeth knew Shanna did it on purpose, mocking her for even caring if she was late, early, or absent. Elizabeth liked school. Mrs. Hoyt made them work hard, but sometimes she would tell them stories of faraway people and long-ago times and her eyes behind her spectacles would become dreamy and lost temporarily before she would bring herself around and say something like, "But enough about the War of the Roses, let us get back to work."

On this morning as Elizabeth tried to make it to the school door before the last ringing of the bell, Marion Pope Hoyt saw her crossing the creek, skirts hoisted, a leather strap wrapped around her school books, her face anxious, and she rang the bell for a little longer than usual. Elizabeth was a sincere and studious little girl.

Mrs. Hoyt, as she called herself—the truth was that she had never been married and was a spinster at forty-three—watched and smiled inside. Mrs. Hoyt had imagined that being a widow would look better on her job application and had carried on with the small deception, inventing a departed husband who had been a railroad engineer in Pennsylvania. At times she could blush with shame for the invention, but no one had ever questioned her and when the subject came up, she pretended that she preferred not to dwell on old memories.

At times, she could no longer even recall the lost idealism that had brought her to the very edge of the country and beyond to teach the unfortunate Indian. Idealism askew. The Indian did not want her school. But she had found another reason for lingering. Unfortunately, that womanly yearning was doomed to be as frustrated as the dream of an idealistic educator. She loved an Indian man.

"Good morning, Elizabeth."

"Am I late, Mrs. Hoyt?"

"No," she lied, consulting the watch she wore pinned to the bosom of her brown calico dress. "Just on time," and they entered the tiny classroom.

Elizabeth slipped into her desk as near to the front of the room as possible. The others teased her about wanting to be a teacher's pet, but the truth was, at sixteen, she was still very short and could barely read the blackboard, squinting from even that near. She brushed her roughly cut black hair from her eyes. Shanna had cut it for her. The new style, her sister had said, was going to be bobbed hair. Shanna, however, continued to wear her hair to her waist and Elizabeth wondered what had really motivated Shanna. Mother had been unable to fix it—"I can't make hair grow, Elizabeth." She had scolded Shanna, of course, but took it as a girlish effort gone wrong.

Jeannie Bear was already asleep at her desk as Mrs. Hoyt began to put arithmetic problems on the blackboard, her head resting on her crossed forearms. Mathematics not Elizabeth's strong point, she had determined to get better at it and tried to pay complete attention. Something classmates like John Mountain Song made difficult. He was not quite right in the head and ugly, although he was affable as a puppy; he constantly made body noises and picked his nose. People said his father had hit him in the head with a stick when John was only four and his father was drunk. Elizabeth didn't know.

She could glance in the other direction and become more distracted so that her calculations went all wrong. Allyn Jefferson sat stiffly in his chair, his eyes dreamy behind his glasses, wearing a white shirt and blue tie. He was fourteen, nearly fifteen, but still came to school every day, which was rare for the boys in the class. His father, Kenneth, was the editor and publisher, printer and distributor of the *Tribune,* a four-sheet newspaper that was printed half in English, half in the Sequoyah's Cherokee alphabet. Allyn had light brown hair despite being a full-blood and a relatively long face that Elizabeth thought made him look like a poet. Byron, perhaps. She had seen his picture in a book but could not read his poetry, the allusions being so culturally distant.

From miles away, Elizabeth suddenly was aware that, as she gazed at Allyn, Mrs. Hoyt had been calling her to the blackboard. Blushing furiously, she went forward.

Some of the children snickered. Allyn sat with dignified aloofness, watching not her but the board. Mrs. Hoyt had to repeat her instructions before Elizabeth set out to solve the first three problems, which she blundered through. Math was not her forte, but that was not it. She wondered if Allyn thought she was foolish. Did Mrs. Hoyt think she was hopeless?

Oddly, some people insisted that Mrs. Hoyt wanted Allyn's father, the newspaper publisher, as a husband, and they laughed, of course. A mixed marriage at that time was unthinkable, even if they were both snooty educated people.

Kenneth Jefferson had graduated from the Cherokee Male Seminary and that was where Allyn intended to go. Meanwhile, he gleaned every bit of information he could from Mrs. Hoyt, who, despite her distant manner, was well educated. People thought Allyn was stuffy—even a sissy. Elizabeth thought the older boy was mature and shatteringly handsome.

Distracted, she had meanwhile managed to multiply 30 × 42 and come up with 1060. The children snickered. Elizabeth returned to her seat, ears burning. It was going to be a terrible day. Now what would Allyn think of her?

Jeannie Bear was awakened to take her turn at the blackboard and Elizabeth began drawing squiggly, agitated figures in her math notebook. It seemed like eternity before the lunch break.

She was first from the schoolhouse and walked to the big sycamore where she sat alone in the deep, warm shade, eating an apple. She became aware of the shadow deepening and the slightest rustling of dry leaves as a soft footfall approached. Startled, she turned and her heart nearly stopped.

"Do I make you nervous, Elizabeth?" Allyn Jefferson asked. "If so, I'm sorry."

"Nervous?"

"I could see you weren't concentrating today." He didn't stutter, but his speech lagged as if he were trying to speak very carefully. A darting dragonfly buzzed past, humming toward the silent quicksilver flow of Otter Creek. Allyn lost whatever self-confidence he had had. He stumbled through his last words like any other fourteen-year-old boy attempting a leap toward manhood.

"I have discussed this with my father and we would be pleased if you would consent to visit us at the newspaper office . . . at our home. Thank you."

He turned then and walked away and Elizabeth sat with her mouth open, the red apple with one bite taken from it elevated in her hand, staring incredulously at his back. He liked her?

And she with her myopic vision and her hair now sawn off, with her ungainly body—slender and well enough put together, but seeming to wish to travel in all directions at once, unlike Shanna's sleek sophisticated progress across a room or through the forest, or when swimming, running, dancing—Shanna could do nothing ungracefully.

He actually likes me?

Mrs. Hoyt was on the porch ringing the handbell. Lunch was over. Elizabeth looked at her apple. The one bite was all she had had for lunch. It didn't matter a bit! She tossed the apple toward an oak where squirrels wound their way down the trunk, eyes bright and cautious, to dine on it. She passed her teacher and went into the schoolroom, failing to notice Mrs. Hoyt's small smile of approval . . . and envy.

"My father," Allyn was saying as he guided the sleek, long-legged bay horse, drawing the surrey toward Broken Post's town center, "is a passionate man. You must forgive him if he goes overboard with his rhetoric."

"Yes," Elizabeth said nervously. She believed she understood what Allyn had said; but out of school when his reticence fell away and he was a young man and not a schoolboy, his demeanor changed, his vocabulary expanded, and she felt herself to be quite young and unknowledgeable.

It was early on a Friday evening, the sky deep crimson and gilt. The silver willows lazed in the sheer blanket of rising river mist. The horse's hoofs clopped steadily, pleasantly on the creek-side trail. It had taken Elizabeth hours, days to bring up the courage to ask her father if she could ride with Allyn to visit his father. Astonishingly, Roy Adair had simply looked up and smiled and said, "Go ahead. Enjoy yourself. Don't stay out too late." An impenetrable look had passed between Roy and Sarah, but that was all there was to it, as if both were secretly pleased.

Shanna, of course, lying on her stomach on the bed reading her movie magazines, had said caustically, "Well, if they let you go, fine. Although why you'd want to go anywhere with that sap I don't understand."

The Jefferson house and the *Tribune* newspaper office were connected by a side door. Together they were no larger than Elizabeth's own small house. Kenneth Jefferson stood at the alley door to his home in shirtsleeves, smoking a curved pipe as they drew up. By the time Allyn had hitched the horse and helped Elizabeth from the carriage, his father had put on a coat and tucked his pipe away, brushed his thinning hair, and lighted the two matching oil lamps at each corner of the small living room.

"Hello, hello, Elizabeth. I hope you are well." Then the father shook hands with his son, something Elizabeth had never seen done before, as if they were friends meeting. The small house had a roughly built stone fireplace where embers glowed dully, a red and black Indian blanket on the wall above it, a braided rag rug covering a portion of the rough plank floor, and little else. Elizabeth had expected more—or something different, perhaps—books piled everywhere, evidence of the man's education, perhaps old newspapers framed on the wall, but the room was nearly primitively bare, perhaps because they were two men living alone. She could only dimly see a second room, a kitchen she assumed, and she wondered where they slept. The fire glowed dimly, the oil lamps sending thin wisps of smoke ceiling-ward. And beyond and just under those scents Elizabeth swore she could smell something else. A woman's perfume. She didn't have to wonder for long about that because from the darkened kitchen, tray in hands, Mrs. Hoyt appeared.

"Hello, Elizabeth," she said with a pleasant smile. And where were her spectacles?

Her dress was of blue taffeta, sleek and narrowly cut, falling to her ankles. And she wore pearls around her neck. Her hair was piled high, and as she passed Allyn and Elizabeth, sitting nervously on the sofa, the scent of the enigmatic perfume became plainer. She walked to Kenneth Jefferson and offered him cookies and coffee from the tray, then turned back to offer the younger people a snack.

Elizabeth could have sworn she saw Allyn's father's hand trail briefly down Mrs. Hoyt's spine toward her hip.

"It certainly is nice to see you here, Elizabeth," Mrs. Hoyt said in a tone different from her schoolroom voice, which the children joked sounded as if it were choked with chalk dust.

Elizabeth stuttered an answer. "It's nice to see you here too," knowing instantly that was wrong. "I'm happy to be here," she amended, growing flustered.

"Well, now, if that's all out of the way," Kenneth Jefferson said cheerfully, "and we're all happy to be here, shall we talk about other matters?"

Elizabeth chewed on her cookies and drank her milk, as uncertain as any young woman of fourteen how to start a conversation with adults.

Kenneth Jefferson started to light his pipe and then, appar-ently out of deference to his female guests, put it away again. The newspaper editor was obviously unhappy about something

His expression was bleak. Mrs. Hoyt, seated beside him, patted his hand.

"Is it the Supreme Court decision, Father?" Allyn was prompted to inquire. His father gave him a surprised look. Allyn knew full well that it was that, but glancing then at the young Cherokee girl sitting near him, he smiled faintly, realizing that Allyn wished to show off his knowledge for her.

"Yes, of course. Forgive me for being distracted, Elizabeth."

"It's quite all right," she said, having no idea what they were referring to.

"Is your response going to be in tomorrow's *Tribune,* Kenneth?" Mrs. Hoyt asked.

"Yes. I'm afraid we're not treating our guest fairly. Elizabeth may not have read the decision yet. Allyn—would you go into the shop and retrieve a copy?" Not only had Elizabeth never read the decision they were talking about, she was only vaguely aware of what the Supreme Court did. In fact, she had never so much as read a single copy of the *Tribune.*

She felt terribly young, uninformed, and overwhelmed. Why had she ever agreed to come to this place? Allyn had gone through the kitchen and into the shop and returned with a broadside sheet.

"Here it is. Shall I read it, Father?"

"If you like," his father agreed.

Allyn cleared his throat and adjusted his wire-rimmed spectacles. He looked over the top of the paper toward Elizabeth. "As I'm sure you know this has to do with the Marchie Tiger case."

"I don't know," Elizabeth said, her voice sounding very small suddenly.

"Certainly your father and his friends have discussed it at your house!" Allyn said, truly surprised. "After all, they are the ones who . . ."

"Allyn!" his father said sharply. "Elizabeth has said she did not know the case."

"Yes, sir. Briefly," Allyn said, "Marchie Tiger was a full-blood Creek who sold the surplus of his land allotment. According to the Five Tribes Act, he had no right to and his heirs wished the land returned to them." His father half-shrugged as if that were enough explanation for now, for the girl and Allyn returned to the paper to read aloud: "The United States Supreme Court has reversed the state court's ruling concerning the rights of Marchie Tiger's inheritors to his allotment land. And has said, 'Our conclusions are that Congress has had at all times, and now has, the right to pass legislation in the interest of the Indians as a dependent people; that there is nothing in citizenship incompatible with this guardianship over the Indian's land, that it rest with Congress to determine when its guardianship shall cease; and while it still continues, it has the right to vary its restrictions upon alienation of Indian lands in what it deems the best interest of the Indian." Allyn tossed the paper aside. "Do you understand that, Elizabeth?"

"Not entirely," she murmured.

"They have made us citizens without our request; now they tell us we haven't the same rights as other citizens where our land is concerned. They can do as they wish. Is this going to be your lead sentence, Father?" Allyn asked, indicating a handwritten addition to the article. When Kenneth nodded, he read with pride the beginning of his father's editorial.

"Three centuries of civilization have not brought the full-blood Indian to the point where his rights equal those of a white man."

No one spoke in response. They sat in silent unease. Elizabeth shifted on the sofa. At length Mrs. Hoyt broke the silence.

"Is that wise, Kenneth? Judge Brant will attempt to close you down again on some technicality. Look what happened after

Joe-Boy Parker was executed—some people have been saying that you incited the murder of Sheriff Lomas."

"My editorial didn't even appear in the paper until after they had found Lomas," Kenneth said, and he seemed a different man now to Elizabeth, more passionate, more formidable. "I will adhere to my beliefs, Marion. A newspaper must speak the truth for those who cannot." Allyn, sitting beside Elizabeth, beamed with pride as he listened to his father.

"Well," Kenneth said, rising. He went to the door and opened it. Standing there, his back to the alley, he lit his pipe, the cherry-scented smoke drifting across the room, "let's read something a little more cheerful. Allyn, find that letter Pleasant Porter wrote about life on the Nation before the Dawes Commission and the allotment laws. Elizabeth might like to hear it."

Elizabeth smiled. She knew nothing about the Dawes Commission either except that it was a bad thing that had tried to take their land away and that Roy Adair refused to be a party to it, he and his full-blood friends.

Allyn emerged from the dark, ink-smelling depths of the building to read a short letter on a yellowing piece of foolscap. He stood beside the lantern and spoke:

"This is Pleasant Porter, Elizabeth, a chief of the Creeks who spoke before the Senate of the United States about the old times.

" 'In those times they always raised enough to eat and that was all we wanted. We had little farms and we raised patches of corn and potatoes, and poultry and pigs, horses and cattle, and a little of everything. In fact, in my early life I don't know that I ever knew of an Indian family that were paupers. There is plenty of them now; there was none then. They were all prosperous and happy and contented in their way, and what more could they want?

" 'I say that I don't know of an Indian family in my early life that were paupers. In those days the ones that would be paupers if they lived now stayed with their kin folks and they made them work. Now, back of that custom of the Creeks was that everybody had to work or leave on the town, and the town had taskmasters who took care of him and saw that he worked. There was not a skulker or one who shirked work among us at then, quite different from what it is now. We had a kind of an Arcadian government then. If anyone was sick or unable to work, the neighbors came in and planted his crop, and they took care of it—saw that the fences were all right—and the women took care of the garden, and wood was got for him, and so on. In fact, everything was done under the care of the people—they did everything and looked after the welfare of everything . . .' " Allyn put the paper down.

"Is that enough, Father?"

"I think so," Kenneth said. He knocked the dottle out of his pipe and returned to the room, closing the plank door behind him.

"Poor Elizabeth," Marion Pope Hoyt said, "she must be thinking this is the oddest visit ever. Elizabeth? When you graduate from our school next year, what are you going to do?"

"I don't . . . work in Tahlequah or stay at home with Mother . . ." she hadn't really thought about it. Next year was so far away.

"You are a special young lady," Mrs. Hoyt said. "You thirst for knowledge. I know this—I work with you every day. I—we—hope you will consider going to the Cherokee Female Seminary at the Masonic Lodge in Tahlequah. They take girls fourteen and over. I would recommend you enthusiastically. We don't want to waste another mind, Elizabeth. The parents hate our school because it is white administered, the children don't see any reason to learn if they can't progress here. You are different; you have to make yourself different."

40

"My parents would never . . . could never. They couldn't afford such a thing."

"I've spoken to your father already," Kenneth Jefferson said. It was difficult to believe the newspaper editor was serious. "He will leave it up to you. The money will come from the tribal fund."

"Do it, Elizabeth," Allyn said eagerly. "I'm going to the men's seminary—I'm leaving when this term is up."

"I can't," Elizabeth shook her head rapidly. All of this was overwhelming.

"We need educated men and women, Elizabeth," Kenneth said. "Just think about it, that's all, please think it over. For all of us."

The ride home was silent, Allyn trotting the bay horse along the river road as the black satin of Otter Creek wound away toward the rising moon. A huge horned owl swooped low and screeched at them as they came too near to its nesting place. Elizabeth glanced at Allyn time and again, waiting for him to explain, to tell her why she had been invited there, what they wanted her to learn, to do, but he spoke only a few words on the three-mile ride home.

Watching her as she walked to the back porch and entered her house, Allyn turned the bay in a circle and headed back toward the village. Elizabeth shrugged and went into the kitchen where Tom and Roy were playing a sort of two-handed solitaire they had invented. Grandfather Deerfoot sat watching them, his face solemn as if he were having his fortune silently told with each newly upturned card.

"How was your visit?" Roy asked without looking up from the game.

"Fine. We talked of a lot of things . . ." she hesitated, "most of it I didn't know anything about, so I just listened."

"Good," Roy Adair said enigmatically. He glanced up at his

daughter and smiled slightly. "That is all good. Go to bed now. Tomorrow you may all go to the moving pictures in Tahlequah. I have to take sawn wood in and your mother will shop."

Surprised, Elizabeth thanked her father and said goodnight. Roy did not really approve of the moving picture show, she knew. It seemed that her world was about to open up in some mysterious way. She felt as if she had discovered a secret doorway and it might lead anywhere.

She found Shanna on her bed, reading a movie magazine as usual. Her hair was pinned up intricately in imitation of some new film star. Father would definitely not approve of that, but Elizabeth said nothing and began slowly undressing. Shanna lowered the magazine, looked over the top of the pages, and raised it again.

"Tina Roberts is going with us tomorrow. You'll have to sit by yourself," Shanna said.

Elizabeth shrugged mentally. Shanna's words hurt as always when she rejected her younger sister; but Elizabeth was too tired, her mind too busy with other matters to complain. She stretched out on her bed on top of the quilt and looked out the window toward the dimly glittering stars, wondering how far away they were, really, and if someone could ever reach them.

Tom decided not to go to the films. He would rather, he said, go out to Wigwam Island with Billy Bird and try to catch that hundred-pound catfish they said lived somewhere along its shaded shores. He also intended to walk past the Paxton farm and maybe see Lorna Paxton if she was in the yard, though he didn't mention that, of course.

Tina Roberts had arrived early, eyes bright. Her father had given her a whole quarter to spend. Shanna and she sat talking on the tailgate of the lumber wagon, Shanna's long hair brushed down again, drifting in the breeze. They would laugh and then whisper and laugh again. Elizabeth watched them from the porch. Her mother emerged from the house, stood beside her younger daughter, and briefly rested a hand on her shoulder.

"Let's go, honey. You'll have a lot of fun today."

"Yes," was all Elizabeth could manage to say. She walked toward the wagon and sat up on the spring seat between Sarah and Roy. She only felt uncomfortable sitting with the older girls.

Roy came out of the house, wearing tight blue jeans, a blood-red shirt, and a wide-brimmed western hat, his hair drawn back into a tail. Elizabeth was watching her mother and she could see her eyes change. She still loved her man, still thought he was the most handsome man on the Cherokee Nation. It was very obvious and oddly fulfilling to know that it was so. Roy clambered up, unwound the reins from the brake handle, and snapped them, starting the mismatched horses—the little roan mare and the old black gelding—toward Tahlequah.

"Do we go past the Cherokee Female Seminary?" Elizabeth asked.

Her father glanced at her from the corners of his eyes. "We could. Any reason?"

"I thought I might like to see it," Elizabeth replied, her eyes fixed on the distance. "I just thought it might be interesting to see."

CHAPTER TWO

She awoke from a dream of silver and silent black to the clamor and glare of color and sound.

Shanna frowned in her sleep. Still in her mind women in silk glittered with a diamond glow, and handsome young men in stiff collars led them dancing gracefully across a polished ballroom floor.

Now awake, she sat and watched the early sun stream through the blue and white checked curtains of her small room. A mockingbird perched in the dusty scrub oak tree beyond the windowsill sang raucously.

Beyond the door pans rattled. Elizabeth was up and gone, her bed made, her teddy bear centered on the pillow.

She sat up, swinging her bare feet to the floor, then with a sigh rose to the color and racketing of the day, rising from the shelter of her bed, leaving the web and whirl of her comforting dreams behind.

Shanna walked to the window and threw the curtains aside, startling the mockingbird away.

The morning breeze pressed her thin cotton nightdress against her thighs. Her hair fluttered across her forehead and into her eyes. Beyond the window the thin brown corn stood withered and bent. The rains had not come in time. Chickens scratched aimlessly at the parched earth. Shanna let the curtains drop.

Snatching up her faded yellow towel and a bar of lye soap,

she went from her room, down the narrow hall, and out the side door.

It was still quite chilly. The persimmon sun rose slowly, glowing through the river mist. The eastern clouds were brass scrollwork against a pale sky.

It was somewhere along that walk down the river path for her morning bath that Shanna made her decision. The exact moment was not defined by any event or thought.

She just knew.

Her plunge into the river became a sort of baptism. The water was cold, but she barely felt it. She stood in the waist-deep water, her long hair draping her, and she smiled. Already the dragonflies, blue and orange, were darting above the river, and the birds had begun to gather to hunt them. Shanna didn't notice them; she did not see them.

She was looking far ahead and far away toward a new world.

She had to tell Tina.

She dressed hurriedly and started off through the oak grove. Reaching the Roberts' house while Tina still lazed in bed.

"Tell her she should get up," Mrs. Roberts said. "Tell her there's work to be done."

Shanna smiled in promise and rushed on to Tina's bedroom door. She flung open the door and raced across the room to Tina's bed, leaping onto it. She propped herself up on an elbow and looked eagerly into Tina's sleepy eyes.

"What is it?" Tina asked through a yawn. "What are you doing here so early?"

"It's not early, ask your mother. I came to tell you a secret, Tina, a very important secret."

"What?" Tina asked, frowning. "What's happening, Shanna?"

"Listen," Shanna said, easing closer to Tina's face. She lowered her voice. "I'm going to Hollywood."

Tina's interest faded. "So am I," she said, sitting up on the side of the bed. "You know that. We've discussed it a hundred times. When we . . ."

"No, listen, Tina," Shanna said with urgency. "We've discussed it a hundred times. Something we'll do one day in the future. I don't mean that." Her voice became a tense whisper. She glanced toward the bedroom door, hearing the whirl of the spinning wheel in the room beyond. "I don't mean 'someday.' I'm going now. Today. I'll be eighteen years old in a week. Old enough to do something. By tomorrow at the latest, I'll be gone."

Tina's eyes searched those of her friend. She started to laugh and stopped herself.

She saw only resolution in Shanna's dark eyes.

"Stop it, Shanna!" Tina said with a smile. "Are you fooling me? Or yourself?"

"I'm not fooling at all, Tina. I've made up my mind. You know all the reasons."

"But now . . ." Tina's voice wavered.

"What's the sense in waiting? Wait for the future? For next year? For one day when we'll be old women looking back regretfully, wishing we had gone?"

Tina rose from the bed. She hunched forward, looking frail and frightened in her pink nightgown. "I'm starting to believe you're serious."

"Completely." Shanna rolled over on her back and smiled up at Tina. Over her head Douglas Fairbanks looked down from a magazine picture, his eyes amused and enigmatic. "Are you coming with me?"

"California . . . it's so far." Tina's eyes wandered the room. "How could we ever get there? Alone!"

"We can walk to Tahlequah. Or get a ride. From there we can take a bus to Oklahoma City. Then we ride the train the rest of the way."

Shanna sounded so sure. Tina stood hesitantly, listening to

the eagerness, the confidence bubble forth.

"Money . . ."

"I have forty-two dollars," Shanna confided. "It's enough. I've already checked on the fares."

Tina remained unconvinced. She sat down in the rocker beside her window.

Beyond it birds cut sharp-winged figures against a turquoise sky.

"But after we get there . . . we'll need a place to live, Shanna. How will we live? We can't expect to get into films in one day!"

"No, not in a day, of course." Shanna said, bouncing from the bed so that the white-painted iron headboard banged against the wall. "But everything is different out there, Tina. There are restaurants, hotels, laundries—oh, all sorts of places where we can find work until we break into films. We can get a little cottage—maybe right on the ocean where we can watch the sailing ships while we have breakfast.

"And you can go anywhere on the streetcars they have." Shanna knew this from the films they had seen. "On our days off we can ride out to the studios. They have a lot of work at the studios too. If we can't be in films right away, maybe we can be seamstresses or extra girls, like Mabel Normand, remember?"

"Yes, of course," Tina said, tugging nervously at her hair, "but it's so sudden."

"It's not! We've talked about it for years."

"But to actually do it . . . what will our parents say?"

"Why tell them?" Shanna shrugged. "I'm not going to tell mine anything until I send them a postcard from California."

"Oh, Shanna!" Tina turned her eyes away. Shanna took her by the shoulders and waited until Tina lifted her eyes again.

"We can do it, Tina. We have to do it now while we're young."

"But we have to tell them!" Tina said in a subdued wail. "You have to . . . what will you tell Wallace?"

"Nothing," Shanna said firmly.

"Shanna! He wants to marry you."

"And so? What do I care." She answered with a toss of her head. "Wallace! What is he? What will he ever be? Another Indian stuck on the Nation. Don't you understand, Tina? We have to go. If we stay here we will die here, old, exhausted, and poor like the land. I am going. Are you going with me?"

Tina couldn't answer. There was rebuke lurking in Shanna's eyes, waiting to be spoken. It was another dare, like those Shanna had always hurled at her in their girlhood.

She had promised to go with Shanna to Hollywood when the time came, but she had not expected the time to come so soon. Certainly not on this bright morning. Perhaps, being honest with herself, she had never really expected it to come. She watched Shanna's eager eyes, searching for some uncertainty, some irresolution. There was none. Finally, haltingly, Tina gave her the only answer possible.

"I'll go with you Shanna. When do we leave?"

With her spirits soaring high, Shanna hurried home to secretly pack the few belongings she meant to take with her to California. She had very little worth taking.

Anything she remembered later could be sent for or replaced once she was established in Hollywood.

Too impatient to follow the sandy path along Otter Creek home, she cut through the oak grove and was immediately sorry. Dipping through a wash, climbing the far bank. She came face to face with Wallace Black.

He was setting a snare when she came upon him. He rose and turned instantly, his broad grin flashing as he recognized her.

"Shanna!"

"Hello, Wallace."

She stifled her impatience. It wouldn't do to have Wallace

Black grow suspicious.

She could tell by the gleam in his brown cow eyes that he assumed she had come looking for him.

He stood thick-limbed and hunched in his faded blue overalls, his grin fixed firmly in place, watching her adoringly.

His hands were thick and callused to cracks. His overalls hadn't been washed recently, if ever. She wondered what his underwear would look like! Someday he would actually expect her to wash them if he had his way. The idea was more than repugnant.

Shanna actually started to gag at the transient thought.

"Let me show you what I've been doing," he said, reaching for her hand.

Her hand remained unoffered; but there was no way to refuse him a few minutes. "I am in a hurry, Wallace. Mother wants me to help her with . . . some mending."

"This won't take long, Shanna. I think you'll be pleased."

"All right. What is it?" she asked impatiently.

"Come along. It's a surprise. You'll see."

Instead of walking beside Wallace, Shanna fell in behind, following the squat, thick man through the trees toward Oak Knoll beyond. Walking behind him, studying his thick waist and heavy hips, Shanna had a sudden ludicrous vision of the man in coat and tails.

He would make Wallace Black look handsome by comparison.

They followed the rabbit run up the side of the grassy knoll to where the old twin oaks cut dreary silhouettes against the powder blue sky.

"Well!" Wallace halted and turned, his arms extended proudly. "Can you see it, Shanna?"

See what? There was nothing to be seen but a small area where the grass had been scraped away and the ground leveled. A few stakes had been pegged into the earth.

There was a stack of medium-sized river rocks piled to one side. Shanna looked it over and then returned her gaze to Wallace's hopeful eyes.

"What am I looking at?" she asked in irritation and saw his eyes fade with disappointment.

"The house, Shanna! Our house. See, here where we're standing is the living room—I know it's a bit small, but we don't need much living room just yet." He walked toward the oaks, pointing out the stakes. "This is the kitchen, you see?" *Where I get to stand sweating all summer long,* Shanna thought. She shrugged with her eyes.

"Well, you have to use a little imagination, I know," he went on, but you see—here is the bedroom. Look at the view from here!"

Yes, the view. The same dusty raw land, the same brush-covered hills and futile farms she had been looking at all of her life. Her mouth twisted upward in imitation of a smile.

"I really do have to go, Wallace. Thank you for showing me this."

His expression grew a little frantic. He lifted his big hands toward her without touching her.

"Don't you see, Shanna. I will build this house for you, for us. I can get work in a sawmill or in the oilfields. I'll get you a few chickens, a couple of hogs . . . you can dress the place up any way you want, and when I get home in the evening, we can sit by the fireplace—that's what those rocks are for: a fireplace and a chimney. I'm starting on that tomorrow."

Shanna didn't even attempt a smile now. Yes, she could see it all: a life of tedium, feeding the hogs, the chickens, waiting for her dirty, exhausted man to come home from the mill or from the oilfields black with grime wanting his dinner, wanting to be pampered, wanting to slobber over her, wanting to get her with child. Everything she did not want from life! Everything she was running away from.

He was only reinforcing her determination to leave. She couldn't even raise any pity for Wallace Black, for any of the dumb mule-like men in the country.

Looking into his hopeful eyes, she couldn't even think of any generous words of parting for him. She just blurted out, "Mother will be waiting."

Shanna turned her back and hurried down the knoll, not seeing Wallace raise a futile, restraining hand, standing there in his crippled dream, watching her slender figure disappear into the shadows of the oak woods.

Shanna slowed as she entered the grove. She was in no hurry to rush home, certainly; only to escape from Wallace Black and his primitive dreams.

She walked on slowly, hands clasped behind her back, watching the sheer gold of the sunlight falling through the foliage overhead. Distantly dry thunder rumbled and she saw a flash of heat lightning. It would not rain; it was only the weary land complaining of its fate.

She passed through the field of stumps left over from the rape of the pine forest where it had been cool and deep and secret before the timber-boom days and soon could see her house below.

Elizabeth was out back, beating vigorously at a rug hung over the clothesline while her young friend, Sally, sat throwing rocks at Bertha, the old sow with the dangling teats.

Bertha paid no attention to the stones as she gobbled through a pile of garbage. Beyond the house Tom was busy burying the garbage not even a hog could digest as fertilizer for the lonesome, scraggly peach tree, which Mother, even now, believed one day would mature and produce fruit like those big blushing Georgia peaches one saw in the fruit carts in Tahlequah instead of the tiny, walnut-sized inedible fruit it usually gave. The peach flowered prettily, multitudes of white blossoms bright and promising, flourishing on its branches; the fruit formed naturally and grew, but it never ripened . . . not here in Broken Post. Most of it fell to the dry ground and rotted, even the birds ignoring it, suitable only for worm food. Yet Mother believed . . .

"Shanna!" Elizabeth lowered her wire carpet beater and waved cheerfully. Sally lifted a hand. Shanna waved lethargically and walked on, passing them in a wide arc.

She was in no mood to talk to children. There was too much to do.

Sarah was waiting at the back door, her hair loose, showing many strands of gray.

She wiped her hands on the dish towel she was holding. She smiled at her daughter but her eyes held a question. There was an odd expression on Shanna's lovely face, Sarah thought. Her mouth was tight, one corner turned up in what was not quite a wry smile, her eyes glittering deeply.

"Hello, Mother."

Shanna's greeting was nearly a sigh. Sarah touched her forehead, frowning solicitously. "Do you feel all right, Shanna? You look tired."

Will she never stop worrying about my health? Shanna thought.

"I am not fragile, Mother."

"No, I know, I know," Sarah said hastily. But in her world there had been so many children—babies—dying of minor illnesses for lack of medicine and doctors. She followed Shanna into the kitchen. The plank floor, freshly scrubbed, still looked dirty with the accumulated grit of years. It was splintered in places, decaying. *Like everything else,* Shanna thought.

"Where have you been?" Sarah asked. "No one could find you."

Why would anyone look for her? She was a grown woman.

Shanna picked up a potholder and looked in the huge iron kettle on the stove. Squash. The heat from the wood crackling in the pot belly of the iron stove was tremendous. Shanna moved away from it. She decided to tell her mother a half-truth to mollify her.

"I was up on Oak Knoll talking to Wallace Black. He's planning to build a house up there." She turned half away to hide the lie in her eyes. "He's got everything graded off and the stakes laid out. He's hauled a lot of river stones up there. He's starting the fireplace and chimney tomorrow."

"Is it nice, Shanna?" Sarah asked eagerly. Shanna turned and forced a bright smile—an actress has to learn these things.

"It will be lovely, Mother."

"I'm happy for you, dear." Sarah hugged her daughter. She smelled of smoke and sweat and only faintly of her lilac powder. Shanna had to pull away after a moment. She stood, her mother's arms still around her, and looked into Sarah's eyes, which were bright with her daughter's projected happiness, with an expectation of chubby grandchildren to come.

She would just have to wait for Elizabeth then. Shanna was determined to never bring children into the hopeless life that surrounded her.

Changing tacks, she said, "I suppose I am a little tired, Mother. If you don't need me, I think I'll lie down for awhile."

"Of course, if you're tired. We can get along without you until supper."

Shanna smiled, gave her mother's dry cheek a perfunctory peck, and went down the hall toward her room. She closed the door very softly, then turned and pressed her back against it, her palms flat on the wood. Slowly a wide smile spread across her generous mouth and she clapped her hands together, throwing herself on her bed.

It was the last day! Incredibly it had suddenly arrived. She lay silently for a time in the reverie of silver dreams.

Abruptly she popped up, energy flooding through her. She dragged her battered suitcase from the closet and stood frowning. What would she take? She had so few decent dresses. The black crinoline she wore to church and the matching hat with its small plume, of course. But what after that . . . ?

She started with her underthings. In tatters, some of them, but they would soon be replaced by fancy chemises and silk stockings, and certainly no one would see these necessities. She folded slips and her only corset hastily—though from what she had observed, the women in Hollywood, with the exception of matrons, no longer wore such things. Everything in Hollywood was much freer—and Shanna had no real need of one with her svelte waistline.

The tap on her bedroom door brought Shanna's head around sharply. Hastily she slammed the lid of her suitcase shut and jammed it under her bed.

"Yes?"

The door inched open and Elizabeth peered in.

"Shanna? I was afraid you were asleep."

"Oh it's you. What do you want?"

"I just wanted to see how you were. Mother said you weren't feeling well." Elizabeth crossed to her own bed and sat on it. Shanna toed an exposed corner of the suitcase farther under her own bed.

"I'm fine. I'm just straightening up a little," Shanna said with annoyance. She aimlessly rearranged a few items on the dresser top.

"You're . . . I hear you might be going away soon, Shanna, is that true?"

Shanna's heart began to palpitate rapidly. She would kill Tina if she had blabbed!

"Who told you that?" she asked with her back still toward her sister.

"Mother," Elizabeth answered, and Shanna's pulse slowed a little. "She said that Wallace Black was building a house for you two on Oak Knoll."

"Oh, that," Shanna said, turning with a relieved smile, "I wouldn't worry about that. It's not going to happen any time soon."

"Promise?"

"Yes, I promise," Shanna said with a relieved laugh.

"I might be leaving sometime next year too, but that would be different. I'd just be going to school in Tahlequah. It seems so far off, and anyway, I haven't made up my mind yet. But I'd hate it if you left. Nothing would be the same without you, Shanna. I don't know what I'd do."

"You'd do just fine, Runt!" Shanna said, giving her sister a playful shove so that Elizabeth toppled onto her back. "But don't worry. I'm not going to marry Wallace Black any time soon."

Or ever.

"Here," Shanna said. Returning to her dresser, she had picked up her porcelain music box, the one with the ballerina in her gold-threaded white skirt. Many evenings she had lain on her bed watching the figure slowly turn to the accompaniment of a tinkling tune. Now it seemed a childish keepsake. "You can have this."

"But, Shanna . . ." Elizabeth knew it was one of her sister's prized possessions. "You're joking!"

"No, whyever for? Call it a birthday present."

"But my birthday's not for a month yet."

"I might forget," Shanna said, shrugging one shoulder.

On the wall behind the bureau was a picture of William S. Harty appearing very rugged, sincere, and competent. Shanna had glued the magazine photograph to a piece of cardboard with flour paste and fashioned a frame of stained lath for it. Now that too seemed childish to her. After all, one day soon, she might meet him in person. She didn't need to clip his picture from movie magazines.

"You may as well have this too," she said, removing the thumbtacks pinning it to the wall.

"Shanna! He's your favorite!"

"I'm not crazy about him anymore. You take it, Elizabeth, if you want it."

"Yes, yes, I do! Thank you, Shanna."

"It's nothing," her sister answered. And it was just that— nothing. Yesterday many small things in the room had importance. But only yesterday she had been a child acting out childish dreams. Today she was a woman, traveling forward into a real and lushly promising world.

It was time to put away the things of childhood.

Once begun, packing the suitcase took Shanna very little time. She took her purse from its hiding place in her closet, counting and re-counting her forty-two dollars. There was then the letter to her parents to write. She worked over it for a long time, throwing three different versions away, finally more out of weariness than anything else, sticking to the bare facts, eliminating all of her soulful revelations.

She folded the letter neatly, put it in an envelope, and tested propping it up in various places for dramatic effect, standing back to study the impact. Finally, she decided to leave it on her pillow at a precise angle. That, Shanna thought, was the most poignant option.

She hid the envelope under her pillow for the time being and lay on her back, hands behind her head, wiggling her bare toes. She was not, she recognized, nervous in the least. Excited, yes, but not nervous. She glanced at the wall where the picture of

Wiliam S. Hart used to hang and smiled.

There was only one thing left to do, but it was still far too early for that, and since she had told her mother she was tired, she closed her eyes and fell off to sleep.

The sun was low when she awakened later and sat up with a deep yawn. She felt the excitement flood back into her and she leaped up, putting on her shoes. Grabbing her shawl, she eased out of her door with a glance toward the kitchen, then slipped out the side door, moving purposefully toward the county road. Already the sky was colored with a faint pink and lower toward the horizon, with a deep purple. She hoped she hadn't slept too long.

Doves winged past, homeward bound as the shadows settled and pooled beneath the trees. She hurried on faster, gripping her shawl tightly.

Ahead she saw smoke rising and she slowed with relief. Duane Silver Fox was still there, and he had a truck to take them to Tahlequah. Shanna knew Duane would do it. He was only half-smart now. Duane and his brothers had gotten drunk one night and Duane had gotten into a fight with some Creeks over near Sallisaw. He had been hit over the head with a two-by-four and kicked savagely while he was down. Now he made his living by collecting stumps and dead wood to burn to make charcoal for which there was a fair market in Tahlequah where a lot of the saloons and hotels had charcoal-burning stoves.

Ahead and to her right, toward Otter Creek, Shanna now saw his red high-wheeled R.E.O. truck and the hummock of earth leaking smoke into the air as the wood underneath smoldered into charcoal.

Duane Silver Fox, wearing faded coveralls and a battered flop-hat, was crouched near the hummock, motionless, his eyes on nothing, thinking his elusive thoughts.

"Duane Silver Fox!" Shanna had to repeat her call three

times before Duane's head slowly turned toward her. Recognition was slow in dawning, but eventually he figured out who she was and he smiled, rising to his feet. He liked her, Shanna knew, and she had no doubt he would willingly give her and Tina a ride to Tahlequah.

It was making her wishes known that presented a problem. Everything had to be repeated at least twice as Duane tried to crystallize concepts and fumble around in his scattered mind for responsive words.

Shanna grew frustrated. On the fourth attempt, resorting to sign language, she made herself clear. "Take me and Tina to Tahlequah when the sun goes down."

The annoying conversation was worthwhile. In the end Duane grinned, pointing at Shanna and then at the charcoal truck, then northward toward Tahlequah.

"I will take you. Sure, I'll wait here with my truck."

Shanna could have almost kissed his lumpy face with joy. She had told Tina that if worse came to worst they could walk to Tahlequah, but the truth was that it was a very long way, especially for two girls in long skirts carrying luggage.

"Thank you. Thank you, Duane. I'll be back. You wait."

Still grinning, Duane Silver Fox nodded half a dozen times. Shanna turned away, hoping the man would not forget by sunset, and hurried on toward Tina's house.

A fire was softly glowing inside the Roberts house. Shanna saw a silhouetted figure pass behind the drawn curtains; the yard dogs came yapping toward her as she crossed the hard-packed yard, but they all knew her and soon quieted down, following her hopefully toward the porch, wishing to slither in toward the hearth.

Shanna knocked only twice before the door swung open. Tina's mother—stout, matronly, her hair pulled tightly around her broad skull—smiled at her. Beyond her Shanna saw the younger Roberts boys on the floor playing checkers by firelight.

"Hello, Shanna."

"Hello, Mrs. Roberts. Is Tina here?"

"Why, no, she isn't, dear," Mrs. Roberts replied. Shanna felt briefly numbed.

"Will she be back . . . soon?" Darn her!

"No, I'm sorry. She's gone over to spend a few days with her cousins over at Cambrish." In response to Shanna's prolonged silence, Mrs. Roberts asked uneasily, "Was it very important, dear?"

"Not really. No. I don't suppose it was," Shanna said.

"Did you want to leave a message?"

"No. I don't think so. She'll know why I came over. And, as I said, it really isn't that important at all."

Which it wasn't. Tina had lost her nerve and run off to avoid facing Shanna. That was all right. Let her hide out and live with regrets forever. Shanna certainly did not intend to. It made her more determined than ever, in fact. She was going to California with or without Tina Roberts.

That evening as the sun sprayed its last blur of color against the western sky and the black velvet shadows settled into the glades among the red hills, Duane Silver Fox's rattling charcoal truck made its way toward Tahlequah and in the passenger seat, clutching her battered cardboard suitcase, rode a silent, quite determined Shanna Adair.

Roy Adair put his axe away in the tilted toolshed Grandfather Deerfoot had built fifty years earlier, paused for a moment to remove his hat and wipe the perspiration from his brow, and started toward his small house for supper. There was a light shining in the kitchen window and smoke curled lazily up from the tin chimney, the wind whipping it away as it rose. He could hear the pleasant sound of Elizabeth and Sarah singing as they finished the dinner preparations.

There was still a last streak of dull crimson low on the horizon to the west, but it was already growing cold. The breeze chilled Roy through his red flannel shirt. Glancing toward the girls' room, he saw the light curtains flapping in the wind. Sarah had told him Shanna wasn't feeling well and had been lying down most of the afternoon. She must have fallen asleep with the window open. The girl would catch cold. He walked that way.

Placing his hands on the windowsill, he leaned over and called in. "Shanna! Are you in there?"

There was no answer, and sweeping the curtains aside, he could see the room was unoccupied. Walking to the back porch, Roy scraped the dirt from his boots and went in.

"Shanna!" he called from the hallway. Sarah looked around from the kitchen, wooden spoon in her hand, white apron over her blue housedress.

"She's in her room, Roy."

"No she isn't, and she left the window wide open."

"Well, when you find her, tell her the chicken's almost ready. You know how she likes chicken."

Roy grunted an answer and turned toward Shanna's room. Entering, he crossed to the window, closed it, and started out again. There was just enough twilight for him to see the white envelope on her pillow. Curiously he picked it up, reading the writing on it.

"Mother and Father."

Roy went to the door where enough light bled from the kitchen for him to read by.

With slightly trembling fingers he opened the unsealed envelope and took the note from it. Carefully, slowly, he read it. Then he re-read it. Then stood holding it limply at his side as he stared out across the yard.

Dear Mother and Father,
    It is important for me to become my own woman. To do this I

must leave home. I will be all right.

 I have made plans. I am not doing this to hurt you, since I love you both very much, but only to do something for myself. I will write when I am settled.

Your daughter,
Shanna

Roy's hand clenched, forming into an angry fist. He crumpled the note in it. After a minute his hand opened and he smoothed the letter out, reading it again in blank disbelief.

"Roy!" Sarah called. "Shanna! Supper's ready, you two, best hurry up before Elizabeth and Tom and I eat it all."

Roy didn't answer. Still holding the crumpled letter, he pushed on through the side door and went out into the backyard. The wind had lessened as the sun sank, but the big oak still swayed and groaned in its upper reaches. A razor-thin line of gold demarcated the western horizon, but the rest of the world was dark. Dark and cold and dismal. Roy stood alone beneath the starry, long-running Cherokee sky, wondering what he had done wrong. For surely he had done something wrong, or why would his beautiful, first-born child have gone. His darling Shanna.

She had all she could have needed. Love, a warm home, food, family, and friends.

Something he had done wrong . . . but what?

Sarah was calling from the kitchen door, and Roy began walking heavily in that direction.

He would have his supper first. Afterward he would sit and talk with Sarah.

By the light of dawn, the bungalows seemed beautiful to Shanna. The night before she had had only a glimpse of them: a shadowed courtyard, the slender vague shape of palm trees, a dark rectangle of lawn. Someone, she remembered, had been strumming aimlessly on a ukulele.

Now, wandering the tiled path around the inner perimeter of the yard, she could capture the details. Eight pinkish bungalows with red Spanish-tile roofs, a line of Mexican fan palms fifty feet tall along the avenue thrusting shaggy heads against the morning sky. There were fragrant white gardenias in bloom and red and yellow roses beside each screened doorway. In the center of the Bermuda-grass lawn there was a fountain in the shape of a cherub with a pitcher on his shoulder pouring water. Well, just now it only spat out sporadically, but that was unimportant. The sun was rising, golden and warm over the mountains. Shanna couldn't see the ocean, but they had said there was an ocean view and she imagined she could smell the sea. It was perfect, just perfect.

Everything she had imagined.

A trolley clanged past along the avenue as she started back toward her bungalow.

She could hear the sounds rising people make, smell bacon frying. The ukulele could be heard again as the little colony came to life.

She entered, the screen banging behind her. On one of the striped living room chairs a dark-eyed girl with long hair and shapely legs sat pulling on a silk stocking, carefully unrolling it as she went. She glanced up at Shanna with annoyance.

"Who the hell are you?" she demanded in accented English.

"Be good, Carmen. This is our new roommate."

In the door to one of the bedrooms stood a frowzy blond in her early twenties. Her hair was pinned up roughly in what had become a tangled mess overnight. She clutched a blue silk Chinese-embroidered dressing gown to her breast.

"Good morning, Maisie," Shanna said.

"Where'd you pick her up?" Carmen asked, finishing the roll of her stocking.

"That card we left on the YWCA bulletin board, remember?"

"I got into town last night," Shanna began. Carmen cut her story off.

"Where was I?"

"God knows!" Maisie said and both women laughed.

"Well, welcome aboard, kid," Carmen said.

Maisie frowned, studying her Mexican roommate. "Where are you off to? Too early for interviews, ain't it?"

"I got lucky. William S. Hart is shooting a little South of the Border oater epic. There was a callout for dusky maidens." She winced. "But, yeah, it's too early. Wherever I was there was hooch and a lot of it."

Shanna listened attentively, understanding only half of the exchange.

"You're going to be in a William S. Hart film?"

"Yeah, well, sort of. There's a few cantina brawls and the bar-room señoritas have to put their hands to their mouths in fear or run out of the saloon or something. If I don't get left on the cutting floor I might appear for a few seconds." Carmen shrugged. "It's rent money."

"It's a start," Shanna said. "I think it's wonderful."

"She thinks it's 'wonderful,' " Carmen said to Maisie.

"Leave her alone," Maisie said, yawning. "I'm going to make some coffee if anybody wants some."

"I don't understand," Shanna persisted as Carmen slithered into a pale yellow dress. "I mean . . . at least you are in a film. And with one of the biggest stars in Hollywood."

"Honey," Carmen said, "I'm just part of the scenery. It ain't a start. There ain't much call for Mexican princesses."

"I don't understand."

"You will." Carmen halted in the act of pinning on a huge yellow hat with a long ostrich plume. "You're kinda dusky yourself. What are you?"

"What do you mean?"

"I mean, you ain't Mexican."

"I'm Cherokee."

"Huh?"

"Indian," Shanna explained.

"Might work to your advantage as long as they keep shooting these damned Westerns," Carmen said. "Hell, they can always use another squaw, right? Mostly they slap makeup on white girls. Makes me laugh. They even make white men into Negroes.

"Ain't many Negroes in California. Besides, they'd rather give some assistant director's brother-in-law a day job."

Shanna had quit listening after the part where Carmen had told her there might be an advantage to being Indian. In her mind's eye she was already playing opposite some handsome hero—a beautiful, mysterious Indian princess.

"I gotta go, kid!" Carmen yelled to Maisie. "No coffee for me. I'll miss the cattle car."

"All right," Maisie said, reappearing from the kitchen.

"So long, kid," Carmen said to Shanna. Picking up a furled yellow parasol, she breezed out of the bungalow.

"She's something," Shanna said.

"Oh, she's all of that. You ought to catch her on a Friday night when she's trolling for bit parts." Maisie sat and tucked her blue gown between her thighs with both hands.

"I don't catch everything you two tell me," Shanna said, sitting beside Maisie on the striped sofa.

"Oh, you will, Shanna—you're still green. It takes a while to catch on to the way things work out here, that's all." Maisie yawned widely and poked at her tousled hair.

"What did she mean, she's going to miss the cattle car?" Shanna asked.

"Oh, God, honey. You'd have to take the trolley out to a studio to understand. Mack Sennet's is the worst. People packed in everywhere, all shapes, all sizes. Men, women, kids being dragged around by their mothers. When you get to the studio it's even worse. Have you ever been to a slaughter house?"

"No."

"Well, neither have I," Maisie admitted, "but it can't be much different. As soon as the gates open to the casting office, everyone charges through like stampeding cattle in a chute. Then you wait and stifle and try not to sweat through your best clothes. Sooner or later some casting director comes through with everyone pressing forward, trying to get under his nose, and he goes, 'You, you, and you, everyone else try again tomorrow,' and damned if they don't!"

"It sounds terrible. Crazy."

"Oh, it is, honey." Maisie smiled weakly. "But then, anyone who comes out here to try to break into the movies must be a little crazy. Coffee's perking," she said, rising.

Shanna followed her into the yellow kitchen. Sunlight streamed through the thin white curtains.

"But surely there are other ways . . ."

"Yeah, sure. You know somebody or you try out on the casting couch."

"I don't understand," Shanna said. Maisie was pouring coffee into two fragile, flower-painted cups. She turned shrewd eyes toward Shanna, shrugged, and answered.

"That's all right. You don't need to. Seriously, honey," she advised her, placing the coffee cups on the miniature round table beneath the sunlit window, "you need an agent to get anywhere. I mean a good agent. God knows there are enough two-bit sharks out there willing to take your money and anything else they can get their hands on and break your heart. I should know," she added, her mouth briefly turning down as she stared into her coffee cup.

Shanna sensed bitterness in her words and asked quickly,

"Does Carmen have an agent—from what you say . . ."

"No, she doesn't. The truth is." Maisie said quietly, "I don't think she much cares anymore. She's gone about as far as she's going." There seemed to be a double meaning to that, but Shanna couldn't penetrate it. "One day she'll likely pack up and go home. Working for rent and groceries is all right for a while, but it can get old. Very old, Shanna."

"I'll never give up!" Shanna said in an explosive whisper. Maisie looked at her as if she had heard those words many times from many girls. She nodded and sipped her coffee.

"You're pretty enough," Maisie said, studying Shanna.

"What should I do?" Shanna leaned across the table, searching Maisie's faded blue eyes. "How would you begin? How do I find a good agent?"

"I wish I knew," Maisie said sardonically. After a moment she added seriously, "Take your portfolio to the best offices, sit there all day trying to look charming and beautiful. Then when they've thrown you out, start working your way down the list."

"How long would that take?"

"Forever, maybe," Maisie said, rising to rinse her cup. "I wouldn't know."

"I don't have a 'portfolio.' What is that?"

"Why, you know, honey," Maisie said, leaning her back against the sink, folding her arms. "Clippings from any plays you might have been in—even high school stuff."

"I never . . ."

"Your very best photographs. Good clothes, good moody lighting."

"I'm afraid I don't have any of those either."

"Jesus, you're serious? Oh, well, then that's the first thing, honey. Go to a good studio, the best."

"I don't think I can afford a good photographer." And clothes? She only had the black crinoline with her. The only good dress she had. It had seemed fine back home, but in Hollywood . . .

Maisie shrugged. "That's my best advice, honey. Find a way to afford one."

"It's that or the cattle car?" Shanna asked with a smile.

Maisie laughed. "That's about it, Shanna. You're starting to catch on."

Shanna was briefly thoughtful. "Maisie, there's one other thing I don't understand. Carmen said I was 'dusky' as if that were bad. What did she mean?"

"Oh, dear." Maisie took a deep breath and let it out slowly. "You are young, aren't you? Look, honey, don't you pay attention when you go to the movies? All of the big stars are white! Haven't you even realized that?"

"I guess I never thought about it . . ." Shanna stammered.

"Well, they are. Look, that's what Carmen meant. She got this bit part because the cowboy hero rides down to Mexico. Just because they need a Mexican saloon girl, maybe to serve the good guy a beer, smile, and get out of frame."

"Still, I mean, there must be parts for . . ."

"For Indians? Sure. Getting shot in front of your tipi or something, dancing around when the good guy's taken captive."

"I am Cherokee," Shanna said proudly. "My people have been civilized for three hundred years."

"Yeah, sure, honey. To the screenwriters you're an Indian, that's all. They're all white, all their heroines, their ideal women are white. Do you really think you could ever get a Lillian Gish role? Don't be stupid." Maisie apologized immediately. "I didn't mean to say that, honey, honest."

"It's all right." Shanna's smile was a small expression of disappointment. "I'm grateful to you really. There are a lot of things I don't know and have never even thought of. I appreciate your telling me."

"I haven't discouraged you?"

"Not even a little," Shanna laughed.

Maisie laughed too and then said, "Well, then, welcome to our club, Shanna. Our poor, pitiful, stupid club."

Carmen Chance didn't return home until after seven o'clock that evening. She threw herself onto the couch and slowly, almost painfully began undoing her shoe buttons. Her yellow parasol lay discarded in the center of the floor.

"How'd it go, honey?" Maisie asked her. Shanna stood at her shoulder watching the obviously weary Mexican girl.

"It was hell, girl. Sheer hell! No one said they were going to have a fistfight around me. Chairs swinging through the air, flying glass. Damn table fell on top of me and I think I took a spur in the hip! If that wasn't bad enough, they had to reshoot it."

"But you're in the movie," Shanna said. Carmen gave her an indulgent smile.

"Yes, kid. If after the final cut anyone can even make me out behind a table with a couple of cowboys brawling on top of me. This," she said with a quick, savage smile, "is what we call acting out here."

"Did you . . . ?"

"Look, I'd rather not talk about it, okay? What's new on the home front?"

"Shanna thinks she might have a job at a shoe store over in Van Nuys," Maisie said. Maisie had bathed and fixed her hair and now looked respectable if not glamorous in a midnight-blue silk dress. "And we are supposed to go out tonight, in case you have forgotten."

"You're going dancing?" Shanna asked cheerfully.

"Well, that's what they call it. It's more like wrestling on your feet with these two slobs."

"Then why go?" Shanna wondered. Carmen shot Maisie an incredulous glance before answering patiently.

"These two guys work for D.W. Griffith, kid! Get it? It's called social auditioning."

Maisie laughed at the definition. "Well, Carmen, if you're going to do any auditioning tonight, you'd better hoist yourself from that sofa and into the bath."

That evening, left alone, Shanna sat at the kitchen table, a cup of coffee at her elbow, and wrote a postcard to her parents. It was incredibly hard. What was there to say, really? She knew that most of all they would want to know why she had done what she had done, what they might have done to cause it, when she would be coming home.

She couldn't explain all of that on a postcard. And they wouldn't understand anyway. As far as when she might be going home—never. Or at least not until she was a big star and explanations were no longer necessary.

She looked at the front of the postcard for a long time—the sunset over Venice Pier with two towering palms in the foreground, the picture nicely tinted by some photographer. Then she sighed, dipped her pen in ink, and wrote:

Dear Mother and Father,

As you can see, I am in California. Hollywood. I have a good job and a nice bungalow with two friends. I will write more soon.

Tell Elizabeth and Tom hello.

Your loving daughter,
Shanna

There was no more room on the card. It was for the best; there was nothing else she really wished to say to her parents. The letter she wrote to Tina Roberts was much more expansive:

Dear Tina!

Everything has gone just wonderfully. Better than we could have imagined. I have a temporary job at a charming little shoe shop. It's plenty of money for me to get by on for now. Certainly more than I could have made in Tahlequah!

I'm living in a pretty little bungalow right on the beach. Talk about luck! My first night here I went to the YWCA and saw a card pinned on the bulletin board advertising this place. My two roommates are both actresses! Can you believe it?

One of them, Carmen Chance is her name, has a starring role in a new Wm. S. Hart film!

My other roommate is a beautiful blond named Maisie Daley. She has "taken me under her wing" and is helping me to put my portfolio together, taking me to a high-class photo studio, and helping me find a really good agent, which you need out here.

Guess where Carmen and Maisie went this evening? To a party at D. W. Griffith's house!

Isn't that incredible?

Really, everything here is so much more bright and magical than we ever imagined. I only wish you had come with me, you little sissy!

Well, Tina, that's about all for this evening. Right now I have to get my "beauty rest" so I'll be ready for the photographer tomorrow. Tell everyone hello.

Your friend,
Shanna

Reading the letter over, Shanna decided that she really hadn't exaggerated that much—just enough to cause Tina to have second thoughts, maybe. Folding the letter, she stuffed it into an envelope and went into the bedroom she shared with Maisie, lying awake for a long time in happy excitement.

At three o'clock in the morning the front door opened explosively and Maisie and Carmen burst in laughing and shouting, two male voices joining in the raucous chorus.

Maisie stumbled into the bedroom, turning on the electric light. Shanna sat up, blinking into its yellow glare.

"Oh, Christ, honey, I'm sorry," Maisie said in a slurred voice. "I forgot all about you."

A slender man with glossy dark hair and a pencil-line mustache was looking over Maisie's shoulder. "What's this?" he said loudly. "Goldilocks? Hank—come see what I've found!"

"Leave her alone," Maisie said roughly. She threw her jacket onto her own bed and turned out the light again, putting both of her hands on the man's chest to push him out into the hall.

"Open the gin, Eddie," Shanna heard her say.

"Already open . . . turn on the light. I want to see Goldilocks again."

The door banged shut, leaving the bedroom in darkness. Shanna rolled over, trying to go back to sleep, but someone had cranked up the phonograph and put a loud record on.

Carmen shrieked. A man laughed loudly about something. Shanna heard Maisie in the kitchen yelling at them to be quiet.

And for just a minute it was quiet, with just the amused low muttering of the men, the phonograph turned down low, but gradually the noise increased again, the music growing louder and louder, the men yelling to be heard above the din. What would her father have thought about this? She tried putting a pillow over her head but it was useless. There was nothing to do but to get up and go out into the living room.

Carmen was sitting on the couch next to a blond man with thinning hair and a comfortable stomach. He had his arm thrown casually over her shoulders. He eyed Shanna in her pink bathrobe in a way that made her uneasy. Maisie was in the kitchen pouring drinks from a pint bottle.

"Wolves, you mean," Maisie said, returning from the kitchen. "Leave her alone, Eddie." She handed Eddie his glass of gin and tonic and, holding her own glass, made the introductions.

"Shanna, this is Eddie Burke. The other character is Hank Shipley."

"Why were you callin' her 'Goldilocks'?" Hank asked, studying the tall raven-haired Shanna.

"The circumstance, not the reality," Eddie said, taking a huge slug of gin. He paused, his eyes growing uncertain as if he weren't sure his statement made any sense.

His expression changed suddenly. He turned to Maisie and asked, "Wait a minute! She's staying here with you?"

"That's right, darlin'," Maisie said, perching on the arm of his chair.

"Well, goddamn! What's that do to our date, Maisie?"

Confused, Shanna asked, "Haven't you already had your date?"

"Part of it, part of it," Eddie said. Hank Shipley burst into harsh laughter.

"Look, girlie—Shanna, whatever—it's like this . . ." the fat man said, leaning forward.

Carmen elbowed him roughly in his padded ribs. "Shut up, Hank!"

The man eyed Shanna dubiously. His gin-clogged eyes protruded like a fish's.

"Hey," he said, "what is this? Is she your baby sister or something you got to protect?"

"Something like that," Carmen said. Maisie nodded her head a fraction of an inch.

Hank turned heated eyes to Eddie Burke.

"You know what I call this, Eddie? A waste of good gin, is what I call it." He rose abruptly, draining his glass. "Let's clear out of here."

Eddie shrugged. "Sorry, Sister," he said to Maisie. Finishing his own drink, he rose and followed Hank Shipley out the open door.

Carmen rose, slammed the door shut, and said, "Good riddance."

"Did I do something wrong?" Shanna asked in bewilderment.

"Nothing, kid," Carmen said. "Don't worry about it a bit. They're nothing but two frustrated Vine Street romeos."

"Well," Shanna said hesitantly, "I'm sorry if I spoiled your evening." She went back to bed, listening to the music that had started up again, very low and soothing now, until she fell asleep.

Carmen, who was still working on the Hart western, had gone by the time Shanna went out into the kitchen the next morning. She mentioned this to Maisie who sat at the table, fully dressed but still unkempt as if she couldn't figure out why she should bother with a hairbrush and powder this morning.

"Yeah," Maisie said, "she couldn't wait to see who was going to knock her down today."

Shanna poured coffee for both of them. She thought she would give anything to be in Carmen's shoes. To be in a movie, even a two-reeler, no matter how small the part. To be able to tell the people back home to watch for her.

"Me and Carmen talked it over last night," Maisie said, slowly stirring her coffee, "and we think we've come up with a photographer for you."

"Oh, Maisie!" and she hadn't even asked for their help. "You're wonderful!"

"Yeah, sure," answered Maisie who knew full well how many hundreds of girls were wandering around Hollywood with their clippings gradually yellowing, their photographs becoming scratched and dog-eared. She poured a dollop of gin into her coffee, astonishing Shanna.

"Anyway," she told Shanna, wincing as she tasted her doctored coffee, "there's this guy we know named Emilio. He's pretty good. No reputation, but he knows what he's doing with

73

gauze and all that stuff."

"Gauze?"

"Yeah, gauze and shadows." Maisie smiled. "They say the camera don't lie. Hardly true. It can be at least coerced into fibbing a little—that's a quote from Emilio."

"You know . . ." Shanna's head was lowered, but she turned her dark eyes up. "I really don't have much money at all, Maisie."

"Yeah, well, who does? Emilio will do it on the cheap if he's asked in the right way."

"You don't mean . . . ?"

Maisie laughed. "No, honey. No 'special favors.' Emilio just reeks of lavender."

"I don't understand," Shanna said.

"You don't . . . my God, honey! Where are you from?"

"Oklahoma," Shanna said ingenuously.

"Yeah, I know that." Maisie sighed impatiently. "I mean, Shanna, that Emilio likes boys, not girls."

"You mean he . . . ?"

"That's right, honey."

Shanna was thunderstruck. She stammered, "But how do they . . . what do they do?"

"I've never been curious enough to ask. I probably don't want to know. All I know is there's gaggles of 'em around Hollywood; they seem to gravitate this way. Which has nothing to do with nothing where you're concerned, right? We just need to get you into his studio and get some photographs taken."

"Yes, of course," Shanna said hastily. She didn't care if Emilio had two heads.

Her mind was already flashing far ahead. Making the rounds with her portraits, a man deciding she was perfect for a part he'd heard of. The studio interview . . . Maisie was watching her with deliberate patience, perhaps reading her thoughts.

"You'll need some clothes," she told Shanna. "You can wear my blue silk dress. Emilio has tons of loose robes down at his place."

"Robes?" Shanna asked blankly.

"You're going to have to show some shoulder, honey." Then, under her breath, she muttered, "Damn."

"Maisie, I'm sorry I'm such a dunce. I really don't know anything. Not anything at all. I've lived down on The Nation all my life. All I really know of films is what I've seen. I'm so lucky I met you and Carmen. I'm grateful that you'd try to help me at all."

"Sure, you say that now," Maisie said cryptically.

Then, more brightly as she rose. Maisie said, "Let me get the blue dress, see if it'll fit at all. Then we'll pin your hair up real pretty."

That, then, was the day that Shanna met Emilio Dan Cruz.

His studio was in Santa Monica, and he really did have an ocean view. Inside the upstairs apartment reached up a flight of weather-grayed wooden stairs, half a dozen women sat fidgeting or filling out cards. Some of them were extraordinarily beautiful ladies, sleek and self-assured in fur wraps and pearls, others of them were rather plain, some almost dowdy, over-dressed and over-painted.

Maisie had called over for Shanna's appointment and she was called in before several of the others, causing glares of annoyance. The studio proper was a tangle of electrical wires and lights, reflectors and painted backdrops like miniature sets. One was a woodsy scene, a second represented a European city—Naples?—a third was an abstract swirl of graceful curves and stark lines.

Emilio himself was a young-old man, thin and hyper-energetic, given to talking to himself as he worked. He wore a loose yellow sweater and his graying brown hair was parted exactly in the center and slicked down. Two curls like miniature horns fell across his extremely high forehead.

He walked around Shanna slowly, examining her as if she were an *objet d'art* on an auction block. "Lovely, lovely," he said. "Love the high cheekbones. Your eyes are very good. Your nose . . . slightly . . . we can compensate for that."

Shanna involuntarily touched her nose. What was the matter with it? Well, she had two "lovelies" and only one "compensate for."

"Okay, let's slip into something else," Emilio said, pointing toward an open dress rack.

"Take the white Grecian robe. That's how I'm seeing you . . ." He looked at the card she had filled out, "Shanna, that's it, right?"

Shanna found the robe easily enough. Looking around for a place to change, she found none. She stood nervously holding the robe, which was sheerer than any chemise she had ever owned.

"I'm a poor man, Shanna," Emilio said with a friendly, toothy smile. "I can't afford a changing room. Go ahead; I won't look. I'll be busy with the camera."

Shanna turned her back. Remembering what Maisie had told her about Emilio, she decided he didn't have any real interest in looking at her anyway. Still she had never undressed with a man in the room before.

Emilio, she saw, looking across her shoulder, was watching impatiently, hands on hips, toe tapping.

"All right!" he said with mild exasperation. "I need fresh plates anyway. I'm leaving for a few minutes—would you please change!" He started toward the door, halted, spun back, and said, "No undergarments either, dear. Ruins the drape of the gown."

For the next hour Shanna had her head shifted, her chin

lifted, the shoulders of the gown pulled down, pulled up as Emilio arranged her like a bouquet of flowers. She held her poses endlessly as he shifted the camera, the reflectors, the lighting behind her and overhead. He put a necklace around her throat, unpinned her hair, tossed it over one shoulder. At one point he did use gauze over the camera lens. Shanna had thought Maisie was joking about that.

Finally, glancing at his pocket watch, Emilio declared, "That's it, darling. Time's up. Get dressed."

"Do you think . . . I mean, how do you think they'll come out?" she asked nervously.

"Darling, Emilio has photographed you. They will be magnificent! You have a marvelous face, Shanna. If you decide to give up on this movie foolishness, you could be a commercial model. With Emilio's help," he added.

"I won't give up on my idea, Emilio, but thank you." She paused reflectively. "If my face is so good, Emilio, why is a movie career such a foolish idea?"

"Did I say that? Yes, I suppose I did. It's not that so much, Shanna. It's just that it's not art. It's . . . well, whatever it is, it devours young women."

"And art, Emilio?"

"Ah! Art seems to thrive on devouring young men." He looked again at his watch. "I seem to have worked into my lunch hour. Let's get a bite and walk on the beach, if you'd like. I'll go out and tell the girls waiting that they have time to go get something to eat as well."

They bought hot dogs at a beachfront stand with a striped umbrella over it and walked to the water's edge. Emilio had the sleeves of his yellow sweater pushed up from his wrists. The sea breeze couldn't disarrange his pomaded hair. He frowned at his hot dog as he slowly chewed a bite.

"Hardly a Coney Island dog, is it?"

"I don't know," Shanna answered. "I've never been East."

"Really?" Emilio said. "Me, I'm a New Jersey boy. I went to New York to try my hand at motion pictures—don't look so surprised. I started with Edison. The Black Maria. I was a pretty fair cameraman. But, you know, with Edison everything was so static. He didn't believe in the camera moving. Everything was one angle; this wonderful invention and he hadn't figured out how to utilize it—well no one did before Griffith. Painted canvas scenery and all that. It was frustrating, really. Like being a stenographer of film." The photographer shrugged, tossing the remainder of his hot dog into the ocean. "I've just made some fish happy—or given him heartburn as well." He continued. "There is no art to motion picture photography. Well," he amended, "maybe Billy Bitzer with Griffith, but God, he's got all the time and money he needs to work with. I had to get out of that business, anyway, everything started to change too fast. Big money came in too early. The producers and bankers grabbed all the power. One day everyone just started packing up and the next thing you know everyone's on the West Coast. Nothing has gotten much better. They're still shooting stage plays without words."

"Some of them are really wonderful," Shanna said.

"Yeah?" Emilio shrugged with the disdain of an artist. "The sets are bigger. With few exceptions, like those Gish sisters—the acting hasn't gotten any better. Pretty faces and fancy clothes. That's all most of them offer."

Shanna didn't respond. She saw nothing but enchantment in pretty faces and handsome, well-dressed men. She sensed Emilio wouldn't be receptive to her remarks on that, so she kept her silence as they walked along the white beach past the gently lapping sea.

At length, she asked, "Why did you say the movies devour young women? It seems to me they have a wonderful life."

"Jesus," Emilio said, "you are young. Some of them, granted, do have good lives. Like Mary Pickford. Now there is one tough little lady. Pinches every penny, like Chaplin. Now he is so damned cheap he tried using his studio carpenters to build his new house. Of course the place started to fall apart like stage flats!" Emilio laughed as if Chaplin had gotten what he deserved.

"Shanna, even the really famous ladies, the big stars, some of 'em, get eaten alive out here. Like Mabel Normand."

"What do you mean?" Shanna asked, slightly flabbergasted. Why, Mabel Normand was the nation's most loved comedienne, famous worldwide.

"Darling, you could fill a swimming pool with the amount of booze she drinks in a week. And just look at her eyes in her new flickers. If you don't think she's strung-out . . . !"

"Strung-out? What does that mean?"

Emilio halted. He looked into Shanna's innocent eyes and said again, "Jesus, you are young! No wonder Maisie is playing mother-hen to you." He took her hand and started back toward his studio, low and stocky on the red bluff above the beach. "I'll get your proofs to you by bicycle courier on Monday or Tuesday at the latest—if I get bogged down in that society woman's portrait. She's very picky. I just don't seem to be able to make her look as young as she believes she is!" Emilio laughed again, a high-pitched, happy sound. "Meanwhile, how about going out with me? A little party. Just a few friends."

"I'd like that," Shanna said, surprised by the invitation but eager to meet people. Then she paused. "Would it be all right . . . with your friends?" she asked, stuttering. She could feel her ears burning, her face flushing.

Emilio frowned, not understanding her at first. Then he did and he laughed again. "It will be perfectly all right, darling. Besides, not all of my friends are psychologically malformed."

"I didn't mean . . ."

"Of course you didn't," Emilio said breezily. "Forget it. I have to get back. I have customers waiting."

When Emilio had gone, Shanna returned to the beach. She stood pondering the limitless Pacific for a long while. Brown pelicans flew low along the surf line. Gulls swirled and screamed above a school of tiny fish. Terns on sticklike legs patrolled the gray of the damp sand, searching for tiny sandcrabs. The breeze was fresh and salt-smelling. So odd, she considered. Here, right here, half of the world fell away. Beyond the limitless sea lay other lands, entire continents unseen, only remarked on her grammar school maps with different-colored shapes in pink or yellow or green.

It all seemed vaguely analogous to her present life. She had, in fact, crossed a sea into the future, found secret fabled islands. And it was all coming with such a rush and roar as the onrushing sea, which was now gaining impetus from some struggling circumstance in the ocean depths, building to a gray frothing series of intimidating crests. There was something suddenly deeply menacing, greatly disturbing about the sea and all of its enormous strength, something similar to the towering gray muscle of a building Oklahoma tornado. She felt herself tense at the sight of the building surf. Her heart beat a little too fast as one massive wave slammed its furious head against the pilings of the pier. With shame, cursing herself and her ancestors for their reliance on and understanding of omens, Shanna lifted her skirts, turned, and hurried away toward the safety of the sea wall and the civilized Venice boardwalk filled with chatting ladies with bright parasols pushing prams and strolling couples glancing negligently at the driving surf.

"Well, how did it go?"

Maisie and Carmen were both at home when she returned. Maisie was in the kitchen—she seemed to gravitate toward that room with dormant domesticity. Carmen Chance, languid and almost faceless with a lack of makeup, lay sprawled on the striped sofa, her long lovely legs uncovered by a carelessly draped red silk dressing gown.

"It went wonderfully," Shanna said, tossing her hat onto the nearby chair. She stretched her arms overhead. "Emilio said the portraits will come out fine."

"You got on with the squidge?" Carmen asked sleepily. Maisie gave her a quelling glance. "Oh, well, personally I like men who are . . . I guess if you never have found him in a closet with one of his little boyfriends . . ."

"Shanna," Maisie interrupted deliberately, "there's a letter for you. I put it on your pillow."

"A letter?"

"From home, I guess."

Carmen sat up yawning and picked up a concealed fifth of gin, drinking deeply from the bottle. Maisie winked and Shanna smiled with nervous understanding. In an attempt to mend fences, she asked Carmen, "Emilio asked me to a party tonight. Do you think it's a good idea to go?"

Maisie and Carmen exchanged glances. Carmen hooked one leg across her other knee and shrugged, burping as the gin touched bottom. Maisie said, "Just be careful. Go slow, honey."

"I don't know what you mean," Shanna said.

"That's what she's trying to tell you!" Carmen nearly shouted. "You don't know nothin'!" She rubbed her eyes and smiled a weak apology. "I'm going to bed." She rose unsteadily and started toward her room.

"Well . . ." Shanna began, but she had nothing to say in response.

"Don't forget your letter," Maisie said. She capped the gin bottle and stood watching Shanna.

"No."

"Shanna . . ." Maisie poked at her mass of yellow hair.

"Yes?"

"Nothing. But have you ever thought . . . maybe you don't belong here."

"Because I'm Indian?"

Maisie just stared. "No, honey. Just because you may be too good for all of these bums."

Shanna again had no answer. Maisie stood indecisively in the middle of the room, cradling the gin bottle. Then she shrugged and quite deliberately crossed to the wall switch and turned off the lights, returning to the privacy of the kitchen where Shanna saw her take a swig from the bottle as well before putting her forehead down on the table. Shanna waited a minute longer and then went to her room. The eerie silver California moon peering in the window held her gaze. She could smell magnolia and night-blooming jasmine and distantly the salt and kelp of the sea.

The letter lay on her pillow and she opened it reluctantly, recognizing the hand. She put the letter down again, threw off her dress, and lay back on the bed, her head on the cool pillow slip, her hair unpinned and free, her eyes vaguely heavy.

Slowly she deciphered the childish handwriting, the letters straggling across the page like weary marchers.

Dear Shanna,

I have now—guess what?—got my Uncle Mack's quarter-section in back of Oak Knoll down toward Otter Creek. Which means we have twenty akres now of corn down. I wish to put the rest of the flat land in alfalffa.

Tina has come over to see me and we sit near the house and talk just about you! It is not reely a house yet, I guess. But, I have done a lot on it except when I am ploughing. We manely just wish for you to come home! I know you wish to be a film star, and everyone knows you are beutiful enough, but this is were you reely belong.

> *Y'rs faithfuly.*
> *Wallace Black*

Shanna stretched out her arm, let the letter drop from her fingers, and drifted off into a deep, serene sleep.

Morning was clear and bright. Shanna's heart was light, her mind sharply alert. She had decided during some half-dream what she had to do now. She would quit her boring, quite useless job of one week at the shoe store. Those hours could be much more profitably spent at the studios or finding an agent. She did not come all this way just to become another hopeful shop girl.

This being Saturday, she felt no need to say anything to Maisie about her decision. Watching Maisie rattle around aimlessly in the kitchen, Shanna came to the conclusion that the blond woman simply didn't have the ambition to carry through with the opportunities abounding out here. Maybe she felt she had given Hollywood her best shot, failed, and simply quit. She said none of that to Maisie, of course.

There was nothing to be seen of Carmen; Shanna didn't ask after her.

"You're still going out with Emilio tonight?" Maisie asked. She was tilted lazily against the wall, coffee cup in hand.

"Of course. Why not?"

"No reason."

"Well, why not?" Shanna asked with irritation.

"I said 'no reason', didn't I? It's just that this is a funny town, honey. It seems like everything is free . . ." She plopped onto the sofa, tugging the Chinese dressing gown up over her shoulder.

"Well?" It was beginning to annoy Shanna that Maisie insisted on calling her "honey."

"Well, a lot of things aren't free. Nothin's free." Maisie's expression altered, her eyes seeming to grow smaller and harder. Now too, Shanna could smell the gin in the coffee across the room.

"I don't know what you mean," Shanna said sharply. "Nothing's free anywhere, is it?"

"No," Maisie said with booze sadness, "not so far as I know, honey."

Shanna stood watching the woman sip her coffee for a few moments and then went back into the bedroom. Not bothering to close the door, she fell back on the bed and watched the shifting sunlight sketch shadows on the wall. Now and then she heard seagulls wheel past; a trolley clanged along the boulevard. She found Wallace Black's pitiful letter and read it through again before tossing it into the trashcan.

She spent hours on her bath, slowly washing, painting toenails and fingernails. Her hair she put off doing until nearly dark, not wanting to muss it. This could, after all, be an important evening.

When the sun did set, casting gold against the low flat clouds and smudging deep crimson on the sea, Shanna heard the toot of a motorcar's horn and went out. Maisie and Carmen were both absent. The bungalow fountain was burbling and the ukulele played as the weekend came to starlit life.

On the sidewalk beneath the fan palm, Emilio stood wearing white ducks, his hands on his hips, hair slick and glossy as usual. At the curb a deeply waxed yellow Packard car idled almost noiselessly.

"I though you'd stood me up," Emilio said. "No one answered the door."

"Oh, well—Maisie and Carmen left without saying a word."

He opened the door to the Packard.

"This is the most beautiful automobile I've ever seen!"

"This is Hollywood," Emilio laughed. He was obviously very

proud of the yellow roadster, however. "I'll have a Duesenberg soon."

He slid into the driver's seat and started the V-12 engine. "This car is used," he told Shanna, "but they tell me it used to belong to Fatty Arbuckle."

"Do you think that's true?" Shanna asked. Emilio eased the clutch out and the magnificent yellow and glittering-chrome car leaped into instant, powerful forward motion down the palm-lined avenue.

"Dear, dear," Emilio laughed, glancing at her. "This is Hollywood. There is no truth here. Or if there is, no one has discovered the point in utilizing it."

The automobile growl-purred its way up toward the Hollywood hills. The night was sea-fragrant and rich with the sweet scent of orange blossoms.

"How in the world can you afford this car, Emilio?"

"Oh, there can be a lot of money in photography—it all depends on the clientele."

Shanna was clever enough to say, "And you won't tell me all of the truth—in Hollywood?"

He laughed delightedly, hit the brakes hard as he realized he had missed the Laurel Canyon turn-off, turned the powerful roadster around, and started off in a different direction.

"Look under the seat, Shanna. The big envelope."

"You didn't . . . ?"

"Took me half the night, but I thought some people at the party might like to see the proofs. I selected what I think are the best ones. Well? Have a look, and tell me what you think."

"You're a dear!"

"For a queer?"

"Stop it, Emilio. You know I meant nothing like that!"

The photographs were really very good. "You've made me look glamorous!" Shanna said in astonishment.

"But, you see, you are," he replied too carefully. "I just taught the camera to capture it."

His voice had lowered and it made Shanna just a little nervous, although she couldn't have said why. Emilio's efforts with the lighting and shadows had produced—she hated to flatter herself, but it was true—exquisite results.

She laughed to cover her embarrassed pride: "I see you have managed to compensate for my nose!"

Suddenly Emilio seemed to lose his good humor. As a matter of fact, he seemed sheepish.

He drove on skillfully, silently. Once he did say as they rounded a bend of the dark canyon road, "Look, Shanna, things have to be done . . ."

"Of course," she answered, having no idea what he meant. She smiled and then her smile faded as she leaned back in the comfortable leather seat. Emilio drove on now with reckless carelessness up the winding road where here and there large, brooding houses sat in near-seclusion with their dark secrets.

They drew into a half-circular concrete driveway high in the canyon. Emilio switched off the engine and with a deeply mellow, nearly-musical after-rhythm, its sound died away to the silence of the dark hills.

The house was large and sprawling, white with a red Spanish-style tiled roof. Four arches stood before the expanse of its front facade. Shanna could hear music from a dance band within.

Later someone told her that a cornet player named Buddy Bolden had started the band. It wasn't until much later that she learned Bolden had formed the first "jass" band in America. Someone told her that Bolden himself had gone mad from the primitive music and been institutionalized for years.

She only knew that the music was strangely provocative and vaguely African. There were two Great Danes fenced in the backyard, providing a bass counterpoint with their barking.

Stepping from the car's running board with the help of Emilio's hand, she looked around the yard. Blooming bougainvillea formed a fringe over the front of the house's face. Strangely twisted star pines stretched toward the warm starry sky. Yellow hibiscus and crimson Camellias crowded long wooden flower boxes.

Emilio, with her photographs under his elbow, led the way to the front door, and as it opened, a tall man in a tuxedo that emphasized the broadness of his shoulders came out to greet them. That was the first glimpse Shanna had of Brent Colter.

His hair was wavy and dark, turning to gray, cut short and lightly pomaded. He had small flat ears and an inquisitive mouth.

"Why, hello, Emilio!" he said, shaking hands warmly. His eyes had shifted to Shanna. "Is this someone I should know, or someone I'd like to meet?"

"This is Shanna Adair," Emilio answered uncertainly. "I brought her along to show her off."

"Did you now?" Brent Colter's eyes shone. "Well, I can help you along there. He looked at Emilio's hand clutching the envelope. "Let me guess—photographs of your new friend." He took the envelope without its having been offered. He took Shanna's hand, startling her; she wasn't used to the instant informality of California yet.

"Everyone in the crowd is here," Brent said, leading them down a paneled foyer with a red tile floor. He had to speak up. The band was reaching a finishing crescendo of brass and drums.

To Shanna it was much like walking through the screen and into a film. All of the men were in tuxedoes or dark suits, the women in clinging silks or satins—half of the younger ones, she noticed, without underwear beneath their gowns. Strands of pearls decorated elaborate hair-dos.

Light from twin chandeliers sparkled on jewelry and glinted off hoisted champagne glasses. Everyone was laughing or smiling with perfect teeth. The music stopped suddenly, and it was almost with relief that she found she could suddenly hear voices around her, shattering the theater illusion.

". . . First things first, Emilio," she could now hear Brent Colter saying. "Get our guest a drink. The bar's that way. I'll take care of the pictures. Wait a minute, Fred Stein's waving at me. What can that old son of a bitch want? Nice meeting you, Shanna." With that he started off across the polished oak of the parquet floor toward a short, balding man with an unhealthily mottled red face and raised glass filled with amber liquid. Shanna just stood and stared.

"Does he always talk so fast? About so many things at once?" she asked Emilio.

Emilio laughed in response. "That's a part of his job, Shanna. You've just met your first real Hollywood agent—and a high-powered one at that. Come on, we'll get a drink."

"I don't drink," Shanna said, but the music had started again and he didn't hear her. He shouted to people across the room, and Shanna followed along in his wake to a serving bar where two Mexican men in white jackets, their expressions blank, refilled trays with glasses of champagne as quickly as they could be poured.

Emilio snatched two glasses from a tray carried by a waiter and handed one to Shanna before she could object. She carried it along like a prop. The music whimpered away and then leaped vigorously to life again. Shanna looked around nervously and then got the courage to take a sip of the champagne. She was left standing alone near a potted queen-palm as Emilio, taking his leave abruptly, went to speak to a thin, bloodless blond man who shook hands left-handed with the photographer and smiled sweetly up at him.

"Dance?" a voice at her shoulder asked and she turned to find a nice-looking young man with curly black hair and a wisp of a mustache beside her. Before she could object that she did not know how to dance, she found herself on the floor with him. She imitated the steps she had seen in films and no one seemed to notice or care that she moved uncertainly from foot to foot.

The night became a whirl of light, music, and dancing. She had another glass of champagne, danced with the young man again, and then with an older man who kept bumping against her with his belly. He said something she didn't catch but she laughed anyway as they spun dizzily through the glamorous mob. She saw none of the really famous of Hollywood. But she thought she vaguely recognized some people from the screen. The night swarmed past. She only wished that Tina could see her now—everyone back home on the Nation. She fell into a reverie, even pretending that this was a film and she was starring in it. Suddenly she found herself in Brent Colter's arms. They were playing a very slow song; he smiled at her, put his lips near her ear, and whispered, "Let me take you home."

"I couldn't! I came with Emilio."

"Well, why do you think . . . all right." Despite his smile, his mouth was tight. "Thanks for the dance," he said abruptly and, with a curt bow, he moved away from her with the music still playing and walked to where a pretty young woman in a sequined pink dress with long fringes at the hem and a narrow glittering band of silver around her hair stood, drink in hand. He spoke to her and she laughed, her crimson lips parting.

The music suddenly ended, and to a smattering of applause, the band bowed and began packing their instruments. People milled and re-formed, gathering in small groups to head for the doors, some calling good-byes as women were helped into their wraps and men finished off one last hastily ordered martini, many of them discussing where to go next to finish the night off properly.

Shanna felt suddenly isolated, an outsider. With relief she saw Emilio, across the room, lift a hand to her and start her way.

There was no sign of their host and so they just tagged along in the wake of the others toward the door and out into the cool and foggy night. Despite the haze Shanna could see stars here and there above the dark, craggy hills and the last faint glimmer of moonlight on the distant sea. In the afterglow of exhilaration, she was too worn out to say anything until the yellow roadster was away from the house, racing along its winding course down the canyon road.

"Have fun?" Emilio asked above the wind the open roadster produced at speed.

"It was wonderful."

"Good." He guided the Packard skillfully through a hairpin turn. "Of course, that's hardly the point in going to these soirees." Shanna looked at him questioningly. "It's all politics, darling. The idea is to meet people, make contacts, make deals. Sell something. Usually yourself . . . or someone else."

"I see." She didn't, not really, but it didn't matter just then. She had had a grand time. Her head was reeling a little from the champagne, with just the beginning of a dull headache at the base of her skull. The Packard hummed along smoothly and she let her head lay back against the seat. Somewhere along the way, without realizing it, she fell asleep with her head on Emilio's shoulder.

Once home, she slipped into the quiet bungalow, removed her shoes and dress, wriggling tired toes, and lay for hours watching the cold, brilliant stars drift past beyond her window. The same stars, the same sky, but she had stepped forward into a magical world eons beyond the one she had known. This was her time, her golden time. She had always pictured herself returning in triumph to the Nation. Now she knew that she would never go back.

Never.

The sun was already on the rise, touching the tips of the leaves on the tallest trees with muted gold before Shanna fell off to sleep to dream her silver dreams.

CHAPTER THREE

From the grassy knoll where they rested, Elizabeth and Allyn could see the two-story brick Cherokee Male Seminary with its handsome rows of Doric columns supporting its portico, the unique and ornate belfry brick and twelve brick chimneys rising above the surrounding live oak trees. Opened in 1851, many of the Nation's brightest young men had graduated from the institution. After burnng to the ground once, in 1889, it was now a proud reminder of Cherokee endurance. Allyn sat now, watching the wispy clouds in the distance, seeing a huge red-tailed hawk sail on the wind currents. His right hand absently stroked Elizabeth's sleek hair that she still wore cut shorter than the fashion. Her eyes were closed behind her round, rimless spectacles. Her head rested comfortably on his lap. Their plans were many. Together they planned to return to Broken Post and build a new school to replace the one neglect and animosity had stolen from under Mrs. Hoyt.

Elizabeth studied geometry—her worst subject—philosophy, history, bookkeeping, and Latin, but her real education she believed came from days like this lazy Saturday when she and Allyn would meet.

He was reading to her from a pamphlet his father had printed at his newspaper shop and forwarded to him. The subject was the infamous 1898 Curtis Act, which, prompted by the recommendation of the Dawes Act, finally suborned the rights of the Indians to maintain tribal government, hold land in common, utilize tribal courts, and forced the Indian, in effect, to accept white law and white traditions, effectively eliminating the tribal way of life. The cause of the rise of the full-blood organizations, the Four Mothers Society of Creek, Choctaw, Cherokee, and Chickasaw, which in time split into two factions, which was said to have twenty thousand members still opposed—sometimes violently—to the advances the Federal government had made upon their nation. The old full-blood society, the Kee-too-wahs, had divided into the Snakes under Chitto Harjo and the Night-hawks.

They actively opposed the despoiling of their land and society. Now it was not uncommon for a person claiming to be 1/64th Cherokee to receive a full allotment of land. Land taken from the full-bloods who wished to continue to live as a tribal unit and live under their own law.

" 'On June 28th, 1898, legislation known as the Curtis Act terminating tribal tenure was passed by the Congress. This was done without the Indians' consent. The Creeks have rejected this law at a special tribal election; the Cherokees steadfastly refuse to admit its lawfulness . . .' "

"Stop that, Elizabeth. You know I am ticklish," Allyn said, putting the pamphlet aside. She had opened her eyes and was tracing a pattern across his lips with a blade of grass. Her eyes were magnified by the lenses of her glasses and gazed dreamily at him.

"You know the importance of learning our history. Isn't this important to you?" he said with a touch of irritability.

"More important than anything in the world. Except you, Allyn." And she rose to kiss him lightly on the lips. She dusted off and sat leaning against him. He smiled and lay her down again, resting on top of her as the sweet scent of grass and wildflowers drifted across the low knoll. He looked searchingly into her eyes and kissed her, this time deliberately and meaningfully until he could no longer hold the kiss without his eagerness rising beyond the breaking point.

"When we are married, woman . . ." he said. That was the way Allyn had proposed to her. Not by asking her directly, but by saying things like, "After you graduate and we are married, we will see if there are tribal funds for a new school at Broken Post." Or, "After we are married, I may not be so easy for you to manage, Elizabeth." And she had accepted it. She had always known they would marry one day. Naturally shy, she knew that was the only way he could approach the subject without tongue-tied embarrassment. Now there was no embarrassment left between them as they lay holding each other lightly in the dream of early summer.

The idyll was broken by the sudden onrushing pop and sputtering sound of a motorcycle.

They both sat up, recognizing the sound and the figure. Tally Red Rock was a student at the seminary who was paying his way through school by delivering messages on his one-cylinder Norton motorcycle up and down the rural roads of the county. He glanced their way in passing and then wheeled around recklessly, one foot pawing at the ground. He started to ride up the hill, thought better of it, and switched off his machine, letting it fall over on its side. He rushed up the knoll toward them.

"Oh, hello, Allyn," he said. Then to Elizabeth, "You're Elizabeth Adair, aren't you?"

"Yes, I am."

"Well, then you'd better get over to the Tahlequah courthouse. Fast. Your mother sent me. Allyn—your father's there too."

"What has happened?" Elizabeth asked.

"Well, it seems they've arrested your father, Miss Adair. Charged him with murder."

Elizabeth felt her knees weaken and for a moment she couldn't catch her breath. "Who do they . . . ?"

"That's all I know," Tally said. "Sorry. 'Scuse me, I got to get to the Chandler farm—their daughter's giving birth right in the corner of the dry goods store."

With that the messenger boy was gone, hopping onto his motorcycle, roaring off down the road in a cloud of blue smoke. Elizabeth and Allyn stood together, immobilized by shock for a moment. Then Allyn tightened the arm he had placed around Elizabeth's shoulders and said grimly, "Let's get going. Thank God my father is there."

"This is all nonsense," Elizabeth said. "My father . . . ?"

"Let's go over and find out what it is. We don't know a thing yet."

The courthouse steps were crowded with a small but tightly knotted group of men. Most of them Elizabeth knew—word must have traveled fast. Black Jack Coodey, drunk as usual, old Cucumber Jack, Elijah Hicks, John Amaoah—all Roy Adair's friends and, as Elizabeth now knew, all Nighthawks, were there. Her mother, distraught, her hair half pinned up, emerged from the courthouse and rushed down the granite steps to embrace Elizabeth.

"What is it, Mother? What's happened?"

"Let's go inside," Sarah said. The men were pressing close around them, trying to get some word on Roy Adair's misfortunes. "Your father's there with Judge Benson," Sarah told Allyn. "You'd better come along."

Inside the courthouse it was cool and silent, the hum of voices, the occasional curse muffled by the heavy oak doors and thick brick walls of the building. Sarah, holding Elizabeth's hand, led the way toward the judge's chambers where they found Kenneth Jefferson, his knuckles resting on Judge Benson's desk, leaning toward the confident, white-haired man opposite, earnestly entreating him.

"Well, what is this going to be, a family picnic?" Benson said

95

sourly as they entered his chambers uninvited and unexpected.

"We apologize, Your Honor," Allyn said diplomatically before one of the women could say anything to spark more trouble. "You understand, I'm sure, that Mr. Adair's incarceration is of the gravest concern to his family."

"The charges are ridiculous," Kenneth Jefferson was saying.

"Now you are disputing both charges, Mr. Jefferson?"

"If Mr. Adair will consent to have me act as his representative, of course I will protest his innocence on all charges," Kenneth Jefferson said.

"Charges?" Sarah said blankly. "Have they come up with something new? Besides this ridiculous murder charge?" she asked the newspaper publisher.

"I'm afraid so," he answered. "Perhaps there is someplace the family and I may discuss this in private, Your Honor?"

"Anywhere rather than here," Benson said sourly. "I'll have the bailiff show you to a conference room."

They were shooed out into the hallway to wait. Allyn muttered, "Benson's already made up his mind, hasn't he?"

"What are the charges now!" Elizabeth asked in distress. Before she could get an answer they saw the bulky bailiff, handgun on his belt, approaching and from the other end of the corridor, Grandfather Deerfoot making his way painfully toward them on hobbled legs, his white hair tied back with a blue bandana, rifle in his hand. The bailiff frowned and walked up to Grandfather.

"I'll keep this for you, grandpa," the big man said, taking the rifle from Grandfather Deerfoot's arthritic hand. Then, rifle under his arm, the uniformed bailiff took them all to a small conference room with a window that looked out on a small oak-studded park where boys were playing a ballgame, their mouths open in shrieks silenced by the window panes.

"All right," Elizabeth said, seating herself in a chair Allyn held out for her. "What is all of this, Mr. Jefferson? Mother?"

The newspaperman told her, "The first charge is that of murder in the first degree. Specifically the murder by torture of one Abel Lewis Lomas."

"Roy did not kill Sheriff Lomas," Sarah said with authority. There was no doubt she knew of what she spoke.

"No," Jefferson said. He spread his hands. "But it is possible he may have witnessed it, isn't it?"

"He would never speak against another Cherokee man . . . if he had seen such a thing," Sarah added hastily.

"He might have to to save his life," Jefferson said carefully.

"All crock of bull!" Grandfather Deerfoot shouted in his thin voice. "Roy no kill Sheriff Lomas. Joe-Boy no kill white man, Jacoby."

"No, but they convicted Joe-Boy," Jefferson reminded them all. "Despite three witnesses who stated that Joe-Boy was playing cards at Shawnee Market that day."

"The law still states," Allyn said, "that no Indian's words can contest that of a white man in court. That's what convicted Joe-Boy, that could convict Roy Adair."

"I don't believe they're really going to pursue the murder charge," Kenneth Jefferson said quietly, glancing toward the closed conference room door. "They'd have a massive Nighthawk uprising, and they know it."

"Because my father is innocent!" Elizabeth said resolutely.

"Precisely," Kenneth Jefferson agreed. "But the second charge . . . I don't know exactly how we're going to defend against a charge of noncompliance. That Roy refuses to enroll for his allotment as demanded by the mandate of the Dawes Commission is beyond dispute."

"He would say as much in court," Sarah said proudly. "He is Cherokee; the land is ours, not for the whites to divide up into parcels and lots as they do in their own country,"

"Precisely," Jefferson said. The room was stifling. The ceiling fan sat motionless. He walked to the window, looked down at the children playing, and decided not to open it. "I do not know how to defend a man who admits he is in open defiance of the law, admits it and is proud of it."

"It is a bad law!" Grandfather Deerfoot said. "It is white law and they pushed it on us here on Cherokee land."

"Yes, everyone knows that. Everyone agrees," Kenneth Jefferson said. He smiled crookedly. "Everyone but the courts."

Later, alone, Allyn asked his father what he had in mind to try to free Roy Adair.

"I think," his father answered, "what they have in mind is agreeing to drop the trumped-up murder charge on the condition that Adair pleads guilty to noncompliance. Which he will do anyway."

"Then why go through all this rigmarole?" Allyn asked.

"To bring Adair to court. To sentence him for his 'crime' as a lesson to all the Nighthawks, all the full-blood Cherokees, to let them know there will no longer be any tolerance for those who refuse their land allotments, that there is no longer any place for free Indians—even on their own land."

"Judge Benson hasn't that sort of ambition," Allyn said. "He's happy collecting his small bribes and visiting the whorehouse. It has to be coming down from higher up."

"Oh, I agree," his father said, now opening the window a little to let in a breeze and the shrill cries of the boys below. "From the very top. I believe Congress is weary of the Indian land question. Once and for all they want to throw 'Oklahoma' open to white settlers and entrepreneurs."

"For God's sake, Father!" Allyn said passionately. "They have already let whites take the timber from our land, let the Texas cattlemen graze their herds here, let the oilmen lease land for their rigs. If the Missouri, Kansas, and Texas Railroad manages to push through this latest piece of legislation, the United States government plans to give them alternate sections in a ten-mile strip on each side of the right-of-way. And it's not their land to give away!"

Allyn blanched a little, remembering that he had first read about this particular scheme in the pages of his father's *Tribune*. Kenneth smiled indulgently at his son's fervor and put an arm over his shoulders.

"For now, let's do what we can do, son. Let's see if we can find some defense for Roy Adair."

"And you, Father, what will this mean for you? The government has already expressed concern over your editorials, calling them inflammatory. Now to defend a Nighthawk in court?"

"An alleged Nighthawk," Kenneth Jefferson said.

"Oh, for God's sake, Father! We're not in court yet—if Roy Adair is not a Nighthawk, the whole organization is a fiction."

"I wouldn't know," Kenneth said with a smile. "As to what this might do to me and the *Tribune*—let's worry about that another time. Now we have to defend Roy Adair in the best way possible."

The mood in the courtroom was dark. Every male observer had been searched for weapons and more than a few were found, the possessors hustled off to the Tahlequah jail.

There were sixteen law officers around and in the building, including Captain Atoka Boone of the Indian police and Marshal George Lindsay Striker, the United States Marshal for the territory. Judge Benson entered the room fifteen minutes late. Elizabeth, seated in the front between her mother and Allyn, swore she could smell bourbon all the way from the bench. Everyone stood briefly.

Kenneth Jefferson had correctly identified the ploy the government was utilizing. The insupportable murder charge had been dropped ten minutes before court was to convene. The remaining charge—no-compliance—was indefensible in the government's eyes.

And it seemed so to Jefferson himself. Ray sat with his head held proudly, dressed in the same blue flannel shirt out at the elbows and twill pants he had been arrested in. Once he glanced at his wife and Elizabeth and smiled. The prosecutor, a small bald man from Wichita named Paulsen, wore a tight celluloid collar and starched shirt with gold studs, a black string tie, and gold-rimmed spectacles. He looked comfortable, almost impatient, as he studied the two pages of scrawled notes on his table. Judge Benson, looking only bored, rapped his gavel twice and everyone sat again.

The court recorder began reading the charge in a gravelly voice, "The people vs. the Cherokee Indian known as Roy Adair . . ." and droned on while everyone fidgeted. In the back of the room Kenneth heard a few Indians murmuring in their own tongue, their sentences sprinkled with vulgarities. Captain Boone of the Indian police heard it, understood it, and walked that way to quietly caution the men to be silent or be ejected.

The trial began.

On the steps of the courthouse Tom Adair sat drawing on the marble with a broken chunk of red brick. He could hear the trial only as a distant droning. Billy Bird was rushing toward the courthouse, his father, Henry Bird, following, his long legs propelling him along the dusty street.

Father and son stopped in front of Tom.

"Hasn't started yet?" Henry Bird asked, his eyes narrowing.

"They started," Tom said.

"Why ain't you in there, Tom?" Billy asked. "I sure would be was it my pop."

Tom shrugged. "Whatever happens, happens. They ain't going to set him loose anyway. How can they?" he asked, looking up at Henry Bird. "He said already he's guilty, didn't he?

Everybody knows my dad wouldn't take no land allotment from the government. They could find a hundred witnesses. Only thing is how much jail time they're going to give him."

He threw away the chunk of brick and rose, dusting his jeans. Then, with a nod, he started away, walking down the Tahlequah street with the wondering eyes of Billy Bird following him.

"Come on," his father said, "let's see if they's seats left."

Tom walked past the ice house, swallowing dust as every wagon rumbled past. He hated the buzz and squalor of the town, the shriek and whir, the people screaming at each other, rushing aimlessly here and there. The only place he felt alive and at ease was in the hills. He and his rifle or his shotgun, or down along Otter Creek, on Wigwam Island. These people continued to call themselves Indians, but look how they lived: a dry goods store where people were gathered for some unknown reason on the boardwalk, peering in the window; a printing press clacking away at the office of *The Tahlequah Tribune;* kids standing in line out front of the National Theater dressed up in their town clothes waiting to see the latest Chaplin flicker.

Beyond the town, smoke rose from the blast furnace on the Seminole Highway and other, darker smoke hovered in the distance, born of the Chickasaw asphalt works. He heard a car coming, heard a claxon scream behind him, and he managed to dodge out of the way just as Crazy Man, driving a new oil-money Dodge Brothers motorcar, careened around the corner at breakneck speed. He would kill someone some day. It was his third car of the month. The first one, a Ford, he had complained would not run and so he bought another, a Buick. The only problem with the first one was that it had run out of gasoline. But then Crazy Man's allotment was sitting right on top of a big oilfield and they paid him one thousand dollars a week for doing nothing. Crazier than Crazy Man were the Snakes—they were like his Dad, too stupid-stubborn to even accept their oil allotment.

Indian pride. And what were they proud of? Tahlequah? Their refusal to grow wealthy? Their lives were rife with prejudice. His father disliked Choctaws and Creeks, blacks and whites, breeds and . . . hell, Tom thought, he didn't seem to like anyone but full-blood Cherokees. He passed Gurney's store where Black Jack had come for reinforcements. Stepping off the porch, he fell on top of his new bottle of whiskey and it broke in his hands, covering them with blood instantly. Black Jack sat up in the dusty street, looking at his torn hands, roaring with laughter.

"Hey, Tom! What're they gonna do? Hang your Daddy?"

Tom walked on without answering. He was dying in this town. He did not want to grow up poor, drunk, and prejudiced. He would not!

He wandered on toward the fringes of town. He passed a tiny storefront establishment pinched between a saddlery and a gun-shop. In the window was a poster showing a soldier with a rifle, bayonet fixed, waving his comrades forward. In the background were three tanks and red fireballs. The recruiting poster said, "Uncle Sam Wants You." Leaning against the doorframe was a young Cherokee staff sergeant, his uniform immaculately pleated, his hair very short and precisely brushed. He smiled at Tom in a friendly way.

"Ready to sign up, buddy?"

"My Grandfather says it don't make no sense to fight a white man's war," Tom answered.

"No?" the recruiting sergeant replied. "Who says it's a white man's war? Do you think the Bosch are going to care if you're white or Indian when they invade this country? The Kaiser's thugs are already bayoneting little babies and women in France. Why do you think it can't happen here? It's your country too, buddy."

Tom shrugged and kept walking. Nearing the creek, he paused as he saw a huge anthill. Red ants and black ants had apparently laid claim to the same patch of sand, because they were biting each other, swarming from point to point, attacking and counterattacking. Tom watched the vast battling ant armies for a long time and then proceeded to the river.

And there she was.

Astonished, Tom Adair halted in his tracks. Lorna Paxton was sitting on the low growing limb of a huge sycamore, her bare feet swinging as she tossed small pebbles from a collection in her hand. She was so slender, so pretty, her mouth generous, her lower lip slightly full, her small ears perfectly formed. Her small girlish breasts gently curved and promising.

"Well," Lorna said without looking over her shoulder, "are you going to stand there forever, Tom Adair, or come up and talk to me?"

"How'd you know I was there?" Tom asked, hiking himself up onto the mottled low-hanging bough beside her.

"Women have their ways, Tom Adair. Why ain't you at the courthouse?" she asked, dumping the rest of her pebbles down, dusting her small, long-fingered hands.

"Nothin' to wait around for. He's guilty. They'll give him maybe a night in jail like they done with them Snakes up north."

"Don't it worry you, Tom? Your own dad?"

"I don't know. If he wouldn't keep this up we could have our land allotment, our own two hundred acres and the law wouldn't bother us no more. As it is, we don't even own the land where our house sits."

"He believes in the tribal way, Tom," Lorna said. God, how her black eyes shimmered!

"Well, maybe that time is gone, Lorna." Tom tore off a broad sycamore leaf and began crumpling it piece by piece.

"Maybe," she admitted, "but maybe he's right. A lot of people get their allotments and then get cheated out of them. Around and about they enlisted breeds, who would go around taking down the names of full-bloods and giving the names of the hold-outs to the Dawes Commission. These slickers would swear that they were the full-bloods and get their allotments. This happened to my aunt. She did not know she had accepted the allotment until a card came to the post office for her. She took it because she did not know what it was, but when she found out she took it back."

"I heard about that," Tom said impatiently. He crumpled up the leaf and tossed it away.

"I got another aunt—you know if you can't write, Tom, how its legal if you touch the pen when somebody signs for you? They come and called her to the fence and when she got close enough they jabbed the pen at her face and when she shoved it away, they called that a legal touching and they ran away and signed her name on the allotment papers."

"I know," Tom said. "Myself, I don't see what's the matter with owning your own land like the whites do."

"Oh, Tom," Lorna said, lightening her tone, "you won't never need no land. You'll always just be roaming the land, hunting and fishing and sleeping out!" She shoved him playfully.

"And what's the matter with that?" he asked. His hand was resting now on her thigh and she gently removed it.

"It wouldn't do for a woman, would it, Tom?"

And there she met his eyes with those deep black eyes of her own. How could any eyes that black shine and glisten like they did? Once Tom had seen a black star-sapphire ring in the Tahlequah store—that was exactly what her eyes looked like in the right light.

"Were you there to watch crazy Alfred Inkatha try to fly his contraption the other day?" Tom asked.

"No, what happened?" Tom's hand had crept back to her

thigh. This time she did not remove it.

"There he was up on Red Bluff over along Otter Creek, tied himself into the contraption, a million feathers I bet, glued to it. We were all cheering and laughing and he waved real proud, you know, and started running off the bluff—which must be a hundred feet high there by his house."

Tom began to laugh in reminiscence. Lorna jabbed him in the ribs.

"What happened, Tom?"

"Now what do you think? He jumped off the cliff and sailed real grandly—for about three feet, then he fell all the way down the bluff, bouncing and rolling. We ran out to unwind him from all the wire. There was feathers and wood everywhere. For a second I thought he was dead, but he sat up holding his head while feathers snowed down and says, 'I guess I still ain't got it right.' "

"Well, that shows you something, doesn't it, Tom?"

"What's that?"

"There's some things that are best left to whites, others that are best left to Indians."

"You're nutty," he said.

"Am I?" Lorna asked. Her lips were very close to his when she said that, slightly parted, and Tom kissed her experimentally, feeling his blood surge. She drew away, smiling.

"You ought to go back and see how your father's trial is going, Tom, it's only right."

"If you'll go with me," he answered.

"If that's what it takes. Help me down, Tom Adair."

By the time they got back to the courthouse and slipped in the back door under the watchful eyes of the deputies, Kenneth Jefferson was ready to summarize before a weary and impatient-appearing Judge Benson. Benson was saying, "I can think of nothing you can possibly present to this court by way of amelioration after the admissions of the accused, Mr. Jefferson."

Kenneth Jefferson rose slowly and, holding a single sheet of folded paper, walked before the bench. He looked down at the floor for a long minute and then lifted his head to Judge Benson. "Your Honor, Roy Adair is charged with not obeying the law of the United States of America to wit: signing for his allotment of land as demanded by the Congress, and instead defying the government choosing to live by tribal law, which holds that all land should be held in common.

"Your Honor," Kenneth proceeded, turning to face the courtroom in general for a moment. "This law was never ratified by the people of the Five Nations. Chairman Dawes of the commission by that name claimed in investigating Indian Territorial rights that the treaties of 1866 had provided for allotment and the creation of a territorial government administered primarily by whites, superseding tribal authority. What Mr. Dawes neglected to state was that those provisions in the treaties had been optional and that the tribes overwhelmingly rejected them. No law can be unilaterally enforced by one nation on another nation's sovereign soil, Judge Benson, and that is what the allotment law is. This is and always will be a sovereign Indian Nation and not a part of this so-called Oklahoma Territory."

The court broke into cheers and Judge Benson began hammering with his gavel.

"That is not the position of the United States government nor that of the Territory of Oklahoma," Benson reminded Allyn's father.

"It wouldn't be," Kenneth said just audibly, but Benson heard him and did not smile. More loudly, he went on. "A law cannot be broken if it does not exist. A law cannot exist if it is not the law within a sovereign nation. Roy Adair cannot have broken any law since none exists."

"A clever, if flawed, syllogism." Benson said.

"It is most certainly not flawed. The stated intention and professed policy of the United States is to annex a free and independent nation."

Again there was an uproar of approval in the courtroom. Kenneth Jefferson rushed on before Benson could interrupt him again. He held up a piece of paper with handwriting scrawled across it. "I wish to read this to the court. It was written by Chitto Harjo to the Congress of the United States in the days when the Creek and Cherokee, the Choctaw and the Chickasaw believed we could hire white lawyers to present our iron-bound case in Washington and protest the loss of our lands and way of life, before the obvious cultural arrogance of the white man and his insatiable greed became nakedly obvious."

"Mr. Jefferson, I caution you. There is a court reporter taking down your words. You are bordering on sedition, sir."

"I see," Kenneth Jefferson bowed his head in mock submission. "I thought I was being patriotic. I apologize.

"To return to the letter of Chitto Harjo, which was written in 1906 . . . for those who do not know who he was, Chitto Harjo, or Crazy Snake, was a full-blood Creek . . ."

"And the leader of the Snake Uprising," Benson said sharply.

"Your honor? Please?" Unfazed, Jefferson went on. "When all had failed in Washington, the white lawyers being in the pocket of the developers, the oilmen, the land for white people, Chitto wrote this letter in frustration. I quote: 'He told me as long as the sun shone and the sky is up yonder, these agreements will be kept . . . He said as long as the sun rises it shall last; as long as the waters run it shall last; as long as the grass grows it shall last. He said, just as long as you see light here, just as long as you see this light glimmering over us, shall these agreements be kept, and not until all these things cease and pass away shall our agreement pass away. That is what he said, and we believed it. We have kept every word of that agreement. The grass is growing, the waters run, the sun shines, light is with us, and the agreement is with us for God that is above us all has witnessed that agreement.' "

Slowly Kenneth Jefferson lowered the letter. "Your Honor— the people of this Indian Nation remind the court that the waters still run and the land we walk over is still the Indians' land to do with as he will. Roy Adair has broken no tribal law. He can, therefore, have broken no law at all."

There was a quiet murmuring and then a cheer of approbation. Men threw their hats into the air and cheered. Cucumber Jack stood up on his chair and toppled over. The marshals and Indian police tightened their cordon as Judge Benson pounded away furiously with his gavel.

Kenneth Jefferson himself had to gesture for silence before the clamor in the court quieted.

Benson, his face suffused with blood, told Jefferson, "I shall retire briefly to my chambers. I will return with a verdict, Mr. Jefferson."

Allyn was beaming with pride; Sarah seemed awed. Roy Adair was trying to hold back a grin as Jefferson returned to his chair between Elizabeth and Allyn.

"Thank you," Elizabeth whispered, putting her hand over Kenneth Jefferson's.

"You were magnificent, Father," Allyn said.

The tension seemed to have gone out of the courtroom. Men spoke in low voice and smiled to one another. In the very back row Tom Adair sat wordlessly beside a nervous Lorna Paxton. Judge Benson was in chambers for a long while. He moved slowly to the bench in his black robes. Marshal Striker strode behind him and now positioned himself beside the bench holding a double-barreled twelve-gauge shotgun. A very bad sign.

Benson did not have to strike his gavel. The court was in

dead silence, awaiting the verdict. Benson looked directly at Kenneth Jefferson and not at the defendant. "Thank you for an entertaining presentation, Mr. Jefferson. It was quite novel and instructive. However, a letter written by a disgruntled Indian is hardly a precedent for any sort of legal decision."

Allyn felt his heart sink. Sarah Adair began to tremble. Tom whispered to Lorna Paxton.

"They're going to give him a night in jail."

"Weighing the seriousness of the crime, carefully reviewing the defense's presentation, I have no legal option but to follow the guidelines set forth by the United States of America and the policy of the Territory of Oklahoma in such matters and find Roy Adair guilty of knowingly and arrogantly violating a statute of this territory." He looked at Roy and their eyes locked. Roy's were black and expressionless, like the charred ends of hatred.

"The court finds you guilty, Mr. Adair. The marshal will escort you to the territorial prison where you will serve a minimum of six years and a maximum of ten years imprisonment for your crimes against the government."

The gavel pounded; the judge returned to his chambers, his exit covered by the shotgun-carrying officer. Kenneth hung his head; Sarah began to cry uncontrollably. Elizabeth was rigid, her face ghostly. Only Roy Adair was able to smile. He waved to them before they put him in chains and removed him from the court to the hoots and yells, the curses and whistling, the stamping of feet of the Cherokee onlookers.

"It's my fault," Kenneth said into the palms of his hands. "I aggravated the man."

"It is not your fault," Sarah Adair said softly, resting her hand on the newspaperman's shoulder. "You told the truth. It is the law's fault."

That did little to console Kenneth Jefferson. He sat with his head in his hands long after the unruly crowd had sifted from the courthouse. When he finally did look up only Allyn and Elizabeth remained.

"Oh well, then" he said, taking in a deep breath that seemed to fill his entire body and straightening his shoulders. "We continue, children!"

He rose and the three walked toward the double doors of the courthouse where still an Indian policeman stood guard.

"What will you do, Father?" Allyn asked.

"First? I am going to write an editorial like none this county has ever seen. Then I'm going to double-run the edition, and if I have to, ride from house to house until every Cherokee citizen is aware of what has happened and what could happen to them. I am," he said flatly, "going to become a seditionist."

Tom and Lorna Paxton walked slowly along Otter Creek. There were pink and white blossoms on the sleek and silver stream drifting slowly away.

"I'm so sorry, Tom. Six years!"

"They'll never do that. They were just trying to scare everybody, make an example of my dad. He'll be home before the week's out," Tom believed.

They paused in a cottonwood grove. The white fluff of their seed clusters drifting like gently settling warm snowflakes. They sat on the creekside grass and watched the river. Wigwam Island was a dark hump against the creek. There was the quicksilver flash of feeding fish and then silence.

"Sons sometimes hide their love for their fathers behind hate," Lorna said. "It's hard for them to admit love."

"What have you been reading?" Tom asked with a harsh laugh. He lay back on the grass, hands behind his head, Lorna looking down at him. "I love my dad, Lorna, truly I do. But what he's doing is crazy. Like a man standing in front of a flood like Moses, yelling, 'Stop! Go back the other way. I defy you!' "

"He feels he's right in his convictions."

"Well, maybe he is," Tom said, "but so what? What good is it doing him to be right? What good is it going to do my mother if they do decide to keep him locked up for years? Nothing is going to change just because he wants to be a martyr for a lost cause." He sat up and winged a flat stone into the creek. "The times are changing, Lorna. Nothing is going to hold back time."

When Tom did get home it was very late in the afternoon. Sarah had kept herself busy preparing a large meal that she realized halfway along no one would eat. Shanna was gone; Elizabeth was at school or at the Jeffersons. Roy . . . oh, God! Roy was not coming home at all!

She sat on the wooden kitchen chair and dabbed at her eyes with her apron, aimlessly straightening the red-checked tablecloth. What had happened to them? When they had come to Broken Post the neighbors had come and helped them build; it was a cheerful time with Roy young and immensely strong and handsome, laughing, driving nails, sawing as the women prepared their meals out of doors in big iron pots and Grandfather Deerfoot regaled them all with funny tales of the old times. The children danced and whirled as funny Black Jack played his ocarina and Lew Slosser beat an upturned tin washtub . . . where had everyone gone?

The answer, if you got to the bottom of it, was that Roy had become an outlaw. Not a pariah, but one too dangerous to associate with in these times when all of the Four Mothers Society agendas had been beaten back by government forces and they had turned to violence and intimidation to try desperately to garner some attention and respect . . . all useless. Joe-Boy Parker had been a good dancer, very quick on his feet. Dead. Black Jack had been young and strong and funny; now he was the town drunk, nothing more. Standing she took a reinforcing breath and with nothing else to do, re-read Shanna's last letter.

At least she was happy and doing well. Maybe she had been

right after all in leaving the Nation, because there was no more Indian Nation. There was nothing.

She rose, hearing the screen door slam as Tom came in. Wiping at her smudged eyes once more, she poked at her hair, adjusted her smile, and went to serve him his dinner.

Tom lay awake on his bed, fully dressed except for his boots. It was close to midnight. He felt that something was about to happen, but he did not know what. He could not sleep. He did not wish to dream.

At five minutes after midnight the horsemen rode into their yard and called out to him.

"Tom! Tom Adair! Come out here."

Tom rose slowly and went down the hall, brushing past his mother who peered fearfully from her bedroom and stepped out into the cool, clear night. There were six mounted men there, dark blurs as his eyes struggled to adjust to the darkness.

"Get your rifle, Tom, we're riding tonight."

"I'm not. I'm not one of you," he told the Nighthawks.

"He's your father," Black Jack, identifiable by his slurred speech, said from behind his black mask.

"I'm not one of you! I don't want to be one of you!" Tom said, spreading his arms in frustration.

"Please, Tom?" Allyn Jefferson asked quietly.

The door behind Tom opened and Grandfather Deerfoot hobbled forward. He handed Tom his .30-.30 rifle and his boots.

"He is your father. We are Adairs. We are Cherokee," the old man reminded him. His rheumy eyes were hopeful, his time-scarred face proud as he held out the rifle with both hands.

"No one's going to be killed, Tom," Allyn Jefferson said from horseback. "We just have to convince the judge that he cannot get away with this sort of high-handedness."

"Allyn . . ."

Someone shushed Tom. "No names!"

"Editorials won't do it, Tom!" Allyn said in a strangely forceful voice at odds with his professorial image. "No matter what my father thinks."

"All right," Tom said angrily. Throwing himself down on the porch, he tugged on his boots and snatched the rifle from his grandfather's hands.

Then he stalked to the barn, feeling his mother's eyes on his back. Now he was one of them! Riding for a cause he did not believe in with men he had no faith in.

One night, this night. For honor, he would ride with the Nighthawks.

He saddled the black gelding and rejoined the men. Someone handed him a mask and he put it on, hiding his features and tightly compressed, angry mouth. He followed them slowly from the yard. They turned north, toward Tahlequah and Judge Benson's house.

Tom rode close to Allyn, still surprised, but, in some way, not overwhelmingly so to find this mild-mannered man among the Nighthawks.

"He won't be alone, Allyn. Not tonight. He'll have Indian police or marshals or both around his house."

"One man, Marshal Striker," Allyn said. "Tom, we don't do these things at random without checking out the situation first."

"No, I guess you wouldn't," Tom said. "Does my sister know about this? Does Elizabeth know?" he demanded.

He had to duck low and slow the black horse as they rode through the cottonwoods, ducking to keep beneath the overhanging limbs. When they emerged from the dark grove, Allyn had moved away from him to ride beside a man Tom identified by his clothes and silver-decorated belt as Cucumber Jack.

It was almost one a.m. when they reached Judge Benson's house.

The two-story white frame house sat in a small hollow next to a narrow rill, surrounded by a low wrought-iron fence. Myriad roses, their scent full in the night, clustered around the house.

One gigantic magnolia tree in full bloom shaded the entire front yard from the falling starlight. There was a single light on in an upstairs room, no sign of patrolling men.

They sat their horses, listening for dogs, men's voices, sniffing the air for drifting tobacco smoke. There was nothing. Allyn dismounted and the others followed his lead.

They fanned out and moved toward the house through the deep shadow, crouched low as they went. Tom felt cold; an entity outside of himself told him to use sense, quit, go home and have nothing to do with these men, yet still he went forward with them. Maybe there was some primitive tribal instinct at work. Then he saw a spark from the corner of his eyes. The blue-orange flicker of flame, and before Allyn's hand could halt the man, Black Jack had set fire to a clump of dry brush and was moving rapidly forward to the base of the white house. Tom heard Allyn curse under his breath and rush forward to try to stamp out the fire.

They were not the only ones who had seen the flame. From a small white shed hidden in the shadows at the rear of the house, they saw the figure of a tall man, rifle raised, emerge to be silhouetted by the feeble light of the stars.

Marshal George Striker, shirtless, opened fire with his Winchester, working the lever of his rifle smoothly. Someone was spun around and knocked to the ground. Black Jack and Sway Tree fired back and Tom saw Striker stagger backward and fall, shot from side to side through shoulders and chest.

Allyn grabbed Tom's shoulder and shoved hard.

"Ride," he commanded as he continued to try to beat out the fire. Upstairs in the house lights flashed on in other windows and there was the sound of rushing feet. There were other men in there as well, despite Allyn's confidence that there were not.

Tom ran toward his horse, not out of cowardice but out of frustration and disgust. They weren't going to kill anyone! Now how do you know that when one group of armed men goes against another? It seemed they had probably killed a United States marshal.

Tom leaped into the saddle of the startled gelding and rode for home at a gallop, still holding his unfired rifle in his right hand. Far behind him now, he heard more shots and then a sharp flurry of them. He rode on.

When he reached home the old black horse was lathered. He was no longer capable of a sustained run like that. It would be amazing if he didn't collapse. One more victim. Tom rubbed it down hurriedly, roughly but thoroughly and walked back to the house. He walked in the front door and past Grandfather Deerfoot who sat expectantly at the kitchen table, smoking his pipe. Tom walked to his bedroom, tore the pillowcase from his pillow, stuffed some clothes in it, and grabbed a blanket from his bed. He walked toward the kitchen.

"Tom?" His mother watched him anxiously, holding her wrapper together at the breast.

Tom opened the cupboard and jammed some tinned food into his pillowcase. Then he turned slowly. "Tom?" his mother said again, plaintively.

"I harmed no one," was all he said. Then quite deliberately he moved toward the chair where his grandfather sat and threw the rifle, clattering, to the floor. "Fight your own fights," he said and left the house, the screen door banging behind him.

She emerged silently from the river and, wiping her eyes with her hands, walked barefoot along the shore of Wigwam Island. Lorna found him just as the sun had nearly dried her hair and dress. He sat alone next to a small fire, baking fish on a stick supported by two Y-shaped upright branches. He looked up at her, smiled hesitantly, and then grew gruff.

"How the hell did you find me?"

"Where else would you be, Tom?" Lorna Paxton asked, seating herself beside him on the mossy log.

"Is anyone else looking for me?"

"Anyone . . . ? No. Only your mother. She sits on the porch in her rocker, waiting for you. She asked me if I knew where you were."

"What did you say?"

" 'No,' of course. But I think she knew I was lying." She nodded toward the fire where the fish crackled and turned golden brown above the flames. "Are you going to eat both of those?"

"Hungry?"

"Sure, I swam from the west shore."

He nodded, that was a long swim for anyone. He was silent for a long time while the flames died to embers. Lorna did not interrupt his thoughts. When he finally spoke it was to ask, "Did he die?"

"Yes. He lived for three days. Then he died. At the judge's. Do you know who shot him, Tom?"

"No."

"It wasn't you, was it, Tom?" she asked, her eyes earnest and probing.

"No. Quit asking questions. I got two slabs of bark over there, they'll make plates for us."

"We have gotten primitive, haven't we?" she asked, laughing.

"Maybe. I don't know."

"Tom, no one knows you were there even."

"Well, you sure as hell seem to!" he snapped.

"I pried it out of Elizabeth. Put on my sad pout." She demonstrated and Tom laughed despite himself.

"That works on women too?" It was Lorna's turn to laugh.

"It did this time. Anyway, Tom, let's go to Tahlequah. Get you off the island for a little while even if you decide to come back . . . I mean," she said hesitantly, "that's all right with me too. I just thought for an afternoon. I have two tickets to the National."

"They must be pretty wet by now," Tom said, looking her over.

"I left them on the other bank," Lorna said, pushing him lightly. "Do I look a huge mess, Tom?" Her eyes were half-lidded now, something warm lurking behind them. "Really a mess?" she tried to say as he smothered her mouth with his own and lay her down on the deep forest grass.

He began to unbutton her bodice. Her hand lifted automatically to stop him and then fell away. Her hair was fanned darkly against the grass, her eyes alive with deep light.

"What's playing?" he asked, kissing her again.

"What!" she asked as his hand slipped under her unbuttoned bodice and found her breast.

"How'm I going to decide if I want to go to the movies if I don't know what's playing?"

She laughed until his kisses and his hands banished the amusement in her eyes and the day became lazy and warm and deep.

"We could have taken the Otter Creek road," Lorna said as they hiked on into the highlands, walking toward Old Man Hill.

Tom held her hand loosely and strode on rapidly.

"I know. I just didn't want to pass anybody I know."

"You didn't want to go near your house."

"Something like that."

"You have to tell your mother something, Tom! Even if you only send a note. I'd take it for you."

"I know," he said seriously. "I will, but just now I don't know what to tell her. I don't know what I'm going to do. Maybe I'll leave town."

"Tom!" Lorna halted, pulling him back by his hand. "You can't . . . now! After today? Besides, where would you go?"

"I don't know." He tugged her along as he started walking again. A cool breeze floated over the knoll, stirring the long grass as it passed, ruffling the leaves in the live oak trees. "My sister Shanna left without knowing where she was going and she's doing fine."

"Tom . . . I love you, Tom. Don't leave me."

He didn't look at her or slow his pace.

"Look! There's The Old Man. Have you ever seen his place?"

"Not close up," Lorna said in a subdued voice.

"Come on, then. Let's go look at it."

They found The Old Man sitting in front of his bark hut, seated on his striped blanket, looking out over the long empty land.

"Is that all he does?" Lorna whispered. "It's spooky, Tom."

"Nah! He's watching for buffalo, isn't that right, Old Man?" Tom asked.

"Tom, that's not nice."

"He doesn't care, do you, Old Man?"

There was no response at all. The Old Man sat watching still, his eyes fixed on some undefined point beyond Otter Creek, across horizon after horizon.

"Well, this is no fun," Tom said finally. "Come on, let's get down to Tahlequah." As they turned to go, The Old Man spoke.

"Did you bury this one? You should have buried this one before the coyotes get him. It's no good to leave any man to get eaten by wild things."

How could he know! How could he know these things perched on this hill?

"Let's go, Lorna. Come on. I don't want to listen to the crazy old man anymore."

Tom was silent most of the rest of the way to Tahlequah. Lorna could not prod him into conversation. She tried to brush and pin her hair on the run without much luck. One long strand looped past her eye and down her sleek throat. She could not read his thoughts. Tom was changing, changing too rapidly for her to understand his moods these days

They passed oil-rich men in yellow suits smoking big cigars, wagons crowded with ragged families of full-bloods hauling their meager purchases home; they dodged three automobiles, leaped over mud puddles in the street, passed the store where Black Jack and his cronies sat drinking whiskey in the alley. They waved at Tom, beckoning him; he ignored them. Lorna could see the tension rising in Tom. The tendons on his throat stood out, the muscles at the hinge of his jaw bulged. He was infused with anger. At whom? Her, himself? Was it a mistake to make love with him? They were nearly beneath the marquee of the National movie theater.

"Look at us, look at this place!"

"Tom, what's the matter?" Lorna asked, bewildered.

"Filth and noise and mud; fancy Indians, ragged Indians. The place roars and farts and smokes. People going nowhere! Filled with racism, dirty politics, hatred, violence, inequities, intolerance. Our only solution is to shoot someone else!"

"Tom," Lorna clutched at his hand but he clenched it into a fist. "You're only hot and tired. Let's sit in the cool of the theater. Simmer down."

"They don't want the white man to run their lives and they act like they're incapable of running their own! But they want to run mine! Oh, yes, they want to run mine. But they can't, Lorna. You hear me, I won't let them!"

"Tom!" He started away from her.

"They won't run mine!" he shouted to the street. Lorna hurried after him. He was marching toward the small storefront office ahead. She couldn't keep up. She slipped, fell in the mud of the street and rose, frantically holding up the tickets, looking back at the marquee, then to Tom.

"Tom! They have Marie Dressler playing. You like Marie Dressler!" Her hair had come unpinned. Mud caked the front of her dress. Passersby looked at her in amusement.

Lorna saw Tom go up onto the sidewalk where a young Indian in a crisp Army uniform came out and threw an arm over his shoulder, smiling at him, saying something. Lorna stood there in the street for a long time, too upset to be embarrassed by her appearance, too absorbed to notice the wagons clomping past, the automobiles swerving to avoid her, to hear the jeers of children, the shouts of the drunken men in the alley. She stood there a very long time, took three steps toward the recruiting office, and then halted. Her hand fell to her side and she slowly crumpled the theater tickets.

CHAPTER FOUR

The clank and hiss and rumbling of the troop train were all new sounds to Tom Adair.

There was a constant buzz along the platform, the crying of women, hearty handshakes from father and goodbye hugs from lovers, people moving shoulder to shoulder. He stood beside an iron pillar with "Platform B" stenciled on a sign, fingered the pass in his pocket, and waited. The recruiting sergeant had given him five dollars and Tom had bought a new shirt and saved the rest for sandwiches on the train. He had not gone home, said nothing to his mother. He had no doubt that Lorna would tell her quickly. Lorna—he felt bad about that. There was just no way of explaining that he had to get out of that town or become crippled by its ways. What did she want him to do? Work at the sawmill and raise babies down on the Nation? It could not have worked, the frustration of dissatisfaction would have overtaken him and in time, like a cancer, spread to her.

Now with a final exhalation of steam the locomotive came to rest on its iron bed and Tom made his way along the platform to find his car. There were soldiers on leave on the train as well as raw recruits. These experienced men appeared confident if not downright cocky, their Sam Brown belts, brass buttons, and boot toes all polished to a gleaming shine.

The coach was full when Tom entered it, weaving from side to side down the aisle as the train lurched forward again, lumbering across the plains. Tom looked for an empty seat, preferably one beside another Cherokee, but it was no time to be choosy.

The train jerked suddenly and Tom plopped down next to a young man with a dark Stetson tugged low over his eyes, slouched down in his seat, arms folded. He wore Western boots, black jeans, and a plaid cotton shirt with snaps instead of buttons. As Tom made an unceremonious landing, the young man tipped back his hat and grinned.

"Sorry," Tom muttered.

The white cowboy nodded back. He had green eyes, and laugh lines or weather marks webbed the corners of them. He offered a hand, which Tom took automatically. The hand was heavily callused from ropes and tool handles. From the way his shoulders filled out his shirt, Tom could tell he had some muscle under it.

"Charlie McCoy," the young man said by way of introduction.

"Tom Adair."

"Glad to meet you. Tom." The young cowboy assessed his new traveling companion.

"Full-blood, are you?"

Tom stiffened just a little. "Yes," he said warily. Charlie McCoy grinned.

"Me too," he said, readjusting his slouch. "Full-blooded Irish."

Tom laughed and relaxed. He looked past McCoy at the window where the yellow land, the small farmhouses, silos, and clumps of blackjack and post oak whipped past at breathtaking speed.

Now and then groups of barefoot boys with dogs yapping at their heels appeared to pretend they were racing the train.

"You know how long this train is supposed to take to get there?" Charlie McCoy asked.

"They told me we get in the day after tomorrow. In the morning sometime."

"I just want to get over to Europe and get some fighting in before it's all over," McCoy said. "I wanted to join up last year, but they wouldn't take me. Said I was too young, and then my Pa made me stay around through roundup."

Tom looked again at McCoy. That meant he had just turned eighteen. He certainly looked older, but he was just Tom's age. Perhaps it was that shadow of a beard McCoy had. Something Tom would never have to worry much about.

"Think it will be tough?" Tom asked.

"Boot camp?" McCoy grinned and shook his head. He lifted his chin, indicating the two soldiers in uniform across the aisle. Both were white, fresh-faced, and skinny. "If they can do it, Tom, I guarantee you we won't have any trouble. Besides," he muttered, tugging his hat down again, "you don't think they're going to be eager to send any volunteers home again, do you?"

Tom smiled. No, he supposed not. But this was his first excursion into the strange world off the Nation. He had his doubts. All in all he was glad he had run into Charlie McCoy.

McCoy seemed to have utter confidence in himself. It would be helpful having someone like that around.

Taking a tip from his companion, Tom stretched out and closed his eyes, letting sleep overtake his nervousness as the train rumbled on.

At one stop near Kansas City they drew up beside another train and all of the uniformed soldiers jumped up, lowered their windows, and began yelling out at the men inside. "Shirkers!" was the most common word after the obscenities. Tom looked to McCoy for enlightenment.

"Draftees," Charlie told him. "It took conscription to get them into a righteous cause. It'll be tough on them in camp, I'll guarantee you."

The camp was a collection of long, unpainted weather-grayed barracks in exact ranks across the nearly barren flats. Here and there the Army had planted sapling trees supported by poles. It was as if, Tom thought, they had cut down a healthy forest for the wood used in the barracks and as an afterthought returned to plant a few scraggly, wind-beaten, non-native symbolic saplings—supported by poles cut from other healthy full-grown trees. Which was very close to the truth. It was wartime; the Army had no time to worry about niceties; and when the war was over the camp would presumably be bulldozed down and the exotic trees would die from lack of water.

The tall, wood-bodied bus from the railroad station rolled in through the main gate past smart-looking MPs. A few recruits in uniform turned their heads to jeer at the new arrivals, shouting "Rainbows!" because they arrived in all different colors of clothing—except Army green.

The bus jolted to a stop in a cloud of its own dust before a two-story building with "Induction" lettered prominently on its front.

"Well," Charlie McCoy said, standing to peer out the bus window, "here we go, Tom!"

From nowhere a huge dour sergeant with three corporals in tow appeared to immediately begin bellowing at the new recruits.

"Just remember," McCoy said as they rose from their hard bench seats to scramble for their possessions, "don't let 'em intimidate you, but whatever you do, don't talk back and everything'll be okay."

Tom nodded uncertainly. He was the only one without a suitcase or some sort of bag filled with belongings from home, but he didn't worry about it. As the recruiting sergeant back on the Nation had told him—"Tom, you aren't going to have any use for civilian clothes for a long while. Everything you got they'll likely not let you keep; anything you really need, the Army'll provide."

The huge sergeant was yelling a series of barely comprehensible commands at them as they stepped from the bus. "Hurry it up! Ain't got all day! Form up here, damnit. Move it. Form up, form up!"

They organized themselves into ragged ranks as the sergeant, consulting his roster, counted heads, shouting out names. Eventually satisfied, he shoved his clipboard to one of his corporals and stood before them, hands on hips, surveying them from under a low-tilted hat.

"I am Master Sergeant Macklin. From now until the end of boot camp, you will address me as 'sir.' You will address everyone as 'sir.' "

A young, nervous man who had come up with a group of enlistees from El Paso raised his hand as if he were in a schoolroom and said, "Excuse me, Sergeant Macklin?"

The big sergeant spun on his heel and marched toward the terrified boy. Macklin leaned so close to the boy that his hat brim touched the bridge of the youth's nose.

"Are you deaf!" Macklin bellowed, "or just plain stupid?"

The boy swallowed hard. "I just wanted to ask a question . . . sir."

"You do not need to ask any questions, do you understand! All of you. Anything you need to know, you will be told. Everything else, you do not need to know!" He turned to his corporals. "Start 'em through."

"What was that?" Tom whispered to McCoy as they began to file raggedly into the induction building.

"I think," Charlie whispered back, "that was our official indoctrination."

"No talking in ranks!" one of the cocky little corporals yelled.

They blundered through the dark, sweat-smelling building,

bumping each other's knees with their luggage, all of them uncertain and vaguely frightened. In a vast, high-ceilinged hall, a pie-faced sergeant stood on a platform waiting for them to assemble.

"Faraday!" they heard him yell and an obsequious private first-class began walking among them, shoving stubby pencils and tags at them.

"These," the sergeant bellowed, "will be attached to your luggage. You will fill out the tags in this manner: last name first, first name, middle initial. If any of you cannot write, Private Farady will assist you."

"My clothes . . ." one inductee blurted out before the sergeant's glare silenced him.

"You will have no further use for your luggage or your civilian clothes. What the Army wishes you to wear, you will be issued. Whatever luggage the Army wishes you to have, you will be given. Is that clear, girls!"

A few men muttered under their breath, but it was clear enough. They belonged to the Army body and soul now.

They left that hall, leaving suitcases behind, and went to another, similar room where they were commanded to strip to the skin. Told to crouch down, they waited like Aborigines as another sergeant with his two assistants approached with canvas-sided carts.

The sergeant, a small and apparently palsied man, old and frail, began to study the alphabetical roster shakily.

"Adair! On your feet. Boot size?"

"Nine, sir!" Tom shouted back, rising, and one of the privates winged a pair of combat boots at him so unexpectedly that they caught him on the side of the head. Someone laughed.

Tom picked up the boots and crouched back down, understanding now why they were on their haunches unless called—to give the two privates a better aim at them. In that manner they were all rapidly outfitted, none of the clothing, of course, a very good fit.

Led to a "barbershop," they suffered through an experiment that was more like sheep-shearing. Then toting duffel bags with their new clothing—green uniforms, green socks, green shorts— they were marched toward an empty barracks while the more experienced recruits hooted at their attempt at marching.

There seemed to be no one in charge of the barracks for the moment, so they sorted themselves out, unrolling the inch-thick mattresses they found on each wire-sprung bunk. There were no pillows. Charlie and Tom took side-by-side lower bunks; Mc-Coy immediately stretched out, hands behind his neck. Tom rubbed his own burred head and followed suit. One of the kids from El Paso had begun to sob and someone yelled at him to shut up.

"Well, Tom," Charlie said from his bunk, "we're in the Army now."

For all that and many minor humiliations, it wasn't really that bad. The Army was processing them at breakneck speed. They needed four million Yanks to whip the Kaiser. The chief instrument in paving their way on the road to war was one Sergeant Frank Joplin. Joplin was their training instructor. He took an immediate and irrevocable dislike of Tom Adair. It was inescapably mutual.

It had begun immediately and for no discernible reason.

Standing in two wavy ranks on their first day at the obstacle course, Tom listened as they were briefed on procedure. Joplin, pacing directly in front of them as he lectured, suddenly halted in front of Tom. His pouched eyes fixed on him. He rubbed his bluish jaw thoughtfully.

"Did you understand all of that, Chief?"

"Yes, sir," Tom answered cautiously.

"Every bit of it?"

"Yes, sir."

"Then you're not going out there and screw things up, are you?"

"I'll try . . . no, sir!"

Turning his back abruptly, Joplin strode away.

"First ten men on the course!" he ordered. Stepping up onto a fifteen-foot high observation platform, he blew the whistle suspended from his neck.

The first squad of recruits started forward, struggling up and over a ten-foot high wall, swinging across a muddy bog on heavy ropes. One soldier dropped into the goo and everyone laughed. The squad jogged on a hundred yards and then hit their bellies to slither through an obstacle of crisscrossed support timbers hung with shiny barbed wire. Then there was a short, all-out dash to the finish line, and that was the end of it. Joplin, hands on hips, squinting into the bright sunlight, observed it all, saying nothing as the young recruits panted toward the finish.

"Here we go," Charlie said to Tom in a low voice. "Don't look like much to me."

"Next ten!" Joplin commanded, and Tom stepped forward with the second squad. Joplin blew his whistle and they ran forward.

Tom had watched the more successful of the soldiers in the first squad, and using their techniques, he scaled the wooden wall and dropped to the far side, second in the squad. He managed to grab one of the two-inch thick ropes on the first attempt and swung cleanly over the bog. He stumbled a bit on landing, but by the end of the hundred-yard dash, he was well in the lead. He hit the dry, hard-packed earth at the last obstacle and wriggled his way around the timbers and under the tangle of barbed wire. Running as swiftly as he could, he finished up the finish-line dash thirty feet ahead of the second soldier.

Panting, sweating with the exertion, Tom rejoined ranks as

the stragglers finished the course.

Joplin stood on his observation platform watching, expressionless.

"Third group!" he yelled. Then he turned toward Tom. He lowered a stubby finger at him and called down. "You go again with them, Chief. Your technique sucks! You promised me you wouldn't screw up, but you did, didn't you?"

"Sir, I was the first . . ." Tom tried to object.

"You're not listening, soldier! I'm not going to repeat a simple order."

"Yes, sir," Tom said between his teeth. He glanced at Charlie McCoy who gave a small shrug.

Then Tom was off again beneath the blazing sun, over the wall, across the bog on the rope—this time he dragged a boot through the goo—then the hundred-yard dash to the tangle of barbed wire, snaking his way through. He was second to the finish line. When he stopped it seemed he was breathing broken glass into his lungs; his heart felt double its natural size as it thumped away in his ribcage. He walked back to ranks, his boots immensely heavy. Joplin didn't even glance at him.

"Third group!" Joplin blew his silver whistle piercingly. With his back still turned, he added in a loud voice, "You better try it one more time, Chief!"

"Sir!" Tom protested in exasperation. Joplin turned sharply toward him.

"That is an order, soldier. A lawful order," Joplin said with quiet menace, and Tom nodded, walking to the starting line, his chest muscles spasming. He caught commiserating glances from Charlie and the other platoon members.

Tom ran the course again and then a fourth time. By the time they were marched back to the barracks, Tom could barely manage to stagger to his bunk where he flopped back with his boots still on, his uniform soaked through with sweat.

"Man, oh, man!" one of the recruits said. "What the hell did you do, Adair?"

"I don't know," Tom muttered. He had his arm thrown across his eyes. The blood still raced through his body.

"Maybe he just wanted to make an example of someone— anyone," another young soldier said.

The young blond kid from El Paso, John Trout, spoke up. "I heard he don't like Indians. Someone said his daddy was killed by Geronimo."

"What's that got to do with Tom?" Charlie McCoy said with heat. He had been pulling off his socks, and now he threw them down in disgust.

"How should I know?" Trout said. "That's just what I heard, that's all."

"Someone ought to report him," Charlie said angrily.

The platoon broke out in laughter. "Now there's a dumb idea, McCoy!"

"He's probably just lucky he ain't a black man," Folsom, a red-headed kid from Dallas, commented.

"There's just no reason to have to put up with crap like that," McCoy, still angry, said. "Army or not."

"Forget it, Charlie," Tom said from his bunk. "I can take anything the son of a bitch can dish out." He paused, rolling his head toward McCoy's bunk. "But thanks for caring, partner."

Charlie grunted something in embarrassment, closed his eyes, and napped until chow call.

That evening after chow, they had their first mail call, the mail from home distributed like everything else in the Army— simply winged in their general direction by an indifferent clerk incapable of pronouncing the simplest of names.

Tom was expecting nothing. Neither his mother nor his father were great letter writers, but to his surprise he was thrown a large manila envelope with a cardboard stiffener. He opened it very slowly as people who receive little mail do. Inside was a very glamorous picture of an incredibly beautiful woman. It took him a minute to realize it was his sister, Shanna, smiling prettily, wearing some sort of loose robe that revealed a smooth shoulder. Over his shoulder Charlie McCoy whistled softly.

"Man, who is that?"

"My sister," Tom answered, still staring at the picture in disbelief. "At least I think it is! She's in the movies."

"If she isn't, she should be," Charlie said with appreciation. The young woman with the white Grecian gown seemed to smile at him as well, her long black hair loose across her shoulders, framing a perfectly proportioned face.

A small group of soldiers had begun to gather, gravitating toward the photograph Tom held in the manner of lonely men everywhere. Tom showed the picture willingly, but refused to hand it around. His stock, he sensed, had suddenly risen.

"When we get back to Oklahoma," Charlie said, resting a hand on his friend's shoulder, "I could use an introduction."

"Sure, Charlie," Tom said hesitantly. He knew what his own father, the family, would think of a white man dating Shanna. He reflected again that a lot of people he knew on the Nation were hardly less prejudiced than Sargent Joplin. Exhausted, he yawned hugely and fell back to go to sleep with one final thought . . .

When we get back to Oklahoma, Charlie had said. Tom realized that no one ever said if I get home from the war. No one was going to die. Some sort of defensive mechanism, he guessed. Then, suddenly, he decided when they did get back he would introduce Charlie to Shanna if she was there. Why not? Charlie McCoy was his best friend, maybe the only white man he had ever met whom he respected and truly liked. Who else, after all, whatever race or color, was willing to back him up against Sargent Joplin? Only Charlie McCoy.

Tom fell off into a strange restless sleep filled with scattered dreams of barbed wire, soaring eagles, and night hawks, of an old man who continued to ask him, "Did you bury this one? It's no good to let the wild things at them," while Tom ran around among all the dead with his tiny shovel, its blade made of rubber and licorice. Lorna kept begging him to slow down, but the dead men kept piling up. Someone had to take care of them.

He awoke with a start, stiff and perplexed. Where in hell was he? Looking down he saw that Charlie McCoy had been tugging at his boot. The dawn light was pale yellow and faded vermilion through the barracks windows.

"Let's go, Tom. Reveille—time to give 'em hell."

"God," Tom groaned. He was stiff and nerveless. He sat up very slowly.

"Come on," Charlie said, rising from his bunk. "Let's get moving—remember, you aren't going to let that son of a bitch have the satisfaction of thinking he's whipped you!"

Muzzily, Tom rose from his bunk. His head throbbed. Soldiers outside were laughing and shouting before being called to ranks for morning chow. No—Charlie was right. He would not let Joplin beat him. He dressed and marched from the shadows of the barracks into the defiant sunlight.

That day was a repetition of the day before. The next six weeks were a long chain of humiliations, punishment duties, and insults, but Tom gritted his teeth and made it through with the support of Charlie McCoy, John Trout, and most of the platoon, all of whom knew he was being singled out for punishment without cause. Each passing day only made his resolve stronger while Joplin seemed to become slowly weary, or at least bored, with riding Tom Adair.

With basic training completed they were to be allowed two nights and days of freedom before being loaded cattlelike onboard a troop ship for Europe.

"Two nights to howl," Charlie McCoy said, adjusting the knot in his tie. He grinned.

"Doesn't seem like much repayment for what we've been through, does it?"

"You've got to take what you can get," Tom said. He finished the shine on his boots, tossed away the alcohol-soaked cotton ball, smiled at himself in the mirror, admiring his dress uniform and the figure he cut in it, and said, "Let's get the hell off this post, Charlie!"

"I told you we'd make it, didn't I, Tom?"

"You told me," Tom said, draping an arm around his friend's shoulders.

There was a short briefing in the conference hall where Colonel Timmons, the post commander, took the podium. He was a short, slightly bent, gray-haired man. He nevertheless exuded authority.

At attention, Tom listened.

"Men, I want you to have a good time," Timmons said, "but any man who gets out of hand will find himself in the stockade. Avoid the abuse of alcohol. I know you will all want to wet your throats . . ." A general laugh echoed in the hall. "Do not disgrace your uniform! Avoid fighting with the civilians at all costs." He cleared his throat dryly.

"I want you to understand that many of the town boys are liable to become quite resentful if you are over-attentive to the local girls. Be careful where you tread. I hope I have made myself clear. Otherwise . . ." he smiled with apparent difficulty or concern, "have a good time."

The colonel turned and walked off the platform and after a few moments, Master Sergeant Macklin appeared, glowering as usual. "Dismissed!" he said, and the soldiers headed for the exits with yelps of excitement, breathing freedom for the first time in many long weeks.

There were three high-bodied yellow buses parked on the parade ground and Charlie and Tom fought for space aboard the second one, which, with a grinding of gears and a lurch, started down the elm-lined dirt road toward town.

They piled off the buses at the station, which until very recently had been a grain and feed store. Three deputies with watchful eyes wearing Texas-style wide-brimmed straw hats watched the young, rowdy soldiers as they disembarked.

The soldiers immediately began moving up the street in twos, in threes, in groups. Tom started to follow the flow of the mob until Charlie put a hand on his arm and suggested, "Listen, Tom, let's get away from this cattle stampede. We'll just end up in a noisy bar drinking watered beer with everyone we already know. There will be maybe two or three girls with all these guys hooting at them. What say we take a side street by ourselves and see where we end up?"

"Sounds good to me," Tom answered, bowing to Charlie Mc-Coy's logic. They left the partially oiled main street with its plank walks and found a long, dusty pecan tree–shaded dirt road that seemed to go nowhere. It was dry and hot, but the shade of the many wind-shifted trees was comforting after the sterility of the post. The clover alongside the road was alive with the humming of bees.

They passed scattered houses behind picket fences. Kids screamed and ran past, playing, throwing balls, or rolling hoops. Overhead a mockingbird was attacking a crow, driving it away from its nest. A small yellow car, so old that it had a tiller instead of a steering wheel, puttered past, an old gentleman with a derby and a handlebar mustache driving, his wife prim in white dress and veiled hat at his side, sitting stiffly as they jounced along.

They came upon a narrow, twisting creek making its way past oak-shaded banks. Upstream they could hear boys screaming as they dived and splashed and swam and teased. There was a narrow, partially overgrown path crowded by blackberries and holly along the creek, and the two soldiers made their way along it, hardly speaking. Sunlight in brilliant patches surrendered to the shadows cast by the big white oaks and poplars. The creek cooled the air as it flowed silver-bright in its course through the sunny morning.

"What's this?" Charlie nudged Tom, who had been paying only half-attention to their rambling course. Looking up, he saw two high-wheeled bicycles tilted against a poplar tree.

And on the bank of the creek two remarkably young, remarkably pretty blond girls, their hair loose as they lounged on the grass, exchanging giggling little secrets.

Both soldiers stood transfixed for a long time.

"Well, Tom, shall we introduce ourselves?"

"Charlie . . . I'm not good at that sort of thing."

"A little practice might help. Besides." Charlie grinned, "what have we got to lose? All they can do is tell us to get lost. Hell, I've heard the word 'no' plenty of times in my life."

How old were they, sixteen, seventeen? Not much younger than they were, really. They just seemed somehow innocent in their white summer dresses with ribbons at the waist and in their loose blond hair. Tom found that his uniform and the last weeks of training gave him a certain feeling of confidence, but without Charlie McCoy he would not have had the nerve to approach the girls.

Together the two soldiers walked down the long-grass bank toward the girls by the rippling stream.

Tom and Charlie removed their caps as they approached. The girls looked up at them with some trepidation, but with obvious interest. Tom let Charlie McCoy handle the opening gambit.

"Pardon me," Charlie said with a small bow. "My friend and

I are from out of town. Could you tell us how to get to Main Street?"

One of the girls smothered a giggle and looked down; the other, apparently the older of the two, answered, "If you're from out of town, you know where it is. That's the only way in or out of this one-horse burg."

"By golly, Tom," Charlie said, turning toward him, "you were right! You see, I just didn't know the name of that street. Sure, we know where it is then, don't we, Tom?" McCoy said, again deliberately inserting Tom's name into the conversation. Charlie sat down on the grass just above the two girls. "My name's Charlie McCoy, and this is my good friend, Tom Adair."

"I'm . . . Mary Lynn, and this is my cousin, Patricia," the older, prettier girl said. "Is Tom too shy to sit down?"

"Tom! I should say not! He's been slightly wounded, that's all. He's just eager to see some of the town before they send us back over to Europe on the troop ship."

"You boys are off to war!"

"Yes, yes, afraid so," Charlie said dolefully. Then he gave them one of his ingratiating grins.

"So we wanted to look around, you know, do something in our last few hours—thing is we don't have an idea where to go." Tom watched his friend incredulously.

"In this town? There isn't much to do. Period."

"Surely there's something . . ." Charlie hesitated as if a thought had suddenly occurred to him.

"Say, maybe you two could show us around a little. All treats on us."

"I really don't know." The two girls exchanged a covert glance.

"Oh, come on. What could it hurt?" Charlie said cheerily. "There must be something to do."

"We could go to the flickers, I guess," Patricia said carefully. "Or get a sundae over at the malt shop."

"Why, sure!" Charlie said expansively. "Why not do both? I don't expect we'll have much use for money in France anyway."

The girls were still hesitant. "We have to have a private chat," Patricia told them. The girls got to their feet, dusting the grass from their dresses, and started back toward the path. Charlie winked at Tom.

"They'll come, Tom."

"Charlie," Tom Adair said, lowering his voice. "I don't think those are even their real names they're using. Didn't you hear the way they hesitated?"

"Who cares what their names are?" Charlie said carelessly, plucking at the grass as he watched the two pretty blond girls. "Anyway," he said with satisfaction, "I'll bet you we're the first two guys in our outfit to have found some girls."

"If they come," Tom said doubtfully.

Just then Patricia came back down the slope alone. "Okay," she said. "I guess there's no harm in it. We have to change clothes first, though."

"Fine." Charlie rose. "We'll walk you along home then and you can . . ."

A quick glint of apprehension lit Patricia's fine blue eyes. "No! You'd better not. We'll meet you at the picture show in an hour. You can't miss it—it's called the Majestic, and it's right there on Main Street." She smiled teasingly then. "If you can find your way to Main Street now."

"We'll make every effort," Charlie said solemnly. Patricia laughed and strode away, holding her skirts up, glancing back over her shoulder at him. The soldiers watched the girls start up the shaded path. They pushed their bicycles instead of riding them, their hips swaying gently in young girl fashion, looking back once or twice to giggle before they disappeared into the shadows of the oaks.

Charlie McCoy clapped Tom on the shoulder. "My friend,"

he said, "we are going to have a terrific afternoon."

Tom was still doubtful, but then, he reflected, that was his nature. With the ebullient and confident Charlie McCoy whistling and breaking into dance steps at times, their caps tilted at a jaunty angle, they made their way back into town. The buildings fronting Main Street held the heat in and reflected it off their faces. Passing rock trucks and hay wagons stirred up yellow dust. On corners they saw groups of soldiers, young and lost, hanging together, uncertain how to approach their freedom. A few of the older recruits stood outside a general store in the shade of a striped canvas awning, drinking beer. They seemed just as uncertain as the younger soldiers, however.

Tom and Charlie walked down the boardwalk, looking for the theater. From time to time they passed knots of town boys who scowled but said nothing. The found the Majestic Theater halfway through town. Tom glanced up at the playbill: a couple of old Chaplin two-reelers he had seen half a dozen times in Tahlequah.

There was a drugstore across the street with a lazily revolving electric fan. It was getting hotter as the day rolled along, and the walk through town in their heavy dress uniforms had done nothing to cool them off.

"Let's go over there and get a milkshake," Charlie suggested. "We can watch the theater from there."

"I thought we were going to take the girls out for a sundae," Tom said.

"We will, we will. But I'm hot now. Don't tell me you aren't?"

"I am, but what if we miss them, Charlie?"

"Why then," Charlie McCoy said, throwing his arm across Tom's shoulder, "we'll just have to find us a couple more. Come on; you worry too much, Tom."

It was amazingly cool in the drugstore. A few soldiers sat idly on the stools along the counter, drinking root beer floats, stirring thick milkshakes with their paper straws, staring at the occasional passing woman on the boardwalk. They saw John Trout in the corner, and the kid from El Paso waved listlessly.

They ordered strawberry shakes and sat at a table next to the wall where they had a clear view of the movie house through the gilded, ornate lettering on the drugstore window. Charlie surveyed the platoon members in their lethargic rank at the counter. He lowered his voice and leaned toward Tom.

"Wait until these sad sacks see what we've found."

Tom smiled. He sipped at the cool strawberry shake. *If* the girls showed up. Otherwise, they would be left feeling more foolish than any soldier in town. Or, at least, Tom would. Charlie McCoy had more confidence than any young man he had met before. Tom knew that Charlie firmly believed that if Mary Lynn and Patricia didn't show up for their date, why, he would simply go out and find some other girls.

"Look," Charlie said, nudging him. "There goes your pal." Tom looked toward the street to see Sargent Frank Joplin strutting past, sweat trickling across his red face.

"I hope we're done with him for good and all," Tom said bitterly.

"And look the other way! Here they come, Tom. I told you they'd show, didn't I?"

Walking slowly down the street, their chins held high as they passed groups of gawking soldiers, came Mary Lynn and Patricia. Charlie drained his milkshake quickly.

"Here we go, boy! Put on a smile and drag out your manly charm."

Chaplin was frisky and funny in his usual peripatetic way. Who had made the decision wasn't clear, but they had paired off Charlie with Patricia, Tom with Mary Lynn. They hadn't even taken seats together on entering the dark theater with its flickering screen-glow.

"Oh, there's two over there," Patricia said to Charlie. In fact, there were six or seven empty seats in a row, and Tom had started that way as well until Mary Lynn took his hand.

"Oh, no," she whispered to Tom. "She knows I can't sit that close to the screen. It hurts my eyes. There's two seats a little farther back."

She led him that way as *The Pawnshop* began to roll on the screen. He still held her hand, so small and soft as they took their seats. She made no attempt to draw away from him. His ear still softly burned from her whisper.

He had seen the film so many times back in the old National that he could nearly have performed most of the routines himself, and so as the film rolled on, he began to lose attention, and began to focus on other matters nearer at hand.

There was a soft lilac scent about Mary Lynn. Intriguing and somehow mysterious, vaguely erotic.

He found his hand freed and he placed it behind Mary Lynn, toying with the short curls on the back of her neck. She turned her face up to him, and as the frenetic two-reeler flickered on, he bent his head and kissed her. Her return kiss was a revelation, open-mouthed, deep, and encouraging. Tom's hand slipped around her shoulder and he held her tightly, kissing her occasionally. Quite satisfied to concentrate on her fine profile, watching her as she followed the film, from time to time laughing out loud in a soft, birdlike voice. He tilted his head, resting it on her shoulder, and let the day pass.

When the lights came up, the four of them rose and emerged into the stifling heat and brilliant light of noonday. Tom stood blinking into the glare of the day, waiting for his eyes to readjust.

"The malt shop?" Charlie suggested. "It seems to be the only cool place around. Unless," he added, "you girls would like to go swimming in the creek."

"We can discuss that later!" Patricia said, laughing.

"You boys did promise us a sundae," Mary Lynn reminded them.

"We haven't forgotten."

Charlie took Patricia's hand and they started toward the soda fountain. Tom reached for Mary Lynn's hand, but she withheld it. There were different rules for the dark theater and the sunny streets, it seemed.

The sun was incredibly bright, white hot. It had to be at least a hundred degrees. Tom's eyes were still sun-dazzled after the dim theater. He was fantasizing about a swim in the creek with Mary Lynn. Would the girls really do it?

He heard an odd thump behind him and then the sound of onrushing boots behind him. He heard Mary Lynn yip, saw Charlie McCoy leap away, and then the first man hit Charlie on the head while another grabbed his arm. Tom was spun around and thrown back into an alley. He stumbled and went down and someone kicked him with a cowboy boot. Tom tried to roll away, but the toe of the boot caught him again squarely in the ribs, this time knocking the breath from him.

There were four of them, all silhouettes against the brilliant sky, wearing cowboy gear.

Tom struggled to his knees and one of them smashed him in the face with a hand that held something heavier than muscle and bone and his head snapped back violently, his mouth filling with blood.

With a shout, Charlie McCoy rushed at them from the head of the alley. He leaped into the pack of town boys, taking them down into the dust of the alley, arms flailing. Tom managed to rise unsteadily to his feet, and the next boy that rushed at him took a fist in the teeth, sending him reeling back.

Turning his attention to a second boy, Tom battered him right and left with both fists. The boys screamed in frightened protest, holding their hands in front of their faces, not fighting back.

"Hey!" someone yelled from the far end of the alley. "Stop it, you boys or I'll call the cops!"

A huge man in a leather apron carrying a length of iron rod had appeared and as he shook the rod at them, the town boys took to their heels, running from the alley, disappearing into the street.

Tom stood swaying on his feet, spat blood, and turned to where Charlie McCoy half-sat, half-lay against the wall of a building. With Tom's help he managed to sit upright, back against the plank wall. Blood leaked from his mouth, tracing rivulets through the dust on his jaw and throat. His blouse had been ripped open, two buttons popped off.

"We whipped 'em, anyway, Charlie," Tom said, crouching down. "We'll get cleaned up and find the girls, okay?"

"You find 'em," Charlie said in a sandpaper voice as he fingered a loose molar.

"Come on . . . are you hurt bad, Charlie?"

"Not hurt," McCoy muttered.

"Well then, come on, Charlie! This ain't like you."

"I believe I've had enough fun," Charlie said. He looked past Tom, not at him.

"You'll be all right in a minute." Tom sat down beside his friend in the thin, hot ribbon of shade cast by the building behind them. "I wonder why they did that. I know these town boys don't like soldiers, but I can't figure . . ."

"You can't figure it out, you damned fool! It's because you're a fuckin' Indian! A fuckin' Indian with a white girl. You can't figure that out!" McCoy rose shakily, bracing himself against the wall as he looked down at the astonished Tom Adair. "You're stupider than I ever thought possible."

"Charlie . . ." Tom started to rise.

"Leave me alone. I could have had a hell of a good day if I hadn't been dumb enough to bring you tagging along with me."

"Charlie." Rising, Tom put his hand on McCoy's shoulder, but Charlie slapped it away angrily.

"I said, leave me alone, damn you!"

Charlie turned and started up the alley, pausing to scoop up two brass buttons. Then, limping, he went around the corner where a few townspeople stood gawking, shoved his way through them, and disappeared into the white heat of the day.

Tom sat down again. Drawing up his knees, he looped his arms around them and stared at nothing. The alley grew silent except for the constant buzz of bluebottle flies around the garbage cans. The ribbon of shade widened, stretching out toward the center of the hot, oily alley.

Finally, he rose. He found his hat, dusted it against his thigh, and crushed it roughly back into form.

He re-emerged on the street feeling weak but strangely and darkly exhilarated. His face was set grimly. He stood motionlessly on the corner, watching cars putt past, men on horseback moving slowly through the traffic. Very distantly he heard a train whistle blow.

"Hey, Adair!" someone called and he turned to see Trout and Folsom weaving their way toward him. Coming nearer, Trout said, "Jesus! What happened to you?"

"Nothing," Tom answered

"Where's McCoy?"

"I really couldn't tell you."

Folsom touched his arm. "Get cleaned up a little," the redhead said. "We found a place you won't believe. Lots of women, lots of liquor."

"Would they serve me?" Tom asked in a taut voice.

"Huh?" Trout was honestly confused. "Man, they been serving us for the last couple hours, right, Folsom? They don't care that you're a soldier. Don't care how old you are."

"Maybe so," Tom said, his eyes still distant. "I could use a place where they don't care what you are. Where they have a lot of liquor."

"Now you're talking!" the blond soldier said. "Give me your hat! What the hell did you do to that?"

"Dust him off a little and he's all ready," Folsom said, his voice obviously slurred. "Lot of women too, Tom. You can have any of 'em but for that little chunky Maria. I've got her staked out for myself."

Trout laughed. "Yeah, I'll bet she's just sitting around holding her breath waiting for you to get back!" he jeered.

"Í don't care about the women," Tom said in a strange voice. "I just want to find a place where I can get all the liquor I want."

The two white soldiers exchanged a puzzled glance. Trout grinned and slapped Tom's shoulder. "We've found it, brother. That's why we came looking for you guys. Come on, let's get you cleaned up and get going. They're waiting for us, Tom!" They began dusting Tom down vigorously, straightening his uniform. At the first pump they came to, they rinsed the blood and dust from his face and hands.

They ended up in a low shack at the far end of town, near the river. The roof was so low you couldn't raise an arm without touching the ceiling. Fifty feet long, it was no more than twelve wide. Here and there a tired, overly made-up woman, none of them under forty, stood smiling or attempting to smile, their worn, flashy dresses exposing most of their muffin-dough breasts. It seemed that half the platoon had managed to gravitate toward the hot, hovelish joint. It was not so hot as it seemed it should be, but still everyone, man and woman, in the bar was glossed with alcohol sweat in the middle of the day heat.

They found two empty stools near the center of the bar. Tom

and Trout sat on them while Folsom stood behind them, searching the long bar, presumably for his Maria.

"What will you have, Tom?" Trout asked above the constant laughter and shouts. One of the harassed bartenders stood waiting, wiping his hands on a dirty towel.

"Get us a pitcher of beer," Folsom interrupted.

Tom's eyes were sullen. The bartender waited impatiently. Farther along the bar two soldiers were waving folded dollar bills and clinking their empty glasses.

"Will you serve me?" Tom asked the bartender, who gave him a quietly exasperated look.

"No, buddy, you can tell we don't serve soldiers here."

The sarcasm eluded Tom. "I'm serious."

"What do you want, soldier? Anyone old enough to go over and help whup the Kaiser gets served here. Would you please order?"

"Tom!" Trout encouraged.

"A pint of bourbon. Any brand." He put two dollars on the bar counter and the bartender went away with evident relief.

"Tom, what was that about?" Trout asked, but Tom didn't answer. With a cry of happiness, Folsom left. Apparently he had spotted the elusive Maria. Trout was left alone with an entire pitcher of beer. Tom's bourbon arrived with a shot glass beside it. He opened the bottle and with methodical deliberateness began putting it down an ounce at a time. John Trout tried to start a conversation half a dozen times, but Tom obviously had no interest in anything but the whiskey and as it went down shot after shot, Trout shrugged, picked up the pitcher and his mug, and wandered off to join other platoon members at a small round table.

A slow warming golden haze began to settle around Tom.

He fell into a numbed silence; it was a very pleasant place to be just then. He ordered another bottle. He had a brief waking dream of a blue-feathered cougar that made no sense. Then Folsom was at his shoulder with a stout Mexican girl so heavily over-powdered that Tom had to draw away from her. Her lipstick was so red it approached black in the lighting. Her jasmine-scented powder couldn't hide the sour-sweat smell of her arm-pits.

"This is her, Tom," Folsom said with drunken pride. "This is Maria."

The girl muttered something and Tom mumbled a meaning-less reply. As the couple staggered away he thought of Mary Lynn's sweet, clean smell and poured himself another drink.

He spun around on his barstool, staring belligerently across the room, shot glass in hand, but there was no one even there to hate or to wish to fight. These were his buddies. They had gone through their small initiation into manhood together, and none of them had ever given Tom cause to hate. He turned back around and poured yet another drink, his head sagging lower and lower toward the bar as the hours slunk past.

Once he did mutter. "And fuck you too, Charlie McCoy," but no one heard him above the constant din.

The golden haze had darkened to burnt umber, and the people who moved through the thickening fog were only shadows and silhouettes. There was some sort of music playing, but it was so distorted it made no sense. It sounded like drums and whistles, rattles and a violin with a string missing.

A girl was at his elbow, speaking to him, and Tom thought at first that it was Lorna Paxton.

That, he reflected, was impossible. She was back in the Na-tion. Still, he thought he should know this woman, but as hard as he tried, he couldn't focus his vision enough to make out her features in the settling gloom.

"What?" he muttered in response to some blurred question.

"I just wondered if you would buy me a drink, honey."

"I'll buy you the whole bar," Tom said. He tried to reach into his pocket for his wad of crumpled bills, but couldn't. He stood, lurched into the bar, spun around, and found himself sitting on the floor. Someone laughed. Someone else called out his name. The girl bent over him.

"You better take it easy, honey."

"I'll buy you a drink," Tom said again. He got hold of the edge of the bar and leveraged himself upright.

"That's all right. Forget the drink, honey," the girl said. "You need some air."

"I know what I need!" Tom bellowed. The girl walked away swiftly, disappearing into the haze. When she had gone, Tom stood braced upright at the bar with both hands. He decided that perhaps the girl was right. As a matter of fact, fresh air sounded like the greatest thing in the world. Having thought that, it became imperative. He needed air, *now!*

He pushed himself away from the bar and started through the crowd toward the front door.

Someone with massive, strong arms turned him around, half holding him up.

"You'd better try the back door, soldier," a disembodied masculine voice said. "It's closer."

Tom let himself be guided that way. His legs were rubbery. The haze had lifted, but his vision was still horribly blurred.

"What's the matter with him?" someone asked. "Get hold of some bad whiskey?"

Tom shouted at the man. "Don't say that! Don't let anybody say that! They got the best goddamned whiskey in the world here!"

Again soldiers laughed. Tom was being propelled on an unsteady course toward the back door. His stomach was beginning to play tricks on him. He could taste rising bile in the back of his throat. Maybe they were right. Maybe he had gotten hold of some bad whiskey! He was about to say that to his escort when they reached the back door. It opened on squeaky hinges and Tom stumbled outside to find himself standing beneath warm sunset skies. The faintest of breezes drifted past. The sky was still clear except for a few thin orange-tinted pennants of cloud low in the west.

He saw two huge black oak trees ahead, surrounded by rusting beer cans and old bottles. It seemed like a good place to go, a place to rest.

He made it only three steps in that direction before he vomited. He bent over, throwing up on his boots and pant legs. The spasms were so violent they hurt his stomach with each repetition.

And they would not stop. In between uprisings he would stagger a few more steps toward the trees.

He could not stop retching, and his head had begun to throb abominably. He had nearly reached the trees when he lost his balance and pitched forward on his face. He didn't even try to rise; he knew he didn't have the strength. He threw up again. It was nearly dry this time, but he felt as if his stomach was coming up into his throat and out his mouth. He lay there groaning, his legs drawn up fetally. His hands between his knees. He could smell his own sour vomit and realized he must be lying in it. It didn't matter; he didn't care.

The sky grew gradually dark. The light breeze increased just enough to cool the overheated day. Once he saw a light spill out of the back door of the bar and he saw two soldiers standing there, silhouetted against the glare from within. Someone called something that he didn't catch and after a minute, the door closed again. It might have been Trout and Folsom looking for him. It might have been two men taking a leak. It didn't matter. No one could have seen him lying there in the pooled shadows beneath the oaks. That suited him just fine. He didn't want to be found, counseled, helped. He realized that for the first time in many weeks he was alone, and that suited him just fine.

He awoke shivering. There was cold sweat clinging to him. His mouth seemed to be full of cactus. There was a garbage stink about him. Tom rolled onto his back with a groan and stared skyward, seeing a silver half-moon through the high boughs of the tree. It took him a long minute's meditation to remember where he was and what had happened.

When he did, an almost electric shock went through him. He sat bolt upright sharply, so sharply that the throbbing headache he had awakened with exploded into a terrible new sort of pain. It was as if someone was driving a spike through his skull. He sat there bent over at the waist, holding his belly, which burned horribly. He peered through the tears of pain toward the back of the saloon, but it was completely dark. Completely silent.

What time was it? He looked at the moon again, trying to estimate it, but these last weeks he had been inside the barracks after dark and lost track of moon-time. It was certainly after midnight, anyway. There were only a few lights on anywhere in the town.

Which meant he had missed the last bus back to the post.

He would have to walk it then. Walk those five miles the way he felt! He had trouble enough even getting to his feet. He stood tilted against the oak tree, breathing in deeply, trying to draw strength from the cool air. He looked around for his hat, but he had lost it again. He smelled rancid. There was drying vomit on his blouse and on his pants.

He stood looking at the stars in the west. "You have become what you swore you'd never become, Tom. A stinkin', drunken Indian!" He cursed himself, excoriated the whites and his ancestors as well.

Calming, he slowed his breathing. Talking to himself, he started toward the main street of Burlington. "Well, so I screwed up. Half the platoon probably screwed up tonight. We have the right. We're on our way to France and to hell, right? I forgive you, Tom old buddy!" He laughed and continued his meandering way, taking two steps sideways for every one step forward, continually falling facedown against the dew-covered grass.

Once, he paused on hands and knees, his head swirling crazily, and to his ramblings added, "And I forgive you too, Charlie McCoy. You son of a bitch."

The streets of the town were dead and ghostly, quite empty. Not a cat or a dog. Behind closed, lighted curtains here and there he saw vague silhouettes or heard muted voices and music. That was all.

Unaccountably exhausted, he sat on a bus bench, head in his hands. The anxiety had returned, the sickness of malaise. He was barely aware of the green truck slowly swinging over to his side of the street. At the squeal of brakes, he lifted his head and saw the military police sergeant approaching.

"Long night, soldier?" the thick-chested Dutchman said, not unkindly.

"Quite long enough, thank you," Tom answered.

"Well, it's over now. Can you stand up?"

"I think so."

Tom got to his feet, using the back of the bus bench for support. He slipped forward, falling against the MP's shoulder. "Sorry," he muttered.

"That's all right,"

Tom noticed the second MP moving up behind him, but didn't understand the significance of it until his arms were yanked behind him and the handcuffs were put on.

"Don't fight us, soldier," the Dutchman said and Tom grinned lopsidedly.

"I assume you're kidding," he answered, and the MP laughed despite the situation.

"It'll be okay, kid. For tonight. We're just going to give you a ride back to the post."

"Fine," Tom answered agreeably, and he yawned magnificently.

"Jesus, he stinks!" he heard the other MP say.

That didn't matter either. He wasn't going to have to try walking the five miles back to the post. No sooner had the MPs gotten Tom into the back of the truck and seated on the bench than he tipped over against the floorboards and fell to sleep.

Morning was cold, gray, and disoriented. Tom awoke on a two-foot wide steel bunk, supported by chains fastened to a cold, gray concrete wall. The cell was four feet by eight.

There was no window.

He felt like hell. His head was a bell tower where huge bells chimed as some sadistic Quasimodo clambered laughingly among the tangle of ropes.

Tom sat holding his head. Beyond the wall he could hear the sounds of the post: men marching in unison, trucks grinding by, and once—oddly—a very large dog barking angrily.

Tom's head came up as he heard the approaching sounds of boots ringing against the concrete corridor floor. Looking in that direction he saw three men walking rapidly toward his cell. The Dutch MP sergeant, a private wearing a sidearm on a white, webbed belt . . . and Master Sergeant Macklin.

They trooped to a halt in front of his cell. Macklin ordered, "Open it up!" and the private produced a ring of iron keys from the back of his belt and opened the cell door. He stepped back immediately to the far wall, hand on his sidearm. Macklin and the Dutchman entered.

Macklin stood staring down at Tom for a long minute, saying nothing. The Dutch MP sergeant stood back, looking at the gray concrete wall above Tom's head.

"Stand up!" Macklin suddenly shouted.

Tom wobbled to his feet, standing at rigid attention. Macklin, crisp and huge, just stared at him with cold blue eyes. Disgust was evident in those eyes and in the tightening of his lips.

"Well," he said at length, "it looks like we failed you, doesn't it?"

"Sergeant Macklin . . ."

"I don't want any answers. I don't want any excuses, Adair. When you were given a pass, Colonel Timmons laid down only a few simple rules. Don't fight. Comport yourself like a gentleman. Seems to me you failed miserably, wouldn't you say?" Tom began to speak, but Macklin roared, "You failed the unit, the colonel, and yourself!

"You don't care, do you, Adair!" He was inches from Tom's face. "The colonel has to maintain good relationships with the townspeople. It is a major part of his job. It is important to him and to his career, Adair. That doesn't matter to you, does it, Adair!"

"Sergeant . . ."

"Shut up! You make me sick, Adair." Macklin's voice lowered, becoming more threatening.

"You had to go into town, and despite warnings, annoy local girls . . . Shut up! . . . get into a brawl with town boys, get yourself so stinking drunk that you passed out and overstayed curfew."

Macklin turned and looked toward where a window would have been in the wall if there were a window. The Dutchman had begun studying his fingernails. Macklin was still seething.

"This reflects on me, Adair, and I don't like having the colonel ticked off at me." He paused for a full fifteen seconds. "I should bring you up on charges and leave you in this stockade until you grow a gray beard. There's only one reason I'm not going to do that, and it's not mercy. It's because we are a training unit and our job is to get as many bodies to France as quickly as we can.

"Your unit is headed for Galveston and a troop ship. You will be with them. You will be under special watch. You will not be promoted to Private First Class. God help the Kaiser."

He had turned and started toward the cell door before he turned and said, "You will be pleased to know that Sargent Joplin has volunteered for overseas duty. He'll be along on the entire crossing to give you any remedial training he deems necessary."

Macklin stormed down the corridor, looking neither right nor left. Tom wavered on his feet, feeling sicker than ever.

The Dutch MP sergeant remained behind. He smiled wryly. "It'll be all right, kid. Once you're overseas it won't matter anymore. Kent!" he yelled to the watching private. The soldier nodded, disappeared for a few minutes, and returned with a clean fatigue uniform.

"Strip down and put these on. We can't have you walking around like that."

Tom removed his crusted clothes as the sergeant watched. Another solider, in the uniform of a stockade prisoner, his head shaven, appeared and disgustedly picked up the fouled uniform with a broomstick, dropping it into a pail.

Escorted back to the barracks, Tom opened the door to find the platoon in a festive mood.

Towels were thrown back and forth as duffel bags were packed and banter and mock fist-fights echoed in the hall. There was a brief silence as Tom entered, a few moments of recognition, and then the uproar began again. Someone was attempting to sing the Marseillaise. Charlie McCoy looked up from his packing, a purpling mouse under his left eye, but he said nothing to Tom.

"Tom!" It was John Trout who approached him first. The blond El Pasoan's eyes were concerned. "God, we thought they'd hang you. Me and Folsom went out looking for you, but we couldn't find you. We knew for sure you were going to miss the bus."

"Thanks for caring, John," Tom said neutrally. He was watching Charlie McCoy's back as he sat down on his bunk. Charlie continued to stuff his duffel bag without turning.

Trout followed Tom's stare. "Well, sure, Tom . . . we're all buddies, after all. And the truth is me and Folsom was feeling kind of responsible, you know?"

"You're not responsible."

"I mean," Trout continued earnestly, "well, we took you to that dive, after all. Well. Okay, thanks, Tom. That's white of you . . . I mean." Trout blushed and lifted confused hands.

"It's just a figure of speech . . . I mean . . ." Trout sat down beside Tom. "You missed it, I guess. We're going to be attached to First Army. And," he lowered his voice and lifted his eyes, "Frank Joplin is going along as our top kick."

Tom just nodded his head in response. His eyes were fixed on Charlie McCoy who was continuing to make unnecessary adjustments to his gear. After a minute, Trout, sensing unease, rose and said, "Well . . . we're glad you're back with us, Tom. I got a few things to see to."

"Sure, John. Thanks."

"Well, sure." Trout wandered away to rejoin the general jubilation.

Tom continued to sit silently on his bunk, watching Charlie at work. For a few more long minutes, he continued to meaninglessly shift articles in his duffel. Then Tom saw Charlie's back tighten, saw him take a deep breath.

McCoy turned suddenly, hands spread. "I'm sorry, damnit, Tom! Okay?"

"Okay," Tom said softly. "You were there for me when they jumped me. If they'd got me down and started stomping me,

I'd be in the hospital right now."

"But when I . . ." Charlie's expression was truly pained, "when I mouthed off . . ."

"I said it's okay, Charlie." Tom rose and thrust out his hand. McCoy took it almost eagerly, and they held a strong handshake for a long minute.

"Okay, Tom," Charlie said with a grin, "let's get going here!"

By noon they were on the bus again, by two o'clock on the troop train south, the boys in their dress uniforms waving out the window to the teasing, flirtatious girls along the way. Tom sat alone in the rear of the last car in his ill-fitting fatigues.

Charlie flopped down beside him, grinning his cowboy grin. He touched Tom's ribs with his elbow. "You ain't seen nothin' yet, Tom. Wait until I fix you up with one of those French mademoiselles!"

"Charlie," Tom said, "don't do me any favors," and he tugged down his cap and slept most of the way to Galveston.

They had begun to call the troopship a floating casket. Ebullience on boarding had faded to lethargy and then to savage resentment. The ship lumbered on for day after day, fifteen-hundred men crammed below deck in hammocks. The stench of the airless, close living became unbearable after awhile.

Below deck the temperature never dropped below a hundred degrees. The pervading smell was of oil and man-sweat, dirty clothing and vomit. The soldiers were seldom allowed above deck. Half of them were seasick the entire way. Men lay listlessly in their hammocks, bathed in their own sweat, wearing only underwear, muttering vague curses, unspeaking until inevitably the discomfort and enforced closeness caused tempers to erupt, and brief, violent fistfights broke out. After a few days on the ocean, these were ignored by those not involved. No one had the energy to try to break them up; besides they were such a common occurrence that they went practically unheeded.

Charlie McCoy had taken the top hammock of three tiers against the bulkhead far away from Tom's. The two seldom spoke. There was no animosity between them, only a lingering disappointment on both men's parts.

"Adair!"

Tom rolled his head toward Joplin's voice. The sergeant stood there in full uniform, sweating like a pig.

"You got engine room cleanup."

Tom sat up, balancing on the hammock edge. He shook his head, pulled his sticky undershirt away from his body, and bounced onto the deck. Joplin's back was disappearing through the forward hatch. Trout, who had the hammock beneath Tom's, said, "Say something, Tom! That's every day since we've been at sea. When's the man going to get off your ass?"

"Complain to who, John?" Tom asked, pulling on his boots.

"That's the Navy's work anyway," Folsom said from across the way.

Tom shrugged. He knew Joplin was still riding him, would continue to ride him, but what was there to do about it? As he had said, who was there to complain to?

He knew full well what it was about. Joplin had never liked Tom, but just as it seemed he was getting tired of picking on Tom, perhaps having picked a new target for his malice, the incident in Burlington had happened. Macklin had to have told him that Adair needed additional training.

And this was it.

The chief engineer, Considine, was a squat, bearlike man with arms blue from fading tattoos.

He simply nodded at Tom as he slid down the ladder to the engine room. One day, watching, he had simply said, "Soldier, you must really have screwed up."

A few of the mechanic's mates waved to Tom. He was getting

to be a fixture below deck now. He got his bucket and mop from the storage cabinet, poured solvent and water into the pail, and began to mop the iron decks. The idea was not only to keep the surface clean, but to get the oil up so that no one slipped and fell going about his duties.

The racket of the huge engines was overwhelming. The thud and thump and roar of them, the massive propeller shafts, the balance wheels and counterweights driving and rotating overhead intimidating. On his first day Tom had been thumped on the head by a huge crankshaft weight.

Since then he had learned to move about in a crab-scuttle, mopping as he went.

The heat was incredible there, the scent of hot oil overpowering. The sailors worked in three-hour shifts to avoid heat exhaustion. Tom's shift was a steady eight hours, despite Considine's attempted intervention.

"Sorry, soldier," the big hairy man had told him. "I couldn't do a thing for you. You're under Army orders."

"It's all right. Thanks for trying."

"You must've really screwed up."

"Yeah," Tom grinned. "I joined the Army."

There was, finally, an end to it. One day the captain of the ship whistled down the intercom and advised them that if they wished to catch their first glimpse of France, all soldiers would be allowed on deck.

It was an uncontrolled stampede of men in half-uniforms, shorts, and undershirts to the upper decks. There was nothing to be seen at first above the murky, constant sea, but after a minute someone yelled and then everyone was pointing and shouting as they crowded the rails. On the horizon a dim mass of deep violet and gray began to rise from the sea. After long minutes it became greener and cliffs took on form and height. A small village with a church's high steeple was dimly visible.

The soldiers' spirits, smothered and repressed, rose again, and an involuntary cheer went up.

They saw nothing of the town when they landed, only gray wharves and gray ships, and once a line of gray-green ambulances with red crosses on their sides, waiting with the returning wounded.

They were packed with incredible haste and unconcern onto a train, and within two hours of landing, they were on their way toward the front, passing bombed-out villages with eyeless churches. Forlorn women and ragged children stood near the tracks, neither waving nor cheering their arriving rescuers.

None of it resembled the jubilant arrival of the Yanks they had imagined and seen in newsreels. The musty, dangerously overcrowded train rushed on past untended fallow fields, smoke-darkened trees, and ruined, deserted villages.

"Way up there," Trout said, pointing over Tom's shoulder, "don't that look like cannon fire to you?"

There was no way to tell, there were only small dark smudges low on the eastern horizon.

"I can't tell," Tom said. He added grimly, "I suppose we'll find out soon enough."

The train rattled on. They were trundled across more empty fields, past more derelict buildings, their roofs missing, their wall shell-blackened. Eventually they came to a wide, murky river slowly flowing toward the sea. One of the soldiers, a kid named Raney, said it was the Seine. No one else knew enough about French geography to agree or disagree. The train rumbled across a low trestled iron bridge. Just to the south they could see another bridge, stark and twisted, its head dipping into the dirty brown of the river like a feeding iron stork.

Just before dusk they came to the end of the line. Looking out the window, Tom saw a square quarter-mile of tents, their flaps fluttering in the smoky evening wind.

"Well, boys, this is it," Folsom said.

Emerging from the train, it became evident that what Trout had pointed out as possible artillery smoke was just that. There were heavy patches of dark man-made clouds on the eastern horizon, and the scent of cordite was heavy in the air.

"Let's go! Let's go!" Sergeant Joplin was yelling. "Form up! It's nearly dark."

They formed themselves into ranks and waited patiently while their fieldpacks were brought up from the baggage cars by French civilians. A new sergeant had appeared carrying a clipboard. He explained how the camp was laid out—there were crude signs on each corner—and gave them their tent assignments.

Trout, Folsom, and Tom managed to stick together along with Raney who had attached himself to their group. Charlie McCoy, it seemed, had decided to distance himself from them.

Starting toward their tent there was a sudden nearby flash like close lightning and a simultaneous thunderous roar. They threw their gear aside and hit the ground, holding their helmets on tight.

"What the hell was that?" Trout shouted.

"Artillery fire!" Tom yelled back. His ears were ringing, his heart pounding crazily. A veteran corporal, helmetless, a cigarette in his mouth, was walking past. He paused, studying the four men on the ground with amusement.

"That one missed by a mile," he said. "What are you doing, looking for a tent?"

Tom nodded. He was sitting on the ground, dusting himself off. He got to his feet and handed the corporal the piece of paper he had scrawled the tent number on.

"Come on," the slim corporal said affably. "I'll show you where it is. Don't worry about the artillery, boys. Those guns can't reach this camp. That's why we're bivouacked here.

Besides, they ain't hardly been firing at night lately. Here ya are," he said, gesturing to a six-man tent with the proper number, B26, stenciled on the side. They thanked the corporal and trooped inside.

Two veteran soldiers sat inside, one coarse-featured PFC cleaning his rifle, the other a bald, nearly eyebrowless younger man wearing corporal's stripes, cards spread on his cot.

"Fresh meat," the older soldier growled.

"Anybody play poker?" the balding kid asked.

Tom tossed his gear on an empty, unmade cot. "Can we get anything to eat tonight?"

"They'll call all the rookies for chow in about ten minutes. How about a few hands of stud?"

"What would we play with?" Folsom asked, turning his pockets inside out. "We got no money."

"That's all right, neither do I."

Folsom laughed. "I guess I'll just stretch out until chow call."

The older soldier asked, "You boys know where you're headed?"

"They told us we were going to be attached to Pershing's First."

"Uh-uh, no, old Black Jack pulled out a week back."

Tom shrugged, "We got no idea, then. Does it matter?"

"Oh, yeah—it matters. You'll find out, boys, believe me."

"Not if we can't do a damn thing about it anyway," Trout said from his cot, and the PFC laughed.

"No, you're right there. I'll give you that."

"Where are you headed?" Raney asked the veteran.

"Kansas City," the big man said. Then he rose and walked to the tent flap to peer out at the glow of sunset, and they could see that he had one uniform sleeve pinned up. Tom glanced toward the card-playing corporal then, and with shock realized the kid had only one leg. The PFC said without turning his eyes from the sunset, "It's your war now, rookies."

At dawn with the skies still colored a vague rose hue, they began to march in full packs toward the east, toward the big guns. They could hear the distant rumbling of artillery pieces now and then, and now and then the faint metallic chatter of machine guns, but they saw nothing of armies engaged at all.

There was nothing to be seen along the road. Only the long, long line of replacements marching silently except for the rattle of equipment. The colonnade of trees alongside the road was as scorched and barren, sterile as old love.

The broken ground they marched over had been churned up into mud and then frozen in winter. Now summer had baked it to brick. Tom saw a horse's legs thrust up from the solid clay and then its hollow-eyed skull, still with the hide on it. A sorrel with a white blaze it had been.

It seemed to be waiting faithfully for its master to come and rescue it from this humiliation.

Perhaps it still wondered why its master had taken its loyalty and driven it into the coils of shredding barbed wire and the chatter of machine guns.

Perhaps its master lay buried beneath the caked mud beside it.

"Where in hell d'ya think we're heading, Tom?"

"To war."

"Yes, but . . ." Trout was sweating heavily. He wiped his eyes with his cuff. "When I write home, I'd at least like to tell 'em where I am so they can find it on a map."

"I don't think you're supposed to do that anyway, John."

"No, I guess you're right. Still a man likes to know . . ."

A man likes to at least know where he is going to die.

Eventually, after they had reached the trenches, they found out. Just south and east of the Marne where there had been recent terrific fighting. They had even passed a sign on the road: "St. Maixent 5km." But if there had ever been a town near here, there was no sign of it, just empty grassless lands with blackened, shattered trees, mile upon mile of barbed wire with rabbit warrens of trenches and underground bunkers behind it. The old soldiers called this the Dead Zone, and considered it good duty. One young sergeant told Tom about the battle at Verdun where 600,000 men had perished and added, "This suits me just fine, all things considered." This area was eerily silent, though signs of earlier fighting were everywhere. The earth was pocked by shellfire where stagnant water pooled. Beyond the coils of wire, here and there, Tom could see a uniformed body, unrecoverable, left to rot in the French sun.

The men in the trenches were more like ghosts than soldiers. Everyone wore a half a uniform or less, most of them in tatters. There were many wearing blood-stained bandages. Some of the soldiers had been living in this very trench for eight months.

The rookies marched through the head-high trench past battle-hardened, grim-eyed veterans to an underground shelter where they were shown their cots. Tom eased his gear off his aching shoulder and nodded to his new bunkie. The sallow man was wearing his helmet, eating from a green tin can with his knife. There was, Tom noticed, a bullet hole in his helmet.

"That was a near thing, huh?" he said. The soldier stared at him blankly. "The bullet," Tom said, tapping his own helmet.

The man continued to stare at him with hollow eyes and removed his helmet. Underneath his skull showed a large depression swathed over with a blood-scabbed bandage.

Trout and Raney had found cots nearby. Folsom was across the dirty, dark bunker. A single kerosene lantern burned dully in the underground gloom. Now and then dirt sifted down through the rough plank ceiling. Folsom wandered to where the others were attempting to store their goods and make up their cots.

"It's a hell-hole, ain't it, boys?"

"Not much like home," Trout agreed.

"What in hell is that stench in the air?" Raney asked. Trout gave him a sick glance and motioned with his head toward a soldier with heavily bandaged legs sitting on a nearby cot. He spoke in a low voice.

"Why, don't you know, Harry? It's gangrene, man."

There were numbers of men, Tom now noticed, sitting motionless in the gloom, with bandaged, festering wounds.

Trout shook his head. "There ain't no way to transport them out of here."

They had barely settled in when Sargent Joplin appeared. He was trailing behind a second lieutenant with a smudged uniform. He stopped directly in front of them.

"Now!" he said, showing off for the officer, it seemed, "we've got replacements for some of your boys out in the trenches. They deserve some rest; my men are still fresh."

The lieutenant didn't say anything; he didn't even introduce himself. He seemed to be miles distant, moving around through some waking dream.

Tom tightened the strap on his flat helmet and snatched up his rifle. They were taken to a position near the center of a forward trench. Standing straight up he could see across no-man's land toward the German lines. He decided it was probably not a good idea to ever stand up straight if it could be helped. There had to be Hun snipers out there somewhere.

He tapped a dozing, bearded soldier on the shoulder and the man slowly opened his eyes, yawning.

"What?" he asked drowsily.

"Come to relieve you," Tom said.

"Really? What d'ya know. First time in a month."

The man stretched and dropped his rifle. He bent over and fumbled for the muddy, disused weapon.

"What do we do?" Trout asked and the soldier stared at him blearily, scratching at his bearded chin.

"Wait, son. You wait."

Then, in acquired bent posture, the soldier lumbered off down the trench toward the dugouts.

Three times that day a single shot was fired from the opposite lines, coming close but doing no damage at that extreme range. Another dirt-encrusted veteran said with a half-smile, "Hermann must've got himself a new rifle. Can't hit nothin'."

"Hermann?"

"That's what we call him," the soldier shrugged. "He likes takin' his potshots this time of day."

"Shouldn't we fire back?" Raney asked in all seriousness.

"Hell no! At what? Their line's about half a mile off. You got a scope? Besides, if you start shooting, you'll have all the boys busting out here, thinking it's an attack. You'd get everyone mighty pissed off." The veteran settled into a sitting position, helmet tilted forward over his eyes.

They stood and sweltered and shifted positions for four hours. Nothing moved in all that time but half a dozen black vultures feeding on something they couldn't see and didn't want to see.

"Now I see why they call this the Dead Zone," Folsom complained, turning his back to lean against the trench wall. He took off his helmet and wiped his sweating forehead with his sleeve. "Don't nothin' move out here, does it? I almost wish there would be an attack."

The veteran tilted back his helmet and grinned up at Folsom. "Last time the Huns came over we lost near three thousand men, son. You don't want to be wishing for things like that."

He pointed toward Folsom's helmet. "And, if I was you, I wouldn't walk, sleep, or eat without that."

Tom continued to stare out over the endless, lifeless field.

"When was it—the last time they came through the wire?" he asked.

"Long time." The veteran soldier stretched his arms over his head. "Hell, must've been two weeks now."

He stood then and grinned again. "Well, since you boys have the duty, I think I'm going to see if my cot's still there and usable." Tom saw the soldier spasm suddenly, saw a gout of blood from his neck, and a split second later heard the report of a distant rifle. The soldier grabbed at his throat and pitched forward on his face in the mud of the trench.

Tom knelt beside the man and rolled him over. He looked up at Tom with cloudy eyes and said, "Well, I guess Hermann's got that new rifle sighted in."

CHAPTER FIVE

There was a terrible racket in the outer room jarring Shanna awake. The sun was already high and bright through her pink curtains. She sat up, startled.

"You cannot go in there!" she heard Maisie yell from just outside her door.

"Well, get her up then!" a man's slurred voice—vaguely familiar—boomed. "Tell her it's Brent Colter come calling."

Brent Colter?

Shanna was up and dressing even before Maisie, her face blurred with sleep, tapped on her door and opened it.

"Company, honey," Maisie said.

"I heard him."

"How could you not?"

"Tell her to step on it!" Brent Colter yelled. Maisie's mouth compressed. She said nothing more. She only shrugged and backed from the room, pulling the door to.

Shanna's heart was racing as she hastily pinned up her hair and splashed on rouge. Brent Colter! Things were moving along at breath-taking speed. In no time at all, really, she had met a photographer, had her portrait shots taken, had them given to one of the most successful agents in Hollywood, and now here he was at her door! He hadn't just sent a message, but had come personally just when Shanna had thought she had made no impression at all on him. The door opened a crack and Maisie reappeared.

"Hurry up, will you? Romeo's getting anxious."

Shanna smiled to herself. The disapproval in Maisie's voice was obvious. She knew that Brent Colter was high if not drunk and it was still morning, but that wasn't it. Look at that Eddie Burke character and that Hank Shipley she and Carmen had brought home! No, Maisie was simply jealous. She had been in Hollywood for a long time and had not one small part to show for it. Within weeks, well maybe months, Shanna expected to be established in films. Not as a great star, perhaps, but who knew? Emilio had told her that Brent Colter was one of Hollywood's biggest agents, and now here he was at her door! The films were seeking her out.

They breezed out of the house, Shanna on Colter's arm, with only a parting wave to Maisie.

Brent had a big black Cadillac, which he drove roughly, shifting gears erratically, skidding around corners. She supposed he was half-drunk. They careened along the Coast Highway, Brent challenging anyone who got in his way. He looked extremely handsome. His wide shoulders filled out the pale yellow sweater he wore over tan-colored slacks. His dark wavy hair with just that touch of distinguished gray was carefully brushed and pomaded. He had a new shave supplemented by a fragrant cologne.

She thought she might already be a little bit in love with him! Now wouldn't that be a fairy tale come true to write Tina about?

"Where are we going?" Shanna asked.

"Anywhere. Nowhere," Brent answered without turning his head. He drove on feverishly, maniacally. "Do me a favor, would you? Open the glove box and get that flask for me."

She did as he asked and Brent opened the engraved silver flask with one hand, drank from it, recapped it, and handed it back to her. He turned off toward Santa Monica, and as traffic forced him to slow the touring car, Shanna asked, "Did you have a chance to look at my portraits?"

"Huh?" He glanced at her, smiling faintly. He nodded. "Sure did, kid! Lovely, just lovely."

He slowed the car as they neared a parking lot along the beach. They weren't far from Emilio's studio, Shanna knew. Brent eased the Cadillac into a space between two Model-T Fords and shut the engine off. Two small kids in one of the Fords gawked at the big car.

"Let's walk," Brent said. He leaned over, took the flask from the glove compartment, and shoved it into his hip pocket as they climbed out.

They walked along the beach in silence, the surf hissing against the pebbled beach. White gulls tumbled through the air, and farther out to sea, Shanna saw a group of five brown pelicans lazily flying southward. Coming to a flat, weather-pocked boulder, they clambered up on it and sat there, Brent cross-legged, sipping from his flask. The sun was warm, the sea calm and glitter-bright.

"I didn't think I'd see you again," Shanna said.

"No?" Brent looked up with curiosity. "Why's that?"

"After I saw you with that blond girl at the party," she replied, looking down at her finger as she traced patterns on the rock.

"Blond . . ." He seemed honestly to have forgotten. "Oh, Nelda. Sure. She's a client, but I don't know." He leaned back on one elbow. "She's a nice-enough-looking kid, but she's got no 'presence,' know what I mean? I really don't think I'll be able to sell her."

"Do you think I have 'presence'?" Shanna asked.

Brent looked her up and down from ankles to eyebrows in a way Shanna found both embarrassing and pleasing. His eyes were very frank when he answered, sitting up.

"Yeah. I think you do, kid. I think you have got it." He handed the flask to Shanna, and nearly without thinking, she took a

deep drink from it. Whatever it was, it burned the back of her
nostrils and flowed like lava down her throat. She leaned
forward, coughing, her fist over her mouth, eyes watering. She
handed the flask back to Brent who had started laughing.

"I really shouldn't drink that stuff," Shanna managed to say
at last.

"Stuff!" Brent said. "That's some of the best brandy money
can buy." He leaned back again.

"Besides," he went on, "everybody should drink it. Everybody
does, at least out here. It's all in learning to go about it."

"Brent," she said, feeling bolder, "how long will it take . . . I
mean, when will you be able to talk to someone at the studios
about me?"

"Monday," he said without hesitation. "Hell, it's in my best
interest. I mean to make a lot of money with you."

His quick, confident response exceeded her expectations. He
smiled at her and stretched out an arm and Shanna leaned that
way, lying down against him as the warm sun beamed down
and the sea murmured contentment.

They dined at a seaside restaurant with huge ocean-facing
windows through which Shanna could watch the dying sun
flush the long-running sea with color and tint the sails of the
incoming sloops. They had green salad and halibut in butter
and lemon sauce and sipped sauterne.

After dinner they walked along the boardwalk, their arms
looped around each other's waists, Shanna's head leaning
against his shoulder. Now and then they stopped to drink from
the flask, and by the time they reached the small, gaudily lighted
amusement park, it was a color-bright swirl before Shanna's
eyes. Half of the rest of the evening was a blur. She could recall
the shooting gallery with the popping of rifles and the ringing of
bells, Brent handing her a huge stuffed teddy bear, a dizzying
ride on a carousel that seemed to spiral into a tunnel of lights

and mirrors and calliope sounds.

Then they were back in the Cadillac, racing along the winding oceanfront highway. She was beginning to feel queasy and exhausted and told Brent so.

"Sorry," he said. The cool evening air swept over them. Brent's arm was around her. "We'll fix you up at my place."

"Y'r place . . . ?" Shanna's voice was thick.

"Yeah, I've got to stop there for a minute. I'll find something to revive you."

"No more alcohol!" she pleaded.

"No," Brent laughed, squeezing her shoulder. "I promise. No more drinks for you."

Shanna closed her eyes as the car rolled on through the night. The car braked sharply and dipped down into a driveway and Shanna's head came up. Even through her mental fog, she could tell this was not the way to the mansion Emilio had taken her to.

"Where are we going?" she asked, sitting up straight.

"My house. I told you."

"It can't be down there. It's up a long canyon road."

"What, that? That isn't my place, Shanna. It belongs to Fred Stein, the producer. Remember that little fat man you were dancing with? It's his place. He hates entertaining. That's all his wife's doing." Brent shrugged. "Fred usually uses me as his official greeter and hand-clasper. Saves him doing it himself."

"I don't . . ." Before Shanna could finish the sentence, the Cadillac veered sharply to the right and lurched up a short driveway to a frame cottage and shuddered to a stop. They sat listening to the engine cool for a moment before Brent leaned over, kissed her lips lingeringly, and drew away, smiling.

"Come on," he said. When she hesitated, he told her, "It'll only be for a few minutes. I want to show you the place. Besides, I promised I'd get you something to fix you up."

They walked up a flagstone path through a stunted cypress colonnade. The face of the cottage was shingled in redwood. Two leaded windows flanked a tall arched door. Inside, the entrance opened abruptly onto one massive room with a very high ceiling. To Shanna's right was a white-bricked fireplace with brass andirons and tools. To the left was a sleeping alcove with a wide bedspread with a purple coverlet. Over this hung a bullfighting scene in gaudy Spanish colors.

"Look at this," Brent said. He took her hand in his and walked her across the coffee-swirl carpet to a set of floor-to-ceiling drapes. He pulled the drawstring, revealing French windows. Beyond was a white-painted deck with wooden deck furniture, then a strip of silver beach and the silky dark ocean.

"It's beautiful," Shanna said.

"It is, isn't it? Want to sit outside for awhile?"

"I'm really too cool," Shanna said. "And a little too tired."

"I promised I'd take care of that," Brent replied. He led the way back toward the fireplace, which seemed to never have been used. No smoke had smudged those pristine white bricks.

There he and Shanna sat on a frivolous white satin settee before a walnut coffee table. Brent opened a sliding drawer beneath the table and withdrew a squat green bottle and a tiny silver spoon.

"What's that?" Shanna asked drowsily. She really could have fallen off to sleep then and there except that her headache was continuing to build. It seemed to grip all of her skull now like a throbbing cap of pain. *Never again,* she thought. *No more alcohol for her!*

"Medicine for the sick and weary," Brent said. He dipped the silver spoon into the white powder in the little bottle, lifted it under one nostril and then snorted.

"I don't understand," Shanna said.

"Nose candy, they call it, dear. Good for almost anything that

171

ails you—including hangovers."

When she looked doubtful, he said encouragingly, "Really. Come on, try a little."

Just then she would have tried anything to get rid of the muzzy, disoriented feeling left by the unfamiliar alcohol, to alleviate the terrible pounding headache. She did as he directed, spilling a little powder with her shaky hands.

There was a sharp burning sensation in her nostril followed by a quick rush of euphoria.

The dim lights in the room, which had been hazy, leaped into sudden brilliance. She felt suddenly alert—more than alert. And her headache was gone in moments.

"Well?" Brent asked, stroking her hair. He was leaning back, studying her intently.

"Well . . ." she said in astonishment. "It certainly did work!"

"Of course it did. Would I steer you wrong? How do you think people show up bright-eyed and ready to work in the morning after parties like the one the other night?"

"I would never have known." She was looking at the little green bottle, at the silver spoon still in her hand.

"Go ahead, help yourself to another snort," Brent told her. "It doesn't cost me much. I've got a discount."

Shanna did, snorting the powder into her other nostril. There was another brief rush of exhilaration and a following sense of well-being and electric energy. She almost wished they were at a party tonight. How she would have danced!

"What is it?" Brent asked from the end of a tunnel, and Shanna realized she had drifted off into a brief waking dream.

"I was just thinking I'd like to dance."

"Would you!" Brent said, rising energetically. "So would I, then! Take off your shoes and I'll wind up the gramophone."

She found herself in Brent's arms, dancing very close as a waltz played softly on the Victrola.

He moved so easily, gliding as he led her across the room. When he turned her the right way she could see the dark ocean with its ruffled white skirts beneath the stars. She leaned her head forward onto his shoulder and kissed his neck lightly.

"We can live here after we're married," she murmured. "Even after you've made me a star. We don't need a big house like Fred Stein's. We can have our own little parties every night. Dance until dawn and have breakfast on the deck . . . we can do that, can't we, Brent?" she asked, drawing back to look up into his eyes.

"I couldn't ask for anything more," he answered with a smile, and he kissed her deeply. They danced on, swaying until the record had ended, waltzing through the bright and magical night.

Shanna awoke to a dry, heated morning. She felt that she was nearly suffocating. Opening an eye, brilliant white light slashed into her consciousness. She rolled her head away from the light, her dark loose hair veiled her face. Opening an eye again, she found that she was sprawled on a wide bed, a twisted purple comforter wound around her like an anaconda.

Her throat felt constricted; her mouth tasted like charcoal dust. She couldn't breathe! She had to sit up. Throwing the coverlet aside, she jerked herself upright on the side of the bed. She was naked and her skin had the feel of dried sweaty effort. She shook her head and looked around.

There was no one else there. She looked down at her body, noticing a bruise on her breast.

Rubbing it absently, she tried to rise. Her inner thighs were so sore that she sat back down again instantly. With an effort, she rose again, very carefully this time.

Brent! The events of the night before—well, most of them— rushed into memory. She called out his name but received no answer.

Her head ached again. Not only that, her hands trembled as she wiped back her hair. She had the odd sensation of being very small. She stepped over her bunched dress and went to the windows, jerking the drapes shut, closing out the diamond-sharp light. Then, on teeny-weeny legs, she walked to the white satin settee and sat in the comforting darkness, her eyes on the drawer where the little green bottle had been. It was gone, but there was a note inside the drawer from Brent.

"Shanna," it read, "it really was a glorious night. Sorry I had to take off early. Business. For us! Took the candy with me. Wait for me if you want, or if not, there's carfare on the kitchen table."

She dropped the note and watched it flutter back to the table. Then she rose stiffly and went to the small kitchen alcove. There was a five-dollar bill on the table there, pinned down by a small chrome salt cellar shaped like an owl.

She felt extremely tired although she must have slept for many hours. Shanna stood numbly in the center of the small kitchen. She wished to God Brent had left her some of that magic powder. Her legs felt now not only very small, but very heavy. Where had Brent gone? It was Sunday, wasn't it? What sort of business could he manage on Sunday? But then he knew better than she, and already Shanna was coming to understand that most business in this town was done at social affairs. Still, he could have awakened her and taken her with him.

No. She supposed not; not the way she felt this morning. She was far from at her best. Of course, the powder would have perked her up, but even then, her clothes were rumpled; she hadn't even a brush, hairpins . . .

Shanna realized she had been standing in virtually the same spot for many minutes. Shaking her head, she returned to the kitchen and started opening cupboards. Opening one, the first thing she saw was a bottle of brandy. The very sight of it caused her stomach to tighten, bile to rise into her mouth. She slammed the cupboard instantly, stood staring at it for a long while, and then opened it again. She reached in and grabbed the bottle by the neck without looking at it.

Anything was better than nothing, and she couldn't feel worse than she did.

And, in fact, it did help. After gagging down the first drink sip by sip, following each with huge chasers of water. She could feel some relief from the soreness and her head began to shrink to its normal size. Sitting at the kitchen table, she poured a second drink and finished that one off more easily.

Rising then, she found her legs more normal although they still were very sore. She took the bottle and a glass of water and crossed the main room. Going to the draperies, she drew them open. There was nobody around on the morning beach. Unlocking the glass doors, she stepped out onto the deck. The sea breeze was exhilarating, racing over her nude body, twisting her dark hair into arabesques.

She realized she was drunk again. Drunk and joyous. She felt wonderfully decadent and free as she sat on one of the white wooden deck chairs, propping her crossed feet up on the railing.

She placed the glass of water on the deck beside her and sat with her eyes closed, holding the bottle of brandy on her naked belly, wishing only that she had started the gramophone before she had come outside.

If people could only see her now, she thought. *If only people could see her now!*

As the sun rose higher, Shanna found the liquor no longer sat so well on her stomach. Brent had not returned and there was no telling when he would. Fumbling into her dress, she pulled on her shoes, buttoned them, and sat on the edge of the bed, tired by her small exertions. Sighing, she rose and tried to do something with her hair, which in the end amounted to no more than stuffing it into her hat and pinning that on.

She considered leaving a note, but couldn't decide what to write. Something flippant? Cheery? Romantic? She felt none of those right now.

She left the five dollars on the table and went out into the brilliant, hazy day. Wobbling along the driveway she reached the Coast Highway and started back southward. Cars whipped past, some honking their horns as blasts of air hit her. A truck loaded with vegetables came so close that it brushed her skirt. A carload of kids came by yelling at her. She ignored them and trudged on. Once a taxi whizzed past, but it was going too fast to flag down.

She didn't pay any attention to the yellow roadster until it swerved onto a turnout overlooking the sea and stopped in a cloud of red dust.

"Shanna!"

She hurried on, waving. Emilio's head was turned toward her, watching with concern as she scurried forward. When she reached the car, he leaned across and opened the door for her.

"I thought that was you," he said, "what in the world are you doing walking out here on the highway?"

Emilio glanced into his side mirror and pulled out onto the road. Briefly, lightly she thought, Shanna told Emilio what had happened. Or a part of it. Emilio's mouth tightened. He looked straight ahead as he motored on down the coastline highway, the sapphire sea shifting and brilliant to their right.

"How could he do that!" Emilio finally said angrily.

"He told me I could wait there," Shanna said. "He left me carfare. I just didn't know how to find a cab or a bus . . ."

"He shouldn't have done it!" the slender photographer exclaimed.

"It doesn't matter," Shanna said, leaning back against the

pleated white leather seat.

"It does to me. This is my fault. All of it. You might have been killed."

"Don't be silly."

"I'm not! I'm the one who introduced you."

"Please, Emilio. It's my own stupid fault, if there's anyone to be blamed, and there isn't really. It's just one of those things that happens."

Emilio didn't say anything else, but his anger was apparent from the way the tendons in his neck stood out and his jaw clenched. He swung off the highway and skidded to a stop sign.

Then he turned toward her house, driving slower on the residential streets.

"Is he going to give those photographs to anyone?" Emilio wanted to know. "Stein, perhaps?"

"I think that's where he went today."

"Do you?" Emilio shook his head as if giving up explanations to a child. He pulled a sweeping U-turn and the roadster glided to a stop at the curb in front of the bungalows. He killed the engine and turned to Shanna. "You know," Emilio said sincerely, "if you change your mind about films, I can still find you work as a commercial model."

"Holding up a bar of soap and smiling at it?" Shanna said. "It wouldn't be the same at all, Emilio."

"No," he said, studying her determined eyes. "I guess it wouldn't be. It was just a reminder."

"Thank you. You're a kind man, Emilio."

"Sure," he said with secret bitterness. "Real kind."

Shanna placed her hand lightly, briefly, on his. Then she opened the roadster's door, got out, and started up the path past the fountain toward her door. Emilio sat there for some time before he started the engine up again and drove slowly down the palm-lined avenue.

"Mother of Mercy!" Carmen said as Shanna went into their cottage. "Look what the cat's dragged in! You look the way I feel."

"Thanks."

"I hope it was fun anyway." Carmen, barefoot and disheveled, sat sprawled on the sofa wearing a loose flower-print dress. "Sit down before you fall down, kid."

Shanna sagged onto one of the striped chairs, tossing her hat down the hallway toward her room. "Where's Maisie?" she asked.

"I don't know. I just got in myself."

"Out late?"

"Up early! Been out working, kid. Got an extra bit for that crazy Larry Semon. What's supposed to be funny about him? Last month he bought a brick smokestack two hundred feet tall and blew it up. It lasts about five seconds on the screen. Is that funny to watch a smokestack fall down? I think he was supposed to have shot it down with a slingshot—some dumb thing."

"I guess it could be funny. He's making money, a lot of people think he is."

"Sure," Carmen said disparagingly. "He's making money, but a comic is supposed to be funny. I mean this guy still thinks kicking somebody in the ass is funny. You know where I was this morning? I mean starting at five o'clock?"

"It's Sunday!"

"That's right, kid. Sunday, and so the bakery was closed." At Shanna's puzzled glance, Carmen explained. "Semon wanted to shoot this scene at a bakery. Not a little studio bakery, but this huge wholesale place he saw. So we all took a studio bus out there, stood around for about three hours waiting for the sun to get right, and then everyone started whacking each other with flour sacks! I got hit three times, and those damned things are heavy! I was supposed to look mad—hell, that didn't take any acting. I was damned mad, flour from head to toe. Now is that funny? No, it isn't Anyway . . . I got a check." Carmen sighed and stretched languorously. "Where have you been, kid?"

"Why, she's been auditioning," Maisie said from the porch. She opened the screen and entered the bungalow. "Isn't that right, Shanna?" She walked slowly across the room; her eyes reflected anger.

"I don't understand," Shanna said, "I wasn't auditioning." Maisie paused before Shanna and just stared down at her. Carmen looked from one woman to the other.

"Hey, you girls," the Mexican girl said, "what is this?"

"Nothing," Maisie said sharply. "Just that our little friend was out on the town with Brent Colter last night. And this morning."

Shanna tried to protest. "There was nothing . . ."

"Right!" Maisie said sarcastically. "Then it was a different Brent Colter. Besides," she said with a harsh laugh, "just look at yourself!"

Then Maisie spun on her heel and walked to her room, trailing the scent of bourbon. They heard her door slam so roughly that the cottage floor shook. Carmen gave a low whistle.

"I thought she was over that," Carmen said.

"Over what?"

"She and Colter—they used to have this thing. He was her agent."

"She mentioned someone," Shanna said in bewilderment. "She called him . . ."

"A two-bit shark willing to take your money and anything else he can get his hands on and break your heart," Carmen finished for her.

"Yes! But she couldn't have meant Brent Colter!"

"Kid, that is exactly who she meant. Take my word for it."

"But she didn't say anything when he came to pick me up."

"What exactly could she have said? Besides, it takes Maisie a little time and a couple of pints to work up to these things."

"Should I go talk to her, Carmen?"

"And what would you say? Just let it lie, kid. She'll get over it."

Shanna started toward the kitchen. She glanced toward the hallway, looking hesitantly at the bedroom door. No—Carmen was probably right. She was bound to know Maisie's moods better than she did. It was all very disturbing, though. Shanna stood at the kitchen window, wondering.

She would ask Brent, of course, but it all seemed quite obvious. Maisie was a failure in Hollywood. She had wanted Brent, but he had refused her. She was simply jealous. As for the idea that Brent was after money! That alone put the lie to Maisie's words. What money did Shanna have? She put the entire absurd episode out of her mind and began to plan for the evening.

Over the next few weeks she saw Brent often. They were careful to avoid Maisie. Brent confirmed Shanna's first thoughts.

"She's a good kid," he told her, "but frankly, I couldn't get anyone interested in Maisie. I had to let her go. And, naturally, she resents it. I just couldn't get anywhere with her."

"Am I getting anywhere?" Shanna asked in discouragement as they sat on his deck at sundown, sipping brandy and watching the sea turn to deep purple silk. "Have you heard anything at all from the studios, Brent?"

"These things take time," he said, smiling reassuringly. "But . . . well, I wasn't going to say anything until I was sure, but I do have a meeting set up with you and an assistant director from Pathe."

"Oh, Brent!" Shanna turned, rising to her knees on the bench. She threw her arms around his neck, kissing his ear.

Brent Colter held up a hand. "Now hold on! Don't get your hopes too high. It's just that he wants to meet you and talk to you. His name's Tony Byrd . . . now give me a chance here," he protested as she continued kissing him. "Don't get too excited. These things don't always work out. But I have a good feeling about this—he wants to take you to a party on the producers' yacht."

"A yacht!"

"I said, calm down, honey. Yes, there'll be a lot of people there, the kind of people who have the contacts we need. It could do you all of the good in the world."

"I'll need a dress . . ."

"Don't worry about that. I'll make sure you're all fixed up. It's an investment in my career too. Hey—" he touched her hand, "This Tony Byrd, he's a pretty handsome guy . . ."

"Don't be silly," Shanna said. She lifted his hand and kissed it. "It's only you, Brent. Only you and me." Brent was true to his word. He was following through for her and he was going to splurge for her clothes and hairdo; what did that do to Maisie's petty theory? For him to be just a little jealous was touching too. There was only Brent. He had brought her to the very threshold of success. All she had to do was step across it. She smiled with her eyes and whispered, "Take me to bed."

Maisie sat on the sofa doing needlework that night the limousine arrived to sweep Shanna away to the yacht party. Shanna wore a black dress alive with sequins, black plumes in her hat, and a loose rope of pearls. Shanna's eyes glittered. She was full of energy and laughter awaiting the opportunity to erupt. She had had four drinks in her room as she dressed and a few snorts from the little silver snuffbox Brent had provided her with. "Just to keep your energy up. We can't have you dragging tonight, it's too important."

Maisie didn't say goodbye or good luck when the chauffeur—chauffeur!—arrived at the door.

The blond was wearing spectacles as she did her embroidery,

and it heightened the illusion of motherly displeasure she gave Shanna as she waved and stepped jauntily out the door toward the awaiting limousine.

The sleek white yacht sat moored on the dark pool of the wide harbor. It was festooned with Christmas lights strung from the rigging of the two masts. Red and yellow, green and blue lights twinkled and were reflected in the still waters of the bay. The gangway itself was bright with tiny white lights. Two men in white uniforms with gold braid protected the yacht from the intrusions of the uninvited. There were a few photographers standing on the wharf, taking pictures of every arriving car and personality. The salt sea scent was heavy in the warm evening air; even thicker was the scent of wealth and power, of perfume and gaiety. Shanna gave one of the men in uniform her engraved invitation card and walked up the gangway, her legs trembling with sheer excitement.

At the head of the gangway was a tall man in a white dinner jacket. He had red-brown hair, a thin mustache, and sparkling blue eyes. "Miss Shanna Adair," he said, bowing from the neck.

"I'm Tony Byrd. So happy you could make it. If you want anything at all, just mention it. Of course, there are several servant girls on board as well."

At a guess, the yacht was eighty feet long. The deck was teak. Handrails of polished mahogany and brass gleamed in the sparkling glow of the overhanging colored lights.

Everywhere were beautiful women wearing diamonds and emeralds. The men were all handsome, their suits impeccably tailored. Shanna could hardly catch her breath. It was madly dizzying. She was steered along the deck, clinging to Tony Byrd's elbow.

"Of course, you'll want a drink."

"Yes, thank you."

He smiled brilliantly and led her to one of the four bars.

Champagne was the drink of the night. Gallons of it in cut-crystal glasses. Some people added brandy from flasks to their champagne. They stood in small glittering groups, laughing. So many voices that Shanna could only catch snatches of conversations, Most of it about films or money. Dazed, she looked around, smiling to herself as she sipped her champagne. This, she told herself, is only the beginning!

She was introduced in rapid succession to many people with unmemorable faces and names, all well dressed and half drunk, but eventually they found themselves in a small group near the bandstand where the tuxedoed band was playing and, looking up, Shanna recognized Fred Stein, the producer. Tony Byrd was making the introductions.

"This is Miss Adair," he said to Stein.

"Oh, but we've met," Shanna said brightly, offering her hand. Stein looked puzzled. "We've even danced together—at your house party," she explained. A ghost of recognition passed through Stein's eyes, and he took a second, more measuring look at her.

Stein was soon hustled away by his very young wife to another group, but Shanna was satisfied. Stein had recognized her, she knew that, and she felt she had made a keener impression this time in her new dress, with Tony Byrd at her side. The next time Brent approached the producer with her photographs, he would remember her. She was sure of that.

She felt greatly excited and suddenly tired. She gripped Tony's arm more tightly and he smiled down at her.

"Can you tell me where the ladies' lounge is?" Shanna asked.

"I'll have one of the stewards show you," Byrd said and he beckoned to a tall Greek in a tuxedo.

She was shown to a cabin, much larger than she would have expected. The furniture was white and gold, delicate; the walls were covered with flocked red wallpaper. A slender blond in silver lame sat before an elaborate mirror, adjusting her makeup. She didn't glance up as Shanna searched for and found a small cubicle behind white louvered doors. She went in, turned the tiny brass latch, sat on an upholstered red stool, and dug the silver snuffbox from her bag. She snorted the white powder deeply, shuddered, frowned briefly with indecision, and then took a second snort by way of celebrating the evening's auspicious beginning.

Back on deck the air was invigorating, alive with laughter and music. The yacht's deck was more crowded now and Shanna couldn't see Tony Byrd around. She wove her way through the crowd, smiling pleasantly, more often than not receiving smiles in return, especially from the men who scraped her with their gazes in passing. The bar was in full cry, but several gentlemen stepped aside to let her pass through. She could read their minds through their eyes; they were admiring her face, her figure. Her presence! She laughed as she thought of that, but it seemed to be true just then, on this glorious night.

Oddly then, there was one brief moment when Shanna believed she was behind the screen of her own imagination. She was like someone—was it Edna Purviance?—being tricked by movie producers and socialites beyond her ken. But then she stopped, pulled herself together, and realized this was, in fact, reality, and she went back through the crowd toward the bar once more.

It was the cocaine wearing off that had momentarily tricked her, confusing reality with her ancient dreams. There was, of course, a cure for that. Another quick snort, this one taken in the shadow of a forward deck cabin with people brushing past her. She still couldn't find Tony Byrd.

Somehow that didn't matter either, she decided. It was Stein she really needed to talk to, after all. He was the man holding the reins.

Shanna took another glass of champagne and brandy without really knowing where it had come from. She thought the very nice man with the dark eyes wearing a blue tuxedo jacket had given it to her. Who knew? What was the difference? She found herself behind the cabin being wildly groped by a man without a face. He pawed at her crotch as he breathed wolfishly. He twisted her nipples and slobbered on her neck. All the time she was looking over his shoulder, trying to find Fred Stein.

She struggled away from the groping man, arranged her shoulder straps, took three steps, and fell over a capstan. Her dress went up to her knees as her head went down to the deck, the glass in her hand shattering. One of the stewards tried to help her up, but she slapped him out of mindless frustration. She struggled to her feet in the bleary night, knowing too many eyes were on her. She cared nothing for the wisps of comment, the stings of indignation.

Shanna stood, puked, and fell, slipping in her own vomit.

For a while then she was conscious of nothing at all.

"Go to hell, Brent!" someone was shouting. Tony—it was Tony Byrd! And Brent was there as well, so everything was okay. They would take care of her, but what were they shouting about? Shanna was sitting on the deck of the yacht with her legs outspread. The lights twinkled darkly. Small waspish remarks drifted past uncollected.

"Go to hell, Brent! If you think I'm paying you for that!"

Paying whom for what? Brent was there and Shanna tried to smile up at him. He hooked her under the armpits and yanked her to wobbly feet. The Greek steward was there as well. Somehow they got her down the gangway to Brent's black Cadillac. Somewhere people were jeering as if a matador had performed a cowardly pass.

He drove too quickly down Highway 101. His face was grim.

"You're a terrible driver, darling," Shanna said.

Brent locked up the brakes on the big car and swung onto a cliffside overlook in a fountain of dust.

"And you aren't much of a bitch," he said very calmly, staring out at the sea. Then he lifted his fist and slammed it against her jaw. Shanna jerked aside. He hit her again. In a wild fury he leapt out of the car, went to her side, and grabbed her ankle, dragging her out onto the ground.

"Brent!" she screamed.

"How stupid are you?" he hollered back. He was panting with emotion. "You're no better than a little child. You just can't figure things out!" He kicked her in the thigh, grabbed her by the wrists, and yanked her back toward the Cadillac as passing cars began to slow and look.

"I don't understand . . . I don't understand," she sobbed. Cocaine and alcohol twisted through her addled brain. The lights of the city and those of the passing traffic were green-red-white bursts. Brent started the car and drove on with stubborn anger.

Coming alert, Shanna began to scream. "Let me out of here! Let me out! My father, my brother would cut your throat."

He didn't even glance her way. Hands locked onto the big steering wheel, he said, "They aren't here, are they? I'm all you've got, you stupid Indian."

She rode in silence after that. Brent barely slowed to put her out of the car at the bungalows.

She staggered, vomit-throated, weaving her way past the fountain toward the bungalow.

Neighbors peered from their windows.

Where was Wallace? He would kill Brent for her.

Shanna reached the front door in a lurching dive and landed on her face as she crossed the threshold. Maisie might not have moved since she left. She still sat with her spectacles on, working with deliberate challenge at her ring-bound needlepoint.

"Well?" Maisie asked. "How did your pimp treat you?" Then without the slightest pause—"Your rent is due."

Shanna somehow made it to her bed, her head spinning savagely as she tried to untangle the events of the evening. Maisie was very angry. That she knew was nothing but jealousy. But she had done nothing wrong! Nothing except what they told her. Brent—well, he was only a man. Possibly he had been jealous too. Crazily jealous.

For one brief, tear-blurred moment she did miss home badly. Mother . . . her head hurt. The room spun lazily. But then, she told herself through the mist and blur of the warm night, she had already accomplished more than anyone she knew. She had made it. And then she slept and dreamed through a strange and only half-haunted night.

It came to her the following morning when, while staggering to the living room, that it was Carmen who was her true friend, not Maisie. After all, they had much more in common.

Carmen was a real actress. True, her parts were small, but she was working several days a week.

Carmen's first words were, "Morning, you should have seen me yesterday! My part in this dumb film was to fall off a stagecoach. Yikes! I don't think my body can afford this career."

Then she broke off, giving Shanna a shadowed glance. "I don't know, kid, Maisie is seriously pissed. She wants some rent money."

"It's Brent, isn't it?"

"No!" Carmen laughed. "I think it's the money!"

Shanna turned away briefly. "It doesn't matter. I don't really need this place anymore. Brent and I are getting married."

"Good." Carmen hesitated. "You know, kid, I can get you some kind of work, if you don't mind flour bags."

"Thank you." Shanna's voice was stiff. Still hungover, she was nevertheless starting to get antsy. There was a slow itch creeping through her body beneath her skin. "I don't think so. I have my own contacts now."

"Sure. Swell." Carmen started trimming her toenails. She looked up at the pretty young Indian girl. There was nothing to say, really. Nothing she would listen to. "Don't you miss your family, kid?"

"No, why should I?"

"I dunno. Sometimes we all do. You never talk about them. I miss my people down in Juarez." Carmen yawned and stretched widely. "Ouch," she said, rubbing her shoulder, "that hurt."

"I don't know why you're doing that kind of work," Shanna said.

"To make a living."

"Yes, well . . ."

"You'd have to know what life is like in Juarez. This is easy."

"You think it was easy where I'm from?"

"I dunno. It doesn't matter."

Carmen lifted a shoulder and thought about the way things had been in Mexico, scraping for tortillas, her brother stealing chickens. There had been only two things a woman could do to make her way. Provide a lot of babies who would probably go hungry or become a whore.

All in all, she considered, being smacked with flour bags was probably better. But, yes, she missed them all—Ramon who had a small truck garden . . . she shook her thoughts aside.

"I have a brother," Shanna was saying. "Tom. He's gone off to the war. And a sister, Elizabeth. She is the clever one."

"I see. Thank you for that little bit. You see, Shanna, I would like to be your friend. The dusky duo. But we can't be friends. If we truly were, I would tell you to go home and you would never listen to me."

Shanna swung around in a controlled fury. "Why would you tell me to go home? Just because you've failed?" And the breach, she knew as soon as she said it, was irretrievable.

Carmen said nothing, but there was a vague fire burning in her dark eyes. Lazily she rose, and with her back to Shanna said, "Pay your rent."

It didn't matter, Shanna thought. None of it mattered. She was on her way to the top and they were going down. Shanna went to her room and took a small sniff of cocaine and waited.

When Brent arrived he was apologetic. His hair was slicked down neatly; he looked, she thought, trim and energetic and very handsome.

"Look," he said immediately. "I was wrong. I was hurtful. I didn't mean to be." Shanna pretended to be piqued for a little while and they made love in the back of the Cadillac and sniffed a little cocaine.

"There's this one guy you have got to meet, Shanna," Brent said, straightening his clothes. "A major man at United Artists. A Chaplin representative. His name is Plainstrom."

There was Plainstrom, then. And Devine. And some short man whose name she never caught. But Brent was always there to watch out for her, even if time seemed to be racing away, drifting into some uncertain future.

Once she saw money changing hands between Devine and Brent, but she only vaguely understood the significance of that. She was adrift on some magnificent chatoyant cloud and hadn't the time to concern herself with small matters. She was a part of the mainstream of Hollywood life, unlike Maisie or Carmen, still pathetically being pummeled by flour sacks or thrown into swimming pools or having cakes dumped in her lap.

Now and then Shanna returned a little smugly to her mental chorus—if only they could see me now!—and it gave her incredible comfort.

"Maisie is really going to be on me about the rent again," she told Brent one August night.

The moon was incredibly yellow and huge in the east above the shadowed hills. Shanna had her head on Brent's shoulder as they sat parked on a tiny secluded overlook.

"Don't worry about it." His fingers drummed on the steering wheel.

"Oh. I'm not!" She sat up straight, crossed her arms under her breasts and leaned forward, looking out at the far-ranging sea. "Why don't I just tell her that I'm moving in with you? We could do that tonight!"

"That wouldn't work," Brent said calmly.

"That was our plan all along."

"Your plan," he said and his voice grew just a little chilly.

"Then get me high," Shanna said with a yawn.

"Not tonight."

She had a moment's panic, then realized he was kidding, he had to be. "Really, Brent."

"Really, not tonight!" he snapped. He started the big Cadillac and let out the clutch pedal so harshly that Shanna's head jerked back as the car started forward.

"You always were a poor driver," she said with a laugh. She put her hand on his thigh, but he ignored it.

He drove down the winding ocean road in his usual wide-open, careening way, and Shanna tilted her head back, liking the rush of summer air over her.

"Really," she said after another mile as she rubbed his leg provocatively. "I need something to get me high, Brent."

Without warning he slammed on the brakes of the big car and it swerved to a stop with the smoke of burning rubber rolling past. Brent sat trembling for a moment. Then he took her by the throat and yanked her head back and forth. He was nearly frothing.

"Don't you understand?" he shouted. "That part is all over! We are all over. That's why I took you out tonight—to tell you that. I can't provide for you forever . . ." His hands slid away from her throat and he wiped his hair back. "Sorry. Truly. I usually don't let myself go like that."

"I forgive you," Shanna said with a forced laugh. She rubbed her throat. "You are worked up tonight. Let's go to your house and relax over a drink."

"No."

"Why not? We can sit on the deck and . . ."

"Because someone else is there! Don't you understand?"

"Someone else . . ." Forcing herself to be calm, she asked, "Who?"

Brent was staring at his hands. "Nelda."

"Nelda?" Shanna laughed. "The little blond?"

"That's right. She's moved in, Shanna."

"Moved in!" Panic and anger mingled in Shanna's mind. "You mean she's your new protégée?" she asked sarcastically.

"That's right. That's more or less it."

"The girl with 'no presence'?"

"That's right," Brent said, still not looking at Shanna.

Without warning she leaped at him, but he backhanded her hard enough to fill her mouth with blood and she leaned back against the door, staring at him with the shock of disbelief.

"Presence," he said with a panting laugh, now spinning to stare at her. "Whatever you did have, that was not it. I can't even sell you anymore. Stealing people's drugs. Drunk half the time. Throwing up on people . . ."

"Sell me!"

"That's right," he said coldly. "God, you are stupid."

"Sell me!" she repeated incredulously. "What about my career?"

"Career?" he said very quietly. "What career? Hollywood is full of whores, dear."

Shanna couldn't think of an answer. Later, she couldn't even recall the ride home. The summer wind had grown very bitter. Maisie was in the doorway, arms folded, watching when Shanna arrived home. She, mercifully, made no comment, asked nothing.

Later Shanna awakened violently. The tremors had begun to set in. Pins and needles over her entire body, her tongue stuck to her palate, cold sweats, hot sweats, thrashing about in the bed, the sheets sticking to her. Rising to throw up greenish bile, dizzily making her way to the bathroom past the silent Maisie and mutely cold Carmen.

For three days she couldn't rise from her bed for more than a few minutes at a time, long enough to drink glass after glass of water. Now and then Maisie would appear, shove a bowl of soup at her, and command her to eat.

When Shanna did get enough strength back to get shakily to her feet, make an attempt at dressing and fixing her hair, she found a stranger in the mirror. Pouched, dark-ringed eyes stared at her hollowly from a gaunt skull.

She sat at the dresser, her forehead on the palm of her hand. She had no money. She had no drugs to help her carry on. She had no friends at all left.

And she was pregnant.

It had all gone too far without going anywhere at all. Yet—she sniffed and raised her head—she was damned if she would give up yet. The Adairs did not surrender so easily. She methodically began to make up her face.

Shanna began making the long rounds of the casting offices, sitting for hours on end in shabby offices with dozens of other hopeful girls. She became exhausted more easily now and she wore her clothing more and more loosely. One day she chanced upon Fred Stein in bowler hat and yellow cravat, and she approached him with a sudden flush of eagerness.

"Mr. Stein! Do you remember me? Shanna Adair."

He looked at her dubiously, glancing at his narrow young assistant for a clue. "I'm sorry, Miss . . . I meet so many people."

"I've been to parties at your house! On the yacht?"

His eyes seemed to focus with recognition, but he shrugged, "I'm sorry."

Shanna's words rushed on. "I'm looking for work, any sort of part at all." She fumbled in her purse. "Let me give you my address. If anything at all . . . ?"

Stein took the scribbled address and pocketed it. "If anything comes up, I'll keep you in mind," he said, sketching a smile. "If you'll excuse us now, we're busy. You understand."

"Of course, but if anything . . ."

"Surely," the producer answered, touching his hat brim. But as the two men brushed past her and started down the sidewalk, she heard Stein say to his companion: "If any parts requiring a drunken, pregnant Indian come up . . .", and the two men began laughing.

Shanna felt the hot rush of tears of humiliation. She could barely see to find her way to the bus stop bench where she sagged and sat crying, trembling until strangers started staring at one another and one concerned little boy asked if he could help the lady. Shaking her head violently, she rose and started making her unsteady way down the street.

There was no point in trying to make the rounds any longer that day.

Returning home, Shanna found the note on the door:

Shanna,

   We are truly sorry to have to do this but the lock has been changed. If you wish to send someone for your things, we will guard them until then. But as things have worked out, we cannot welcome you back into our home.

                                  Maisie and Carmen

Shanna stood staring numbly at the note for long minutes, absorbing the impact of it. From the bungalow across the way the ukulele player began a ditty. A screen door banged. Two young girls with corn-tassel yellow hair ran past laughing. The fountain hissed, gurgled, and sputtered.

There was nowhere to go.

Emilio Dan Cruz opened his cottage door, his eyes registering surprise, then concern and finally dismay. He put his arm around Shanna's shoulders and led her into the sunlit orange and black living room of his house.

"Sit down, Shanna," the photographer said.

"Emilio . . ."

"Sit down," he said more sharply, "unbutton your shoes and rest for one minute. Drink a glass of lemonade. Then we can talk."

Meekly, she complied. Emilio bustled around in the kitchen. Shanna heard the tinkling of ice, the splash of lemonade into the glasses. She closed her eyes again against the sunlight, which was bright against the tessellated sea. Far out, once she saw the head of a sea lion as it surfaced for air.

"Here," Emilio said gently, handing Shanna her lemonade in a frosted glass. She took it shakily, smelled it, and realized it was only that—lemonade. She placed it aside on a low Chinese-red table.

Emilio lowered himself onto one of his burnt-orange overstuffed chairs facing her. He crossed his legs in a way Shanna thought was decidedly unmanly, and waited for her to begin.

"I need a job." She blurted out. Emilio was watching her patiently, but she could tell, appraisingly. She saw his head make the tiniest of negative shakes. Leaning forward, hands clasped between her knees, she went on earnestly. "You always told me I could be a commercial model."

"Shanna . . . those were different days," he said uncomfortably.

"Not so very long ago at all," she persisted, but she saw in his eyes the same reflections she saw this morning in her looking glass. "What have I done?" She began to sob uncontrollably.

Emilio didn't move to comfort her; he did not speak.

Finally, lifting her face from her hands, Shanna sniffed and said, "I have no place to go, Emilio. And I'm . . ."

"Obviously."

"May I please! Can you . . . ?"

"Of course," the photographer said quickly. "At least until the baby is born." He hesitated, trying to make a decision. Then with a constrained smile, he rose and said, "I have a neighbor who usually has an extra bottle of gin. I'll go over and see what I can do. But I am doing it to help get you well, not to start you off on the roller coaster again. You must quit, Shanna! You must. Some people cannot drink. You are one of them."

"I will! I promise you. I know I have to quit," she said, but Emilio could see the eagerness in her eyes, the need she had for that one next drink. Shaking his head, he got to his feet, walking along the sandy boardwalk to his next-door neighbor's cottage. And, looking back, he could see Shanna at his window, watching him through parted curtains.

The letter read:

Dear Tina,

These are the saddest days of my life. I told you about my husband, the young director, Brent Colter.

Dear, dear Tina—tears fill my eyes, making it hard to write—he has been killed in a boating accident in Mexico. I can't go on out here without him. Worst of all—or happiest of all—he has left me with a baby son! My heart is broken, and I must come home to the Nation.

Y'rs,
Shanna

"And what," Tina asked Wallace teasingly as she placed the letter aside, "does this mean for us? Your one true love is returning." She sat on her husband's lap. A fire glowed softly in the stone fireplace built by Wallace Black's own strong hands. The little house on Oak Knoll was warm and tight. Rain pattered down outside, a gentle, soothing rain. Wallace hugged Tina and answered.

"I'm sorry for her, but it means nothing, Darling. Nothing to our happiness. You are my wife, Tina, and a good wife you have been. I have only sadness for Shanna, no other feeling." Then as the fire they had purposely let burn low sputtered and died to golden embers, Wallace scooped up his young bride and carried her off to the bedroom he had built for her as the gentle rain slanted down.

CHAPTER SIX

The Dead Zone. That's what they called it, and for days and weeks on end nothing happened. There were no major German advances here, unlike the warfare on the Meuse or Belleau Wood. They were away from the major offensives. Men continued to die, of course. At times there was fierce shelling, but this was largely ineffective and the German commanders seemed disinclined to waste ammunition on the non-war in the zone. Gangrene and the cholera that swept through the trenches took more lives. Some men died from malnutrition or undiagnosed illnesses, from untreated wounds and scurvy. For the most part there was only squalid inaction in the area. The sniper known as "Hermann" had picked off six more doughboys with his Mauser rifle with the telescopic sights. Five of these had died.

For the most part Tom lived in unalleviated tedium. It was not so much a war as a test of endurance. The glaring sun and rotten rations by day, the bedbugs and lice at night—there was no relief from those. Someone had come up with the theory that dousing your head in kerosene would rid you of lice. And it was tried, until someone pointed out what would happen if flame was nearby.

No one had a theory about the bedbugs.

It was the night duty that got to Tom the most. A shadow, any shadow, was an approaching Hun patrol. It was all he could do at times to restrain himself from just opening up with his

Enfield rifle, shooting at the ghosts, driving them back.

Sargent Joplin still had not let up on him. His favorite trick was to slip up behind Tom and give out a series of what he considered Indian war-whoops.

"You see Custer out there yet, Chief?" he would ask and then go away bellowing laughter, having amused himself with his wit.

"The man's just a damned sadist," John Trout said.

Tom, unfamiliar with the term, just shrugged.

"How long are you going to let it go on, Tom?"

"Have you got a solution, John?"

"No," Trout had to admit, "I guess not."

Charlie McCoy was around often, but something was missing from their old relationship, had been since Texas. Tom wanted desperately to rebuild their friendship, to say something, but what? "It wasn't my fault, Charlie"? McCoy already knew that. Anything else seemed pointless.

Many hours the two men stood side by side in the trench, staring out at no-man's land, saying nothing at all. The silence and the days lingered motionlessly. Nothing moved beyond the trenches except the constant vultures feeding on war's carnage.

Then, on the 13th of August, the artillery opened up and shells began to fall through a screen of smoke and the Germans began their advance. The Maxim machine guns opened up, and the gray-uniformed Huns, rushing against the barbed wire, fell by the hundreds, or by the thousands.

No one was keeping count. Artillery shells rocketed into the trenches, blowing bodies aside.

The underground billets were ripped apart; the sick and wounded awaiting the never-arriving transport from the front were torn to shreds by shrapnel and buried under falling earth as the dugouts collapsed beneath the onslaught of the bombardment. Tom saw his first Germans and began firing as rapidly as possible in sheer dread. The ghost continued to surge forward through the black cotton of the smokescreen; there seemed to be nothing that could stop them as they rushed onward through the roar and blur of the gunpowder-scented day. Tom shot three Huns, thirty . . . thought he had shot that many; no one could be sure in the tumultuous scramble, the fierce battle over meaningless land.

The lieutenant walked calmly down the line, his tunic unbuttoned, his face too calm, with almost a maniacal leisure to his gait and orders.

"Fix bayonets, men. Fix bayonets."

Tom fumbled with his belt sheath, grappling for his bayonet. He fixed it finally with shaking hands, yet at that moment, for unknown reasons, the Germans broke off the offensive and disappeared into the smoke, leaving hundreds of their dead and dying on the field.

Tom turned his back and leaned against the side of the trench, sagging down. Then he gave a yelp and leaped up. Their habitat destroyed by the artillery fire, thousands of rats rushed through the trench, mindlessly seeking refuge.

They squealed and thrashed; soldiers tried to club them down with their rifle stocks. It was another exercise in futility. The rats disappeared as quickly as they had come.

Out on no-man's land someone was screaming in agony. Another soldier chanted something endlessly.

"It's the Lord's Prayer in German," Raney said.

"Can you see him?" Tom asked.

"Second coil of wire. No helmet."

"Should we . . . ?"

Tom didn't have a chance to finish his thought. A dozen men down the line, Joplin raised up, adjusted his ladder sights for range, and fired. The chanting stopped.

The lieutenant, his tunic now buttoned, his eyes as wide and wild as before, tramped back down the trench.

"First platoon! Third platoon! Counter-attack on my signal."

Counter-attack? With what possible result? Leaving their men draped over the German wire. Tom was second platoon. They and the fourth would remain in the trenches and provide covering fire. "Counter-attack for what!" he yelled.

"That's the way battles are won, Chief," Joplin said. "Pursue and defeat."

"You're volunteering to go then!" Tom screamed. Sweat streaked his dusty, powder-marked face. Joplin said nothing. Trout touched Tom's arm and said in a low voice, "Don't make things worse, Tom."

"Guess what?" Tom said belligerently, "I've had it. Finally had it with that bastard." He wiped the sweat from his eyes. His face was smeared with powder smoke, a small cut over his eye trickled blood. "What is Joplin going to do to me? Bust me? Send me home? Screw Sargent Joplin and his mother!"

"Tom . . . you got to settle down a bit," Trout said, but Tom had started after Joplin.

Unexpectedly, Charlie McCoy positioned himself between Tom and Joplin.

Speaking past Joplin's fixed bayonet, Charlie said hurriedly, "It's the shooting, Sarge. He's just upset."

"He damned well better be." The livid sergeant was interrupted by the lieutenant now looking composed and angry.

"Is there some problem here, Sergeant?"

"Nothing I can't handle, sir," Joplin said menacingly, his eyes still fixed on Tom Adair.

"Then handle it later! If you haven't noticed we have other things to worry about just now."

"Yes, sir!" Joplin snapped, standing at magnificent attention, an anachronism in the muddy, bleeding trenches. Still glowering, he waited until the lieutenant had gone and then stormed away.

Charlie McCoy whistled softly. "Damn, Tom, you do push it to the limit."

"The bastard's getting to me," Tom answered roughly. "He's been trying to do it—now he has."

Trout and McCoy glanced at each other. Something was getting to Tom. Whether it was Joplin or the war itself was impossible to tell, but he was getting sharp-edged, harder.

"Here we go," Raney said, arriving breathlessly, and at a signal from the lieutenant's whistle, the first and third platoons went up and over from the trenches, rushing headlong toward the coiled barbed wire and the shell-pocked charnel house of no-man's land.

The smoke and confusion began again. The Maxims opened up and Tom wondered how the machine gunners could avoid shooting their own men. It was a sort of controlled panic. The gunners were firing only out of a horrified survival instinct.

The German artillery barrage began again almost immediately. Missiles were whistling through the air, exploding so near at hand that every man in the trenches was rendered temporarily deaf. The ground underfoot swayed with the impact of the heavy shells.

Out on no-man's land, men fell in lockstep, ghosts vanishing to join the ghosts from the other side in a silent dance of death. Tom screamed, "This is insane!" as rank after rank of men died.

But no one could hear him above the thunder of the guns.

It fell suddenly, eerily silent. Munitions expended or assault repulsed, the big German guns ceased firing.

Slowly the ghosts began to return through the haze of burned gunpowder. Tom saw the lieutenant watching as their first and third platoons straggled in, shouldering their walking wounded along. The officer's expression was one of dark regret. He, after all, had sent them over in this meaningless tit-for-tat game of advance and retreat. He walked away, hands behind his back, his lips moving soundlessly.

Joplin, in contrast, seemed nearly joyous. As Tom watched in horror, unable to move quickly enough to halt him, the sergeant snapped his rifle to his shoulder and fired, the report of the .30-06 loud in the settling silence. A man far out in the day-gloom of smoke toppled forward, dead.

"Got me that Hun!" Joplin shouted.

"How in the hell do you even know what side he was on at that distance!" Tom yelled, spinning the NCO around to face him. "I couldn't tell!"

"Come on," Joplin chided, "your people have great eyes, right?" Joplin laughed inappropriately. "I could smell him, Chief! There was a strong smell of sauerkraut on that one."

When Joplin strode away, Tom spoke under his breath, not noticing Charlie McCoy at his shoulder. "I swear I'll kill that son of a bitch before this is over."

Then Tom walked away toward the ruined bunkers, dragging his rifle behind him. McCoy just stared at his fading back. Trout, who had also heard it, said, "You know what, Charlie? I think he means it. We've got to keep an eye on Tom."

"Won't do no damned good. He's an Indian. They got their own way of thinking. Once Tom's made up his mind to do something . . . I reckon he'll do it."

McCoy walked away, leaving Trout to think about matters. There damned sure was enough opportunity to do the man in if the grudge went that deep. What puzzled him was why Joplin wouldn't let up on Tom. The danger signals were obvious. Tom might as well have been walking around with a red flag flying. To Trout it seemed the height of folly to continually antagonize a man with a rifle in his hands. But then, John Trout was a man without prejudice and no real idea how deep racial hatred could run, even to the point of destroying common sense. Trout shrugged it off for the moment and got back to his post, still worried, but not alarmed.

The breaking point came that evening. Joplin, strutting through the trenches, hand on his sidearm, stopped in front of Tom whose face was grim and wan these days.

"The lieutenant wants some volunteers, Adair. You're one of them."

"Volunteers for what?"

"Dog tag recovery. Somebody's got to get them off the dead men out there. I volunteered. So did you."

"You mean . . ." Tom looked at the smudged, sunset-colored landscape of no-man's land, the barbed wire shadows long and deep and menacing.

"That's right, Chief. We're going out there. Don't worry about it. There's still some kind of sense of honor in the Hun lines. They won't open up once they see that's what we're up to. Or so the lieutenant says." Joplin grinned bestially and leaned nearer. "Afraid, Chief?"

Tom didn't answer. Of course he was afraid. Would Hermann be watching from his position in the German trenches, rejoicing as the two misinformed Americans walked boldly out into his field of fire? Tom stared at Joplin. The sergeant was still smiling as if it were all a joke, as if he were putting Tom on some ridiculous punishment detail. But this time the taunting sergeant was actually going along, putting his own life in jeopardy. Tom began to wonder for the first time about Joplin's sanity.

"When?" he asked.

"Five minutes. Let's move out while there's still some light left."

"Right."

And so, with the dusky smeared reds of nightfall in the western skies, they moved out onto no-man's land, their En-fields cradled in their arms as they crawled forward on their bellies past the dark ribs of wire shadows. Chips of sunshine, small and tired, fell across the dark battle-scorched earth. Tom realized something he had not noticed before. It was the time of evening when birds should be winging their way homeward against the sunset sky, but he had not seen a single bird since arriving at the trenches—except for the dark, crooked-necked vultures. But then how could even a bird be so stupid as to try to nest in this Satan land of blackened trees and man-made moonscapes?

Joplin pointed at something, a still, dark mannequin form, and Tom crawled in that direction, sweat stinging his eyes, his elbows and knees growing raw. A young soldier he had never met lay sprawled and blood-caked and broken against the futile ground. Tom removed the dog tags from his neck and started on again.

No one fired from the German lines. Not even Hermann—if there was such a person. Maybe there were dozens of snipers, all Hermanns. Maybe Hermann had been killed in the counter-attack. Maybe Hermann, if he ever had existed outside their imaginations, truly was a soldier with a sense of honor.

These were only casual thoughts. Tom concentrated at the job at hand, crawling on as rapidly as possible through the mud and bloody slush, under the rolls of barbed wire as rapidly as possible as the sunlight faded and the land darkened. At first he gently removed the dog tags, unfastening the chain clasps or lifting the chain up and over the heads of the dead. But after awhile his sensibilities wavered. He found a soldier staring at him without eyes and as Tom reached for his tags, he swore he saw the man's lips move. He was dead! There was no doubt that the man had to be dead, it was only a trick of twilight and shadow, wasn't it? But Tom just jerked the tags from the man's throat and crawled on across the broken ground, dry-mouthed and ashamed.

Thereafter he yanked the tags from men's necks like a blind

harvester. He didn't look into their faces anymore. What if they were alive, half of them?

The sky was nearly dark. A night bird descended to the field. He could see Joplin not far away at the same grim task. But Joplin . . . was smiling.

Joplin was kneeling over a body, but even in that light, at that distance, Tom could tell the dead man was a German soldier. He couldn't see what Joplin was doing. His hand worked in a curious sawing motion. Was Joplin savaging the body, searching it for war souvenirs? What!

The sergeant began crawling back toward him. It had grown too dark to continue. Joplin signaled to Tom and they began crawling back toward the safety of the trenches.

Tom's pockets jingled and clinked with the dog tags of the ghosts. The sun died without a last flare of color. A weary, exhausted sun. They tumbled finally into the trench. Hands reached for Tom. He tried to stand, but his legs were too rubbery to support him. He sat on the cold earth, emptying the recovered dog tags from his pockets into his helmet.

The whispered call to mess was passed down the line, and one of two soldiers started toward the dugouts. Trout stood over Tom, shaken himself at the sight of the dozens upon dozens of dog tags.

"Tom . . . ?"

Tom looked up. His eyes were deep hollows in his skull, his hair hung into his face. "I don't want to do that again, John. Never!"

Charlie McCoy had drifted down the line and had went to his haunches beside Tom, placing his hand ever-so-briefly on his shoulder. He said nothing; there was nothing to say.

Then, incredibly, there was a war-whoop in the air and Joplin appeared, dancing crazily, waving something over his head. He threw it down onto Tom's lap, and they all saw immediately what it was. Joplin had scalped a dead German soldier.

"Jesus!"

"No, Tom!"

It was too late for Trout's warning. Their restraining hands couldn't hold him down. There was a loud buzzing in his ears. His eyes were unfocused but wild. He leapt to his feet, drew back his rifle, and drove the fixed bayonet deep into Joplin's guts. He withdrew the bayonet and started to thrust again, but hands held his shoulders and Joplin was already staggering back, clutching his belly with both hands. He looked as if he were about to say something, but it never rose to his lips. He simply sat down roughly and died. There was one brief moment when his face had registered surprise, and then—inexplicably—a sort of smugness. Then he was incapable of facial expressions of any kind.

"Oh, Jesus Christ, Tom!" Charlie McCoy cried out.

Tom didn't respond. Perhaps shocked by his own action, he simply sat down, grinning in a macabre, humorless way.

"Jesus, Jesus!" Charlie said repetitively

"What are we going to do, Charlie?" Trout asked, grabbing his sleeve.

"How the hell do I know!" Charlie answered, shaking off Trout's hand.

"No one saw it but us," Raney said, looking up and down the trench, quiet and still as purple dusk changed to night. "Most everyone's in the bunkers chowing down."

"Maybe we can just get rid of him," Folsom said, nodding toward Joplin. He was sweating although the evening was chilling rapidly.

"At least wipe the blood off your bayonet!" Charlie shouted wildly. "Tom, aren't you listening? We're trying to help you."

Tom remained seated next to his victim, the same crooked grin on his face.

"He can't hear you. He's in some other world."

"I say we just get rid of him," Folsom repeated, more excitedly, but more quietly. "Drag him up and over."

"And what in hell do we tell the lieutenant?" Charlie asked, waving a hand in exasperation.

"He won't know," Trout said. "Haven't you noticed the way he's been acting? He's a shell-shock case for sure."

"We have to have some sort of story!"

"Hermann," Raney suggested.

"What?" Charlie McCoy removed his helmet briefly and ran a harried hand over his hair.

"Sure," Trout agreed instantly. "We'll tell him that Hermann picked Sargent Joplin off."

"No one's heard a shot," McCoy argued. He stood watching the apparently unrepentant Tom Adair in the settling gloom.

"We could fire off a round," Raney said.

"Don't be stupid. That might start the Germans shooting. Besides, anyone who's not a moron would know the shot came from our lines."

"Forget the shot. It's a good enough story anyway," Trout said. "The lieutenant is only half here, anyway. Besides, you think he's going to go out and check the body if we drag it to the wire?"

"It'd be a bitch—dragging Joplin out there. What if the Huns see us? They won't know what we're up to. It might look like an infiltration maneuver," Raney said logically.

"We either risk it or see Tom in front of a firing squad," Folsom said, "for doing what, God knows, he had provocation enough to do." He looked skyward. "It'll be black-dark soon. It ain't a huge risk. We just take him to the first strands and shinny back."

"Then you three do it," McCoy said with restrained anger. "I intend to survive this damned war. I'm not risking my neck to save his.

"Jesus Christ," he said, "what's the matter with you, Tom?" He leaned down then and yanked the dog tags from Joplin's neck and tossed them into Tom's helmet with the others.

"And someone bury that," McCoy said, gesturing toward the scalp without looking at it.

Despite his words, Charlie McCoy helped them to do the job. First he took Tom's bayonet and thrust it numerous times in the earth to remove the blood from it. Then he picked up Joplin's legs and Trout got the sergeant's shoulders, and with Folsom and Raney keeping watch, they managed to hoist the dead man's body up and out of the trench. In the cool stillness, they dragged the corpse along over the churned earth until they reached the first coil of barbed wire, half-expecting a shot from the German lines at any moment.

They did not speak. Even their labored breathing seemed loud in the quiet night. It was, McCoy thought, a strange ritual, delivering the dead to the battleground. Charlie slipped on the uneven ground and fell into the wire, the razor-edged rusty steel ripping his arm. He cursed and dragged himself upright again, feeling the hot trickle of blood.

They crabbed their way back much more rapidly, hoping that some trigger-happy American soldier didn't mistake them for the enemy.

With relief, they tumbled back into the trench and stood trembling. McCoy walked directly to Tom despite realizing how high his anger was running. He hovered over Tom and said, "Now we've done that for you, you dumb bastard. I feel like kicking your teeth in, but I won't. Live with it, you dumb Indian!"

Those were the last words Charlie McCoy ever spoke to Tom in France.

Tom did not return to his dugout and his cot that night. He sat sleeping in the trench, holding his rifle between his legs, from time to time drifting into uneasy dreams. The Old Man came to sit with him, and he asked Tom, "Did you bury this one, Adair? The wild things will come and get him. It is not good to leave a man unburied so that they can tear him apart."

Tom awoke with a start. The yellow glare of coming day erased his attack of panic, but did not erase the dream from consciousness. He got stiffly to his feet and prepared to fight for another day.

Oddly, no one ever asked what had happened to Sargent Frank Joplin. Men, after all, were disappearing mysteriously every day. You only asked after your friends. Joplin had had none to ask after him. Someone from Command arrived one day and the lieutenant was taken away not long afterward. Someone said he had gotten a psycho discharge. Some said Tom Adair should get one as well, but it seemed that privilege was reserved for officers.

Their new commanding officer, a Captain Short, was fresh from the States. Blunt, direct, well groomed, his hair cut in short needles, he nevertheless was a man of common sense. He ordered no assaults across no-man's land. His attention was focused on formalities and grooming.

Tom said nothing, interacted with no one.

At times there would be a brief German barrage, but it seemed they were half-hearted. Short in duration, these shells never even reached the trenches. Maybe their ammunition was low.

Maybe the gunners were conscripted fourteen-year-old boys without the necessary skills to produce war. Maybe they knew it was all over.

The major action that month had taken place to the south. Trout said, "Good thing we weren't attached to the First. I heard old Black Jack Pershing took a million men into the Argonne."

No one knew exactly where Meuese-Argonne was with any certainty. It was years before Tom learned that Pershing had crushed the enemy there with only ten percent casualties on the Allied side. One hundred and seventeen thousand men had been killed. It was considered a victory.

"The seed and hope of the next generation," some English writer had said. "The bravest and the best. The flower of their generation's hopes." One hundred and seventeen thousand men's grieving widows, lovers, mothers, friends. Tom found himself sitting alone one silent morning with a blood-red sky running far across the broken land. He was crying silently for no particular person or race, but for all humanity, for all races and nations. All of it a futile expression, of course; he even found himself hoping uselessly that Hermann, whoever he was, had made it through unscathed, even though they had invented him themselves out of countless sniping incidents until he had acquired mythological life.

Now and then these days, daring pilots in biplanes with English tri-circles painted on their wings and fuselages would buzz low across no-man's land. From up there, Tom thought, it must look equally futile and so distant that the warring factions resembled ants—red and black—fighting over some tiny sand-hill.

They continued to fight their numbing war in the Dead Zone. Their own youths wasted, some of their own best left to rot on the killing fields of France. Then one orange and golden morning, it was suddenly over. Up and down the lines the word "armistice" was passed like a sacred host, given from one man to the next. All of them were priests; all of them were sinners. If there had been anything to drink there would have been ten thousand deliriously drunk soldiers in the trenches.

Tom watched them all laugh and slap each other on the back, break into jigsteps and holler to the skies. Tom watched this silently. Something had gone wrong with the war and he wasn't quite sure what it was.

There were a few late volleys, a handful of sniper shots slowly waning; "Hermann" or someone like him trying to kill one last Yank; someone who had not yet gotten the word, perhaps, but it was over, outside of what their superiors—the generals and the politicians—were calling "incidental casualties." With a strange whimper a deep silence settled in across the French countryside, and one day a German officer in a smudged tunic appeared, walking across no-man's land, waving a white flag. He surrendered his sword to Captain Short, and they knew finally that it was over, all of it.

The long voyage home was in fact only a matter of minutes. That is, it seemed so to Tom; he had divorced himself from the concept of time. It had no meaning to him anymore, hadn't for months and months. He slept the days away, emerging only at night to wander the deck of the hulking steamer. It was against regulations to be on deck after dark, but what were they going to do? Shoot him? Send him to another war?

Tom stood and watched the bleak endless sea and the frothing wake of the big transport ship, wondering if anything at all had been accomplished. Surely a man should at least learn something, gain some new insight, have formed firm comradeships, found new depths of his soul . . . he had learned nothing. The world was as flat and empty as when he had begun. Perhaps even more empty, flatter yet. He had found new friends and lost them all just as rapidly. He had killed a man for no reason. He had nearly been killed himself . . . where in war was the glory men spoke of? He had seen nothing resembling glory in the faintest way.

He had made himself a pariah without really knowing how.

No one spoke to him; he was the only man in the platoon, in the company, in the entire expeditionary force, who was returning home an undecorated buck private! There should have been shame involved, but Tom felt no shame any more than he felt elation about returning to the States. He had one friend; a man whose name no one knew, a man with bandages over his blind eyes who spoke in monosyllabic mumbles. Tom would sit sometimes and hold his hand, listening as the wounded soldier tried to explain his life and his soul and his longings for love, children, a future in broken words. That was all the friendship he could find and all he needed. The rest of them could go to hell.

Manhattan Island was a stinkhole. Someone told him there were 130,000 horses in Manhattan. It seemed there were at least that many Model-Ts and buses weaving down Broadway, all their farts and stink mingling to form a brown, putrid haze. Soldiers and sailors were everywhere, strutting down the sidewalks, glorying in their survival, women of dubious integrity and laughing availability attached to their arms.

Tom stood on a lonesome corner, jostled and ignored, a stranger now in what supposedly was his country. The Negro woman who shouldered into him had protuberant lips very deeply painted in a bright crimson hue. Her skirt was tight enough to show every line and curve of her hips. She smiled and made a mock apology and Tom followed her home.

She called herself Vera, but there were different initials on her embroidered things. As soon as the door was closed behind them on the third-story cold-water flat, Tom went to his knees, pried under her skirt and yanked her panties down.

He took her on the floor and then on the bed, thrusting until she cried out with astonished pain.

"Take it easy, soldier! God's sake." She lay there, head lolling, lips parted to show fine white teeth. She smiled, this time with genuine pleasure. Tom didn't look into her dancing brown eyes. He watched himself entering her.

"Come on, big boy, slow down," Vera laughed. "I'm getting sore."

But Tom would not slow down. He couldn't. He made reckless love, but he was making it only with himself. He stopped abruptly without reaching a climax. He sat up, leaving a sudden vacuum in Vera's body and a quizzical expression on her honey-colored face. She sat up as well, pressed her soft dark breasts against him, kissing his shoulder.

"It's all right, honey. Say! Why don't we get a sandwich or something? Later you'll want some more of me."

She rose, smiling. And swayed across the room, her lipstick smeared crazily across her face. She turned the radio on and some of that new "jass" came across from some Negro station.

Tom got up out of bed. He stood naked staring out the window. Manhattan swarmed past beneath him. He wished he had his bayonet.

"Honey? I'm going to make some coffee. Want some?"

Tom turned slowly around. The girl was out of focus. She seemed to be . . . someone else. She was naked and dark. He stared at her breasts with their dark nipples and at her pubic hair, suddenly repugnant.

"Honey? Are you okay?"

Vera smiled and stretched out her arms and Tom slammed his fist into her face.

She staggered, fell down, and sat, her legs spread, her mouth bleeding. Tom took her then, completing the act as she cried and writhed beneath him.

"Are you crazy, are you crazy!"

He saw that one of her front teeth had been knocked loose. He spilled himself all over her dark thigh.

"Are you crazy! Why are you doing this to me?"

Tom got to his feet unsteadily; he found himself nearly unable to breathe. He stood straddling her. He felt like spitting, but his mouth was too dry.

"Why do you think?" he said. "Because you're a fuckin' nigger!"

He found his pants and pulled them on. He emptied his pockets and threw a handful of crumpled bills at her. Vera lay crying and humiliated. With other men she might have gotten up and clawed their eyes out, but some instinct told her this one might very well kill her, and so she closed her eyes and wished for some sweet memory that never came.

On the street, Tom waved a cab down. He realized he had lost his hat, left it under Vera's bed. Out of uniform, soldier! It was so damned funny he began to cry.

"Where to, buddy?" the Polish cab driver asked.

"Oklahoma," Tom told him.

"It's a dreary little remembrance, isn't it?" Mrs. Hoyt said to Elizabeth and Allyn as they poked through the dilapidated schoolhouse, which hadn't seen a student's eager face in two years. Allyn had shooed a pair of raccoons and a nesting owl from the rickety building earlier that morning. The desks were overturned, vandalized and neglected. Outside the big cottonwood where a swing for the children had been suspended had been split by lightning and was in its last precarious stage of existence. The skies were gloomy, the wind bitter cold. All of this reflected their common gloom. Nevertheless Elizabeth and Allyn were determined to build the Cherokee school despite government interference.

Mrs. Hoyt shook her head and dusted off the teacher's chair behind the desk with its carved graffiti. "I really did have such high hopes all those years ago, when the Cherokee council hired me, I was proud, actually, considering the Cherokee history of education."

"In the days when we had our own schools," Allyn said. Looking around the one-room school, Allyn himself had doubts. Only Elizabeth was buoyant and positive.

"Come on, Darling," she said, lifting her husband's glum chin. "We all agreed to give it a try. It needs to be done. The children out back here, Broken Post children, Two Lakes, Riverford—they have no school nearer than Tahlequah."

"Of course," Allyn said, still looking desolate. He forced a smile. Elizabeth knew exactly what her young husband was thinking. How had things come to this state?

It was all very simple, and quite devious in its way. The Five Tribes Act had been passed by Congress. That had abolished the tribal courts, the ability of the tribes to levy their own taxes, and the United States' complete control over all oil, coal, and asphalt, timber royalties, and grazing rights. No tribal treasurer received or dispersed moneys after the passage of this law. By extension, the Indian inadvertently lost control of his schools. The Secretary of the Interior ruled that his control over royalties and revenues invested him with the responsibility for the management of territorial schools and the old schools were no more.

"We're in violation of the law," Mrs. Hoyt said. "Opening the school on our own."

"We're in violation of some new law every time we do anything for our people these days," Allyn said with some heat. "When is the government going to build a new school for the locals? Tomorrow, never? No, it is up to us."

"Well," Elizabeth said, knowing when to interrupt Allyn's anger. "We have to do something about the roof, that's for sure."

"Cucumber Jack can help us," Allyn said. "I've talked to

him." He held up a hand. "I know he's a drunk, but he has a lot of experience. If someone gets hurt, it will only be him."

"He works hard when he's sober," Mrs. Hoyt put in. "We've had him to our house once or twice to help out."

"The supplies?" Elizabeth asked.

"There is still some money hidden away in the tribal funds."

"We don't have to worry about a teacher, that's something," Mrs. Hoyt said, standing, dusting off her skirt. "We've the best we can get in Elizabeth."

"I still wish you'd help me get started," Elizabeth said, adjusting her spectacles, "with your experience!"

"You know my eyes aren't that good anymore, Elizabeth."

Allyn said, "If you wouldn't insist on proofreading every edition of the *Tribune,* it would help."

"It has to be done," Mrs. Hoyt said. "That frees your father to write, and he must write! There has to be someone, somewhere in Washington that will listen and realize they are stealing the Cherokees' heritage from them."

"All it's going to do is get him killed," Allyn said in an uncharacteristically bitter voice.

Elizabeth forced merriment into her voice. "So the roof can be done. I can sweep out and paint in here. I'll get a couple of the local boys to help me."

Allyn smiled thinly and put his hand on her shoulder to let her know he appreciated her trying to pull him out of the doldrums. They went outside again to try to assess the extent of the damage to the outside of the small white schoolhouse, and it was then that Bill Bird, riding his small roan horse bareback, approached them, raising a hand. The bucktoothed kid seemed pleasantly surprised to see the three together.

He halted the horse, remaining mounted. He nodded and said, "You're really going to open it up again, huh?"

"That's our intention, Bill," Elizabeth answered.

"Well, I think it's great. Now." He grinned. "A few years ago you couldn't have dragged me in to no schoolhouse hog-tied. Now I'm at the sawmill, I see them that can do numbers and write are gettin' ahead of me fast."

"You could still come, Bill."

"Me?" he laughed. "Elizabeth, I reckon I'm too old to sit with a bunch of kids. And too big for those little desks!" He paused, looking wistfully at the school. "Besides, I got to go to work every day."

"I'd be happy to tutor you, Billy," Elizabeth said. "Evenings, weekends."

"Really?" Bill seemed surprised and delighted.

"I would as well," Mrs. Hoyt said.

"Any of us, all of us," Allyn added. "Just let us know when you're ready, Bill."

"Why, damn all!—pardon ladies." He took off his wide-brimmed hat and scratched his head. "I guess I never considered before that a growed man could get some education. Sure, why sure, I'd be glad of the chance, if you can stand a slow student. Sure, sure, I'd like to give it a try." He replaced his hat and turned his horse away. He hesitated one moment, deciding, then held up the horse and said, "Elizabeth, I seen Tom. He's back in town."

"Back in town? When? Where is he, Billy! He hasn't been to the house, not even to tell Mother he was all right."

"I just seen him once last week, Elizabeth. I don't know where he is for sure." Then Bill nodded, and still looking as if he had given up a confidence, rode slowly away toward The Split.

"I've got to find him," Elizabeth said, gripping Allyn's arm.

"It sounds like he doesn't want to be found," Allyn said.

"They say it takes soldiers awhile to readjust, Elizabeth," Mrs. Hoyt said. "Maybe you should leave it up to him . . . when he wants to come back."

"You could tell your mother," Allyn suggested. "Put that worry out of her mind—that he might have been killed."

"And give her a new worry to take its place! No, Allyn, I think I'm right. I have to find him, talk to him, anyway. Then, if he doesn't want to come home—well, no one can do anything about it. But I've got to try. For Mother. For Tom."

Everyone has a place called "home." It doesn't necessarily mean you want to go there again or that anyone wants you back, but it's a place you understand, where the language is familiar, a place where—with any luck—you might encounter one familiar face to welcome you.

Tom stepped from the bus and waited in the dust swirl. Looking toward the depot he saw no one but a pair of baggage handlers lazing in the shade, a yellow dog beside them, panting in the heat. He shouldered his duffel bag and with the campaign hat set at an angle, began slogging uptown. Tahlequah looked the same as when he had left. It might have been only yesterday for the unchanging, dusty, smelly aspects of it. He strode evenly down the plank walk, which had been nailed down in his grandfather's time and went directly to the recruiting office. A man of forty or so, his pale hair worn long, slicked back, stood in the door, smiling greetings to the passing Indian youths who ignored him one and all.

"Morning, soldier!" the recruiting sergeant said by way of greeting. "Tough over there, was it?"

Tom put his duffel down and asked, "Where's that young guy, the tall Indian used to work here?"

"Why? Did you have a reason for asking, soldier?" the blond man asked affably.

"Yeah. I want to punch him in the nose," Tom said. The recruiter laughed.

"I guess I can understand that. But he ain't here. He went

active and got himself killed at Verdun."

"I see," Tom nodded. He turned his back to the sergeant and stood for a moment, staring at the crowded, horse-smelling street.

"You live here?" the recruiter asked.

"Why?"

"Nothin', except I bet you're glad to be home."

Tom nodded, saying nothing. He stepped off the boardwalk, dodged a surrey driven by a silly young girl in yellow, and trudged on. Passing the general store he was hailed. Stopping, he turned that way to see Cucumber Jack, John Red Fox, and Two-Fingered Catawba Arnie squatted near the rain barrels, empty whiskey bottles scattered around them, a full one being passed. Tom started that way.

"Thought that was you, Tom!" Cucumber Jack said, rising. He wiped his hand on his jeans and offered it to Tom. "Boys, you remember Roy Adair's kid, don't you? Give him a drink."

Two-Fingers half-rose and gave the bottle to Tom who measured it and then took a long, long drink, drawing approbation. "Knowed you was a man now," Jack said. "How did all that shooting go, Tom? Kill many whites?"

Tom ignored the question. "Is my dad out?"

"No, Tom, he ain't. Kenneth Jefferson, he keeps trying appeals and all that, but old Judge Benson, he won't bend on it. In the old times I guess the Nighthawks would take a hand, but not now." He shook his head. "They kinda broke up the Nighthawks with what they did to Roy."

Tom tossed his duffel down into a patch of shade and sat on it. He fished into his pockets, pulled out some folded bills, and told the men, "Next bottle's on me, if you can spare one more drink out of that one."

"Seen your sister, Elizabeth—say, Tom, you probably didn't know! She married that Allyn Jefferson—isn't that man a puzzle?

Always thought he was a spectacled egghead. Next time I seen him he was night-riding with old Black Jack."

"What happened to Black Jack?"

"Well, Tom, they hung him for killing Marshal Striker. They weren't no witnesses but they hung him just the same."

Tom took a drink of the sun-warmed, raw whiskey and lowered his head, handing the bottle on to John Red Fox. He took a drink, peered at the bottle, and said, "I'll get us another, men," picking up Tom's money from the ground.

"My sister married him, huh?" Tom asked.

"Yeah, all legal and proper. You mother holding a big bouquet of roses—I just seen it from the outside of the church. Wasn't invited, didn't belong inside anyway. Must be six months back, didn't nobody write you?"

"There wouldn't have been any way for a letter to get through," Tom said. John Red Fox was back from the store with a new bottle. He handed it to Tom as provider and he opened it, took a swallow, and passed it on to Cucumber.

"Yeah, she and Allyn got some idea about starting up the old school back of Fletcher's Pond. Askin' for trouble with the law, but I guess they're going to try. They wanted me to do the roof—want to help, Tom?"

"No, thanks." He was feeling the warmth of the sun, the inner glow of whiskey. He could have laid down there in the alley and slept right then without a second thought.

"You need a place to sleep?" Two-Finger said, "I got me a spot in the feed and grain store loft."

"No, thanks. I'll sleep out. I'm used to it."

"I'll bet you are!" Cucumber laughed, reaching over to slap Tom's shoulder. "And it would beat sleeping in them trenches, wouldn't it?"

Tom nodded. As if anyone had ever actually slept there. It was as if he hadn't had any sleep for many months. None at all.

All of the sudden with the warmth creeping through him, Tahlequah didn't seem that bad at all. There was no one sniping at him anyway, no bedbugs, no artillery fire. He took another drink from the passed bottle.

"Hear anything about my other sister?" he asked Cucumber.

"Shanna? Nope. Not a word. I thought she was still in Hollywood making movies. We just been waiting to see her name up there," he said, framing the marquee of the National Theater with his fingers.

"I guess she is still there. Maybe I'll go out there," Tom said in a fading voice. He slid down, stretched out on the dirt of the alley, using his duffel bag as a pillow.

"Why not? You're no stranger to traveling now. Was I as young as you, I'd consider it. Why not . . ." Two-Fingers touched Cucumber Jack's arm and put a finger to his lips. Tom was asleep. "No wonder," Cucumber thought, "boy's been fighting a war, plain beat up mentally, emotionally." The three older Indians passed the whiskey bottle and let the day pass in silence.

Tom awoke with nightfall. It wasn't cold, but he felt a chill. Disoriented, he grabbed for his Enfield rifle, panicked briefly when he could not find it, and then saw motorcars and horse-drawn buggies rolling past his line of vision, drawing him back to reality. He was in Tahlequah, not France.

A church bell rang six times, annoying him. He eased up onto his duffel bag and peered around through his splayed fingers. Cucumber Jack was sprawled on the alley floor, an empty bottle beside his outstretched hand. His silence was beyond sleep. He wasn't going to wake up again that night; he was completely passed out.

"Screw this!" Tom said to himself. "I'm better than this," and he started to get up, but his legs let him down and he toppled sideways, his face skidding against the gravel and sand of the alley. "Oh, well!" he told himself, "I thought I was!" And he began

221

to giggle as he crawled to the wall of the general store and slowly dragged himself erect.

He followed the alley, bouncing from wall to wall as he made his way to the back door of the store. The door was closed, but there was a ribbon of light showing under it. He pounded on the door with the heel of his hand. "Open up!" When there was no answer, he yelled again, "Open up, damn you!" and began pounding again.

Finally, he heard approaching footsteps and a young, dark-haired clerk he had never seen before opened the door. "Sorry, sir, we can't serve you at this door."

Tom stifled a laugh. "Would you rather have me come around and troop through the front of your store? Give me a bottle of whiskey—no, give me two," he said, handing the kid a wad of bills without counting them.

"Just a minute," the clerk said, closing the door in Tom's face. He was gone four or five minutes before returning with two fifths of whiskey stuffed into a paper bag. He didn't offer Tom any change and Tom asked for none. He turned, slipped, and stumbled off the porch to the dark alley, managing somehow to maintain his balance and keep from breaking the bottles.

Tom walked slowly toward Otter Creek, forgetting his duffel bag and his friends. He found a spot beneath a huge sycamore where no light at all penetrated from the starry, moonless sky, and sagged to the bank, breathing rapidly. It took him a full minute to fumble the cap on the whiskey bottle open. The river flowed by in inky progression, with only here and there a silver highlight from some distant, bright star.

He drank the whiskey and leaned against the tree. It was utter contentment, he thought. No guilt, no one to apologize to, no worries, no snipers, Texans, officers, Nighthawks, women, freeloaders. How could a man alone with a bottle of good whiskey be anything but content?

Mutely he watched the murky river. His mood darkened gradually, and he wanted to curse someone, but he could think of no one but himself.

He needed to see her.

He needed to explain everything to Lorna Paxton.

Perhaps not tell her about Vera, but about leaving, about Joplin, about the horror of dead men's eyes, about how it felt to walk around this earth knowing you have misplaced your soul.

Unfortunately, he was drunk, knew he was drunk. Yet, when else would he be able to tell her? He had to be drunk to speak of those things, to make her see how it felt deep inside where the dark thing had taken up residence in his soul's quarters.

"Think about it any longer and you'll never go," Tom told himself, and so he made a massive effort to hoist himself to his feet and start off on a meandering course toward the Paxton house, far along the creek toward Broken Post.

The rim of the rising moon was showing above the scattered hills by the time Tom reached the Paxton house.

He stood in the deep shade of a huge oak staring at the small two-story house like some pilgrim reaching a nearly legendary shrine.

It seemed like an image from some distant time. Yet it had sat there, unchanging, unremarked for all this time. It was Tom himself that was from another time, another sphere.

He took a deep drink of whiskey, placed the bottle at the base of the oak tree, and started forward across the sparse lawn. Roses grew here and there, their locations marked by rings of white-painted rocks. There were no blooms; the only scent was that of earth and water here on the bank of Otter Creek.

He was undetermined as to what to do. March triumphantly up to the front door? He looked down at his uniform, the knees torn out from a fall. He lifted his eyes to Lorna's bedroom window. It was lighted, but dimly, a lamp turned low. The house was so silent he could hear the breeze shifting the leaves of the trees. The moon, sneaking into the sky, now crested the roof of the house and made Tom realize he had been standing there indecisively for a long time.

The light in Lorna's room was suddenly brighter. She had turned up the wick. He saw a vague, curved silhouette behind the curtains. It caused his heart to throb heavily. She really existed! She was still here, a flesh and blood woman. He didn't hesitate any longer.

Tom darted through the shadows, swung into the low branches of the elm tree, and clambered to the second-floor porch, sliding onto it easily. Silently, he moved to her window and tapped.

"Lorna," he said softly, and then realized his voice, nearly a whisper, couldn't possibly have been heard inside the room. "Lorna!" This time his voice was too loud and he expected doors to open, dogs to bark, lights to go on. Nothing of the sort happened, but the silhouette froze in position, moved softly to the window, opened it an inch, and spoke to him.

"Who is it?"

"You have so many beaux you can't tell who might have come calling?" he laughed.

"Tom?" There was a long pause. Then more quietly still, she whispered, "Tom Adair, is that you?"

"It's me," he said. Again too loudly. His fingernails alone touched the glass of the window.

There was another long pause. He thought she had slipped something on, a robe, and then the window opened and she leaned her head out between the wind-fluttered curtains.

"Go home," she said. Lorna's hair was down around her shoulders in a deep cascade of temptation.

"How can I?" he asked with a smile. His boot slipped under

him and his head came up hard against the upper frame of the window. "I need you."

"You need too much, Tom."

"Huh?"

"You didn't need me when I wanted you. You don't need me at all. You need a dream and you have no dream."

"Lorna . . . this is me!"

"I can't even talk to you now. You're drunk," she told him.

"Don't I have the right?"

"Knock on my door when you're sober. Like any other visitor."

"Don't I have the right to get drunk after all I've been through?"

"I don't know. But you don't have the right to be drunk here. This is my home. Go away now, Tom," she said quietly but with authority, and the window closed and was latched. Tom lifted his clenched hand as if he would slam it against the glass, but he lowered it to his side and stared at the curtained window into his past and started slowly away down the elm tree, anger covering his rejection. He missstepped on the last branch and fell headlong against the earth.

Tom looked around quickly to see if anyone had seen him, but the house remained dark and still, some ancient monument to ancient memories. He staggered across the yard, tangling himself in a rose bush, and then continued on to the oak tree where he searched for a full five minutes for the whiskey bottle he had hidden nearby. Finding it at length, he settled down against the trunk of the tree, a few quick drinks of the fiery cheap whiskey reaffirming his thought that a man alone with his whiskey was the happiest man in the universe. He cursed Lorna Paxton inordinately and then began to cry silently.

★ ★ ★ ★ ★

"No one knows where he is," Allyn told Elizabeth. The alley was dim and smelled of urine and garbage. Cucumber Jack was awake and the other men were curled up against the wall of the general store, passed out between bottles. Tom's duffel bag, his name and serial number stenciled clearly on it, was beside Jack who had been using it for his pillow.

"Ask Jack again—obviously Tom's been here!" Elizabeth said with frustration. "Tell him my mother needs to know."

"I tried," Allyn said. "He just doesn't know."

"Where would he have gone?" she wondered aloud as they walked back to the street where Allyn untied the reins to their rig from the hitching post. Tahlequah had grown suddenly silent and dark except for the secret places where lost souls congregated.

"Lorna Paxton's?" Allyn asked. He had helped Elizabeth into her seat and sat with the reins held loosely in his hands.

"He wouldn't . . . well, maybe he would," Elizabeth said. "I don't know my brother now, I suppose."

"How could you? At any rate, I don't think we should go over there," he said, pulling his watch from his pocket, glancing at it, shaking his head.

"Elizabeth—you'll have to let him do this in his own time, in his own way. There's a reason he doesn't want to go home just now, and we can only guess at what it might be. The war has done strange things to many young men. All we can do is be grateful that he's come home alive, well, and give him the time he needs to resolve whatever problems he has. And be there for him when he does return."

"I know it," Elizabeth sighed and rested her head briefly on Allyn's shoulder. "I hate it when you're so right—and so logical. He's my brother, it's different for me, you understand?"

"Of course but chasing him all over the county and demanding he do what we think is right for him is an exercise in futility."

"There you go being logical again," she laughed.

"You're tired, Liz. The school, Tom . . . let's get some rest."

He backed the bay away from the rail and started the rig up the street. There was still a light burning in the office of the *Tribune*, Allyn's father continuing the quixotic mission to bring the authorities to an understanding of the Indians' position. And Marion Hoyt would be there with him, bringing him coffee, reading the proofs of the scathing editorials Kenneth Jefferson continued to pen.

"She's so devoted to your father," Elizabeth said. "I will never forget the shock of meeting at your house, out of school. I had never thought of a school teacher having a life outside of the classroom."

"Now you know, don't you," Allyn said, letting the horse find its way for a while as he kissed her and stroked his wife's back. He took control of the horse again. "I know what you mean. I was too young to understand myself. But she is good for him— good to him."

"She's quite a woman, is Marion Pope Hoyt," Elizabeth agreed. "She came out here to teach Indian children, and when they took control of the Indian schools away from us, still she held on and tried her best. No money from the tribal fund. No money from the government. And darn little attendance! . . . Allyn!" Elizabeth shouted and her hands grabbed for the reins.

Startled, Allyn reined in, confusing the bay horse, which had been trotting easily, homeward-bound. Tossing its head, ears twitching in annoyance, the bay halted. Allyn looked at his wife in bafflement.

"Elizabeth, what in the . . . ?"

But Elizabeth had hoisted her skirt and stepped from the carriage. They had passed the dark figure on the road; with the

227

fantastic shadows of the moonlit night shrouding it in anonymity, still she was instantly recognizable. Madonna and child in the deep silence of the Oklahoma night. Elizabeth yelled, "Shanna!" and began to cry even before the struggling woman in black, the child in her arms, answered her and began making her way toward the carriage.

"God, Sis," Shanna said, throwing herself into Elizabeth's arms, "I never realized how long the walk home was." Then she smiled, her eyes deep and moonlit. "Don't crush the baby."

Elizabeth opened the corner of the blanket and looked down into the peaceful, unformed face of an incomparably beautiful baby. Why would it not be, with her mother's beautiful fragile figure and dark mysterious eyes.

"Come on, Shanna," Allyn said, smiling down at the baby himself. "Let's not keep this little tyke out here in the night. Where were you planning on going?"

"Home, Allyn," Shanna said. "Home."

CHAPTER SEVEN

The baby continued to cry. Sarah Adair walked it from one side of the front room to the other. The fire burned very low in the rock fireplace. Outside the new sun spread a golden sheen over the grasslands.

"I think Brent is hungry still, Shanna," Sarah said as her daughter flitted across the room, brushing her long glossy hair.

"Oh, Mother!" Shanna said in exasperation. "You think he's always hungry. He's had breakfast."

"Maybe he just wants to nurse," Sarah said, looking down at the crying infant.

"That spoils them. I read that somewhere. Besides, I don't have any milk anymore," Shanna said. She stood before the oval-framed mirror, pinning up her hair. "He had milk in a bottle. With oatmeal added. I've left you another bottle. Just put it in a pan of water and heat it. He'll be perfectly fine."

Sarah put the baby to her shoulder and patted its back comfortably. Shanna had finished hastily pinning her hair. She was positioning a tiny black hair on her head, tilting it this way and that as the baby cried.

"I can't believe you people don't have a telephone yet," she said with a sigh. Sarah looked up sharply. You people? "Honestly. To have to go all the way into Tahlequah to send a wire. You know all my clothes are still in Los Angeles. If Maisie and Carmen haven't worn them all and ruined them. Those people aren't exactly clean."

"You always said you liked them—in your letters," Sarah said.

"Oh, well," Shanna said, "what was I to do, worry you? Besides they were so snoopy, they would have read my letters given half a chance. Especially Maisie! I told you how jealous she was of me and Brent!"

"Several times," Sarah said.

"Anyway," Shanna said, tossing her brush onto the table beside the mirror. "I have to send a wire. I need those clothes, all of my things. Things Brent gave me. I can't believe I have to ride a horse into town! Will we never get civilized here? In California I could have called a taxi or taken the trolley. I don't know why you people can't even afford an old Model-T."

Sarah said nothing; she was so happy to have her wandering child back. The truth was with Roy still in prison, she could barely afford food from week to week. If it weren't for Elizabeth and Allyn helping her. She could not work the garden anymore. Her fingers were beginning to curl with arthritis; the pain in her joints was terrible sometimes. She was old, suddenly old.

"How long will you be gone, Shanna?"

"I couldn't say. Don't worry, though. I won't be terribly late, and the baby does have his bottle. Goodbye, Mother," she said and, kissing Sarah on the cheek, she swept out the door, walking toward the barn where Roy's saddled black gelding waited.

The baby continued to cry. Sarah sat and rocked him. After a few minutes, she heard Shanna's horse trotting away. The room was still; the yard was filled with the clucking of chickens and the occasional squeal of a piglet. Sarah looked down at the baby who still squirmed uneasily. No, he was not hungry, not in that sense, she thought. Glancing toward the door, she began to unbutton the bodice of her dress. Then she put the restless infant to her breast and let its mouth find her nipple. Its finely lashed eyes fluttered and then closed in contentment. Sarah sat there for a peaceful hour, dry-nursing the tiny boy.

Shanna rode swiftly along Otter Creek, the wind in her face, feeling free, as she had not for a long time. There were no demands on her here, no obligations, no need to be anyone but herself, and even that, in her own mind if nowhere else, was a gilded image, a symbol of success. She had gone into the great Other and returned in sadness but hardly defeated.

She liked her new image; it fit her well, she thought. Tragic figure; broken-hearted but hardly bowed by misfortune. The creek was rapid and silver-blue, the trees bright and alive in the changing light of the early morning. She rode on quickly, exultantly.

"Tom!"

He sat beside the creek, back against a tree. A lonely soldier in a torn uniform, a dirt-streaked face and dark, suspicious eyes that watched her as she dismounted. Then he rose in astonishment.

"My God, Shanna!"

"Dear, dear Tom." They clung to each other for a long minute, scarcely able to believe it. "No one told me you were back!" Shanna said.

"No one told me you were! But then I haven't seen anyone," he admitted.

"Afraid to go home?" she asked, holding back a smile.

"I guess so, not in the way you think."

"Maybe just in the way I think," Shanna said. "Me too. I wouldn't have—but I have a baby, Tom."

"A baby! Really!"

"Yes. Brent Colter . . . oh, you wouldn't know. My husband died and I had no place left but home."

Tom scratched at his chest. "A kid? A boy? Well, damn me. Listen," he said, "I know you probably wouldn't—but I have a bottle of whiskey over here. If you'd let me toast to the baby. If

231

you wanted to join me. You probably wouldn't, Sis, but . . ."

"Bet me I wouldn't, Tom! I can't think of anything in this world I could use more right now."

"Well, how we have changed, huh?" Tom said, laughing, and the two of them walked toward the creek, leaving the black horse to graze on the spring grass. Sitting on the banks of Otter Creek, Tom opened the bottle and offered it to Shanna. "Sorry, I kinda forgot to bring my crystal along," Tom said.

"I've seen enough crystal glasses to last me a lifetime," Shanna said, raising the bottle to her lips, taking an admirably deep drink.

Tom whistled. "Wow. Hollywood style, huh?"

"Hollywood style." She leaned back on one elbow, tossing her tiny hat aside. "Next time you run across some of that stuff, Tom, pick me up a bottle. They still look funny at a woman who needs a drink back here."

"Not like Hollywood?"

"Not like Hollywood—but I don't care to talk about that anymore, okay?"

"Sure. I can understand that."

They sat in silence for a time, drinking, the sweet scent of grass, and the smell of the glittering creek in their nostrils, the warm sun dropping golden coins through the leaves of the oak.

Tom said, "If you knew how many hearts you broke . . ."

"The picture?" Shanna laughed. "That was nothing."

"It was to them—there," Tom said, handing her the bottle once more.

Shanna asked quietly, looking out across the creek toward Wigwam Island, "Was it terrible, Tom?"

He hesitated and then shrugged, "About as much fun as any war, I guess."

"Isn't it strange to be back?" she said, plucking a clover flower, studying it thoughtfully.

"Halfway around the world, you and I, and when we come back everything is still the same. Nothing changes here at all, does it?"

"Nothing," he agreed and now he closed his eyes. His words were slightly slurred. How strange it was to be sitting drinking whiskey with his sister, and there was not a word, a look of censure in her eyes. How much she must have seen in Hollywood.

"Tom!" Shanna sat up anxiously. "You know all the boys in town, don't you?"

"Well, I should say so. Why?"

"I wanted to ask you a favor. It may sound terrible, but you would know—or someone you know . . ."

"What in the world is it, Sis?" Tom asked, taking another drink from the bottle. He held it up to the sunlight, gauging its contents. "Come on, you can tell me."

"Are you sure?" she asked in a strangely coquettish voice.

"I said yes, didn't I? Tell me what it is, and then I'll ask you for a favor."

"A trade?"

"Sure," Tom said. "Ask me first."

"Okay," Shanna said. She paused then lunged ahead. "I want some cocaine, Tom."

"Jesus, Sis," Tom said, truly shocked. Shanna rushed on.

"It's legal, Tom, isn't it? As legal as anything. As legal as this," she said, holding up the whiskey bottle. "I need it. After Brent died a doctor gave me some and I got kinda—hooked—on it. It was an accident. I was down so low. That's why I can't nurse my baby, but I could never tell Mother or anyone but you. If you could please! . . ." she said, clasping her hands prayerfully.

Tom was silent, looking into her eyes. He took a deep drink from the bottle and decided. "Okay. I know men hooked on that damned morphine from the war. Pain. I can understand it. I know some people. I'll do it, Shanna."

"When?"

Her eagerness startled him. "Today. I promise, okay?"

"Okay," she sighed with relief, taking her turn on the nearly empty bottle. "Now—what was the favor you wanted, Tom? Anything, anything at all and I'll do it."

"You might not want to . . ."

"I said anything. Look what you're doing for me."

"Okay." He looked out across the creek and took in a deep, cleansing breath. When he turned his eyes back to Shanna's, he said, "I want you to get Lorna Paxton for me."

"How many does that make?" Allyn asked Elizabeth as he drove the buggy toward Tahlequah and his father's house.

"Only nine, I'm afraid," Elizabeth said, looking up from the enrollment forms in her hand.

"I suppose we can't blame people. Still, it's disappointing."

"No, you can't blame them. I thought I had Mrs. Blue Elk convinced, but then her husband came home. He demanded to know if it was a government school and I said no. Then he wanted to know if it was a tribal school, and I had to tell him no again, not strictly."

"It's our school," Allyn said.

"Exactly. He wanted to know how we were going to support it. And," she smiled at her young husband, "if it were legal in the first place."

Allyn nodded. "There's the rub—is it or isn't it? We're certainly not going to get any state certification. You should have told him the truth—we are trying to establish a tribal school without actually calling it that. A private seminary for young Cherokee boys and girls."

"Which is probably illegal. Probably—we sure can't take the

chance of asking the bureaucrats in the capital. It cannot be a public school; if it is a private school, we have to admit children who aren't Cherokee."

"Which I personally have nothing against," Allyn said. "Only, then we have to be chartered by the state—which I do object to."

"We're fighting a losing battle, Allyn," Elizabeth said.

"Ah," he said with a smile, "but we are fighting!"

In earlier years when the only law had been tribal law, the Cherokee children had an education far superior to that of any white or black in the Nation. Simply, they had raised their own taxes and built their own schools, educated their own young. The presence of an alien population brought in as laborers or skilled professionals caused thriving development of the white men's towns throughout the Nation. These came to be important shipping centers for coal, timber, and cattle, but only the Cherokees provided for the incorporation of these towns. As a result, there was a drastic difference in the physical appearance of Cherokee towns and that of the speculators, the "invaders." The Cherokee was here to stay, the interlopers were there to reap a financial harvest and move on. There were no city taxes except in the Cherokee townships, hence no schools, no police or fire protection, no sewers, no city lighting. All of this had changed with involuntary citizenship, with the involuntary loss of tribal control. The Federal government had come and "saved" the Indian from himself. And the Nighthawks, the Four Mothers' Society, The Snakes could only offer brief and futile armed resistance to being collectivized and seeing the end of a people's way of life vanish.

Now, not through their own choice, they were a state and no longer a great Nation.

They sensed something wrong immediately upon driving into Tahlequah. There were groups of kids running up the street, men scrambling toward them . . . "Allyn! It's the newspaper office," Elizabeth said, gripping his leg tightly. Allyn nodded; he had already come to the same conclusion. Snapping the bay with his whip, they raced on toward the office of the *Tribune*. Allyn saw a familiar figure lounging in the shade of the post office's awning.

"Isn't that . . . ?

"Yes," Elizabeth said, "it's Tom. There's no time to worry about him now. Hurry!"

There was a crowd in front of the *Tribune*'s offices, peering in through broken windows.

Allyn guided the horse up the rear alley, halted it, and leaped from the buggy, assisting Elizabeth.

Inside all was chaos.

Kenneth Jefferson was sitting in his living room holding a bloody cloth to his forehead.

Mrs. Hoyt, displaying an anger Elizabeth had never seen, hollered at the gathered crowd. "Go away! We don't need any gawkers around here. Please! Just go away, people."

Allyn went to his father and knelt down beside his chair. "What happened?"

"Hooligans," Kenneth Jefferson said. He pulled the rag from his forehead to refold it and Elizabeth saw a huge lump there, bisected by a cut that went through the scalp.

"You need stitches," she said. "I'll get the doctor."

"I don't need . . ." the publisher tried to object.

"You do when I can see bone through the hide on your head, Mr. Jefferson. So unless you want me to do it with my sewing kit, you'd better send me for the doctor." Wearily, Jefferson nodded his agreement.

"Glass everywhere," Mrs. Hoyt muttered. She already had a dustpan and a broom.

Allyn stopped her—some of the glass shards were more than

two feet across. "You'll cut yourself. I'll get it later with gloves," he told her.

"Get out of here!" Mrs. Hoyt shouted at a few lingering onlookers. Allyn smiled at his father.

"Protective, isn't she?"

"Hooligans," Kenneth Jefferson muttered again. He was in no mood for jokes. The printing press had a scar from a hurled rock; the font lay spilled across the floor. Glass was everywhere. Both front windows had been broken out.

"Kids. Do you know who they were?" Allyn asked.

"Did I say kids!" Kenneth said in the rage of pain and frustration. "Not unless we have kids six feet tall wearing a uniform."

"Dad?" Allyn was shaken by that information.

"Yes, it was the Indian police. I saw Atoka Boone myself! Saw him! He was standing there, pretending he knew nothing about it. Hands on his hips, looking up the street. 'Seems to be a problem here, Mr. Jefferson,' he said to me. A problem! I should think so when the local police throw rocks throw the windows of a man's business to try intimidating him. Well, Allyn, they do not know me all that well, do they! I will not be intimidated."

The publisher had exhausted himself with his tirade and he sagged back in his chair, Mrs. Hoyt holding the cloth to his brow. Allyn stood in the doorway leading to the press and stared at it glumly. "What was yesterday's editorial?" he asked.

" 'Release Roy Adair'," his father said. "And I won't quit demanding they release him!"

"The state elections are next month."

"Yes."

"Judge Benson doesn't seem to want any negative publicity about his fitness to be state senator."

"Benson?" Mrs. Hoyt asked.

"Who else? His aspirations are growing. Atoka Boone is in his pocket. The trial of Roy Adair was a farce, very unpopular.

Benson doesn't want people reminded of his handling of the case now."

"That hardly seems enough . . ." Allyn fell silent as Elizabeth entered, leading Dr. Sharpe, a pock-marked, arrogant man with absolutely no bedside manner but quick and professional in his diagnoses and surgery. He walked directly to Kenneth, tossed the rag away, opened his black bag, and removed a bottle of carbolic.

"This will hurt," he said and mopped the publisher's split scalp with the searing carbolic acid.

Kenneth jumped, his hands tightening on the arm of the chair and his eyes going instantly red. Before the sting had subsided, Dr. Sharpe was busy with his needle and suture. Elizabeth turned away, stepping to the alley door.

"I see two or three of these a week," the doctor said, stitching up Allyn's father as if he were quilting. "Kids throwing rocks at each other. This one must've been a big one."

"Fist-sized," Allyn said. He was still staring at the office, the shattered windows, still thinking dark thoughts about Captain Atoka Boone.

As if his mind could be read, Allyn's father spoke up, "No one rides nights in this country. Not anymore."

"No," Allyn agreed, although it was tempting. Very tempting. But he had Elizabeth now. Besides, his father's word was law— that was the way he was raised. The doctor looked up and blinked.

"Lots of people ride at night around here. See 'em all the time," he said in confusion.

"Then I was wrong," Kenneth said pleasantly. "Must be that the bump on the head has me speaking crazily."

The doctor finished his stitching and applied bandages. Shown to the bathroom, he scrubbed his hands and left. Mrs. Hoyt and Elizabeth slowly cleaned up the glass and scattered font. The curiosity seekers had gone; the sky beyond the shattered windows was a hazy purple. Allyn had gone to find wood to board them up with. He and a neighbor boy nailed up the sheets of wood, surrendering the office to darkness. Elizabeth lit a lamp and picked up a discarded editorial by Kenneth. Reading it, she was astonished.

Kenneth watched her, his hands hanging limply over the arms of the chair as she read it by lamplight, her brow furrowed.

"Yes," he told her without Elizabeth's asking, "I am sincerely investigating the possibility."

Elizabeth re-read the editorial. It was a request from the Cherokee people that they be allowed to flee the onerous land allotments of the government and return to their tribal way of life. It began, "We are informed that the white people came to this country to escape conditions that were not as bad as the present conditions our Nation had sunk into; that he went across a great ocean and sought a new home to avoid things that were distasteful to him. We ask now that we be permitted the same privilege. If we might accept our undesired allotments of land, those given out indiscriminately to unborn children, to blacks, to whites, to outlanders of all sorts, some of whom like one young lady recently awarded an allotment in Tahlequah, was as apple-cheeked and fair as a Gainsborough portrait. We might sell them back to the oppressive government of Oklahoma and purchase a tract of land in Mexico or South America where we might resume our traditional, that is to say, tribal way of life with no man's interference . . ."

"Kenneth!" Elizabeth was shocked, "But you have always been the one to lead us, to say we must continue to fight for what is ours."

"What is it?" Allyn asked, entering. He stripped off his gloves and took the sheet of newsprint with its unfinished editorial from Elizabeth. "The Jacob Jackson proposal," Allyn said, referring to an elderly, university-educated Choctaw who had presented this proposal to a senatorial committee when the certainty of losing control of their own destiny began to mature among the people of The Five Tribes.

"Yes." Allyn closed his eyes. His head was throbbing massively. "I am starting to be persuaded that it is the only way, Allyn."

"Not for me—I respectfully disagree, Father. This is my home. What do I know of South America?"

"What did our grandparents know of Oklahoma when we were herded west along the Trail of Tears? And what alone held us together? Our people. The tribe. The Way."

"The government will never agree to such a plan," Elizabeth said practically. "Secretary Garfield rejected it in 1908, the Federal government will again. The white man's conscience can not permit us to be driven for a second time into exile."

"What conscience?" Kennneth Jefferson said bitterly. The others traded glances. Never, resolute as he was, had any of them heard raw bitterness arise in Kenneth. "I have a letter here—" He fished in his vest for a handwritten document.

"What is it, Father?" Allyn asked.

"It is the letter Black Jack wrote to the president when he was tried for treason and for murder."

Dear Sir,

As I want you to hear from me, a Tahlequah-town Cherokee Indian, as fullbloods we held a meeting there as this treaty between the U.S. government & Indians was made long ago and I am under the treaty raise my children as I have already told to you. I have made elect the chief and also light horsemen ready to make my sign through the Indian nation but your citizen is what trouble me so, cause my citizen in trouble your citizen arrest my citizen without any reason any-one know of. I am doing perfectly right as what treaty was. I am not disturbing any U.S. government nor break any law whatever. I am right line, but your citizen what trouble me. I wrote you about it but it is your citizen. I ask you as you said any-one bother in your nation I would tend to that clear out of my nation as you said as this gentleman what bothers so his name is Judge Benson and his dog who is Atoka Boone who call themselves the law suppose to be. As you see this letter to please answer it right away. I am a friendly worker for the Cherokee Nation.

They sat in the dim silence. Mrs. Hoyt brought Kenneth a cup of tea. He smiled his thanks.

"Surely you're not going to print this," Elizabeth said.

"Yes. Of course I am, it is document of our times, of the truth of them."

"Father," Allyn asked. "Have you a file with all of these documents? If so—you realize how Benson will view all of this in an election year. The man is running for state senator! You have made yourself into his enemy, a barrier to his ambitions."

"And that is exactly what I am," the publisher said, sipping his tea. "And what I shall remain until we are driven from this land. I don't take the plan to emigrate lightly, Allyn, but if we cannot get rid of these new carpetbaggers, what are we to do? My father," he said inconsequentially, "fought for the Southern cause. There were many Cherokee regiments in that war. Jefferson Davis had promised our eastern lands in perpetuity should we prevail. One wonders at times how long Washington, D.C.'s memory is. One wonders how we could have fared worse under the Confederacy."

Allyn looked at Elizabeth and an understanding passed between them. Kenneth was speaking emotionally at the moment, and not logically, they both knew.

"You're tired, Father. A rap on the head like that—the body needs time to recoup. We will let you sleep now." Rising, they nodded to Mrs. Hoyt who took their hands in gratitude.

"Will it be all right?" Allyn asked Marion outside. "Do you want me to stand watch?"

"They wouldn't dare come back tonight, but thank you, Allyn. Thank you." Then impulsively Marion Hoyt went to tiptoes and kissed Allyn on the cheek before turning back from the alley, slipping indoors and closing and locking the newspaper offices.

"Allyn?" Elizabeth said anxiously as her husband climbed up into the buggy to unwrap the reins from the brake post.

"I know. He's tired, dear. And he's had a shock. He's not entirely himself, one thought twisted on another. He is searching for a way out. Defeat is not easy to face, and that is what we are looking at, Elizabeth. The Nighthawks could not win, the lawyers with our treaties in hand, the letters to Presidents . . . it is one more lost battle."

Elizabeth rested her head against his shoulder as Allyn clicked his horse into motion. "We, then, Allyn? What shall we do?" she asked from the starlit closeness.

"We?" Allyn laughed and snapped the reins, picking the bay from his lazy walking gait to a snappy trot. "We shall fight on!"

Darkness was crowding the colors of the garden. An owl dipped low, changed its mind, and swooped away on broad, silent wings. Lorna watched its heavy, dark silhouette against the dying sunset and wiped her hands on her apron. Gathering up the rose stems she had been pruning, she started toward the back porch of the house.

"Hello, Lorna," a voice called to her from out of the settling dusk. It was a familiar voice, but one not readily recognizable, like a voice-shadow in some murky dream. Lorna squinted into the shadows and then smiled. Shanna Adair!

"Heaven's sake!" Lorna exclaimed. It had been so long and

Shanna and Lorna were never in the same crowd anyway. Lorna, Jeannie Bear, and Elizabeth had been great friends. Shanna and Tina Roberts had been the older girls, far superior. Lorna could still remember Shanna telling them that their dolls couldn't come to their party because their clothes weren't pretty enough. All those years ago.

Shanna walked toward her from the tree shadows, both hands extended. Lorna Paxton was a pretty girl and knew it, but Shanna in her green satin, her long hair brushed over her shoulders, was beautiful! No wonder she had become a Hollywood star. The two women embraced. Lorna moved back to arms' length to study Shanna. The lines of her throat, her face were perfect. Her eyes were lively and over-bright, defying the slight darkness around them. Lorna had seen how Shanna photographed from the pictures she had sent Sarah and Elizabeth. Still, despite the sparkle of her eyes, Shanna looked tired beneath the surface. Well—why wouldn't she, losing a husband, bringing a child home to care for alone?

"You look wonderful, Lorna," Shanna said. "May we sit for awhile?" she asked, nodding toward the back porch where Tramp, the shy Yellow Labrador pup, watched, wagging its tail uncertainly.

"Of course! But don't you want to come in to the parlor?"

"The air is so fresh," Shanna said. "We can see Otter Creek from there, can't we?"

"You sound as if you missed Broken Post," Lorna laughed.

"Maybe. Maybe just a little," Shanna said as they started that way. They went up the two steps and Shanna scratched the pup's head, and he, knowing this was welcome company, lay watching, head on his paws.

"My!" Lorna said, settling onto the glider beside Shanna. "You certainly surprised me. Are you sure you don't want some lemonade?"

"No thank you," Shanna said. She sat looking through the sycamores to where the creek rolled on, endlessly, timelessly, still vaguely violet in the twilight. She decided to barge ahead with no more small talk. "I've come to speak for Tom, Lorna."

"Tom . . ." Lorna tripped over his name. "I have spoken to him," she said, regaining her stiff composure.

"That wasn't Tom, Lorna. You know that," Shanna said, turning to Lorna Paxton, taking her hand between hers. "He's been through a dreadful time, a horrible war."

"And so he had to ask you to speak to me!" Lorna scoffed. "The brave soldier. He had to get drunk to talk to me!"

"Yes."

Lorna stared at Shanna in the darkness. The dog watched them both, eyes rolled high in his skull. The nightbirds had begun to sing in the trees along the river. Shanna tried to explain.

"He was afraid, Lorna. He has been gone so long. He tried to get his courage up with alcohol and then ruined his chances of telling you how he felt."

Lorna shot back immediately: "How he felt! He never cared how I felt, did he?"

Shanna was honestly taken aback. "He went to do his duty, Lorna."

"His duty to whom? For what? He didn't care about his duty to me, Shanna. Not a bit. He left me pregnant! Do you understand?"

"I . . ."

"No, you don't. He is your little brother. But he is a man, oh, yes—at least in that respect. Duty—he ran off and left me." Lorna had begun to cry and both women found it uncomfortable.

"Did he know?" Shanna asked.

"No." Lorna snuffled, lifted her eyes, and stared off into the distance, at the stars above the trees, the coming rim of the moon. "How would he know? He never asked me. He never wrote in all that time."

"They couldn't write, really. The way I understand things," Shanna said.

"Never!" Lorna's laugh was derisive.

They sat in silence on the glider for a long while. Without looking at Lorna, Shanna asked, "What happened—to the baby?"

"There never was a baby. I missed my period one month, then the second. I went to the drugstore and bought a hundred quinine pills and took them by the dozens . . . I eventually had a miscarriage."

Shanna didn't answer. She wanted cocaine. She wanted Brent. She wanted . . . not to start crying, which she did anyway, and so did Lorna. What a pair of fools!

"I guess I'll never have to worry about contracting malaria!" Lorna said and somehow they both managed to laugh through bitter tears.

"Will you give him a chance?" Shanna asked. The night had gone still. The mosquitoes had started to drift in from off the river and the flycatchers were swooping through them. A bat winged past, a quick dark shadow, ate his brief meal of insects and returned to hell. There was a rising breeze that dispersed the insects, and started the willows along Otter Creek to shift and sway. The rising crescent moon showed sharp and bright above the plains. Lorna still had not answered.

"Yes. Tell him I will. Tell him I don't know if I can love him any longer, but I will see him."

"That's what she said," Shanna told Tom. He passed the whiskey bottle to his sister.

"Tell me again, tell me exactly," he said, rolling onto his belly, propped up on his elbows against the damp grass on Otter Creek bank.

"Tom—" Shanna laughed, her spirits very high again. She had had one more sniff of cocaine, one more drink of whiskey. "I told you three times! Now it's up to you!"

"A baby . . ." he shook his head and fell into a brief dark reverie. "How in hell was I supposed to know?"

"Well, you know what causes that, don't you!" Shanna teased darkly and Tom shoved her shoulder until she rolled onto her back and lay staring at the sky.

"That's not what I mean, Shanna—what happened, well that's between two people and it happens, right, else none of us would be on this planet, right? But I wouldn't have hurt her. I wouldn't have abandoned . . ." he broke down into drunken tears briefly. "A little baby."

"Well, tell her, hot-shot!" Shanna said with mock-roughness. "I've done all I can, soldier."

Tom sat up, silently watching the night. He took another drink of whiskey. "Yes," he admitted, "you did all you can do. I need to talk to her. But not tonight, huh, Sis?"

"Not tonight, Brother."

Tom was deeply silent. The bottle sat on the grass between them. Neither touched it. It was a long and sad and enormously important night. "Hard to make a step forward," Tom said carefully. "Easier to stay where we are."

"Yes." Shanna had stretched out on her back, arms spread wide.

"Is Brent okay—baby Brent?" Tom asked. "It's near midnight."

"Grandmother's watching him, of course he's all right," Shanna said a little sharply.

"Yeah, I guess so." Tom fell into dark reverie again. "I wonder, Shanna, was it a boy or a girl baby?"

Sarah sat with the baby before the low burning fire. Elizabeth and Allyn had stopped by briefly on their way home and told her about the vandalism at the *Tribune* office. Now they were gone and the house was as still as it ever was. Just the low moaning of the prairie wind.

Roy was not there with his booming laugh and his crazy friends and the night's boisterous merry-making blending into a season of love-making. There was only one tiny infant in her arms. Had all of the good days, the fine nights, faded into age so soon?

When the screen door on the porch opened with a bang and the accompanying sound of riotous laughter, Sarah jumped to her feet, her heart pounding. But she recognized the laughter, and it had been so long since she had heard it . . . she walked across the firelit room to the bright kitchen to see Tom and Shanna together.

"We've come home, Mother," Tom said and he walked to her, hugging her around the baby.

"Tom, you're drunk."

"Yes, Mother," he said, taking a staggering half-step backward.

"Come home, Tom. Lord, come home," Sarah said and Tom nodded, banged his shoulder into the doorframe between kitchen and living room, and curled up before the fire. In minutes he was asleep.

"I'll take the baby," Shanna said, and she held Brent as her mother with a shake of her head threw a warm comforter over her wandering son.

"Where was he, Shanna?" Sarah asked her daughter.

"In town. Afraid to come home," she answered.

"How could he be . . . afraid?" Sarah asked in confusion. "This is his home!" She watched her sleeping son in the torn uniform, his hair tousled, his face streaked with dirt. "Was it the war, Shanna? Tell me the truth. The war?"

"Yes, Mother. The war. But he's home at last."

Sarah nodded. She sat on the faded red rocker, her hands folded, watching her son by the dim light of the golden embers. Shanna had forgotten for a moment where she was. The tabloid in the faded light with its deep shadows, was an Old Masters' scene. It failed to touch her reality. She had been standing still for a long moment, forgetting who she was, which way her room was, whose baby she held. Shaking her head violently, she walked down the familiar, unfamiliar hallway to her room and placed the sleeping baby in his crib. Then, fully dressed, she fell onto the bed in the utter darkness and cried, not remembering for whom she cried.

It has nothing to do with the war, Mother!, she wanted to scream.

She loved her mother too much to do that. It was that she and Tom knew the small, grimy, useless corner of the world they inhabited for what it was. A hopelessly dead end to life, to joy, to love, to experience or success. The hogs grunted in the pen beyond the window, the moonlight shined through the curtains, no duller, no brighter than it had been before Hollywood. Restlessly, angrily, she rolled over and pounded her pillow flat with her fist. Only Tom knew. She felt like waking him up, sitting up all night long drinking whiskey and reliving what very nearly had been . . .

Very nearly.

Well, Tom at least had the hope of getting Lorna Paxton, a good girl. She would coach him on that, tell him what a woman thinks and wants to hear, as for herself . . . she sat bolt upright! As for herself, who could say her career was over? That she had dragged herself back to the Nation defeated? She still had her contacts, her friends.

She could write Emilio. He would give her work. And Tony.

Fred Stein! There was no reason she couldn't begin again and this time she would know the ropes. She could get her stomach flat again easily. She was young and this time she could not be beaten. It was that or this dingy, useless, dust-ridden, cancerous Nation. She would write Emilio a letter that very night. Only one thing had to be done—the baby had to be cared for.

But, by who?

Not Mother. She was getting too old. She would never understand. Who? She looked toward the cradle where the baby lay peacefully sleeping. Brent—funny—whoever your father is, he does not want you. That was the way with men. She spent one long desolate minute wishing that his father was really Brent Colter. Stupid, empty wishes!

But who could take care of the baby? Give him a good home? . . . Tina Roberts. Tina Black!

Why not? It was just a matter of coming up with a story both of the Blacks would believe.

Wallace would accept anything, she said, there was no doubt of that in Shanna's mind.

Tina . . . that was a little more difficult. Tina was not a stupid woman. But it could be done. It could be done. Shanna rolled over against her cool pillow and watched the rising moon through the ink-black branches of the lonesome oak for a long minute, then wriggled happily, pulled up the blanket, and fell off to an undisturbed sleep.

Tom woke up stiff and cold. The fire had long ago burned out, the wooden floor was rough and chilled by the night. He didn't move for a long minute, trying to establish in his mind just where he was. So many nights sleeping and waking in odd places in cold and mud and desolation—he could have been anywhere. He moved very slowly. He sensed no death there, no enemy steel. Slowly he began to recognize articles around him in the cool dawn light. No!

He was home. By God! He sat up too sharply and his head protested. He sorted out the events of last evening bit by bit as he sat in front of the cold hearth, the comforter draped over his shoulders.

He had talked to Mother. She had accepted him back into the house. She had known, of course, that he had been drunk . . . thinking of that made Tom wonder if he had hidden part of a bottle out somewhere. He needed his Johnny-wake-up just then. His mouth was glued shut, his pulse beginning to race, his hands to tremble.

Lorna! Shanna had spoke to Lorna for him. Maybe there was even hope in that area. That meant Shanna was here as well. He rubbed his forehead, trying to put the pieces of the puzzle together. There was a baby. He knew that. Shanna's baby. He didn't even know she had been married. Lord, what else had happened while he was in France!

His mother was sleeping in late, uncharacteristically. Or maybe she slept in longer these days. With a groan, Tom rose, shedding his comforter. It was cold in the early morning and he hugged himself. He thought about starting a fire, but decided to do first things first. He still couldn't remember . . . he wiped back his dark hair with both hands and went through the kitchen to the back door. Opening it, he felt a rush of icy wind. He went out into the garden and began a search. In the roses, perhaps? No, all he found there was a way to rake his hands on the thorns. Under the porch? That was where they used to hide things from their parents. He looked underneath. One summer he and Shanna and Elizabeth had hidden there when the biggest, roaring tornado in memory had raked the county, destroying three houses and many outbuildings. They had laughed and played as the massive dark funnel cloud moved past within a mile of their home. Tom remembered not being able to catch his breath as dust and confusion reigned outside. It had been safe under the porch.

And there it was—his bottle of whiskey, only a third down.

Where could he drink it? Not anywhere his mother would see him. He knew she would say nothing, that was Sarah's way, but he didn't wish to make himself smaller in her eyes.

Shanna's room! Of course. Elizabeth no longer lived at home. Shanna and he understood each other's small weaknesses. He tip-toed to the back of the house and went to her window, rapping lightly on the glass.

"Shanna," he whispered. When there was no response, he called her name louder, and eventually a tousled head and wan face appeared at the curtains. She looked momentarily angry, but Tom grinned and held up the bottle, and Shanna pointed eagerly toward her bedroom door.

Tom went in the back door, down the short hallway, and slipped into her room to plant himself on the bed.

"God, you're a life-saver," Shanna said. Tom opened the bottle and let his sister have first drink. She sat beside him, shuddering as the raw whiskey hit bottom.

Tom looked across the room at the little white cradle where the baby still slept. "I didn't even know you had a baby. Did you tell me? I can't remember, I was pretty drunk."

"I don't know. I was pretty drunk," Shanna said and they briefly shared muffled laughter.

Shanna stopped herself abruptly. "Oh, God, my head."

In her night dress she went to the bureau and took out a bottle of aspirin. She dumped half a dozen into her palm and put them in her mouth, washing them down with a large slug of whiskey.

"Wow," Tom said. "What does that taste like?"

"It's awful, Tom, it's truly awful," Shanna said. "But give me about ten minutes and my world will begin to stabilize. Want some?"

"I'd better, I guess. We can't get drunk before breakfast, Shanna."

"No! Just enough to get us up and functioning, right? Tom," Shanna said, "that man you got the coke from—has he any more?"

"I don't know. Maybe. I could ask. Do you need it that much, Shanna?" Tom asked with concern.

"Not really," she laughed, tossing her head so that her raven hair fell in a silky cascade down her back. "It just brightens things up for me. You know, I didn't have an easy delivery with . . . Brent," she nodded toward the baby who was now beginning to stir, small fists clenching and unclenching.

"I don't know anything about those things. I know women can die in childbirth. It was pretty terrible, huh?"

"I almost died myself!" Shanna said, seizing the dramatic. "One more drink, Tom?" she asked, reaching for the bottle.

"Sure, why not. One more then maybe we ought to make coffee for Mother."

"She likes to do it herself—but, oh, well, why not." She took another drink from the quart bottle, which now was down to the halfway mark. "The thing is," Shanna said, returning to her earlier thought, "I don't have any money for coke. Until my husband's will is probated, I'm virtually penniless—that's one reason I had to come home," she said quite seriously.

"I can ask. But I don't know," Tom said. "You don't have anything left—from the movies and all?"

"All that went for funeral expenses, Tom," Shanna said.

"I see . . ." Meditatively he stared at the floor, then glanced at the baby and took a healthy drink of whiskey. "Maybe I can loan you some, Shanna. I should still have some of my separation pay." He laughed, "I'm afraid to look in my pockets to find out! God knows where I've been throwing the stuff around."

"You should save some for you and Lorna," Shanna said.

"Lorna—you don't think she'd take me back, do you?" he asked hopefully.

"Maybe, Tom. I know she loves you. Take it from a woman."

Tom nodded, his morning suddenly brighter. The whiskey and aspirin were working. The new sunlight was dancing in the upper reaches of the oak. Robins and the inevitable mocking-birds hopped from branch to branch. A squirrel twisted his way up the trunk of the tree.

He rose and opened the window. The morning air was not so cold, so dismal. When he turned back his sister was standing in front of her dresser, dipping into the white powder in the engraved silver snuffbox.

"I thought you were out of that," Tom said.

"Not just yet." She sniffed and held her nostril pinched closed. "But I will be. Tom—I don't want to get sick just now. I need to keep the pain down for just a little while longer. Just a little while. There's too much I have to organize still—for the baby."

Sarah awoke later than usual. The sunlight streaking her bed brought her to morning. She stretched out a hand automatically, but Roy was not there. There were unusual sounds in the house, which had been like a tomb as she lived on her own, by herself and for herself. Singing!

She heard singing in the kitchen, and she came suddenly alert, remembering.

Tom and Shanna had come home. The baby was in the house!

Sarah rose, brushed and pinned her hair rapidly, put on her morning coat, and walked to the kitchen where the smell of cof-fee being boiled greeted her.

She halted in the doorway.

There were broken eggs on the floor. The coffee boiled over in the granite pot. Shanna and Tom were dancing, singing a strange jazz song. Off to her right, in Shanna's bedroom, the baby was crying unremarked. Sarah's smile faded from her lips. She walked across the house, through the living room where Tom's comforter lay near the hearth, one corner smoldering on the embers. She tugged it from the fireplace, stamped on the blackened material, and flung open the front door to step out into the blood-colored sunrise.

The land was sere and yellow. The hogs snuffled at her from their pen. The gaunt black horse was nuzzling clumps of nutritionless bunch grass. Even this land was not theirs. The government had not given it to them because they had not accepted their allotment. What had been given to them was taken away. Raucous laughter rose from the kitchen. A frying pan rang as it hit the floor. Sarah could hear the baby crying.

She walked slowly across the brick-dry front yard. The peach tree with its tiny withered fruit stood there pathetically dwarfed. She walked to the grinding wheel, unused and silent, the pleasant, utilitarian sound it made of stone on steel only memory. Sarah picked up the hatchet that sat on the gray wooden bench beside it and recrossed the yard.

And she swung it at the trunk of the damnable peach tree. Useless, withered relic her grandmother had brought from the South, carried on a wagon all along the Trail of Tears to the new nation. And she struck the tree again and again, tears blinding her vision until a hand gripped her arm and stayed a cutting arc of the razor-edged steel.

"Now you have caused me some work, woman! Find some tar and some burlap. We'll try wrapping it again."

Sarah turned. Astonished, grateful tears filled her eyes. She could hardly see him. Her hands, her lips, her body touched him and felt him, assuring her he was real. "Roy, oh, my God, Roy!"

"Yes." He said nothing else. He held her close and for minute after minute they did not speak or move or even look into each other's eyes.

"How . . . ?" she asked worriedly.

"I didn't escape!" he laughed. "It is election year, Sarah. I am a token. Only that."

She knew his touch, his eyes. But his hair had gone gray and his face was creased, his cheeks hollow. "Was it hard, Roy? Very hard."

"Being away from you was hard, woman!" he laughed, and she saw that one of his front teeth had been knocked out. "For the rest of it—bah! I am a warrior."

"Yes, you are, Roy. You are my warrior." She was wiping her nose on the collar of her nightdress, dabbing at her eyes. Through the tears she manufactured a smile and told him, "Tom is here. Shanna is here. She has brought us a grandson, Roy!"

"A baby! Really. Let me see the little one. Has she brought a husband too?"

"He is dead, Roy. She doesn't like to talk about it."

"Oh?" Roy was briefly dubious. He could read his wife's tones, her eyes. He shrugged mentally and placed his arm around her shoulders. "I'm sorry—but let me see my wandering children and the baby!" he said expansively. "I am home! And it is too fine a morning to waste chopping down trees."

Breakfast was a clouded affair. Sarah had scrambled eggs and sliced bread for Shanna to toast. Tom and Shanna both appeared edgy. Roy misread their behavior and thought perhaps they were ashamed of him. They spoke in desultory tones, the two younger Adairs glancing at each other meaningfully from time to time in a way Roy couldn't quite understand. It was a strange homecoming for him.

Later, when they were alone and Roy voiced his concerns, Sarah felt compelled to tell him the truth. "They were ashamed,

Roy, like children caught in a small crime. They were both very drunk."

"At this time of the morning?"

"They were both very drunk. Tom has been in town for weeks, wandering the streets. He only came home last night. Shanna is not taking care of the baby."

Roy began to get angry. She could see the heat rising in his black eyes. Sarah put her hand on his wrist. "Please, Roy. Don't say anything, not just now. I felt I had to tell you. You seemed to believe they did not want to see you when, in fact, they just feared your disapproval. Please? For me, Roy? Say nothing."

"All right," he agreed reluctantly. In his time he knew what his father would have done. Lay the law down to Shanna, take Tom into the backyard and convince him physically whose house this was, whose rules they were to live by. But Sarah, he knew, needed to have her babies home, at least for a time. To be a family for a little while even if a part of it must be a sham.

"All right."

Sarah brightened. "Elizabeth is married. You knew that of course?"

"She has been good about writing. I want to see her today. And Allyn and Kenneth. Kenneth is getting himself into extreme danger, I'm afraid," Roy said. "He has suddenly become a man possessed by the quest for freedom."

Sarah only smiled at Roy. Was there ever a man so possessed by that quest as Roy Adair?

Quietly she begged him, "Roy? No more, please. No more of the Nighthawks, no more of the Four Mothers." Her eyes were damp again. A single tear trickled down her cheek and he wiped it away with one finger. He kissed her cheek and then her hand. His own hands were trembling as he answered, and she knew how much it cost him to promise her. It was not fear of the government, of personal consequences; they had not intimidated him and never would. It was love for her that made him give his word.

"No more." He rose then. "I still have not seen the baby!"

Shanna found herself entangled in a web of invention, distortion, and plain twisted lies. Her parents asked her about the baby, its father, her life in Hollywood. She had grown so used to evasiveness that she was certain she tripped herself up continually. Her father, now fascinated by the baby, seemed to not notice as he delighted in the tiny toes and fingers and continued to make the baby gurgle a laugh. Her mother, she was sure, did notice. And the whiskey was wearing off. Her eyes went continually to the bureau drawer where the snuffbox rested. There was no way to get to it!

Why did she have to go through this!

She didn't belong here any longer. She belonged in Hollywood where it wasn't necessary to go through these childish explanations and evasions, to smile when she didn't feel like it at all, to coo over the baby who was only an accident and an anchor to her aspirations. Looking out the window once, she saw Tom among the cottonwoods taking a drink of his bottle. He caught her eyes and laughed and she shook her fist at him. He shrugged and laughed again.

When the baby had been thoroughly examined, changed, worn out by Roy's play, Shanna told them in a low voice, "I'd like to go see Tina and Wallace if you can watch the baby for a while."

"Wallace Black?" Roy said. "Did he ever finish that house up on Oak Knoll? He always was an ambitious young man. Steady."

"Steady," Shanna said silently. Where would his steady have gotten him on the Coast? He would have appeared to be just what he was, an ox, an ignorant, pathetic hick.

"And Tina Roberts married him!" Roy continued. "She's done all right for herself then. Shanna, you should have caught him while he was after you."

"Probably," she said irritably. Then, since she had to change her clothes, she managed to get them both out of the room. She immediately lunged for the drawer. There was very little cocaine left in the snuffbox. She snorted what she could, wet a fingertip and ran it around inside the silver container and smeared the residue on her tongue. She felt better—but not enough better.

Tom had to come through for her. One more time.

Slipping out, she managed a cheerful goodbye to her parents and tracked down Tom who was sitting against a wind-ruffled cottonwood, plucking petals from a daisy, looking as contented as a wood elf.

"Bum," she teased, sitting down beside him, reaching for the bottle, which had no more than an inch of whiskey left in it. "You could have come to my rescue!"

"How?" Tom peered into the sunlight. The cottonwood tree's leaves rustled in the breeze, turning silver where the sun hit their underside. "A least you got through that—I still haven't had my talk with Dad."

"Why would that bother you? You're a man. You can come or go as you please."

"I would have to talk about the war, Shanna. To Father war is a tragic reality entered into with full consideration."

"And?" Shanna took another drink.

"And—my war was a petty, dehumanizing ritual of blood lust that took more lives than any catastrophe of God's or man's devising, all for the sake of a meaningless dispute hidden deep in the Balkans."

"Then why, oh why, did you go, Tom?" Shanna asked, gripping his knee, looking into his whiskey-bright eyes.

"Oh, hell, Shanna! Why do we go anywhere? It seemed to be . . . away."

And she understood that, and they shared the rest of the

bottle in silence as the cabbage butterflies and iridescent dragonflies lazed above the garden, and the killdeer sang in the stubble grass.

"Well," Allyn said as he slowed the bay horse. "Is that who I think it is?"

Elizabeth who had been half-dozing on this lazy morning along the Otter Creek trail, lifted her head and answered, "Yes, it is. Shanna! Shanna! It's us!"

Shanna stopped, holding her breast, breathing heavily. Years ago the walk to Oak Knoll had seemed a minute's dash through the pines and over the fields. Now it seemed mile upon mile away. She waited for the buggy to pull up alongside her in the heavy shade of the river trees.

"What are you doing, dear?" Elizabeth asked.

Allyn tipped his hat. "Need a ride?"

"You have no idea," Shanna gasped. "I was going to see the Blacks. Is it that hot, or am I that old—or have they moved Oak Knoll farther away since I've been gone?"

"Climb in," Allyn said as Elizabeth scooted over on the bench seat of the buggy. "Your father is home?"

"Yes, he is," Shanna said, still breathless, as the buggy started on again. "We had a lovely visit."

"That's what we were told—that Roy came in on the morning train. It seemed too good to be believed."

"He's home. He said Benson had him released because of the election coming up."

"That sounds like the judge," Allyn said.

"He and mother are just . . . wonderfully happy. Tom's home right now too, Elizabeth," Shanna told her sister.

"Just like the holidays," Elizabeth said, adjusting her spectacles. Unconsciously she touched her shorn, shoulder-length hair as she looked at her sister's raven-black tresses glossed to nearly deep blue by the sunlight, rich and extravagant. Men must pine to run fingers through it. And to have her magnificent black eyes turned upon them . . . ! Elizabeth shoved her nascent jealousy aside.

"This is fine," Shanna said, pointing to Oak Knoll road, now graded and widened due to Wallace Black's efforts. They could just see the corner of the house and its stone chimney rising above the trees on the knoll.

She walked slowly up the road. Well known to her, it seemed so much steeper than it had a few short years ago. Short years! No, there was eternity separating this excursion from her last visit to see Wallace's intended homesite. The house was not impressive, but it was well built, strong and unassuming like Wallace himself. Shanna rapped on the door, but there was no answer. Tina, she saw, had planted daffodils in wooden half-barrels along the walls. There were young jasmine plants struggling to grow in the shade of a juniper tree, their soil damp and mulched. A geranium sat on the window ledge. Shanna could see a canary in a cage hanging from the ceiling, and a large, comfortable fireplace, its mantle decorated with pewter cups and a straw cornucopia, its mouth bright with wildflowers.

There was no answer at the kitchen door with its woven welcome mat and hanging bronze bell, either. Shanna circled the house slowly. She should return home, she knew, but she felt suddenly extremely tired, all of her false energy fading. She would just rest for a little while and wait for them; surely they would be home soon. She walked a little way into the oak grove with its carpet of moss and bright green struggling new grass. Finding a shadowed vine-hung nook, she fell to the earth and curled up, falling off to sleep.

"Tom!" Elizabeth stepped from the buggy almost before Allyn had braked to a stop and she rushed to her brother, throwing her arms around him. He smelled of whiskey and of sweat, she found, but he was home. There must be a period of readjustment after what he had endured, she supposed. Allyn walked to him and shook his hand firmly.

"Well, you're still in one piece," Allyn said with forced joviality, holding Tom at arms' length. On the porch Sarah and Roy had appeared, Roy with a fresh shave, a clean shirt, his hair brushed back and Elizabeth uttered a little cry of joy and ran that way.

Allyn hesitated a moment. "Tom, a letter came for you through the newspaper office. I guess they figured someone would know you."

He gave Tom the letter, patted his shoulder, and went off smiling, waving to where Roy waited, his daughter hugging him. The letter was from El Paso, addressed care of the *Tribune*. Tom opened it slowly.

> *Dear Tom,*
>
> *How are you, old buddy? I have no idea how things are going for you up home, but while I was gone my Daddy built up his little machine shop to something quite big, on defense contracts mostly. Anyway, we have gotten to be a fairly large concern down here, manufacturing oil drill bits among other things. I guess Daddy is going to take a huge chance and let me manage our Plant Number Two! If you get to where you would care to come down here and learn the business, Tom, I could use you.*
>
> > *Best to y'all—your friend,*
> > *John Trout*

"Any good news, Tom?" Allyn asked hopefully as he returned from talking to Roy. He nodded at the letter in Tom's hand.

"Nothin'," Tom said, crumpling the letter. "More white man's bullshit," and that sounded so little like the Tom Adair that he had known that Allyn was stumped for an answer.

"Well . . . sorry," Allyn finally said. Tom almost seemed afraid of something.

"Yeah. Allyn," Tom asked. "I need a few bucks. Can you help me for a while?"

"I've got . . ." Allyn started to look through his pockets.

"Like fifty dollars," Tom said. "I've shot my separation pay, Allyn."

And there was the constant need for whiskey. And the promise to Shanna that he would tap his cocaine source again for her.

"Fifty . . . I should talk to Elizabeth about that much," Allyn said.

Tom grew suddenly mocking. The alcohol was wearing off and he was growing edgy.

"Now you got to ask the woman before you can make me a loan? Always thought you were a man, Allyn! I've seen you ride with the Nighthawks, remember? Did you have to ask her then—say, 'Oh, darling, may I ride with the boys tonight and kill someone?' "

"Tom, you're making a mistake. In those days I was making a mistake." He breathed in slowly and out again slowly, glancing toward the porch. "One time, okay? The next time I will discuss it with my wife, do you understand—that is the way our marriage works."

He scrawled a check to Tom and ripped it from his checkbook without glancing at it. "The bank will take care of you, Tom."

"Okay, thanks, Allyn. Sorry if . . ."

Allyn interrupted him. "Just remember what I said and try to take care of yourself!"

"Allyn!" Elizabeth was calling from the porch. "Come on, honey, we're going to see the baby."

"All right!" he hollered back. Then to Tom who was folding

the check to jam into his pocket. "Please, Tom—be careful for all of them. They care."

Supper was very plain. Pan-fried homemade bread with cheese melted on top and one fried duck egg for everyone. Sarah apologized the entire way through the cooking and the serving until Roy stood and took her in his arms, "Woman," he said, "do not apologize for what is properly my fault. Besides, this meal is the best I have eaten in months and months—and served with far more love."

Roy went on over supper. "I'll find some extra work and get the farm back in shape. Why, if Tom helps me, we'll have no worries whatever."

Allyn and Elizabeth were silent, although they smiled conditionally. In all honesty, they knew no one in this county could risk hiring Roy Adair. That was inviting trouble from the law-enforcement people and the courts. Nor was Tom likely to be of help in getting the farm back on its feet. Sarah wondered aloud once where her son could be, but no one seemed to know.

Allyn, of course, did, but he wasn't about to say anything to disrupt Roy's homecoming.

The meal was adequate. Again, Sarah noticed, people struggled with conversation over coffee. No one wanted to ask Roy to relive his time in prison. He, in turn, had been gone too long to know about the local events. It was the same, Sarah considered, as wanting to ask, not asking, Tom about the war, asking Shanna about her dead husband and Hollywood. Something had changed. These conversations after supper had always been so easy in years gone by. Now it seemed everyone was huddled inside his own cavern of secrets. She knew that Roy loved her, that he was happy to be home, but the jail years had done something terrible to him. She could watch his eyes as his mind drifted away and she could see dark, terrible thoughts there, like creatures crouched in some secret, horrible forest.

All of their heads lifted as a rider came into the yard. He was riding hard, whoever he was, and he seemed to hit the ground before his horse had even halted. Boots pounded across the porch and a fist banged on the screen.

"Allyn Jefferson!" It was Billy Bird, his chest rising and falling rapidly, his shirt drenched in sweat.

"Yes, Bill."

"You'd better come quick, sir. They done set fire to the *Tribune* office and your Father is hurt real bad!"

The bay horse was frothing as they drove headlong down the Otter Creek road toward Tahlequah, Allyn using the whip constantly. Elizabeth hung on grimly. From a mile away they could see a dull orange glow against the night sky. Racing into town they encountered crowds of people standing, watching the flames from the *Tribune* office, and were forced to slow drastically, to Allyn's frustration. The pumper truck was in front of the office, but it was obvious that its thin stream of water was too little too late. The false front of the building had charred and collapsed into an ashen heap that covered the boardwalk and half of the street. Glass, blown out by the heat, littered the dark earth as well. They could get no closer than half a block away.

Allyn handed Elizabeth the reins and leapt from the buggy to rush toward the nearest fireman.

She saw him grab the harried fireman's arm and turn him, saw a few short words exchanged, then Allyn ran back to the carriage.

"He's at Dr. Sharpe's."

Allyn backed the horse, which was frightened by the smoke and flames, and then turned it back up the street.

Doctor Sharpe lived in the Maybelle Hotel on the ground

floor. His shingle was hung outside the alley entrance and they found him emerging from his surgery, drying his hands on a towel.

"Hello, Mr. Jefferson."

"How is he?"

"Badly burned. Second-degree, mostly. Some inhalation. Some solid object apparently fell . . ." The doctor was interrupted as Marion Hoyt came out of the other room, her face ghostly pale, her hands trembling as she touched her throat nervously.

"You have to help him, Doctor!"

Sharpe shook his head. "There's really nothing else to be done, Mrs. Hoyt."

Marion Hoyt seemed only then to recognize Allyn and Elizabeth. "He's been hurt," she said pathetically in a child's voice. Then she turned and re-rentered the dimly lighted room. Dr. Sharpe shrugged and shook his head and Allyn and Elizabeth went in behind the woman who was obviously in shock. When Allyn saw his father, he could well understand it.

The visible skin was burned black. His head was swathed in bandages, including a patch taped over his right eye. His arms were wrapped as well. Tom approached the bed carefully and took his father's hand. It was very damp, and his squeeze brought no response. Kenneth's breathing was ragged and shallow. Marion Hoyt had sunk to her knees and remained there weeping, her hands clasped prayerfully. Allyn turned away sharply and stalked from the room. Elizabeth called after him, but he did not stop.

Elizabeth hurried from the room, following him to the alley where she found him standing, staring into the star-clustered sky.

"Allyn?"

"He's not going to make it," he said somberly.

"You don't know that! It will be a while before we . . ."

"He's not going to make it," Allyn said in a distant voice. "They finally killed him—a better man than any of them ever dreamed of being."

Allyn's voice began to rise strongly at the end of the sentence and Elizabeth could feel the anger rising in her husband.

"We don't know what happened, Allyn. It could have been an accident. A lamp turned over."

"We know," Allyn said firmly, turning to take his wife by her shoulders. "We know what happened without having been there, don't we?" He started for the buggy and Elizabeth hurried after him.

"What are you going to do, Allyn?"

"Borrow a gun and kill Judge Benson."

"Tom, no! You can't. Would your father want you to do that or to remain and fight the good cause for him!"

"It has to be done. A man has to do these things." He shook his arm free of her hands and climbed into the buggy. She rushed to the other side and sat beside him.

"What are you doing? You can't go with me."

"I am," Elizabeth said.

"I won't take you into danger."

"Take me!" she began to giggle hysterically. "I wouldn't have anything left if they kill you, if they lock you in prison. Let them kill both of us—that's the easier way for me!"

Allyn looked directly ahead, up the dark alley. A few revelers laughed behind the saloon.

He took an extremely deep breath and wound the reins back around the brake lever. "Don't sit there," he said in a sorrow-roughened voice. "My father is dying. We ought to be beside his bed when it happens."

CHAPTER EIGHT

The tree was as black as sin but brilliant silver stars decorated every branch, dancing through the misty air. Far away the moon awakened lazily from her sleep and lifted dim eyebrows above the horizon.

Where was she?

Shanna came suddenly alert and she sat up sharply. She had been sleeping in the open, under a massive wide-spreading oak tree. God! Where was she? She held her head and then peered around. It was full dark; nightingales crowded the trees, chirping, bounding from bough to bough in bird rituals known only to them.

Oak Knoll. She was on Oak Knoll, and . . . looking to her left through a half-opened eye she could see a house that she took for Wallace Black's. She rose and smoothed her skirt.

Her mouth was full of sandpaper; her eyes ached. A light burned in a window of the house.

Smoke rose in a thin, lazy curlicue from the stone fireplace. Shanna started that way, staggered, and halted, pulling herself together, rehearsing her entrance, her story. This hadn't seemed to present an ordeal when she had been high. Now it seemed like an impossible task.

She took a slow breath and started for the front door of the house.

She knocked, heard muffled voices and muted approaching steps and Tina opened the door to the house.

"Shanna!"

"Hello, kid!" Shanna said cheerfully. "Okay to visit for a while?"

Tina glanced toward the living room where the fire burned brightly. Wallace called out to her, "Who is it, Tina?"

"It's Shanna Adair," Tina answered. "Come in, Shanna. Did you walk all the way down here?"

"I got a ride from Allyn and Elizabeth," Shanna told her. Tina was obviously ill at ease.

That was too bad. Shanna had come on a mission, and she would complete it. She followed Tina into the small living room with its overstuffed furniture—far from new—and braided rug.

Wallace, in stocking feet, peered at her and then rose, smiling hesitantly.

"Shanna. It's good to see you, do you want something to drink?"

"No. No thank you, Wallace." Shanna seated herself without being invited and she leaned back with a sigh. "I'm sorry, I'm bushed."

"Just sit, then," Wallace said.

"I get tired easily still," Shanna said, touching her abdomen meaningfully.

Tina sat on the arm of her husband's chair, hands clasped and waited. She knew Shanna very well. "What has happened, dear?"

"Really? To get right to the point," Shanna said, leaning forward, her eyes intense in the firelight, "I have to go out to Los Angeles again. Brent's business affairs are still in a mess. The bank needs my signature; the beach house is still on the market. The will is being contested by some relatives of Brent's back in New York. I thought our agent was going to handle all this, but he seems, really, nearly incapable of doing his job."

"Quite a mess, huh?" Wallace said, his face sincere and

understanding.

"Quite! Here is the thing," Shanna said, rushing on. "I can't subject little Brent to a trip to the Coast and another back immediately. Then what am I to do with him out there? I can't take him to business meetings and . . . well, I don't know what to do. Mother is too old to take care of him. She does try, but, well, I've seen some lapses of memory when I was a little concerned for the baby."

"What are you asking us to do, Shanna?" Tina Black asked coolly.

"Why, honey," Wallace said, "she wants to know if we can take care of the baby until she gets back from Hollywood."

"Yes, that's it," Shanna said with relief. Tina was shaking her head slowly. "We'd have to think about it, Shanna. Discuss it in private. We can't promise you anything."

"Oh, I know, Tina. That's all I was hoping for. He's really a good baby, and it will be just for a little while."

"When would you be leaving?" Wallace asked.

"I'm waiting for a letter from my agent. It should arrive in a few days."

"Well," he said, "I don't see why we couldn't . . ."

"We'll have to discuss it privately, Wallace," Tina interrupted.

Shanna rose to her feet and put on her most imploring manner, smiling at both of them, but letting her eyes linger longer on Wallace. "If you could possibly . . . I'd be forever grateful."

"Yes," Tina said. "Are you sure you wouldn't like some tea? Or a little something to eat, Shanna?"

"No, really! I couldn't put you out. I'll leave now. But if you can . . . well, I'll let you two decide," she said.

They both walked to the front porch and waved goodbye as Shanna started down the path toward the road. When the door closed, Shanna hoisted her skirts and ran silently back toward the house, standing beside the living room window. She could hear Tina's voice.

". . . I know her. I don't think much of the idea, frankly."

"Honey," Wallace replied. "She is an old friend. A neighbor. She's having a tough time right now. We really must help her out. What kind of friends would we be?"

Shanna backed away from the window, smiling to herself. That was settled then. Tina was a strong woman, but she wasn't going to win this argument with Wallace's generous heart, nor would she push it. Shanna knew both of them very well. Brent was off her hands for the time being.

She dashed homeward, the rising moon lighting her way through the creekside trees. She wondered if Tom had come back with more coke yet. It might yet become a fruitful, satisfying evening.

The Adair house was dark and silent when she reached home. Only a single low-burning lamp in the front window. Maggie's new litter of pups came rushing to meet Shanna. Four months old, clumsy and unrestrained, they tangled themselves together as they ran. One fell on his chin and grunted with surprise. They leaped for her attention, but she was too weary to play with puppies and she shooed them away. Maggie herself arrived around the corner to see what the disturbance was. Her back was mangy, her teats sagged almost to the ground.

"Getting a little old for this, aren't you?" Shanna said. "And where in hell do you find these men?"

"You don't have any trouble, do you?" Tom asked from the darkness of the porch. He was sitting alone on the glider in the shadows of the awning. "A dog'll always find his bitch."

"Bitter tonight, are we?" Shanna asked. Her spirits brightened in a sudden leap as Tom held out a small blue phial to her. She sat, exhausted on the glider, spreading her heavy skirts. "You're a treasure, Tom."

"Yeah. I didn't mean anything—what I just said. You're right, maybe, I'm a little bitter tonight . . . Here—this is free." He handed her his bottle of whiskey.

"You owe me five dollars for that," he said, nodding at the cocaine.

"I know, I know," Shanna said. She drank deeply and gratefully from the bottle, and as Tom watched carefully sprinkled a little powder on the web between her thumb and forefinger and sniffed it deeply. "I was afraid you wouldn't make it," she told her brother, returning the bottle to him.

"I almost didn't. Everybody's in town. Elizabeth, Allyn, Mother, and Dad. Mother's got the baby."

"What happened!"

"They killed Kenneth Jefferson," Tom told her. His eyes were glazed, Shanna could tell even by the poor light.

"No!" Shanna was truly shocked. "Who? Benson and that crowd?"

"Who else?"

"What are they going to do?' she asked in a hushed voice. "The men?"

"Vote," Tom said derisively.

"The Nighthawks, I mean!"

"I know who you mean—they're going to vote. That's what they do these days, those old bold warriors. For myself," Tom said, rising to place his hands on the porch railing and look out at the dark land, "I believe I might just kill Judge Benson and Atoka Boone."

"Tom!" Shanna was astonished. His intent was unmistakable, his words conversational.

"Well, why not? They damn well deserve it and everybody knows it." He lifted his bottle, shrugged, and drank it, peering through the brown glass at the moon now growing smaller and brighter in the high sky.

"Tom?" Shanna asked in a whisper. "When you were in the

Army, did you have to kill people?"

"Yes, dear," he said with a deprecatory laugh. "That was the job, wasn't it?"

"But did you," she asked intently, accepting the whiskey bottle from him, "did you just shoot a lot of bullets at them or did you ever—you know, have to look right in a man's eyes and kill him?"

"I looked right in a man's eyes and killed him." Tom said, remembering, and they both fell silent for awhile.

"Did you go by Lorna Paxton's again?" Shanna asked more lightly.

"I tried to see her. No one was there."

"It certainly wouldn't do much for that quest if you went out and killed Benson and got yourself hung, Tom."

"No," he agreed. "I don't suppose getting myself hung would do much good for anything. But, then again, maybe everyone would be better off if it happened."

"Don't talk like that, you fool!"

"All right." Tom sat on the glider again and closed his eyes briefly. He had at least discarded his uniform. He wore his old red checked shirt and a pair of trousers that seemed too snug on him these days. She could see his mind was still ruminating on the impulse to kill. He was just drunk. It would pass. Benson probably had a dozen bodyguards around him if he had indeed done what Tom believed.

"I'm going to go again, Tom," Shanna told her brother.

"Where?"

"Back to California. This," she waved a hand toward the dark and empty land, "is no place for anyone. There's nothing here, is there?"

"No," he agreed. Tom Adair sat holding the bottle of whiskey between his legs, rocking the glider minutely, buried deep in his own dark thoughts.

Shanna felt compelled to be light. She shoved his shoulder. "Well, for you! Sure. There's Lorna and . . ."

"And what, Sis?" Tom asked deliberately.

"There's Lorna," she said. "That's more than I have here."

"When are you going, Shanna?"

"I'm just waiting for a letter. Then I'll pack up and go West again. I'm going crazy sitting around here. It's all right for Elizabeth, I suppose."

"She's better than we are, Shanna," Tom said in an even voice. "She is better. She wants to fix things—for other people. She and Allyn, they're better than you and I. We're a pair of cowards." He smiled, winked, and raised the whiskey bottle to his lips.

"Oh, give me a drink of that too!" Shanna laughed, "You coward, you!"

Tom was meditative, studying the moon that was slowly glossing the land. "A man could hunt by that moon," he said.

"Once we went after grouse by moonlight, Tom, remember? Dad and Black Jack too, all of us kids went along."

"I remember. That was the winter it was so cold the grouse couldn't fly and we just went out on the ice on Fletcher's Pond and threw nets over them. Practically the whole tribe was there. We got something like two hundred in two nights."

"Right! It was such fun for us kids all bundled up, but the men were dead serious. I felt so sorry for the dumb frozen birds, though."

"I felt sorry for us later," Tom laughed. "Did you ever think a person could eat so much grouse! Mother must have gone mad trying to figure out new ways to prepare them."

"They were good. I remember she would take them and wrap them up in pastry blankets. She told us it was like putting the little birdies in their beds. 'Course you didn't have to pluck them all, you man!" Shanna laughed.

"Yes, well, you never went hunting with Dad. I shot my first deer when I was nine and he made sure I gutted it and packed it home by myself."

"I couldn't do that. I don't like blood, Tom," Shanna said with a shudder.

"No."

Shanna sniffed some more cocaine and again drank from the bottle. They had been dancing around the topic for long minutes—now she asked him directly: "Are you really going to do it, Tom? Go hunting?"

"I think so, Shanna."

"I wish you wouldn't." She only glanced at her brother and then turned dreamy eyes toward the starlit sky. He would do what he wanted. She would do what she must. They were two of a kind.

Shanna had dozed off in the middle of a sentence. She had been talking about playing along the river. The story was something about Jeannie Bear going swimming with naked boys.

Tom never got the end of it. She was snoring now through fluttering lips, her head lolling on her shoulder, looking quite a bit younger than she liked to believe she was. Tom got to his feet, staggered a bit, and kissed her forehead. Then he went into the house and took his .30-30 rifle from the rack, jammed a half a box of cartridges in his jacket pocket, and slowly slipped out of the house into the heavy shadows, the puppies following him along for a quarter of a mile before they got tired and returned home.

The quickest way to the judge's mansion was straight through Tahlequah, but that was where Roy and Sarah were, that was where the Indian police would be watching, and a man with a deer rifle walking down the middle of the street would draw a great deal of attention. He started instead toward The Split. He would circle far behind Judge Benson's house. No man could find him in those hills. The moon was bright enough to find your way if the paths had been walked since boyhood. Tom walked the trails easily by the faint moonlight glow. How many years had he known them? The rifle was light on the sling across his shoulder although he switched it from time to time to prevent a rub burn in the morning. He passed the schoolhouse where Cucumber Jack had unloaded his lumber prior to repairing the roof. Most of it was used stuff, but there was some bright new pine that Tom suspected had been lifted from the sawmill.

He trod on, past Fletcher's Pond and toward The Split. The whimpering behind him caused him to stop, to turn.

One of those stupid long-legged furry pups had followed him for a mile. Tom cursed at it, tossed a stone, and started on. He began to climb the ridge route toward Old Man Hill and The Pines beyond, the route toward the Judge's bloated house on Tahlequah's north side.

The whimpering came to him again and Tom sighed, sat down on a granite boulder, and waited while the four-month-old black and gray pup with the huge feet caught up to him, belly going low to the ground, tail wagging furiously, a trail of pee in the dust behind it.

"Stupid," Tom said, letting the pup maul his fingers with small, needle-sharp teeth and lick madly at his hand with a small, rough tongue. "Come so far you don't know how to get home, do you? Counted on me to take care of you?" The pup rolled over on his back, turning a freckled fat belly up to be scratched.

"Not this time, pal," Tom said, rising. "This walk's way too long for you. You figure out your own way home or figure yourself for a coyote's dinner."

He started away, walking faster, but it did no good. The small pup ran after him, his paws becoming raw from the excursion.

Still, faithfully, it trusted in Tom to provide for it.

"Jesus!" Tom muttered, looking heavenward. "It's always something."

Looking up the trail, he thought of one possible solution to this unwelcome development.

"Come on, pup. I'm going to introduce you to a new friend. If he don't eat you, you'll be okay."

Tom hoisted the pup and, holding it under one arm, he walked the ridge trail toward The Old Man's camp.

"Old Man!" Tom yelled as he approached the camp. Maybe he was dead by now—no one had mentioned him; but there he was, sitting in front of a fire that could have been placed inside a teapot, watching the night and the stars and eternity.

"What have you brought me, Adair?" The Old Man asked in his wavering voice. "A dog, a fine puppy?"

"How do you know that? How do you know who's coming?" Tom asked. He sat down beside the fire, placing his rifle aside. The puppy went immediately to The Old Man to scuffle with his dark, heavily veined hand.

"I know how you walk, Adair. I have heard you walk many times. I know what a pup-dog smells like. Nothing else smells like a pup-dog."

"I want to give him to you if you want him. Or leave him here for awhile."

"I will keep him. He will be a good strong dog."

"Good." Tom rose and The Old Man's hand stretched out. His eyes were bright in the firelight.

"Stay here for awhile too, Adair. You don't want to kill nobody."

"But you could be wrong," Tom said. "There has been an injustice."

"There always is an injustice," The Old Man said. The pup had fallen asleep on his lap.

"You want to kill someone to be rid of trouble—maybe you want to kill yourself, Adair."

"Don't be foolish, Old Man."

"I'm old. Old people are always foolish to the young. Kids are silly; old people are foolish. But we are all part child, part age-old. I think you want to kill yourself. Whatever you do, you better wait until you're sober."

"What makes you think I'm drunk?" Tom grew truculent.

"Pup-dogs smell. Whiskey smells."

"Yeah, I guess so." Tom leaned back on both elbows. "How old are you, Old Man? You have always been here, they say. What's your name, anyway?"

"Old Man." The ancient Indian smiled briefly, deeply. "I am Memory, Adair. A people has to have a memory. I am that."

"What do you remember?" Tom said, almost tauntingly. "They all say you remember buffalo, that you look out there for them to come back."

"Do they? Maybe that is their memory, then. I remember the cool spring in the southern forest lands where our people came from, the lazy creeks wandering through the pine forests where magnolia grew and the raccoon and beaver swam and the puma roamed, and we lived our own lives in a quiet way. All of those things."

"You're crazy." Tom was silent for a minute then asked, "How come I dreamed of you one night. Far away. I was in a war and I thought of you and you said, 'Did you bury this one?' "

"Is that what I said?" The Old Man shook his head. "It was your dream, Adair. Dreams are very powerful, you know. If the dream meant something, only you can decide what it was."

"But it was you!"

"Maybe," The Old Man shrugged beneath his thin blanket. He rubbed the pup's small floppy ears between his thumb and forefinger. "This is a good pup, Adair. Thank you for bringing him to me. I wouldn't kill anyone tonight if I were you. Also," he said, rising, the pup in his hands, "there is a lion who comes around here. Not a big one like the swamp pumas we knew when I was young, but a nice cat. Please don't shoot him either. I leave food out for him. He doesn't want to kill anyone. His family wants him to go home alive. So don't shoot him either."

Then The Old Man left, walking to his crude bark hogan, and Tom sat watching the tiny fire.

He should be on his way. He should take care of the judge and Boone. He yawned and his eyelids dropped heavily. He thought he heard a far-distant puma scream, a puma with blue feathers, but that made no sense. Yet he was only dreaming and he quit fighting it, tugging up the blanket The Old Man had spread over his shoulders as the moon rose higher and silvered the land.

The dawn had been a bleak, quite moody gray, the tendrils of crimson above the eastern hills only a terrible reminder or a spreading foreboding.

The funeral was very small. It was as if no one wanted to be associated with Kenneth Jefferson, his work, his passion, his passing. Elizabeth and Allyn, Sarah and Roy, the inconsolable Marion Hoyt were the only participants. A few observers hung back in the mist of the morning gloom, hats in hands, watching. That was all. They had all forgotten what Kenneth had fought for, it seemed. Or perhaps the instant he was buried he was simply forgotten, as all are. It seems, Allyn said, only the evil are long remembered.

"We have to do something for her," Elizabeth told her husband, meaning Mrs. Hoyt, but there was nothing to be done. They gave her a ride back to town in their buggy and dropped her at the Maybelle Hotel. All offers of assistance were refused.

"I am going home," Marion Hoyt said in a wintry voice. "I

have not seen Ohio for a long time. I should go back to my people in Ohio."

Then she turned and walked up onto the boardwalk and into the shadowed hallway, a tiny, fading woman whose dreams had escaped her.

"Sad," Allyn said as they drove south, out of town. He was watching the townspeople, bustling around about their normal business, hardly a one giving a thought for Kenneth Jefferson who had devoted most of his life to improving their lot. "Oh, well," he said. "Who is really remembered beyond the second or third generation?"

"We'll have to see that he is," Elizabeth said. "In some small way."

Allyn agreed, "I intend to. The first business of the next edition of the *Tribune* is going to be a eulogy. A definitive, and I hope productive, eulogy in that people will be reminded again who holds this county in his greedy grasp."

"Allyn!" Elizabeth gripped his hand. "You are going to continue the paper?"

"It has to be done. To not do so is to betray his memory."

Elizabeth nodded, knowing that he was correct. "Where . . . ?"

"I'll have Cucumber and his sons help me. I can rent a small office in the Elks Lodge. I've already talked to Sonntag about it. Of course, I won't be able to help you at the school as much as we had planned."

"We only have three students, Allyn," she reminded him.

"Yes. Well, that's three more than we had. The newspaper can continue to invite parents to send their children over. A lot of people may not even know it has reopened."

"And so we are playing with fire again ourselves," Elizabeth said.

"And so we are," Allyn said. He was silent for a long while as the buggy rolled on, the light breeze lifting the horse's mane and tail, the shifting mirrors of the creek bright and new in the morning light. "Elizabeth—I intend to run for state senator."

"Allyn! You have said nothing."

"I've been wrestling with the idea. I think I only decided this morning. At my father's graveside when I realized what we will inherit—and deserve to if Judge Benson is elected."

"He'll fight back," Elizabeth said with concern, but Allyn's mind was set.

"Yes, I suppose he will, won't he?"

The bay horse reared up abruptly and darted into the woods despite Allyn's firm grip on the reins and Crazy Man roared past them, tooting his horn, his red car swinging from side to side over the entire road.

"I swear . . . that son of a . . ." Allyn sat trembling. The bay still jerked and kicked nervously in the traces. "I saw him the other night. Driving blind in the dark. He doesn't know how to turn the headlights on, it seems. He shouldn't be allowed on the roads."

"When you are senator," Elizabeth said soothingly, "we shall pass a law that everyone must be licensed to drive."

"Yes." He managed a smile. "When I am the state senator."

Tom awoke to sharp daylight. The sky was a startling blue with only a few high horsetail clouds, wispy and ghostly, in the east. He sat up, throwing the old striped blanket from his shoulders. His head ached abominably. There was a little eager puppy between his legs suddenly, wiggling, wetting, licking. It tried to bark but its little yaps were small and unpracticed.

"He thought you were dead, Adair," The Old Man said. "Does your head hurt? Here," he said, giving Tom a cup of strangely scented herbal tea. "This stuff will help if you didn't drink too much."

Tom nodded, shoved the pup away, and sipped at the tea. The Old Man took his usual position, letting the pup maul his hands. The tea seemed to do some good. Tom felt oddly at peace this morning, his anger faded. Still his head ached.

"Do you know what day this is?" Tom asked.

"I don't know."

"What a 'memory,' " Tom said derisively.

"Well, in my day there was no calendar, you know. I never saw a clock until I was your age. It seemed like a lot of foolishness to me," The Old Man said. "I know when I am hungry. I know when I am tired. If I want to go somewhere, well, I get up and go there as I can. Maybe sometimes I stop for a day or more and fish or just to enjoy a place I have found with a deep pool and fern on the sunny slope. Besides," he said, more enigmatically, "why measure something that doesn't exist?"

"Time?" Tom asked, perplexed.

"Only young people think there is such a thing. The old know there is just swimming in the heavens."

"You are crazy," Tom said, finishing his tea. "In town they'd lock you up."

"Yes!" The old Indian laughed. "Did you hear the cougar last night? I told you he was coming."

"Did he have blue feathers?" Tom asked, wondering immediately why he had said that.

"No, I don't think so. Maybe yours does. Mine is the ordinary sort. He was near to you; he wanted to paw your head to see if it was a melon with hair, good to eat. The pup cried and hid under my blanket. Maybe that was why I thought you might be dead this morning."

"My God! You let a mountain lion paw at me? You could have shot it—you have my rifle!"

"Oh, he found you were no good to eat. If there's an itch on your scalp, that's what it was. You drank so much you slept through it. How could I kill it, anyway? We are brothers."

"Fine, foolish man! I'm your brother too."

"Yes, that is true, but he would not hurt you. He just wondered what you were, why a man was sleeping alone in the open like that. Maybe he thought you were dead and no one had buried you."

"Should've shot the bastard," Tom said, handing his cup back to The Old Man who filled it again with the tea, which had a calming effect.

"No, I do not kill these creatures. When I was a young man I used to hunt all the time. Back in the South. I could walk all day and see a hundred squirrels, a thousand rabbits, fifty deer, a dozen bears: when I was hungry, I took one. Now I don't see so many wild things. We outnumber them. I see ten white hunters trying to shoot one buck deer! I went to a white man's house once—it was raining like cold hell and I wanted to beg for some flour to keep me alive.

"Oh, these people were nice for white people, they let me stand awhile by their fire, but all over this man's wall I saw a hundred sets of antlers, the stuffed head of a cougar with glass eyes. In a case he had a hundred rifles. You would think the man would be fat from eating so much game. He was not fat. He killed for the antlers and the tails. He called them trophies. Dusty dead things now, and now he is gone too and the animals could not provide more young for others to see or to eat when the hunger times come."

"You make me tired with your talk, Old Man," Tom said.

"I believe that. I haven't had so much talk for a long while." He was silent for a moment, rolling the puppy from one spot to the other while the dog snarled and entered a mock-fight with his blanket. "This will be a good dog. You should have kept him, Adair," The Old Man said, tweaking the gray and black puppy's ear.

"Our bitch has had a hundred puppies. We can't keep 'em all."

"I see. Where do you have to go, Adair? You aren't going to kill some more men, I hope?"

"No." Tom was suddenly sure that he would not. How drunk had he been? Did he really have that much indignation and rage against Judge Benson or was he trying to justify something in his own miasmic existence somehow. He no longer knew. The day seemed pleasant; the odd tea had soothed his rancor and replaced his need for drink with a curious calm. He sat with his arms looped around his knees and looked into the distance across the plains.

"What do you see, Adair?"

"Nothing," Tom said with an edge of anger. "I'm not a crazy old man."

"No. There is nothing," his host agreed. "Who has said there cannot be peace in nothing, though?"

"You are crazy."

"I don't know—could be," Old Man said, "All things could be. I am here. Below people are running around drunk, wanting to kill each other. Maybe I am crazy. What do you think, Adair?"

"I don't know. Maybe."

"Do you have a woman, Adair?" Old Man asked.

"I don't know right now."

"Well, you have to go get her pretty soon, Adair. To find out."

"Why? You are crazy—first you tell me there is no such thing as time, now you tell me I have to go find her quick."

"Young women, Adair. They have time in their bodies. When they begin to blossom, their body tells them time has come. When that happens you have to be there or some other young man will."

"If that's the way she wants it, then . . ."

"No! It is the way it is. Her body is made to do this. Listen,

Adair, to what I tell you. It is your time too. Do you want me to tell you why? You will have a little boy, looks just like you. He will not remember to button his pants or wash his hands. He will watch everything you do. He will want to go hunting with you. You will be, for that time, his God. You can do nothing wrong in his eyes. Or there will be a little girl, look just like the woman you love. Her hair all brushed and having a ribbon in it. So tiny and she smiles at you. And you are her daddy, her God, and can do nothing wrong. Then you will not wish to kill, to fight, to wander. You will forget whatever made you so mad."

"An extreme solution," Tom said ironically.

"Extreme? No, it is what happens. Why would you want to kill? Killing because you are angry does not take the anger away. You have tried that already, Tom Adair. Listen to a crazy old man."

Tom walked home through the fading glow of twilight. At the schoolhouse Cucumber Jack and his sons were still working, the striking of hammers, the biting sounds of well-stroked saws loud in the air. He avoided the school and walked on home.

He went in through the front door and hung his rifle on the gun rack. Sarah sat there, before the window lighted by the last glow of day, her sewing in her hand. She looked at him, asking no questions.

"Mother," Tom said, and he went to her, knelt down, and put his head on her lap as she stroked his dark hair in the silence of dusk. When he did rise, he saw his father had come into the room. Roy struck a match and lit the lantern wick.

"A person could go blind in here," Roy said.

Tom rose, wiped his eyes unashamedly, and went to his father. He stuck out a hand and then was pulled into an extraordinarily strong embrace. Roy spoke softly, "Are you home now, Tom? Home from the war at last?"

Tom nodded. "I have to get cleaned up," he said without looking at either of them. "I'll be going over to talk to Lorna Paxton if you don't mind."

He had nearly made it to his room down the dark hallway when a hand reached out and grabbed him, spinning him around. "Tom!" Shanna said. "Where have you been? I've been going crazy."

"I was just out walking the hills, that's all."

"Did you bring anything . . . I need a drink. Tom, I need coke really bad now."

"I haven't been to town. I told you," he said to her through the gloom. Her eyes were bright and searching in the darkness.

"But you're going, aren't you?"

"No." He hesitated. "I have to go see Lorna. It's more important now."

"Tom—" Shanna laughed, "she'll always be there. Later, tomorrow!"

"I have to go now," he told her. "Sober. It's important to me, Shanna."

"What about what's important to me?" she said shrilly. Then she looked to the end of the hallway, stilled her voice. Her fingers were nervously dancing on his arms. "I helped you with Lorna. I need your help, Tom."

"Shanna . . . ?'

"All right! To hell with you, then. Give me ten dollars and tell me who has it. I'll go myself."

"The baby . . ."

"The baby is gone, Tom," Shanna said. "I gave it away. While Mother and Dad were at the funeral. I let Tina Black take him. Now I have to go to California. Now! But I'm sick, Tom. Really! I'm so sick!"

"I can't, Shanna!" He tore her hands from him. "I haven't got any money!"

"Who has it, Tom? I can get it," she said with pathetic eagerness.

"How?" Tom asked with increasing apprehension. Had things gone that far with her?

"I can! A loan. I'll ask Elizabeth."

"Does Mother know—about Brent."

"She doesn't know anything. That's why I have to leave now! That's why I have to keep my courage up—or they will kill me again!"

There were voices in the kitchen now, Roy and Sarah discussing dinner. Tom heard the word "baby." He rifled through his pockets, found three one-dollar bills, and shoved them into Shanna's hand. "That won't be enough for cocaine. You can buy a bottle of whiskey."

"I can get more. Who's got it, Tom?" she pleaded. "Who?"

"Joe-Don Turner," he blurted out. "Ask John Red Fox where to find him."

"John Red Fox is a thief."

"Don't ask him, then!" Tom said too loudly. He heard inquisitive words from the kitchen.

"Listen," he said in a taut whisper, "that's the best I can do, Shanna. That's all I can do." He walked down the hallway to his room, leaving his sister standing there in a quandary. Moments later he heard the back door bang angrily and Tom started that way—maybe he should have . . . but that impulse sagged. He started back toward his room. No more could be done. He would clean up, eat, see Lorna if she would even talk to him . . .

Shanna's door was open when he passed her room heading toward the back door, and a letter, ripped in half, its pieces strewn across the bed and floor, lay there. Tom hesitated. Better to pick it up, he decided. It was certain to be something Shanna wouldn't want Sarah to find. He bent and picked up all of the yellow scraps, looked uneasily at the empty crib, the packed suitcase, half concealed under the bed, and went out.

He closed his door and with a shadow of guilt, pieced together the letter. It was from Hollywood. Someone named Emilio had written. Was that her agent? Tom put the letter aside for a moment, then, gritting his teeth, he lit his lamp and sat to read it.

Dear Shanna,

I don't know what to tell you, really. I never expected to hear from you again after you took the baby and left my house that foggy morning. You could at least have told me you were leaving. We all expect too much of gratitude, it seems.

In answer to your rambling and elusive letter—dear, do they have cocaine back in those dreary hinterlands as well, or was that all alcohol talking? (Which does remind me, I did find out what happened to my silverplate. Hugh Gore returned it—he is a dear! And swore he never knew it was mine, and I believe him. That he only was trying to help you, as strung out as you were.)

I forgive you for that. I just can't quite forgive myself for much. Taking you in was just an attempt at resuscitating my nearly moribund morality, I'm afraid. Dear Shanna—didn't you really know? We all teased you about your age and your back-ground, but you must have known more than you let on. In any event—I was Brent's pimp, you see? Through my studio I would find "possibles" for him. In turn he would pimp to the directors, the producers (well, actually third-tier underlings, nobodies, we let them call themselves whatever they wanted.) Did not Brent and I both tell you how it was we were able to afford these big cars and have the contacts we do? Or try to tell you—you were in such a haze most of the time.

Dear, you know I wasn't making that much money shooting pictures of baking soda. I am sorry—the "commercial model" offer I made you would have turned into something much more tawdry than that as well. The sort of photographs that do not circulate in magazines. But my latent conscience was touched by your incredible naiveté.

As far as finding work out here now? I certainly can't take you in. There is Charles to consider—and he was in a rage the last time I let you stay here, while the baby was arriving. Brent—that was such a terrible idea it was funny—forgive me.

He gave that blond person (what was her name?) the boot and set up with a redhead who turned him into the coppers—I don't even remember what for, I think he beat her up—it's been so crazy out here. He may have gone to jail, I'm not sure. Fred Stein? The man never even knew your name, Shanna. I can't think of a single scrap of hope I could give you. Those who don't know you do not care. Those who did know you no longer care to.

If that is cold, it is my assessment. It would be an utter waste of your life to come back to Hollywood. Wasn't there some clod back there named Wilber or Wallace or something like that whom you had hooked? Maybe you should consider trying your plentiful charms on him again and selling while the market is up.

Late news! Maisie has gotten a film part—second girl in a Gloria Swanson pic. I'm happy for her; she was so patient. Carmen has gone back to Juarez. I think she is going to marry some tortilla merchant; I didn't get the story straight. Anyway, she had her purse full of gringo dollars, well earned after all the pratfalls she took, so she'll be all right too.

I have to go! Charles is knocking at the door. He gets so impatient! I wish you well, Shanna, really. You do have the baby! That is something to appreciate and grow with and do for. Au revoir!

Emilio

Tom dropped the letter and got to his feet. He grabbed his denim jacket from the closet and started toward the front door.

His mother and father were sitting at the kitchen table, drinking coffee.

"Dad, I have to go to Tahlequah. Can I take the roan?"

Roy, surprised, nodded. "If it's important. Take the black. He's quicker."

"I think Shanna has him," Tom said, and his father's puzzlement deepened. Sarah asked, "What about the baby?"

"The baby's all right, Mother. Tina Black has it. Don't ask me any more questions, please, because I don't have any answers. I just think Shanna is in trouble."

"Want me to go?" Roy asked, getting to his feet instantly.

"No, Dad. It's nothing you could help with, believe me. I'm sorry, I have to go." Before the last words were out of his mouth, Tom walked into the living room, took his .30-30 from the rack, and was out the front door, jogging across the yard toward the barn. The black, as he had expected, was gone from its stall. He hurriedly saddled the roan, swung aboard, and started through the moonlight toward Tahlequah.

What was she thinking? What was she doing? Why had she lied to him, the only one in the family who would listen and understand no matter what the trouble?

"Why did I let her down?" he asked himself aloud. He drove the horse on, much faster than the little roan was used to running these days.

Shanna would already be in Tahlequah, in The Alley, a place no decent woman should be.

John Red Fox, Two-Fingers, and the rest of them would be roaring drunk by this time of day.

There was no telling what Shanna would be walking into. Tom, for himself, couldn't care less about any of them, but his sister did not belong back there. He rushed on down the Otter Creek road. All he could hope for was that Shanna had made a leisurely trip of it.

She hadn't, of course. The lure of cocaine had propelled her on faster and faster, whipping the black gelding to a foam.

What was she to do? Not go to Hollywood? Stay here? Admit she had given the baby away? Live in mortification the rest of her life, beaten, humiliated . . . she had to have coke. And whiskey. She could think so much more clearly when she was high, when her mind was above the clouds, deep into the rainbows above where everything was more ordered. And imminently sensible. One just had to ascend to that height, to look back and see how petty all these matters were, how easy it was to transcend care and clarify objectives.

Entering Tahlequah, she slowed the lathered horse and trotted it toward the general store and the alley behind it. What a fantastically ignoble place to encounter salvation.

Leaving the shuddering horse at the rail in front of the general store, she walked into the alley, the black dress she wore leaving her practically invisible in the deep shadows. She knew she should be frightened, but her need overcame her fear. Besides, despite her maturity, Shanna still sheltered some girlish illusions. Among these was that no man in the country would dare lift a hand against Shanna Adair.

Easing her way into the alley she suddenly tripped over a log lying there. What was . . . ? But it was no log, it was a man's leg and a hand shot out and grabbed her ankle.

"Who the hell is that?" the man demanded in a deeply slurred voice. "Can't even sleep in this town no more." Then his fingers told him that it was no man's ankle he had in his grip and he said, "Say! What have I caught?"

Shanna yanked her foot from his grasp and demanded irritably, "Where is John Red Fox?"

"Who wants to know?" The man sat up in the darkness.

"I do, now tell me, will you?"

"Who are ya, lady?"

"My name is Shanna Adair," she announced.

"Adair . . . ?"

"You know, Chivo," another man's voice said. "The famous movie star. Come all the way from Hollywood just to see us. That's thoughtful, wouldn't you say?"

From the darkness another man approached. He reeked of whiskey, vomit, and other excrement. "Is that you, Two-Fingers?" Shanna asked.

"See, they don't forget me," Two-Fingers Catawba Arnie said, "even when they get famous."

"Where is John Red Fox?" Shanna asked, feeling just a little edgy now. "It's important. I need to see him."

"Maybe we don't know," a third man said. Shanna knew him as well. It was a half-breed they called K-Bar, for a Texas ranch he had once worked on.

"Maybe you don't," Shanna said, her chest growing a little tighter. All three men were now on their feet and closing a circle around her. "That's all right then." K-Bar took two more steps toward her. "Tell him to back up, Two-Fingers. Maybe he doesn't know who I am."

"Oh, I know," K-Bar said. "Adairs, sure. Bunch of famous Nighthawks. Big men in their day, huh? Roy Adair—I seen him. Looks like a little old gray-haired jailbird."

"Wait just a minute," Shanna warned. "Talking like that won't do you any good in this county."

"No, her brother-in-law might write a nasty piece about you in the newspaper," Chivo said.

"Oh, that's right, paper done burned down." He put his face inches from Shanna's, but she refused to back away. She was frightened enough to turn and run, but something kept her dignity and fearlessness intact. Chivo grabbed her wrist and twisted her resolve. She tried to pull away from him.

"That don't leave no one to scare us except her drunken

soldier brother," Chivo said. "Give him a bottle and he'd sell his own sister out."

"Or maybe," Tom said from the head of the alley as he cocked his lever-action Winchester, "he'd come along after her and blow your brains out."

There was dead silence in the alley. Along the late street a buggy went past, trace chains chinking. A dog yapped across town.

"You want me to start shooting or you want to clear out . . . not you Two-Fingers. You others, get! Now!" Tom shouldered the Winchester Model 94 and the two drunks fell over each other racing for the end of the alley. "Now, Two-Fingers, my sister asked where is John Red Fox?"

"He's right back by the meadow. Hell, Tom, we were just funnin'!" Catawba Arnie said. He stepped forward, grinning, his arms outstretched. Tom brought the walnut stock of the rifle up under his chin and slammed the man back. Two-Fingers fell to the alley and stayed down, blood running from his broken mouth.

"Now get out of here!" Tom hissed at his sister. He stood over Two-Fingers, his chest rising and falling.

"Why should I now?" Shanna asked like a spoiled child. "You've eliminated that problem. I know where John Red Fox is."

"Sis! I'm not kidding. No man likes to be humiliated. Not even bums like these. They'll get their second wind, get a little more courage under their belts, and they'll be back. Believe me, I know."

"By then I won't be here, will I?"

"By then—damn you, Shanna!—I won't be here either."

He glared at her for one minute out of the dark mustiness of the alley shadow, then gave it up. "Here," he said, jamming three folded dollar bills into her hand. "I found these in my room."

"Thanks, Tom," she said with true appreciation, softening Tom's anger.

"Yeah. Go do what you have to do . . . Shanna, I know why now."

"Why what, Tom?" she asked brightly.

"I read Emilio's letter. Don't you want to come home with me and talk it through with the folks? We can think of something. Besides, you told Tina you just wanted them to babysit for a couple of days, right? We can get the baby back. No one has to know."

"No one but me, Tom," Shanna said and her voice trembled just a little. Tom waited, but it was a pointless hope. She kissed him goodbye and walked off toward the foot of the alley, toward the meadow where John Red Fox and his magic powder could be found.

The breeze that fluttered past the white lace curtains in the parlor of Judge Benson's house also helped to dilute some of the noxious blue cigar smoke hanging in the air like wispy platters. Judge Benson himself was not a smoker; in fact, he deplored cigars and was already wondering how Emma, his maid, was going to rid the furniture and wall hangings of the stink. Larry Morrisey, however, was addicted to the things and Benson was not going to say a word to alienate the state committee chairman. He and his associate, Swillinger, the able publicist, were going to get Benson elected to the state senate. A little stale cigar smoke could be suffered for that assistance.

"I am worried about this Allyn Jefferson sweeping this county, Judge Benson. He does in fact control the only newspaper of any influence," Morrisey was saying. A stout man with legs so thick that he seemed incapable of crossing them, he sipped at his brandy.

His white, unmanaged eyebrows were arched as he studied Benson with clear, searching blue eyes.

"Is that ethical?" Swillinger asked. A narrow, impatient man who was constantly shifting positions, his twitching made Benson uneasy. "In effect editorializing for himself?"

"It's been done before," Morrisey said, "besides, ethical or not, it's legal."

"He's already a sympathetic figure," Swillinger said, thinking out loud. "Death of his martyred father, whatever . . . has he ever actually accused anyone of deliberately killing Kenneth Jefferson?"

"No, but it's been implied," Morrisey said, relighting his cigar. "My information is that no one did actually try to kill the man, though it appears the fire was intentionally set," Benson told his guests.

"Okay," Swillinger said with nervous hand gestures. "Popular local family. Full-blood Cherokee as I get it?' Benson nodded. "We can assume then that he's got that vote locked."

"Whites? How divided are they down here, Benson?"

"My people assure me that most of them can be convinced that having a state senator who would continue to fight for tribal sovereignty in the capitol is contrary to their best interests."

"Then we have the breeds and the Negro vote undecided, right?" Benson nodded. "So then—can we begin a newspaper campaign of our own? I understand this Jefferson is starting from scratch. Some of his fonts were even melted and new ones have to be ordered . . . all that gives us time, to my mind," the publicist said. He leaned back, apparently pleased with his suggestion.

"It could have been done," Morrisey agreed, "a few months

ago. Now we're fighting against time. At least Allyn Jefferson has a printing press. We don't even have that. Let alone an editor—who also knows the Cherokee language and is ready to move to Tahlequah for what any idiot would recognize as a short-term operation."

"It is time, gentlemen," Morrisey said, crushing out his cigar in a delicate teacup and grunting to his feet. He walked to the window, slammed it shut, and stood staring out the window at the wind-shifted walnut trees. "We don't have a lot of time. We need control of this county, Judge Benson. We are counting on you to pull your weight here."

"I certainly intend to," Benson said huskily.

"Is Jefferson absolutely certain he wishes to be a state senator?" Morrisey asked.

"Of course, Larry." Benson looked surprised but wary.

"I mean, Judge, is there no way he could be convinced that this is not the proper way to channel his ambitions? To have it demonstrated to him that perhaps a political career may not be in his best personal interests."

Judge Benson nodded his grim understanding. "I suppose I know people who might be able to talk to him, to convince him that he is in an area he might not fully understand, that he might not fully comprehend the hazards of such a life for the uninitiated."

"I suggest that you have these people talk with him, Judge Benson. Make sure they speak bluntly. We have little time for subtlety at this late hour."

It was too cold. It was too dark. There was only the faintest silver of the stars, tiny and distant, glimpsed through the river fog. Shanna missed a step and fell roughly onto her shoulder. She lay beside the creek road for a minute, taking in slow breaths. Then, rising again, she wiped her hair from her eyes and went on, holding her side.

She felt sick. She felt terribly sick and weak. She had not eaten that she could recall, yet she had thrown up plenteously along the way. It was all the fault of that stupid black horse. It must have shaken its reins and gotten free—unless someone stole it. That made her angry briefly. It then occurred to her that perhaps she just had forgotten where she had left it tied. She thought about going back to Tahlequah, but turning around she couldn't even see a faint glow from the town. She must have been halfway home. At least halfway. Maybe Tom had taken the horse with him.

She fell again and quit thinking about the problem of the horse. She landed on one knee and one elbow. Rolling over onto her back on the dewy grass, she felt she might as well stay there all night. Maybe by morning . . . no! By morning she would just feel like oozing hell! She unbuttoned three buttons on her dress and reached into her camisole. Her hopes lifted a little.

She found the paper cone John Red Fox had put the coke in. Was it empty? No, it couldn't be, she reasoned. Why, then, would she have saved it?

Sitting up, she carefully opened the paper and peered at it by the feeble starlight. She couldn't tell what it contained, if anything. Putting it directly to her nose, she took three mighty whiffs, feeling the rush of cocaine. She waited a minute, rubbed a moistened finger around the inside of the now-depleted supply, and licked it off. Rising, she started on again, feeling more buoyant. She had neglected to rebutton her dress and her hair hung down unrestrained on the right side of her head.

That was just enough to get her home, Shanna decided. Just enough. Then she would find Tom—he always had a bottle— and she would be able to sleep until morning. By then she would have come up with some sort of idea of what to say to her parents.

The baby! She had to get the baby back. Tonight. Tom was right; Brent was all she had left just now. Her mother and father would believe them if she said Tina had just been watching it for the evening . . . because. Because Shanna just felt she needed a little break from it. Certainly.

Why wouldn't they believe that?

All right, how far was it to Oak Knoll? What time was it now? It didn't matter if Tina and Wallace were asleep. She would have a story to give to them by the time she reached their house. She hurried on, her spirits much higher. She would work everything out eventually. She had just planned this move too quickly, counted on people who obviously didn't give a damn about her, the traitors.

There was a strange rumbling behind her and Shanna stopped and looked back down the road, but there was nothing there. She stumbled on. She could tell Tina . . .

Shanna heard a roaring sound, a shuddering, the whine of metal on metal, and the car rushed out of the darkness to slam into her body with the force of a dozen sledge hammers. She was tossed to one side, down the creek embankment. She tried to fight through the agony of pain for consciousness, but the battle was already lost and she tumbled into a well of blackness.

Crazy Man had tried to swerve at the last second, but still he had barreled into the woman in black. He had careened off the road and slammed his car into a sycamore tree where it rested now, front wheels propped off the ground, spinning at forty miles an hour. He had bashed his head on the dashboard and blood was in his eyes. Dazed, the Creek knew something must be done. He had killed a woman! Damn his laziness for not having learned to use the headlights. He had stayed out later than he intended, drank more than he meant to, and decided to drive home anyway. If he went fast enough, he had reasoned, he could beat the setting sun, but the sun had gone on and he kept his foot down on the accelerator, driving wildly down the Otter Creek road, swerving from side to side, sometimes losing sight of the road entirely as he continued to steer with one hand and tried to turn on the unfamiliar headlights with the other.

"The woman!"

He leaped from the open car, fell to his hands and knees, and crossed the road, scrambling down the river bank to where she lay inert and huddled. He approached the small figure fearfully, cautiously, and prodded her with his fingers. She did not move. He could not see her breast rising and falling with respiration. Her legs were bent at crazy angles under her skirt.

He got to his feet and wailed to the sky, stood breathing heavily, his shoulders trembling.

Then he started up the road at a dog trot, searching for help on that lonely stretch of road.

CHAPTER NINE

The first house Crazy Man had come to was the Adair farm. Gibbering, shaking, he had told his story, pointing up the road. Before he had finished, Roy had his boots on and was rushing from the house toward the barn. Sarah stood holding her throat, fighting back tears.

They both knew who it was. They could hope not, but they both knew. Women alone did not walk the Otter Creek road at night, not usually. And Shanna had been dressed in black.

They had found her crumpled and unmoving, lying on the dark grass at the river's edge. Roy had carried her to the buckboard and they had driven steadily, quickly to Tahlequah where they roused Dr. Sharpe from a heavy sleep and followed him to his surgery.

Tom had been home, found the hastily scrawled note, and returned. Roy only nodded to him.

Sarah took his hand as he sat beside her. None of them spoke, none of them slept until with dawn coloring the eastern sky, Dr. Sharpe appeared, rolling down his sleeves, his face drawn and pale. As one, the family rose.

"Well?" Roy asked tersely. The doctor shook his head slightly.

"She'll live, Mr. Adair," Sharpe said and Sarah released a breath she hadn't realized she'd been holding. Sharpe added uncomfortably, "I don't believe she'll ever walk again, though. Her legs are too badly damaged. Perhaps another doctor, with better facilities, could give you a better prognosis. For now . . ."

He pulled out his pipe, swung open the door, and lit it, saying without turning back to face them, "I did what I could."

Sarah's words rushed out, "I'm sure you did. We all know that, Dr. Sharpe. And maybe . . ."

The doctor turned toward her and the expression in his eyes cut off any real hope. All he could say as if it were any consolation was, "I didn't have to take her legs off, at least. For a while there . . . I didn't have to take them off." Then he went out into the dawn-lit alley to stand by himself, puffing his pipe, pondering a physician's constant limitations in the battle with mortality.

It was almost two weeks before Shanna could be taken home. Allyn and Elizabeth took her in a borrowed wagon with a mattress in the bed. Sarah had cleaned and brightened Shanna's room, adding flowers, new linen and bedspread, putting up new frilly blue curtains on the window. Shanna noticed none of this as they placed her in her bed and the family gathered around. She was silent, her eyes distant. There was absolutely no way to know what she was thinking. She would talk to no one, not even Tom. She asked for no food, no drink, and was content to let them do as they liked with her. The doctor came every few days and pronounced her as fit as could be expected.

At the kitchen table over coffee, Roy looked toward Shanna's room and asked the doctor, "Are you sure she can speak? She hasn't uttered a word since we brought her home."

"She can," Sharpe said. "It's the shock still. Maybe she doesn't really recognize everyone—perhaps she no longer feels there's a point in conveying a thought."

"I don't understand that," Roy Adair said. "She knows we are her family. We would do anything for her."

"Then at this point," the doctor suggested, "it is probably best to let her maintain her silence."

Tom was sitting on the small back porch where the shade still lingered into early afternoon, mending a piece of harness with rawhide and a heavy needle. He heard the buggy approaching, squinted into the sunlight, and recognized the driver. He called over his shoulder to his sister. "Elizabeth! You'd better come out, we have company."

Elizabeth, who had been doing Shanna's laundry on this day before school began again, appeared behind the rusted screen, wiping her hands on her apron.

"Who is it?" she asked.

"Tina Black."

"Oh, my!"

"Oh, my is right. That's why I called you, Sis. You can handle this. I haven't an idea what to say." He started to leave, placing his work aside on the bench, but Elizabeth came out onto the porch.

"Oh, no you don't! You're not deserting me now," Elizabeth said, grabbing the back of his belt.

They waited, standing side by side in the shade of the awning as Tina drove her buggy to the porch.

Tom stepped from the porch to take the reins and loop them around the hitchrail, patting the fine sorrel gelding Wallace had purchased for his wife. He saw the basket on the floor of the buggy, a small hand lifted above the blue blanket.

"Hello, Tina," Tom said. He helped her down from the buggy. She smiled and walked to the other side of the vehicle to pick up Shanna's baby and carry it in her arms to the porch.

"My, it's warm. Surprisingly warm," Tina said, seating herself on the wooden bench.

"It is, isn't it?" Elizabeth said. "Would you like something cool to drink?"

"Not just now, no, thank you."

Tom had stepped back to the porch and now, with his hands in his hip pockets, legs crossed at the ankles, he leaned against one of the uprights, smiling meaninglessly. He kept giving Elizabeth nudging looks; someone had to get to the point of the visit sooner or later.

"May I hold the baby, Tina?" Elizabeth asked.

"Oh, of course! You are his aunt, after all!" Tina handed the little boy over and Elizabeth, unwrapping his blanket, let Brent take her finger and grip it. She smiled down thoughtfully.

"What has happened," Tina said in a rush, "is that we thought maybe having her baby with her would help Shanna to get well quicker, encourage her, that is."

"That is very thoughtful of you," Elizabeth said. "Truthfully, she can't take care of him right now," she said, handing the baby back to Tina.

"Well—at least she'll want to see him, I'm sure." Tina sighed, "Maybe I am thirsty."

Tom said, "I'll get some lemonade for you," and went into the house.

"The truth is, Elizabeth, we have gotten used to having the baby around already. Wallace loves him. I . . . ." she turned her eyes down, "haven't been able. I don't know if I will ever have a child of my own."

"I'm sorry."

Tom had re-emerged with a glass of cool lemonade for Tina. She thanked him and said, "To tell you the truth, we—no, I should say I, Wallace never doubted her—thought that Shanna was meaning to go to California never to return and just decided to give the baby away."

"Oh, no," Elizabeth said, "I'm sure not!"

"Of course not," Tom chipped in. "She just had some business to take care of. She knew you would take good care of the baby while she was gone."

"You have always been her best friend," Elizabeth said to Tina who was rocking the baby, her expression worried.

"Well, for awhile I was put out," Tina said, "because I thought that, you see. Then as the days passed, I prayed I was right—that we'd just get to keep him and raise him as our own. Now," she said, tears brimming from her eyes, "I just don't know what to do. Wondering from day to day! Oh, Elizabeth, what should we do? Tom?"

"Nobody can decide but Shanna," Elizabeth said. "She just won't communicate about anything. Knowing that her legs are crushed and feeling that her future is blank and pointless—especially as concerns Hollywood and the films—she doesn't really seem to want to concern herself about life anymore."

"That's what I mean," Tina said carefully. "Does she want . . . would having the baby around help her to get well; or would she rather we continue to take care of him . . . ?"

"And for how long?" Elizabeth said with understanding. "To have her suddenly change her mind after months, years even?"

"Yes," Tina said, thankful to Elizabeth for understanding. "Now, of course, the baby wouldn't know. But after a period of time . . . I am just confused, Elizabeth. I wish she would talk and tell me what is best for her, best for Brent."

"We can try asking," Elizabeth said. "I don't know what else to say."

"Your mother and father have a say in this too."

"I know Mother. She would understand." Elizabeth glanced at her brother. "Tom?"

"You talk to her, Sis," Tom said. "It's more a woman's duty . . . you know what I mean."

"All right," Elizabeth said, rising.

"Should I come too? Bring the baby?" Tina asked.

"No, I don't think so. Not just yet," Elizabeth said.

She said that because no one who had not seen Shanna lately could enter that dark and airless room without being shocked at the figure propped up on the pillows of the bed. Shanna had become only a memory of a woman, outside of time, a creature of the darkness without a voice or ambition, without life, though her heart pumped and her eyes, dark and deep, followed any movement around her.

Elizabeth entered the room, doing so quickly, careful not to let too many seconds of daylight into the cavern where her sister lay motionless, the drapes drawn. A soundless, lifeless tomb for the living. Elizabeth forced a smile, added some mock cheeriness, and walked to the chair beside the head of Shanna's bed.

"Hello, dear! Feel like going outside for a while? It's a clear bright day. A picnic day. Remember when we girls used to have our little picnics over by the duck pond? How serious we were with our dollies and cookies and tea. Those were glorious days, weren't they?"

Shanna had not so much as moved a finger, had not smiled, frowned, acknowledged that she was being spoken to. Elizabeth went on with sham anger. "The doctor thinks you ought to get up, you know. Your blood is just pooling in your butt, Shanna! Air and sunshine are what you need."

Raising no response with her mock tirade, she went on, approaching her subject slowly.

"Tina Black is here. She'd like to talk to you." There was a slight negative movement of Shanna's head. "Come on!" Elizabeth encouraged brightly. "Tina Roberts! How long have you two been best friends? Forever."

Shanna stared straight ahead. Elizabeth threw away caution and leaped ahead. "She wants you to see the baby. She wants to know if you want Brent to stay with you. She doesn't know if she's supposed to keep him or for how long. She's afraid you'll get well and want him back when he's old enough to make it very hard on him. What can I possibly tell her? You have to do it, Shanna. He's your son!"

Shanna's jaw moved. The illusion was that of a long unused door creaking open. She glanced once at her sister and then returned her gaze to the ceiling. Her words were clear, precise, and absolute.

"Tell her to go away. I do not have a son. I never have had a baby. Whoever says that is a liar. Tell her to go away and never come back!"

"Shanna!" Elizabeth was shocked and yet pleased. Shanna had not spoken since the accident.

Now she was at least communicating. "We have to discuss this. He's such a good little boy, a perfect baby. Let's at least delay the decision until we can talk it through, right? The decision is up to you, of course, but let's talk about it. Later, if you're tired now. All right? Shanna?"

The cajoling, the coaxing did no good whatever. Shanna would not say another word. She closed her eyes and drifted away into her dream castles, wherever they were, whatever they meant to her silent world. Silver, silent, and doomed.

Frustrated, Elizabeth went out onto the porch. Tina looked up anxiously. Tom watched her with hooded, expressionless eyes.

"She would appreciate it if you could continue to watch Brent for awhile, Tina."

"Can I talk to her?"

"She is very tired. She's fallen off to sleep again."

"Do you think . . . ?" Tina asked anxiously.

"I think that she will give up the baby, Tina. She just doesn't feel well enough to take care of him."

"I understand," Tina said, her face a mixture of anxiety and hope. Elizabeth took two steps and hugged her.

"Maybe you don't, honey. But it will be all right. Really. Shanna knows you love the baby. She only wants to do the right thing for everyone."

Tom helped Tina back into the buggy, holding the horse's bridle as she arranged herself and the baby. Then Tina waved cheerfully and turned the rig toward Oak Knoll and home, leaving Tom and Elizabeth on the porch, arms around each other's waists. When she was out of sight and the dust from the buggy had settled, Elizabeth lifted her eyes to Tom and asked, "God, when did we become such liars?"

"I don't know." Tom grinned, "For people who are new at it, though, I think we did a pretty good job!"

Elizabeth stood on the porch of the tiny schoolhouse ringing the hand bell, watching the last of her fifteen students scurry toward it. "Old Mrs. Jefferson," she had heard one of the young girls call her the other day and she was struck by it, by the rapid rush of time. Yesterday, the blink of an eye ago, she had been the child and Marion Hoyt had been "old Mrs. Hoyt."

Elizabeth smiled and turned toward the schoolroom, the students quieting as she entered. She caught a glimpse of herself in the window panes. Allyn had finally convinced her to let her hair grow past her shoulders, but it did not suit her. Bobbed, she looked as if someone had just taken a pair of shears, grabbed a handful of hair, and cut it all in one stroke. Wearing her glasses—which were becoming more and more necessary, she looked, she felt, like a strange, gawking, blinking, confused undergraduate. Her black hair was now long enough to pull into a bun, but it seemed to make her look more "school marmish" than ever. Even now, from time to time, she could envy Shanna who had known ways to somehow wring out her exquisite beauty, even though a comparison of photographs would show the sisters had very similar facial and physical characteristics. It was a residue of girlhood, Elizabeth knew, some jealousy that would probably remain forever—Allyn told her always that she was every bit as beautiful as Shanna had ever been, and that was enough. Even if he was lying through his teeth!

"This morning," she said, facing the class. "The first and second graders will please take out your math books . . . Just a minute, please."

Elizabeth smiled. Her oldest student was just arriving on horseback, still dirty from working the nightshift at the lumber-mill, books in his grimy hand, eager apology on his bucktoothed mouth.

"I'm dam . . . sorry, Mrs. Jefferson. I was working overtime."

"That's perfectly all right, Mr. Bird. Try to see it doesn't happen too often. Now then," she went on as Billy Bird squeezed his lanky frame into one of the small desks, "as I was saying: the first and second graders . . ."

Bill remained behind after school was out and the young ones had gone screaming out into the bright light of freedom. He was in the doorway, books in hand, shoulder against the frame.

"Elizabeth?"

"Yes, Bill?"

"I got a friend at the mill. He wants someone to help him with a problem. I figured if you and Allyn can't, nobody will."

"What kind of problem?" Elizabeth asked.

"Well, the government took his land for an oil allotment. They owe him a percentage for the last five years. They ain't give—given—him a thing, and he don't understand it. No one understands it. What can he do? Go to Benson's court? He wants to write to the government direct, Elizabeth. Can you help him?"

"They've just cheated him out of his oil allotment! Is that what you mean?"

"That's the way it seems, Elizabeth. He don't know what to do."

"Well, sure, bring him by the newspaper office or here, and . . ."

"He's here now, Elizabeth. He been waiting for school to let out."

"He's been here all day! Billy, you should have told me earlier."

"I suppose," Bill said with some shame, "but he didn't want to interrupt your schoolin' the kids."

Elizabeth shoved Billy out the door, "Well go get him now, you big goat! Let me talk to him."

She saw Billy Bird go toward the oak grove and watched as he gestured and in a few minutes he emerged with a small older man with hunched shoulders and a knobby, broken nose.

He kept his eyes turned down as he approached the school and Billy practically had to drag him up the steps and onto the porch.

"He's kinda scared, Elizabeth. Scared they'll come and beat him up for complainin', but he don't know what to do—his family needs taken care of."

"Of course." She put out a hand. "I'm Elizabeth Jefferson."

"Robert Winterbuck," the old man said, keeping his eyes down as he took her hand in his gnarled, weather-cracked grip. "They won't give me none of what they promised, Miss. The Texans, I mean. They chased me off my own land with rifles. I talked to this here Atoka Boone who is supposed to be our law and it was like talkin' to the back end of a jackass. I just want to write a letter to the Agency for Five Tribes—those are the fellows who are supposed to help us out."

"All right, let's go up to my desk. Pull out a chair and think of what you want to say," Elizabeth said.

"I know what I want to say, if you just spell it down for me. Write it just as I tell you, Miss, so they will know its come from me. Then I can get the help I need."

"All right," Elizabeth said, and she settled behind her desk, dipping her pen into the ink well. "Go ahead and tell me what you want to write."

The old man sat staring at his hands for a moment, then he nodded his head sharply and began, Elizabeth's pen trying to keep up with his unhappy torrent of words.

Robert Winterbuck began his letter:

"I will write to beg advice. I want to know all about my royalty and I will find out soon how my oil wells are producing or find out about all the runs.

"There is something wrong or else crooks might have cause of it. I hope you fellows will look into it and find out, please. I suppose to know all about my place, my own land, and here I don't even know.

"I believe there is a crook somewhere, I can't locate him, so I beg you agents with all my heart to help, please. You know cannot trust a thief, a liar, not even a robber or an outlaw, but I can trust my own kind, the good people. I need little money.

"I wish I could get my money soon when I really need it. You guys want to hurry up a little and whip up and send me some money please. I want you to mail my checks every first of each month or send it every second. I work mighty hard for my own money every day. I work until I have all kinds of boils and carbuncles and sores of every kind, but I do not get my government money. I love you men just same as I love my own country and all my people. I love you all same as I love the stars and stripes. I love America with all myself. I cannot love or serve my America and salute my flag enough. I am the true American on all the Earth. Well, I hope you all would send all my money please. And I want you to track of my land and my oil wells too, all about my farm and my royalties. I ought to be a rich Indian now. I need a new house on my homestead so that when I got married I can take my wife to my own house. You fellows

look into it. I am yours for everlasting with great loves and wishes."

"It is so sad. There is no end to it," Elizabeth said, bowing her head. She sat with her shoes off in the plush red chair, watching Allyn as he re-read Robert Winterbuck's letter. "He was so sincere it breaks my heart, Allyn. How many people are there out there, sincere and trusting? We used to wonder why your father kept those massive files on mismanagement of tribal funds, the allotment cheats—now, I wonder how many, many millions of dollars have been withheld or simply stolen. I wonder, sometimes, if the fire wasn't started to destroy those records. Letters like this one."

Allyn walked to her, handed her back the letter, which Elizabeth folded most carefully and put into an addressed envelope. "And where will you end up?" she said to the letter as if it were a living thing.

"It has to end. It must end," Allyn said strongly. With his glasses now removed, standing in front of the sundown-reddened window, his profile was as sharp and bold as that of any ancient Indian warrior, Elizabeth thought. And he had as much to fight for.

"Read this one," Allyn said, handing her a letter with scorch marks on the border, "I managed to save this from my father's burned desk. It's from a Creek Snake. You'll notice he writes not Oklahoma, but Indian Territory."

Okema, I.T.
Secretary of Indior
DEAR STEPFATHER,
    I request you a few reasonable words to tell me something about Wilson Jones and John Jonas was sent to Washington as delagates for Creek Nation and they word tell sun down and had the Bill Pass two houses. Bill was an old treaty of 1832. If

the Bill was Pass the houses, please send me a copy of it. Well you the man looking over Poor Indians. What have you find out about and what you gone to do about it. Are you look after them or you wont do it. Are Have you don Report on it. If you did, in this matter do write me about it. I am welcome to your works. If you have take care of the Poors, I'm respecting was this. Yours all had said the home of the Indians be west of Arkansas River. This is what your all have said.

In the treaty your have syned in the year of 1832, June 9. This treaty will be life as long as the sun rise and go down and as long as grass grew. And as long as the sky don't fell to the earth. As long as the water runs. The home of Indians will be there for ever. The big flat bottom land of West bas of Arkansa River. To-day the sky is still in the air yet, and grass grew yet, and water run yet. In regard this matter. In mistaking write. But you man know all this matter. So fill out what I want and answer. I remain hoping to hear in earliest date. Yours ever.

Respect

P.S. Answer this letter and tell all about what I ask. I'll be much suprized.

"Oh, Allyn!" Elizabeth said. She was near tears. "What can we ever do for all of them!" Allyn was seated on the arm of the red chair and her head was against him, his strong arm around her. "We have come into the fight so late. It seems it is already over."

"Only when we say it is, dear. Only when we surrender."

Elizabeth removed her spectacles and looked up at her husband through the blur of tears and the haze of her uncorrected vision. "Remember, Allyn," she said, "I asked you not to go into politics, pleaded nearly. They might hurt you, is what I said."

"Yes."

"I was wrong. These people have no one to fight for them. With one voice in the senate . . . I am on your side, whatever you decide. We cannot let them down; they are our family too. We have to work on."

"Even in a doomed cause?"

"Is that what it is?" she asked.

"I don't know. My father didn't believe so."

"Did he think that, or did he know it was just, won or lost? Won or lost, Allyn, we have to fight for what is right as long as we are able."

"Our cause, won or lost?" he asked with a smile.

"Yes. Won or lost," Elizabeth said and he leaned over and kissed her lips, turning down the lamp with his free hand. There was a time to fight, the wise men said, and a time to love.

"I haven't a bloody idea in the world suddenly," Tom admitted. He kept his hands on Lorna's waist as she perched on the low bough of the sycamore where they had talked so many, many days ago. "I used to at least think I knew what I was doing, where I was going. Now—I haven't got a clue and it's starting to scare me."

"And you want me to go with you? Into this mystery? No, Tom," Lorna said shaking here head. "No woman would. You have to figure it out. Have some idea. A reckless dream, a small, everyday nothing of a plan—it doesn't matter—but some idea of what you are going to try. Then maybe a woman . . ."

"You!"

"Then maybe a woman would agree to marry you and follow your plan through to the end."

Tom looked off across the silver water. The sun cast an exquisite golden lace against the ground beneath the trees. "Would she?" he finally asked.

"I would think so, Tom. Yes."

He took her and lifted her from the bough and kissed her deeply and lay her down softly against the dark earth and new grass, stroking her gently, his eyes growing deeper. Lorna looked into his eyes and smiled.

"No," she said.

"No, what?" he asked as he lifted his leg over hers, their thighs meeting in warm agreement.

"Just, no. Once bitten, Tom . . ."

"You're not shy," he said, trying to lighten the moment, but the moment had already passed and he knew it. "Lorna," he said, sitting up. "I need a good woman to guide me. You say a woman needs a future to look toward. Which has to come first? Can't you trust me? You do love me," he said. It was half a question, which her smile answered wordlessly. "I have to do something to prove my love for you! That's not trust and love," he said angrily.

"Isn't it?" Lorna asked and he softened again, stretching out beside her, kissing her gently.

"I guess it is," he said. "I guess so."

"Then?"

"You're a tough bargainer, Lorna Paxton!" Tom said, laughing.

"Yes, I am. Well?" she asked, teasing his lips with her finger.

"Sure you don't want to live on Wigwam Island with me?"

"Pretty sure," she answered. "We're getting a little too old for that, Tom. I don't care to be Mrs. Huckleberry Finn." She was silent for a few moments. "I'm not asking you for much. If you can't do it, I understand. I'll always love you."

"But not marry me?"

"Make a movement, Tom. Any small movement. Shake the war off and start a new life—any kind of life, and I will be with you as a wife, thick or thin, till death."

"Do you mean it?" he asked very seriously and her head

moved just a fraction of an inch.

He kissed her then and got to his feet and Lorna, sitting up, asked him, "Are you leaving me so soon?"

"Yes."

"But why, Tom? It's early yet."

"Because I'd rather have you forever than spend an extra hour with you, Lorna Paxton. I have things to do." And then he leaned over, kissed her once again, and started up the path toward the Adair farm while Lorna sat watching, a guileless smile on her lips.

Tom swung open the front door and entered the house. "Elizabeth! You here still?"

"Just barely," his sister said, emerging from Shanna's room, pinning her hair up. "I'll be late for school if I don't get out of here. Try explaining that to tardy students. Look, I've changed Shanna's bed and given her soup and . . ."

"Have you sent your mail into town yet?" Tom interrupted.

"No. Billy Bird takes it after class usually," she answered.

"All right, then." Tom said. "I just want to write a letter. Do you have an extra stamp?"

His actions were frenetic. He was digging through the kitchen drawers, searching for paper and pen, envelope.

"Tom!" Elizabeth laughed. "What in the world are you doing!"

"Can't find anything is this damned house," he said, opening and slamming a couple of drawers shut. Elizabeth watched and waited, repressing a smile.

"Anything I can help you find?" she asked.

"Well, for starters—where is that damned letter from John Trout? I thought I might write him a letter."

"What's the rush, Tom?" she asked and Tom knew she was teasing and it just didn't matter. "After all this time, I mean . . ."

"Elizabeth—quit being a sister and be a pal. Where in the hell is that address? I need it."

"You've made up your mind, Tom?"

"Yes!" He was overloaded on stress and energy—directed energy for the first time in a long while. He smiled sheepishly as he carefully closed the last kitchen drawer.

"Tom, can I be your sister one last time before I'm your pal?" Elizabeth asked. She stretched out loving arms to him.

Tom went to her and hugged her tightly.

"How did you know?" he asked.

"Stupid," she answered. "Why don't you just carry a big sign around with you?"

"Saying?"

"Saying—'I surrender! Lorna Paxton has hooked me.' "

Tom laughed and let his hands flop helplessly to his sides. Elizabeth asked—"Are the demons truly gone, Tom? Because if they aren't, it's no good, you know?"

"They're gone, but if I told you who exorcised them you'd never believe me."

"No?"

"No, not in a million years."

"All right. Just be sure, Tom."

"I'm sure, now."

"Is she?" Elizabeth asked.

"Yes. We had a talk this morning. We didn't say everything the right way, organize and define it all, but she is sure, Elizabeth . . . now, damnit! Where is John Trout's letter?"

"Gone. You tossed it away. But Mother wrote down the address. I'll get it for you if you quit hopping around like a madman."

She paused. "Are you sure you want to go to Texas, Tom?"

"Hell, no! I'm just sure I want Lorna. Isn't that enough?"

Elizabeth had hurried off to the school. Sarah and Roy had

315

gone into Tahlequah to pick up the weekly supply of groceries. Tom paced the living room for a long while. How had it come to this? He was afraid. Ashamed. Daunted?

He wanted to see his sister who was lying in her bed no more than thirty feet from him. But she was no longer his sister; they had had such fun. Illusory fun, he supposed. Alcohol fun. He didn't know how to categorize it, but they had been so close for a time when they were both so hurt by their experiences in the real world outside. He hadn't even realized that until he saw the letter to her from that person in California; he hadn't even realized which direction he had been drifting in until a stupid old Indian who had always been a subject of mockery in his life had opened a window and let him peer out to see a ravaged and empty Tom looking in. He wanted a drink, and he dared not take one. He wanted to not talk to his sister, and had to!

He crept more than walked down the hallway to the closed door where Shanna slept, or dreamed, or watched the empty day. She would not talk; who knew where she dwelt now.

Alone, in dreams of glamour, broken in love, cheated of life, empty without her child, angry, renascent, bitter, neglected, desperate or determined and powerful beneath her facade of uselessness. Tom no longer knew her. He approached her as a well-meaning stranger.

Tom rapped once on her door. A meaningless gesture; she would not answer the knock. Then he stepped inside. The room was musty and empty. Shanna was there but was not. Tom felt like flinging open the curtains, raising the window, letting life and air into the room, goading her into animation. Existence. Shanna was the spark of their family, the woman alive. When all else seemed dry and hopeless, Shanna was always there with her wild ideas and projections for the future, some quite fantastic and far too bold, crazy, immeasurably beyond what they could hope to achieve, but she was always there with her ambitions and her huge appetite for life. When they had all been content with what they had, with what life, the government, God, or Fate had handed them, it was always Shanna who had looked past and beyond and told them life could be captured, tamed, reorganized, and made one's servant. Tom had never considered that before, but now he did. Shanna had always been their reminder that hope was a part of life and if she had bent, snagged, or even destroyed her own attempts at that hope, still she had been there among them, a driving if disturbing force.

Now she had given up on her own dreams, and in some distant way, it caused Tom to feel that his own dreams could never be realized. He had to speak to her, and he sat in the silent gloom at the head of her bed, his hand caressing her beautiful sleek dark hair.

How . . . ? He lunged blindly ahead.

"Hi, Shanna," he said softly. "Tired? It's a nice day out—if you wanted to go. There's that new wheelchair, never been used," he said with a smile, nodding toward the woven wicker chair in the corner of her room. "I'd wheel you around the yard a little—hell, we could even go down to the creek if you wanted."

There was no answer and Tom felt a little anger seep into his words, "Damn, Sis, you can't stay in here forever. Like some little old lady fixin' to die."

Ashamed of his outburst, Tom sat silently for a minute, hands on his lap. How did anyone know how she felt, after all? How much pain she might be in, how much of her mind was left.

He looked around the room, his eyes never really fixing on a single spot.

"I think I'm going away, Shanna. Texas. El Paso, or at least it looks like it. I think Lorna is going to go with me. Marry me." He thought he saw his sister's eyes shift, but in the darkness he could not even be sure of that. "You know, if you got up and started moving around, you could be maid of honor! Unless

Lorna has another idea. I don't know. I guess I'll have to talk to her about that. I'm sure she'd think it was a great idea."

It became obvious he wasn't going to get any answer. He rose and stood over her, a dark empty woman in the bed. "Damnit, Shanna!" he said, unable to help himself. "You're breaking Mother's heart. Everybody's! I don't believe you can't talk, don't want to get up. Where's the old fire?"

But still he got no answer and he turned slowly and made his way out of the room and went out the back door, slamming the screen behind him.

The buzz and squalor, dust and rumble of Fort Gibson, on the far western border of the Cherokee Nation along the Arkansas River, made Tahlequah seem quaint and colorful by comparison. Allyn drove the buggy steadily on while Army trucks and hooting kids in Model-Ts rolled past them, blowing claxon horns to try to startle the bay horse. Allyn was a strange mixture of moods that morning. Determined, cheerful, worried, and curious. Elizabeth, at his side, shared most of those feelings with her husband.

They had discussed this journey endlessly, weighing pros and cons, the necessity of it, the probable futility, the detrimental aspects. The convention of the full-bloods of the Cherokee Nation had been called by the old tribal chiefs. The Fort Gibson meeting was determined to find ways and means of restoring the old tribal order, broken and trampled by the Federal government despite all promises of sovereignty given and passed into law by treaties dating back to 1832. The official notice, received by Allyn at the *Tribune*'s office, proclaimed their goal was a restoration of the old order, "Just like we were before statehood, a common title to all Indians."

There were risks to attending—in fact, it could almost be declared a seditionist meeting, a gathering of secessionists, but it was doubtful the government even knew of the meeting or took it seriously at this late date.

More risky was having Allyn's attendance at the conference publicized just as his race for the state senate seemed to be on track, his popularity among the constituency apparently far ahead of Judge Benson's.

"You will be seen as a maverick," Elizabeth warned him. "A man divided. How can you represent the state of Oklahoma on one hand and favor tribal independence on the other?"

"I do still favor tribal law. How else can I gain a platform to speak for the people unless I have the white man's podium," Allyn had answered, but there was hesitation in his answer. The contradiction was obvious. Alienate the white government by advocating tribal independence, alienating some of the full-bloods by seeking a position in the white government.

"It only seems contradictory," Allyn had told a supporter in Elizabeth's presence. "The Cherokees have always had a strong allegiance to the government when it has allowed us to live as we wish, it is the same with me. I am a patriot; but I am a Cherokee first."

Elizabeth doubted many people would understand that. It might seem as if Allyn was playing both sides of the fence, seeking opportunity for personal advancement wherever it presented itself. Representatives from across the Nation would be at Fort Gibson. In the Cherokee Hills there were still three thousand living in dire poverty rather than submit to government regulation of their laws, schools, and tribal life. There were still Creek Snakes living in tiny decrepit cabins at the Old Hickory Stomp Ground who preferred their communal life to all the allotments the government could press upon them. Still Snakes and Nighthawks existed in the Territory, though they had no true power anymore. The and the U.S. marshals had been working diligently to eliminate them by law or by force.

Allyn's invitation to the meeting had come to him because of his father's well-known work for the tribal cause. And because it was known that in his younger years he too had ridden with the Nighthawks.

Roy Adair had been invited by separate invitation, but he had given his promise to Sarah when he had been released from prison. They had never taken his pride, but he would not let them take him away from his family again. He had respectfully and regretfully declined, feeling in some obscure way that he was denying his heritage and tainting his manhood.

"Well," Allyn said as they halted on a knoll away from the busy military road below them and looked toward the town of Fort Gibson, a jumbled collection of boxlike structures and dark winding road, to the silver-blue Arkansas River winding its sinuous way southward, a ferry visible here and there and one grand paddle-wheeler, a relic of its time, tied to the dilapidated wharves. "Here we are, dear. Civilization."

"Frightens me in a way," Elizabeth said, holding Allyn's arm tightly, curling close to him as the cool spring breeze shifted the long grass on the knoll. "However will I stand the 'civilization' in Oklahoma City when you are senator? I'm just a simple country girl." Her voice mimicked a child's. Allyn laughed and kissed his wife.

"We will survive, dear . . . simple country girl! Those politicians' wives don't know what they're in for."

"It will be all right, won't it, Allyn? All of it?" she asked seriously.

"Of course! What a question. What prompted that?"

"I don't know," she said. "I had a sort of cold tremor creep up my spine just then. A premonition?"

"You're cold, that's all," he said, putting the buggy shawl around her shoulders. "Or," he said brightening, "it could be the first sign of pregnancy."

"It could, could it?" she laughed, snuggling closer to him. "And how in the world could something like that have happened?"

The U.S. Grant Hotel on Riverfront Street was elderly, well maintained, and nicely appointed. Gingerbread decorated the front porch, which faced the river two blocks away.

The room the Jeffersons were shown to was clean, bright, and fresh. They had not unpacked before Allyn took his wife to their bed and lay her down, stroking the sleekness of her body from breast to thigh, slowly unbuttoning her dress, nuzzling her throat, kissing her deeply as they made slow, careless love. There were four hours until the meeting and they let them linger in forgetful warmth.

The rifle was an ancient Springfield .45-70 of the type once familiar to every U.S. soldier and all of his Indian adversaries. They were no longer common, even on the frontier, having been replaced almost universally by lever-action Winchesters and Henry rifles. This particular weapon had ladder sights, faded bluing on the barrel, and chips in its walnut stock. None of that mattered; it was destined to end this day at the bottom of the Arkansas River. The eye behind the sights was clear and alert. The marksman had several hours to wait, but he was a patient man and sat silently on the rooftop of the Camden Yards brickworks across from the Grant Hotel, legs folded, rifle across his lap.

"We can't be late," Elizabeth murmured from out of a sated half-sleep. Allyn was coiled against her, his thigh over hers, his arm across her breasts.

"No," he said in a muffled voice.

"Allyn!" She jostled him playfully. "Really, dear. You have to look over your speech again."

"I know," he said, forcing his eyelids open, sitting up in a sleep-drugged daze. "I'm awake."

"Let me get dressed," Elizabeth said. "I'll go down for some coffee."

"All right," he said, rising reluctantly. "You're right—you're always right." He stretched out her arms to embrace her but she rose, kitten-quick from the bed, laughing.

"No you don't! You'd start again. I know my husband."

He rose naked and walked to the window to stare out at the rose-tinted skies above the river.

Elizabeth dressed very quickly. Her eyes were bright, her cheeks still flushed with love-making.

As she sat pinning up her hair, he walked behind her and embraced her again.

"I do love you so," he said.

"Yes, and you're interfering and getting funny ideas again," Elizabeth said, glancing at him in the mirror. She put her brush down. "Start getting dressed. I'll be back in five minutes with a pot of coffee."

Reluctantly Allyn let his hands fall from her shoulder, sat on the bed, aimlessly looking at his clothing scattered across the floor, and scratched his head. "I mean it!" Elizabeth said in her school teacher voice and he smiled, nodded, and began pulling himself together, giving her one last lingering look as she went out into the hallway, closing the door behind her.

He had gone over the speech a dozen times. He doubted if he would even need his notes, but he took them anyway, folding them up and placing them in his vest pocket as Elizabeth finished straightening his tie for him, jerked down on his jacket, and went to tiptoes to kiss him.

"All right," she said, looking at the watch pinned to her bodice. "No time to delay now. Ready?"

"Ready," Allyn said, putting on his glasses. The sky outside was a dull violet. A streak of pale amber lined the western horizon as they stepped out onto the wide porch of the hotel. They linked their hands together. Allyn took a deep breath, smiled, and said, "All right then, here we go. Into the future."

He took one step more and the rifle shot boomed out, stilling his voice. He crumpled to the porch, blood streaming from his chest. The desk clerk rushed out and then retreated. On the street a horse reared in its traces and citizens fled for the shelter of surrounding buildings, eyes lifted upward. Elizabeth collapsed next to Allyn, unconsciously covering his body with her own.

His eyes were open. His glasses were askew, his mouth filled with blood. There was a look of wonder in his eyes, a word unformed on his lips. His chest rose and fell erratically. From up the street someone with a badge was running toward them. Elizabeth looked up and yelled frantically, "Hurry, for God's sake! They've killed my husband!"

The Adair house was steeped in gloom. Tom crept through it like a silent ghost himself, afraid to make any noise at all, to disturb the dark spirits there. Shanna lay alone in her bedroom, more silent than Death, perhaps wishing for it to come to her and embrace her in dark arms.

After two shaky weeks in Fort Gibson, Allyn had been carted home. Elizabeth could not take care of him, teach school, and attempt to run the newspaper, which was now a one-sheet affair, the type set by a well-meaning, bumbling apprentice from Tulsa named Baumgartner. Allyn lay in Tom's room, still racked with pain. He refused morphine or any heavy pain-killer. Now and then in his sleep he would cry out in pain, waking himself, apologizing profusely. The slug had ripped through his lung, narrowly missed his heart, and torn a gaping hole in his back, shattering the scapula irretrievably. His right side would be forever paralyzed.

Three days earlier word had come that he had lost his bid for the senate. Judge Benson had won the seat as, apparently, voters had decided not to vote for a man who was crippled and possibly dying. Allyn seemed to accept all of these setbacks, with some dismay, assuredly, but he accepted them. Yet some of the life seemed to seep out of him as he sat day by day in pain, never really mending, his future a blur of irresolution.

Tina had quit bringing the baby around. Although Sarah had been given an open invitation to go up to Oak Knoll to visit little Brent, she had gone only once. She had told Tom, "I cannot see him. He has his home, his parents. My daughter has said he is not her child. How can it be of my blood, then? I am a nosy old woman visiting." Nothing Tom or Elizabeth said could change her mind although it was obvious it broke her heart. Roy worked aimlessly around the farm, a farm that legally was not even his since he had never accepted his allotment from the government; yet no one had come around to threaten or harass him, out of pity, guilt, or Roy's known status with the still-active Nighthawks. He had aged rapidly in prison, and the sweeping changes in his life, in his family, had aged him even more.

They were desperate, cold times. The change, when it came, was from the most unexpected direction.

At mid-day Tom, Elizabeth, and Allyn sat in the garden, under the awning of the oak tree's branches. Ducks waddled around, quacking at each other, running from the newest litter of the ever-fecund Maggie's pups. Elizabeth sat holding Allyn's hand as he stared aimlessly across the yard toward the river, his thoughts lost in some impenetrable reverie that seemed in these days to approach despair. Tom was perched on a stump nearby, endlessly whetting a hunting knife with his pocket-sized carborundum stone.

Each lost in personal mists, none of them heard the stranger's approach. The shadow crossed Tom's as the man halted within a yard of him and he turned around wearily.

"Well, as busy as always, I see."

Tom turned, gaped, rose to his feet. Shook his head in sheer disbelief and cried out, "Charlie McCoy!"

"It's me, pal! What d'ya say?"

Charlie's hand came up, but Tom ignored it and threw his arms around Charlie, pounding him on the back, pausing to give wild introductions all around.

"What in the world . . . I never thought to see you again, Charlie. Not after . . ."

"Not after the unit broke up," McCoy finished for him. "Well, I'll tell you why, Tom . . . mind if I sit down first? They told me in Tahlequah how to get here, but no one told me how long a walk it was."

"Sure, why sure, Charlie." Tom waved a hand toward the stump, wiping back his hair as he stared in disbelief at Charlie McCoy.

"I'll get you a drink," Elizabeth said, rising, "Mr. . . ." She paused, noticing for the first time.

"Reverend McCoy."

Tom hadn't noticed it either, but there was Charlie McCoy, old cowboy McCoy wearing his collar reversed. And his right sleeve pinned up. Tom took a moment to gather that all in. It was incredible and now plain puzzling.

"Just call me Charlie," McCoy said. "All right, Elizabeth?"

"Just Charlie." She nodded and went into the house, leaving the three men together.

Charlie sat on the stump, wiped his brow, and smiled. "I was hoping it would be all right, me coming here," he said to Tom who was leaning against the oak, one heel cocked up behind him.

"All right! It's great!" Tom said, meaning it. "We had times, but . . ."

"But we had times," Charlie said with a smile.

"You two fought the war together?" Allyn asked.

"We were there together, sir."

"Is that where . . . ?" Allyn nodded at the empty sleeve of McCoy's jacket.

"Yes, afraid so," Charlie answered. Elizabeth had reemerged with glasses of lemonade on a tray. Serving all around, she seated herself next to Allyn.

"But, Charlie!" Tom said. "How—I mean I was there!"

"Yes, how did you get wounded?" Allyn asked. Coming from him, a man obviously crippled himself, Charlie McCoy took no offense. He shrugged.

"It was just a little bit of nothing, sir, as so many things that turn our lives around can be. One night I tangled with some barbed wire on what we called no-man's land. Well, it bled a lot, but I thought nothing of it. As the weeks went by, however, it began to grow sore and bother me. We had no sulfa, no medicine to speak of, and no one who knew how to administer them. By the time I got back to the States I had full-fledged gangrene in that arm. That, the surgeons knew full well how to deal with." He shrugged. "It's been so long ago, it doesn't matter anymore."

"Barbed wire!" Tom was stunned. "When you . . . ? God, Charlie!"

Elizabeth and Allyn looked at each other, knowing there was something more to the story than either ex-soldier was willing to talk about. They could have guessed forever and never have figured out that Charlie McCoy had lost his arm dragging a corpse from the trenches to keep his friend from being placed before a firing squad for killing a superior.

"Well," McCoy said quickly to Tom, "we can tell our war

stories another time. Let's not leave present company out of things?"

"But you're a minister!"

"Yes. I know, Tom—don't give me that look. It is something between my God and myself. One day it just seemed the right thing to do, the right way to go—for me."

"And you just happened to be passing through?" Allyn asked.

"Oh, no, sir! I live in El Paso now. I have a small but compassionate congregation. John Trout happens to be one of my parishioners—imagine his expression, Tom, when old Trout saw me up at the podium. I thought he was going to strangle. It was everything I could do to keep from laughing in the middle of Mark 7. But," he went on, "Trout said you had written him and we thought rather than have him write back, I'd just swing on by—I had a conference in Oklahoma City anyway—and perhaps Tom and I could go on together to El Paso."

"I think it's wonderful!" Elizabeth said.

Tom was thinking other thoughts. "Charlie—about your arm . . ."

"Yes? I've thought about it many a time, Tom—after I got through the inevitable self-pity—that I was a lucky man. I could've gotten my head shot off over there. It could've been me that Hermann fixed his sights on."

"Who?" Elizabeth asked, perplexed.

"The enemy. Many boys died over there. Me, I'm alive and I have God in my life. I'm a lucky man." His eyes seemed to be fixed briefly on Allyn's gloomy face, but nothing was said. Was this a small unspoken sermon? Tom couldn't penetrate it that deeply. He was just happy that McCoy was here. When he looked back on all they had been through, their disputes and the bad times, still it was possible that Charlie was the best friend he had ever had in this world.

"Well, Tom," Elizabeth asked, "are you going to go with

Reverend . . . Charlie?"

"I don't know." It was very sudden. "There were things I've been planning—Charlie, I think I'm going to get married. If she'll still have me."

"And so?" Charlie asked, tapping a finger on his clerical collar. "What d'ya think this is for, Tom?"

"Wouldn't that be something?" Allyn asked, becoming animated although the pain was still obvious. "Your best friend marrying you and Lorna?"

"Lorna, is it?" Charlie said. "Yes, I seem to remember that name from late-night barracks talk. From everything you said she is a lovely person. So you still have a chance with her?"

"She's said yes," Tom answered. "I just need . . ."

"I'll guess," Charlie said. "A job, a house, a destination. Tom, between me and Trout we've got all of that waiting for you."

"Tom?" Elizabeth said.

"I'd have to ask her. If she said so . . ."

"The wedding should be here in front of your family," Charlie said. "Tell her to pick the date."

"You beat all, Charlie!"

"Do I? No, Tom, I'm just a doing man, not a waiting and hoping man. You should remember that much about me from the old days." He smiled at Allyn again. Again Tom thought it was a meaningful smile.

"Yes," Tom said, "you were a doer, Charlie." He turned to his sister. "There was a time, Elizabeth, when I was afraid to talk to a strange girl, but Charlie McCoy . . ."

"Long time ago, Tom," Charlie said hastily. "But you have forgotten one promise you made to me."

"I don't get you, Charlie?" Tom said, obviously baffled.

"Well, in town they said she was living here. You promised once you'd introduce me to that beautiful woman who broke all of our hearts in boot camp."

"Shanna! But . . ."

"They told me that too, Tom," McCoy said. "And what has that to do with anything? Dreams are dreams. Sometimes, I believe, reality can be more beautiful and substantial."

It was Elizabeth's turn to object, "Reverend . . . Charlie, you can't understand."

"That she was injured? That she is hurting and afraid?" Charlie asked. "I believe I can, Elizabeth."

"But not the depths of it."

"No. It is her darkness, not mine." He rose and smiled at Tom. "Still—you promised me, Tom. I've waited a long time to see this princess."

With heavy trepidation Tom shrugged and he and Elizabeth traded looks bordering on despair.

"Tom," Charlie asked, "is it for her or for me that you resist my selfish impulse? If you think my seeing her will harm her, I will not. If you think that I will be somehow disappointed or even offended, you are worrying about nothing. Believe me."

"All right. Come ahead then, but expect nothing, Charlie."

"If I expected nothing in life, I would end it myself. Come on, lad!" he grinned, slapping Tom's shoulder. "This is the most pessimistic crew I've run into since the Dead Zone!"

Then Tom led him into the dark hallway and through to the darker enclave of Shanna's room. He knocked very softly and then peeked in. "All right, Charlie," he said, stepping aside.

"This is my sister, Shanna. Shanna!" He swung the door open wider. "This is my friend Charlie McCoy. Remember me talking bout him? The Irishman who loves the ladies. I've brought him by to see you."

She did not yell out, cringe, cover her head. Shanna lay as still as ever, the blankets over her breast, her arms still and lifeless above them. Charlie nodded. "Thank you, Tom. Won't be needing you now."

Then Charlie entered, shut the door, and sat down beside Shanna. It was ten minutes by the clock before he said a word. The two of them alone in that dark and airless room.

"Damned stuffy in here!" Charlie said, dragging a finger around the inside of his collar. Shanna did not respond. "Feel like opening the window? They say you don't like it open. Why would that be? Life is outside, Shanna. Small animals, friends, family. Oh, well, I'll leave it closed for now if you like."

He wandered the room. On the dresser was a framed photograph of Shanna taken in Emilio's studio. Not the one McCoy had seen before, but obviously taken at the same session. There she was, smiling provocatively if innocently, her sleek hair merging into smooth pale shoulder, her expression distant and commanding, the posture of her body seemingly that of a lioness in crinoline, ready and able to instantly rise and stalk, to bring down and devour.

"Well," Charlie said, "no matter who he was, he certainly was able to capture your spirit."

He walked to the window and, without asking, swept the curtains aside, letting sharp flat beams of light into the room, cracking the window to let in the crisp air. Shanna's body jumped.

"What's the matter? Prefer it closed?" he asked, but there was no answer and she settled back, turning her head away from him. "I need a little light and air in my life."

Again he sat beside her without being asked and went on, "Miracles, Shanna—how I believe in dreams and miracles. But there are all sorts of them. Those we only imagine can never come true. Those we approach and live through always have a chance of becoming reality. Don't you think so?"

Charlie went on. "I know Tom's told you. Lord, how you made the men dream when they saw your photograph. You were a light in our drab days at camp. You are still a light out of the darkness for your family. They know you. They hope for you. Know what, Shanna? I think there's been enough of this lying around in the dark," McCoy said, getting to his feet. Her eyes made negative movements.

"Tom couldn't have told you. He just found out today. I'm a minister, Shanna, do you see my collar? Only trouble is," he said with an old Charlie McCoy grin, "I'm still kind of new at it and sometimes I revert to my old ways. We're going visiting."

Outside the house, Tom's head spun around; Elizabeth got to her feet. Allyn gripped the arms of his chair tightly as if it were tilting under him. The shriek from inside the house was piercing, wild, and frantic. They looked toward Shanna's window. The window had been flung wide open and the curtains thrown apart. The scream came again, was muffled and then became a whimper.

Tom started toward the back door, wondering what he had done, when the screen swung open and Charlie McCoy backed through it, towing Shanna in her wheelchair.

"She wasn't sure she wanted to come outside today, but we discussed it and she saw my side of it," Charlie said.

Shanna's face was furious, her eyes smoldering. Suddenly she began sputtering a stream of incoherent invective. Tom started toward her, hand outstretched. Elizabeth shouted at him.

"Tom! He's right. Leave her alone!" Elizabeth turned around and crossed her arms beneath her breasts and Allyn heard her say, "I'm tired of babying her too."

From the barn Roy had come running. Rounding the corner of the house, his ax still in hand, he looked from the porch where Shanna sat fulminating in her wheelchair, trying to strike at Charlie with her fists, to Tom frozen in confusion, to Elizabeth who stood behind Allyn, half-smiling.

"Father," Elizabeth said. "I don't think you've yet met our friend, the Reverend McCoy."

"No, no I haven't," Roy said, his eyes drifting with amusement to where Shanna sat, shouting for help. Roy looked at the scratches down McCoy's cheek and said, "I see you have been hurt a little, sir."

"I don't move as well as I did with two arms," Charlie said, touching his face.

"No. What are you? A Christian minister, McCoy?" Roy asked.

"Yes, that's right. I am."

Roy grunted, looking again at his outraged daughter. "One day I would like to hear you preach, Mister."

Tom said with respect, "Well, Charlie, you did say you are a doer, I guess, by God, you are."

Allyn had asked Elizabeth to take him aside. Hobbling on a cane, he walked toward the river with her. The sky was sunbright, quail called from the underbrush. The river glittered silver-bright. Allyn looked back toward the porch. Shanna had quieted now. No one was heeding her cries of alarm and there was no point in railing against the universe and her ill treatment forever.

"It was all that simple," Allyn said in wonder. "Why didn't we think of that?"

"Sometimes it takes an outside perspective," Elizabeth answered.

Allyn said thoughtfully, "I suppose so . . . Elizabeth, I have been thinking . . ."

"Yes?"

"That darned Baumgartner, he doesn't know what he's doing, does he?"

"He can set type," Elizabeth answered, "but he can't spell! He doesn't know the Cherokee language. Of course," she said, "he tries. He is competent at what he does. Lord, Allyn, don't think of firing him!"

"No. I didn't have that in mind. I agree with you—he's good at what he does, very quick at setting type, but he is not a newspaperman. The *Tribune*—my father's paper. We no longer have strong editorials. We—I—have been letting it die. I won't fire Baumgartner. How could I? At least he has kept the paper going. What I need to do is thank him . . . and then, get back to work."

"If you think it is time, Allyn," Elizabeth said, standing near him, her hands on his hips. Allyn's eyes were on Shanna. She was so angry she had forgotten to be silent and was venting her thoughts a mile a minute as Tom and McCoy studiously ignored her complaints, exchanging war stories. It was intentional, Allyn was sure. Shanna still could not stand to be ignored. He smiled softly at his wife.

"I think it's time. I need to work. Now, let's rejoin the others."

Arm in am they walked back toward the porch. Shanna's tirade had tired her. She sat watching the sunbeams through the trees, the galumphing puppies.

Tom had been watching his sister and he now said in a low voice to Charlie McCoy, "Do you know what, Charlie—I think I actually saw her smile."

"You've seen nothing yet, Tom," Charlie answered. "I am going to make that woman smile, and laugh, and shout for joy."

"What do you mean . . ." Tom was taken completely unaware. He thought he caught his friend's intention then. "You can't mean it, Charlie."

"Why can't I? I'm a minister, not a monk."

"You don't even know her!" Tom objected.

"No. I guess that will come while I'm teaching her to laugh. I am," he repeated, "a doer and not a waiting and a hoping man."

"Why," Tom said, looking at Charlie McCoy's earnest face, "would I not believe you?"

CHAPTER TEN

Twilight was silent, a splurge of colors spread across the dusk-bound sky, birds cutting quick dark silhouettes against the mammoth canvas of heaven. Tom rocked evenly in his chair. Elizabeth sat in silence beside him, listening to the gentle sounds of approaching night: the river lapping the banks at the ford, the cooing of nestling dove, the last bark of dogs as darkness gently settled.

"Well?" she said finally to Tom, "it has been a day."

"It has been," he agreed. "Are you sorry it's over, Sis?"

Elizabeth thought it over. "Maybe so, Tom. Maybe. We all hate to see good things pass, good times. But they do, don't they? It's wrong to try to hang on to them when their time has come to fade away," she said, looking toward the sunset sky.

"I guess you're right," he admitted. "I've hung on to too much. Maybe Dad has too."

"Maybe all of us." Elizabeth was quiet for a long minute. "The past is to be remembered and honored, not to be relived. It can't be. Not really."

"No."

"The way of the Cherokee—the old way of the Cherokee—is gone, Tom."

Startled, Tom looked at his sister. That was not the way Elizabeth had viewed things in the past. She went on. "Oh, it is, Tom . . . It's the truth. The Nighthawks can't bring it back, our defiance, our pride, dreams can't bring it back. Maybe those times weren't even so good as imagination paints them. It's time, Tom. Not the white man, not politics, not oppression that has taken our way from us. Time conquers everything. If there had never been a single Indian war, still we couldn't have stood against time. We still would have seen and coveted the new things of our time—movies, automobiles, radios. Just as our ancestors coveted iron pots, rifles, bright beads. Things they did not have. People progress, or at least move on, wanting . . . whatever time might bring."

She looked into her brother's eyes, "And sometimes what progress brings is a new way, every bit as good if not the same as the cherished old."

"You and I, Elizabeth?" Tom asked, "what do we do? I do cherish the old. I do hope for the future. What do we do, woman?"

"We remember what was and honor it. We step forward fearlessly into what will become whether we wish for it all or even understand it all. Tom, the past is not our only life. We are here now. The Cherokee will be as strong and as proud as ever. But we must live on, in our time."

The sun was very low, his shadow stretching out before him against the short grass on the knoll where he sat watching the gathering dusk. It had been a day. The sun had risen in a flourish of flame and passed overhead, hot and yellow, and then it had set slowly, becoming a hazy wash of crimson and deep gold, fading to purple. The Old Man had thought of many things on this day, and seen much. The pup dog, eager and hungry now, ran up to him wagging its tail, nuzzling his leg. The Old Man left his memories for the day and rose, walking back to his sleeping place, the pup at his heels. It had been a very good day.

EPILOGUE

"... and so you see, Tina," the letter concluded, *although we all fought through a lot, we survived it and were happy with what life had given us. As you know your father, Brent, stayed with Wallace and me, growing up on Oak Knoll until he got older and Broken Post was too small to hold him. He married your mother and went to work for the aircraft company, and you were born. Your real grandmother, Shanna, became Mrs. McCoy—I know you did meet her once, the pleasant older woman in the wheelchair. Maybe at that time you didn't even realize really who she was. You certainly have her looks! You are a beautiful woman too. I write these few things for you so you will have something to remember us by. May your life be beautiful and full.*

Your grandmother
Tina Black.

The rain had let up and the sun had finally broken through. Outside, the world was coming back to life. Tina walked to the window and saw Amy Charles below. Opening the window, she waved to her and called for her to wait. Then the letter was folded again and placed back in the trunk to be read again some other rainy day. This was their day for the living: Tina and her friends. It was their world now and their time.

ABOUT THE AUTHOR

Paul Joseph Lederer was a native of San Diego, California, and attended San Diego State University before serving four years in an Air Force Intelligence arm during the Vietnam era. He traveled widely in the United States and in Europe, Asia, and the Middle East.

He was the author of *Tecumseh, Manitou's Daughters, Shawnee Dawn, Seminole Skies, Cheyenne Dreams, The Far Dreamer,* and *North Star.* His most recent contemporary novel was *The Moon Around Sarah,* published by Robert Hale, London.